The Hunting Season

By the same author

Total Eclipse
Summertime

The Hunting Season

ELIZABETH RIGBEY

MICHAEL JOSEPH
an imprint of
PENGUIN BOOKS

MICHAEL JOSEPH
Published by the Penguin Group
Penguin Books Ltd, 80 Strand, London WC2R ORL, England
Penguin Group (USA) Inc., 375 Hudson Street, New York, New York 10014, USA
Penguin Group (Canada), 90 Eglinton Avenue East, Suite 700, Toronto, Ontario, Canada M4P 2Y3
(a division of Pearson Penguin Canada Inc.)
Penguin Ireland, 25 St Stephen's Green, Dublin 2, Ireland (a division of Penguin Books Ltd)
Penguin Group (Australia), 250 Camberwell Road,
Camberwell, Victoria 3124, Australia (a division of Pearson Australia Group Pty Ltd)
Penguin Books India Pvt Ltd, 11 Community Centre,
Panchsheel Park, New Delhi – 110 017, India
Penguin Group (NZ), cnr Airborne and Rosedale Roads, Albany,
Auckland 1310, New Zealand (a division of Pearson New Zealand Ltd)
Penguin Books (South Africa) (Pty) Ltd, 24 Sturdee Avenue,
Rosebank, Johannesburg 2196, South Africa

Penguin Books Ltd, Registered Offices: 80 Strand, London WC2R ORL, England

www.penguin.com

First published 2006

1

Set in 13.5/16 pt Monotype Garamond
Typeset by Rowland Phototypesetting Ltd, Bury St Edmunds, Suffolk
Printed in Great Britain by Clays Ltd, St Ives plc

A CIP catalogue record for this book is available from the British Library

ISBN–13: 978–0–718–14563–7
ISBN–10: 0–718–1456–3

Acknowledgements

My warm thanks to Beverley Cousins and Louise Moore, Mark Lucas, Peta Nightingale and Nicki Kennedy. Thanks also to Franklin Johnson and Ed Jackson of Utah and James Monro FRCS who shared their knowledge so generously without any idea of how much they were helping to shape and inspire this novel. A special thank you to Dr Deirdre Wright, for whom *The Hunting Season* became more demanding than any patient. Any oversights, mistakes and wilful disregard for facts are all mine.

Prologue

It is night. It is not late. It is still early enough for pedestrians to feel safe out on the street. Of course, they are not safe if the night is dark and the street has no sidewalk. There are many dangers for pedestrians in these circumstances.

You might be driving home from work. Your mind might still be at your desk or you might be thinking about the home which awaits you. Perhaps this small gap in your life, between home and work, between these two lives of yours, is a place of private refuge. It is the only time of the day you are alone. Your body settles into the curves of the car seat. You relax. You drive loose-limbed, one-handed.

Or maybe you are a stranger. The street is new to you but you are confident. You are following directions others have given you and anyway, you know you have plenty of time to get lost and find your way. You relax. You drive loose-limbed, one-handed. You switch on the radio. Occasionally a clause, in words or music, invades your wandering thoughts, steering them this way or that.

You might, of course, already be lost, uncomfortably lost. Anxiety has begun to twitch at your scalp, plucking at hairs. Your body has straightened, your shoulders stiffened. You drive with both hands on the wheel, elbows locked. You are alert, watching, waiting for a sign or a landmark. The sign, you anticipate, will tell you where you are and then you will feel your confusion lift, suddenly, like fog.

Or maybe you aren't lost and you aren't going home and you aren't following directions but there is some other reason why you are driving through this stretch of forest, right now, tonight, on the edge of this town, in this state, at this very moment. Maybe no one knows you are here and maybe only you know why.

The road is unthreatening. It is thickly wooded, with occasional gateways leading to isolated houses. The road is familiar, because you travel here daily or sometimes, or because you have travelled many like it.

Maybe you take the corner a little too wide or drive a little too close to the forest's turfy edge. Or maybe the pedestrian is out too far in the road. Afterwards you will have days, weeks, months, years to examine and re-examine the precise dynamics of the event. But the fact is that you have turned a corner and, instead of the dark road stretching ahead of you, there is a pedestrian. He is in front of your car.

The running man is lit freakishly by your headlights and he appears in them as suddenly and shockingly as a ghost. He is wearing running shorts and running shoes and probably he was already running, running when your engine idled at the downtown traffic lights, running when you felt the city's solidity disintegrate into suburban spaces and shadows, running when you turned into this forest road, and he is still running. But right now he is running to get out of the path of your car.

The headlights seem to trap him and the brief paces he has time to take are strangely towards your fender. In that second you notice, of all things, his elbows. They are working like big pistons to carry his body out of your path. And you see his prominent jawbone, made more prominent because he is gritting his teeth, pointing his jaw in the direction of safety at the side of the road. But he cannot avoid the car and you have no time to avoid him either. Your right leg careens like a mad horse on to the unyielding brake but you already know it is too late. There is going to be an impact. For a part of a part of a second, it seems to you that this impact, its sheer inevitability, is something which you have been steering towards all your life. For your whole life you have been hurtling decisively but probably unknowingly on a collision course. Now you know. Here is the collision.

You grip the wheel in both hands and brace yourself against your seatback.

The man's body shoots on to the hood of the car, head first, so that his face rushes towards yours for a split second, and in that terrible moment your eyes meet. His are wide with terror. In his you see the knowledge of his imminent death. And you know, too, that you are going to kill this man. He is about to be killed by you. You look at each other in fear and horror.

Maybe your reason for coming to the forest had something to do with this man. Maybe you knew he was going to be here. Maybe you had already decided what was going to happen tonight. Even so, what you feel now is the same fear and horror of the driver who was innocent of all intention. Terror, it's the same for everyone, the guilty and the innocent.

And then the man's head collides with the hood of the car, just in front of the windshield. Behind him you see his legs fly up like some flimsy fabric caught by the wind, a child's kite, say, or washing on a line.

There is a moment which is lyrically gymnastic, when the man seems to be poised on his head on the hood in front of you. All the time you are braking. There is a screaming noise in your ears, the scream of the brakes, the scream of the man, your own screams, the radio; afterwards you will have a lifetime in which to wonder who was making all that noise.

Then, when the car still hasn't stopped but has made a

significant contribution towards stopping, the man's body is flung far ahead of you. You know it must be moving very fast but it seems to fly in slow motion. The feet and legs are still high in the air. They must be held there by a supernatural wind, there can be no other reason for this man to remain feet uppermost as his body travels headlong, head first, in a graceful trajectory towards the earth.

Does the body land at the same moment the car stops? It would be a fitting end to the hideous but curiously balletic syncopation between driver and victim. At any rate, there is silence now, the deepest of silences.

You might get out of the car to examine the man's condition, call the emergency services, and generally play the good citizen. You know that this action and all subsequent exemplary behaviour can never change what happened in the space of a few seconds tonight on this dark road but you could do it anyway.

Or you might not get out of the car. You might instead remain tightly locked in your warm cell. By staying inside the car you minimize any evidence of your involvement in the event and you can minimize it still further by, for example, going to the car wash. A cursory glance at the hood tells you there are no dents immediately visible, at least through the windshield. If there really are no dents and you never take this road again, how is anyone investigating the death to associate you with it? You can drive on now and no one will ever know.

You go to start the engine and realize that it's still running and the radio's still playing. You pull slowly, cautiously, around the body. As you pass you stare down at it, although you do not wind down the window or stop the car to do so. The man lies with his head nestled against his own shoulder in a manner so like a puppet that you are certain he is dead. You want to look for longer, search for signs of breathing, but now you must hurry.

Shaking, your breath uneven, your thoughts frozen, you drive down forest roads in a wide circle back to the town. You are squeezed through the car wash on a slow-moving belt which you are powerless to control while brushes as mighty as dinosaurs prey on the car's exterior. You could pay through a window without even climbing out of your car but you choose to open the door and cross the asphalt. Your legs, as you walk, feel uncoordinated. You try in vain to remember the precise point in each pace when you should lift the next foot. Are both feet momentarily on the ground at the same time? You have walked for years without think-ing about it and now you can't exactly remember how. You stumble twice before you arrive at the cashier's. As you reach for your money you are aware of the tug of each muscle at your ribs. As you look for the right coins your eyes, which have seen too much tonight, seem to bulge, their lenses unfocused, struggling to work in concert. While you wait for your receipt, you allow yourself a glance back at your car's fender. Your heart thuds. The fender shines with water. Its surface is waxy smooth. It is unmarked.

You drive home, taking a circuitous route, nowhere near the forest. You drive into your own garage and the door closes behind you, and you look around at the lumber stored on the rear wall and the hanging electrical cables and the leaf rake and the snow shovel. All inanimate objects, placed here by you, but they seem now as complicitous as old friends. You switch on the overhead light and reach for the power flashlight. The garage's privacy is almost palpable. It is a poor cousin to the rooms in the main house but its dark, cold, silent windowlessness gives it a special status. Because now it shares your secret.

Shielded by its walls, you examine every inch of the car's fender and hood. Unmarked! Unmarked, except by the smallest of blemishes for which any number of explanations is possible, explanations more acceptable than the truth. It is incredible that the event has left no footprint but re-examination confirms your first findings. Both you and the car are unmarked.

The Kill

I

It was spring and the earth was warming up. The hospital authorities were, as usual, slow to respond to this annual event and the heating, in the older wards and offices, had not yet been turned down. Its level was not adjustable by any individual. You could switch your heater off and feel cold or leave it on and feel hot.

'I'm hot,' mouthed Matt's patient when Matt leaned over his bed in the almost dark, almost quiet hospital and asked him how he was doing.

You could hear the roar of some other patient's television. A comedy programme, actors shouting their lines over the audience's laughter. Further away was the clang of metal on metal, a night trolley making its rounds.

Matt explained about the heating.

'We're all hot in this part of the hospital, Mr Zoy,' he said, knowing that it was worse, far worse, for Mr Zoy, who could not take a shower or drink an iced tea unless someone brought him one and then held it while he sipped it, who could not open the fridge door and feel the blast of cool air in his face while he wrapped his fingers around an icily wet can of beer.

'I'm so hot I've been wondering if I'm not dead already,' rasped Mr Zoy and, while Matt debated how to reply to this, added, 'I wish I was. Dead. I want to die now, doctor.'

Matt was silent. He could have just left Mr Zoy's room right then without a word. The old man would have been unable to stop him, to complain. But it was Mr Zoy's helplessness which kept Matt at this patient's bedside. He could not bear to abuse the power his position, his health, his strength gave him. He had been called in tonight to another patient and now he regretted the impulse which had halted him by Mr Zoy's room on his way out. It was perhaps a month since Mr and Mrs Zoy had sat in Matt's office and asked him, politely, to kill Mr Zoy when the time was right. They had explained in simple, practical language, that the final humiliations of Mr Zoy's illness were something they both wished to avoid.

'You can't ask me to do that,' Matt had said. 'I have to live with myself afterwards.'

'We're not requesting anything wrong. We're simply asking you to abbreviate misery,' said Mrs Zoy, a high school English teacher whose voice was strong and clear. 'If Anthony doesn't want you to do it, if he chooses to wait for death, then he won't ask. But if his pain and distress become unbearable, we hope you'll respond with humanity to his request for help.'

Matt's reply had been non-committal. He had felt discomfited when the Zoys had gone away thanking him, as though they had succeeded in securing his agreement to their plan.

'I'm ready now,' said Mr Zoy as though he, too, had been remembering that conversation in Matt's office.

Matt switched on one of the small lamps at the bed's end and lifted Mr Zoy's notes from their holder.

'I want to die,' repeated Mr Zoy. 'It's time.'

Matt studied the notes. They charted the patient's final decline. Matt guessed the man still had a week of suffering ahead of him.

'Please,' said Mr Zoy. 'While I have a little dignity left.' He had been the principal of a grade school. Matt remembered his own grade school principal, an immensely tall figure who had wandered the asphalt at recess, watching pupils, talking to them, interesting himself in them. He had seemed steeped in children's lives, seasoned by their growth.

Mr Zoy was waiting for Matt to look at him. Matt chose instead to stare around at the darkness of the room beyond the lamplight like a man searching for something. The city glowed orange through the window but he knew that not far away, invisible now, lay the great, dark shapes of the mountains. High in the mountains lived Matt's father. Without even looking at Mr Zoy's face, Matt sensed that the man was regarding him now the way his father sometimes did, with the calm gaze of knowledge, a knowledge acquired over many years, the knowledge of what Matt would do next.

Matt blinked and searched the window's square of sky for stars. He could see none. The universe seemed entirely dark. Of course, Matt knew the stars were there, masked by the earth's bright lights the way the present masks the past. Nearby, the shapes he could discern in the man's room (the TV, the closet, the spindly-legged chairs which lined the far wall in case more than one visitor showed up at once) seemed laughably prosaic.

When he finally turned back to the patient he found that the old man's eyes were still fixed on him. The similarity between Mr Zoy and his father was disconcerting now. How had he failed to notice it before? Maybe because Mr Zoy had lost a lot of weight. His face had become gaunt but you could see his strength, just the way you could see Hirsh's strength from the lines of his face. And Mr Zoy's look had something of Hirsh's dignity, too. He was not pleading or demanding but there was a light in his pupils. The light expressed desire. It was desire to die, but still it was desire.

'Your eyes are bright,' observed Matt quietly.

'Too bright to die?' whispered Mr Zoy. 'Is that it? Is that what you're saying?'

During his years in African field hospitals, Matt had seen many deaths. Sometimes death lingered, occasionally it even loitered, but it never seemed to visit patients whose eyes shone like Mr Zoy's. The vulture might circle but when it saw bright eyes, it always flew on.

'Spare me any more, spare my wife's suffering. I've done what I need to do and said what I need to say. Help me just to slide out of this world gently, gently,' whispered Mr Zoy with a lilt to his voice which made Matt wonder if he wasn't quoting a poem or a song.

Matt studied the patient's chart. He asked, 'Are you in pain now?'

'Oh yes,' sighed Mr Zoy, closing his eyes. And when he briefly reopened them it seemed to Matt that their light had faded a little. He thought about calling Mike Salinski, the patient's oncologist. Although still a member of the team managing the Zoy case, Matt had, as surgeon, handed over day-to-day control to Salinski. Matt glanced at his watch. Mike Salinski was a good doctor but, as Matt knew from experience, was liable to be drunk after eight in the evening.

'We'll increase your pain relief,' Matt said. He called a nurse and waited with the silent man in the silent room.

'Would you like me to phone your wife to come?' asked Matt.

'No,' said Mr Zoy.

The patient with the TV must have switched it off. Outside the night trolley was still. Mr Zoy's breathing was laboured. His eyes were closed. He appeared to be asleep. The hospital's mechanical hums and whirs seemed briefly to have ceased. Matt felt himself to be entirely alone in the building with the dying man. When no nurse came he got the key to the dispensary.

On his return, he found the patient's sited line blocked, and it was hard to find a place in his thin arm to inject. His veins were like faint streaks of crayon. Finally Matt inserted the needle into one of them. He pulled back gently on the syringe until the bevel of the needle was darkened by blood. Then he injected 200 milligrams of Zornitol.

Mr Zoy seemed unstartled. He appeared still to be asleep but, when Matt withdrew the needle, he opened his eyes and something like a smile spread across his gaunt, unshaven face.

'Thank you, doctor,' he said sleepily. 'Your humanity triumphed. There was no other doctor I could ask.'

Matt stayed with him a while, watching as sleep engulfed Mr Zoy. He saw the man's cheeks soften. His breath grew even. Matt thought about his father again and he knew that Hirsh never would have done what Matt just did. Hirsh had been a renowned family doctor in the city. Probably patients had pleaded with Hirsh to end their lives but Hirsh would have adhered strictly to his principles, kindly but firmly. He would never have killed a man.

This uncomfortable knowledge drove Matt from Mr Zoy's bedside.

'Goodnight,' he said softly. He turned out the lamp. He did not withdraw the patient's notes from their holder or the pen from his pocket. He closed Mr Zoy's door. His feet sounded loud in the empty corridor.

He rounded a corner and there was a night cleaner, clad in green, his fingers coated in plastic and his face masked. He looked up from his trolley as Matt passed, his eyes searching Matt's face. Disconcerted, Matt nodded to him. The man did not respond but, over his mask and from behind a big bottle of green fluid, he continued to stare. It seemed to Matt that there was an accusation in the man's dark eyes.

As he drove home he told himself that although he had forgotten to record the injection that night and had not even signed for the Zornitol in the dispensary, he would do so immediately on his return in the morning.

He now tried to think ahead to tomorrow, to the patients he must see and the small administrative backlog he aimed to clear. But his mind kept returning to Mr Zoy's dark room at the hospital as though his thoughts were a balloon bobbing at the end of a string held in the thin but steadfast grip of Mr Zoy.

'Your humanity triumphed,' Matt reminded himself but the words could not still his unease. This sensation increased as the city passed. The shadows between street lamps and around the closed shops in the malls seemed thicker and darker than usual. The automobiles on the used car lots assumed a new shapelessness in the night air.

In his memory, Mr Zoy's room was swathed in a darkness he knew it was impossible to achieve at the hospital in reality. Instead of injecting powerful drugs as gently as he could into the old man's arm, it seemed to Matt that he had been mercilessly punching Mr Zoy's pillow, or even Mr Zoy himself. His hands sat heavily on the wheel. They felt too big, as though he had new fingers or the old ones were impossibly, violently swollen. Even the car seemed to smell different. It smelled of decay, like a damp, leafy forest. This stretch of road was briefly without traffic, a small wrinkle in the city's ceaseless surface of noise and movement. Matt felt himself to be completely alone.

By the time he drew up to his own garage, Matt wanted to turn around and go back to the hospital to check on the patient. A lower dose of Zornitol would have diffused Mr Zoy's anxieties and assured him a good night's sleep. Why had he foolishly allowed himself to fall prey to Mr Zoy's demands? By studying a drug manual he could work out the correct dosage of antidote to reverse the effects of the Zornitol. Except it might already be too late.

He brushed clumsily against the snow shovel and the leaf rake hanging on the garage wall as he let himself into the house. There was a light on in the kitchen. The rest of the house was dim. He paused, listening to the silence, then crept into the bedroom. Denise was asleep. Her limbs lay neatly, even her hair hung in tidy hanks down the pillow. Night-time's strange monochrome accentuated the lines which defined her cheeks and her chin. She was beautiful, fine as something drawn and perfected with a sharp pencil.

Next to Denise lay Austin. He had started walking about six months ago and then last month he had learned how to climb out of his bed and now, at eighteen months, he had begun to use these two skills most nights to find his way into his parents' room. He slept in disarray. The bedcovers were twisted around his legs and his arms were up on the pillow submissively as though someone in his dream had shouted: Halt, you're under arrest.

Carefully, Matt lifted the small boy and carried him back to his own bed. Austin snuffled and gave the shadow of a cry, then rearranged himself without waking.

'Your humanity triumphed,' said Mr Zoy's rasping whisper inside Matt's head. 'There was no other doctor I could ask.'

Matt felt both tired and unable to sleep. He opened the fridge door and was at once aware of its icy breath on his face. He reached inside without looking and his fingers wrapped themselves around the cold curve of a beer can.

He sat very still at the kitchen table, drinking the beer slowly so the air molecules around him remained as undisturbed as possible.

He closed his eyes and leaned his head on his hands, rubbing his temples a little. When Denise did this for him it felt good but tonight, alone, the movement was not soothing because he knew that tonight a man would die and that he, Matt, was responsible for this death. And at the very moment he acknowledged this to himself, he smelled a damp, woody scent, the combination of growth and decay. He knew the smell with a kind of intimacy, recognizing it from the forest where he had spent his boyhood summers and where his father lived now, up in the mountains. His temples throbbed. He was looking down a long, dark well and here in the well he was a boy again. He knew this because the trees which surrounded him seemed so large, their trunks swollen. He peered between the trunks and he could see, indistinctly, a car. It was a red car. His right leg felt unsteady with the pain of some recent blow and he shifted his weight off it and looked around the other side of the tree trunk. His eyes watering with effort, he was now able to discern the dim shape of a figure inside the car. He waited for the figure to move, or to get out, to call or even, absurdly, to laugh a big, deep, bellowing laugh. But the figure did not move, just as he had known it wouldn't, because the person in the car was dead. There had been a death and it was Matt's fault and now he had a secret which he must keep hidden for ever.

Matt blinked once, twice. His heart was beating hard as though he had been running but he was sitting, not standing, he was a man and not a boy, and here was the kitchen in the house he shared with his wife and son. Its lighting was bright and clinical. He did not close his eyes again until he was certain that the car would not reappear but even now, distanced by time and geography from the red car, the sense that something immense and irrevocable had happened did not leave him. Mr Zoy. Mr Zoy might be dead by now. He wanted to call the hospital and ask about the patient. He picked up the phone. Then he put it down again.

He slipped into bed beside Denise in a way that barely redistributed the bedcovers. He wished that she was awake so he could talk over what had happened with her. He talked over everything with Denise. And then, as he fell asleep, he was relieved not to have told her. What had happened tonight was the kind of thing you didn't tell anyone except, maybe, if you trusted them enough, another doctor.

2

The following morning, Denise switched on the weather report and then reminded Matt to take a coat because, although Salt Lake City was getting warmer every day, there was still snow in the mountains. For a minute Matt stared at her and then he remembered. He wasn't coming home tonight. He was driving to his father's house in the mountains right after work.

'I wish you two were coming,' he said.

Denise smiled and shook her head. 'We'll wait until the weather's better,' she said. 'Trying to keep warm and stay vigilant up there is too exhausting.'

Now that Austin was old enough to scamper around all over the old house, Denise and Austin joined Matt less often when he visited Hirsh. On their last trip, Austin had tugged at some of the electrical wires which had been dangling dangerously for years, nearly lost a finger in a mousetrap and found poisoned peanut butter which Hirsh had laid for some small, unwelcome mammal and then forgotten. Plus, the living room didn't really warm up unless the fire was alight but the fire was the greatest hazard of all.

'Okay,' agreed Matt reluctantly. 'Next time, then.'

Whenever he drove up the mountain alone to see Hirsh these days, he absurdly sought reassurance that Denise and Austin missed him. Denise said they did, of course, but it seemed to Matt that they managed his mountain absences as smoothly and painlessly as they managed his daily absences at the hospital. On the other hand, when Denise ran one of her music therapy weekends, he and Austin felt something like a small bereavement. Matt would look forward to the weekends, to the things he would do with his son, but the little boy's yearning for his mother swelled so rapidly and palpably that by Saturday lunchtime it had robbed all Matt's plans of oxygen and there seemed nothing they could do but wait together for Denise to come home. Once Matt had started counting how many times Austin asked when Mommy would be back but he had stopped after thirty.

'Anyway,' said Denise, 'you need a restful weekend with Hirsh. You look exhausted.'

'I thought I go up there because my dad's old and he needs me to help with the heavy jobs and because I'm supposed to be persuading him to move somewhere more sensible,' said Matt, shuffling coats around in the closet. He was looking for his thick mountain jacket.

'Sure you do,' said Denise, opening another closet and drawing the coat out as though it had just leapt into her hand. 'It also happens that you come home relaxed and rested.'

Matt looked at her reproachfully. 'But I miss you and Austin,' he said. Denise put her arms around him. She was tall and slim and she played the flute and Matt thought that when she moved she looked like music and that even when she stood still her long body had the elegance and mystery of musical notation. They had been married for more than two years now and he never saw a woman who attracted him more.

She said into his ear, 'I don't want you to go. Don't think that I do.' Her words and her warm touch softened his body. He felt as though he were made from pieces of Austin's luridly coloured play dough.

13

When he reached the hospital he wanted to go right to Mr Zoy. He stifled this urge. He checked on the patient he had operated on last night. Then he went to the dispensary, passing Mr Zoy's room. The door was shut and a cleaner in dark green scrubs was standing outside. In the dispensary Matt signed out 200 milligrams of Zornitol and, since there were only 100-mg phials in stock, then stated that he had administered 150 mgs and disposed of 50 mgs. A resident countersigned without even reading it.

In his office Matt found his secretary kneeling precariously on his rotating chair, her back to him, screwdriver in hand.

'I'm sorry,' she said, not looking at him but perhaps seeing his reflection in the window as she leaned over it. 'I mean, excuse me, but I come from Washington State where we actually open the windows from time to time.'

'We used to open windows here in Utah,' said Matt. 'Then we discovered air conditioning.'

'Air conditioning is fine,' said the secretary, 'if someone switches it on. Right now, what we have here in the old part of the complex is heating. Too much heating.'

She set to work with the screwdriver. Matt took off his jacket and pulled up the sleeves of his pale blue scrubs. Today it was too hot inside even to put on a white coat. He took the notes which were stacked on his desk and shuffled through them standing up while his secretary's broad body gyrated with the chair whenever she succeeded in turning the screwdriver.

'You want me to do that?' he offered.

'Nope. I alone get to upset that bald moron in Buildings Admin.'

Amid the patient files, Matt found one labelled Zoy, Anthony. He pulled it out and, still without looking at him, his secretary said, 'Bad news on Mr Zoy. He died in the night.'

Matt felt his heart land somewhere hard. He heard the thud and his own sharp intake of breath.

'I mean, are you surprised?' asked his secretary, who amused herself reading patient notes and liked to discuss them with him sometimes.

'Well, no-oh . . .' said Matt carefully. 'But I'm sorry. I liked him.' He was looking at the nurse's neat writing at the back of Mr Zoy's file. Respiratory failure. Death: 12.25 a.m. That was about forty minutes after Matt had said goodnight to him. Matt's heart continued to thud. He tried to still it by taking deep breaths.

'Mr Zoy's family have requested a meeting with you,' said the secretary.

Inside his ribs, Matt's heart scudded again like a tin can someone was kicking down the street.

'You mean, his wife?'

'The wife and son. The son's asking why his father died so suddenly. Unbelievable. As though the poor old guy had years to live when anyone could see he was due to check out anytime soon.'

'Did you schedule a meeting?'

'I gave them eleven o'clock. Technically, of course, you can't make it but I figured you'd find the time. Matt, are you okay?'

She was looking at him now. Her fight with the screwdriver had loosened some of her blonde hair. Her large, round cheeks were red with effort.

'Don't I look okay?' asked Matt. He remembered how Denise had told him this morning that he needed a rest.

'You look weary. You look the way guys look in Washington State when they need someone to open the window. What time did they call you in last night?'

'Nine, ten o'clock. A high school kid with a knife in his spleen after a fight.'

'I've just been reading the file! Major skin slashes, knife in his spleen and guess what? Marjory says that when the kid woke up there were two police officers waiting for the details and the dork wouldn't talk. Can you credit it?'

She dropped the screwdriver on to the rug and then lifted the entire window from its frame. Matt hurried to take it from her and lean it against the wall. Cool air was rushing into the room. It didn't ruffle his hair but its touch had that kind of familiarity. The secretary marched out triumphantly, dropping her screwdriver into her purse and ostentatiously wiping her hands.

On the desk sat Mr Zoy's file. Matt debated whether he should now add details of the injection he had given before the man's death. The file would be checked and signed out by one more doctor who would scarcely look at it. Unless, of course, an autopsy was requested. The high concentration of Zornitol in the decedent's blood could be explained if Matt declared that he had injected only 150 mgs. The fact that the patient had died forty minutes after the injection would be harder to ignore.

He hovered by the file for a moment, feeling the fresh air circling his cheeks.

The secretary reappeared in the doorway.

'I hate to tell you this but it is now five minutes to and you already have three patients waiting in line,' she reported. 'My, but they're eager beavers this morning.'

'Okay,' said Matt, grabbing his white coat and heading down the dingy hallway to the examining rooms.

The first patient was a straightforward lymph node biopsy, the second had been treated for bowel cancer but a solitary secondary tumour had now been detected in her liver. Matt took notes and told them their operations would be scheduled as soon as possible. Before the third patient could enter, his secretary stepped smartly into the room, holding a coffee in one hand and a file in the other. She pushed the door shut behind her with her foot.

'It's the son,' she said. 'I gave him eleven o'clock but he's demanding to see you now.'

Matt knew whose son she meant but felt it was appropriate to appear confused.

'Mr Zoy's son. Mr Zoy who died last night,' she hissed, slapping the Zoy file down in front of him.

'Is Mrs Zoy here?'

'No. And there are a lot of other people waiting for you and he has an appointment at eleven o'clock, and excuse me but the people outside are alive patients and his father is a dead patient and so I think he can wait another couple of hours.'

But the door had opened and a large, fleshy, fat-cheeked version of Mr Zoy was standing between the secretary and the hospital chaperone.

'I asked you to wait,' the secretary informed him fiercely.

'But . . .' he blurted out, 'my dad just died.' He looked like a confused child. His cheeks swelled as though he were about to cry. Matt, who had been wondering what to say during this meeting, felt an unfamiliar stinging sensation behind his eyes. For a fraction of a second he smelled a dark, dank smell of the forest and it seemed that there were trees all around him, but he was already getting up and walking around the desk in his office, knowing without thinking about it what to do with this unhappy man.

'Come right in,' he said, taking the man's arm and leading him to a seat. 'I'm very, very sorry about your father. I know he was an exceptional person.'

The secretary and the chaperone melted away, leaving the smell of coffee. Matt thought about how Mr Zoy had calmly, without aggression or antagonism, placed his request to die. Probably he had an urge to fight death but his need to spare his family the suffering of his final days had been greater. Yes, he had been an exceptional person.

The son was crying now. His body was large and his sobs filled the room. Matt passed him a handful of tissues and then opened another box.

'It was so sudden!' said the son when he could speak, raising a wet face to look at Matt. 'He wasn't supposed to die yet. We had a lot of things to say to each other and we didn't get them said.'

'That's how most people feel when someone dies, even if the death was expected like your father's,' Matt told him. He wondered if he would feel that way after his own father's death. There were things he knew he should say to Hirsh but somehow the time was never right. He had resolved to speak on many occasions but something always stopped him. He decided, right now, that he would say the unsayable, ask the unaskable of Hirsh next time he saw him. He would do it this weekend.

The man had started to cry again.

'I didn't tell him how much I loved him!' he gasped, snatching at the words between sobs. Matt tried to imagine himself telling Hirsh how much he loved him. But that was the kind of thing you didn't say. You just didn't talk to the old guy about love.

When he opened his mouth to speak, Matt detected something heavy in his own voice, as though it were a loaf of bread someone had sliced too thickly.

'You didn't tell him. But,' he suggested, 'maybe your father knew anyway.'

The man scrubbed at his face with the tissues until they became a small, soaking ball. He held this out helplessly to Matt, who took it and threw it away and gave him some more tissues.

'And . . . and . . .' heaved the man, 'he didn't tell me either. He must have meant to tell me he loved me, but he didn't have time to do it.'

'Maybe he subscribed to the view,' said Matt, 'that some things don't need to be said.'

'No, no, he died too suddenly. He hadn't finished the things he meant to do.'

'He was ready to die,' Matt said.

As if he had flicked a switch, the man's face changed. It grew thinner, sharper, and his eyes looked small and bright. Matt remembered the eyes of Mr Zoy as he had asked Matt to finish his life. Matt had thought they were too bright for death but death had come anyway.

'Did he tell you that, Dr Seleckis?' demanded the bereaved man. For the first time, his voice held no sign of disintegration and he threw back his head a little and ran a hand through his hair in a gesture that reminded Matt of a rearing horse. 'Dr Seleckis, did my father tell you he was ready to die?'

Matt felt hot. He wished his secretary would appear with her Washington State apple cheeks and her capacious purse and produce from it a screwdriver with which, right now, she would dismantle the window of the consulting room.

'Your father knew he was going to die, Mr Zoy,' he said.

'He knew, sure, but was he ready? He didn't even say goodbye, for God's sake.'

'That's too hard for some people, for many people.'

'He wasn't ready. They were going to try some new

treatment on him. Dr Salinski said so. He said it could give my dad a few more months, maybe a lot more.'

Matt was startled by this. He said, 'There's nothing about further treatment in your father's notes.' He hoped he had read the notes properly. He wanted to grab the file right now but the man was already demanding more information.

'Did he say he was ready? When did you last speak with him?'

'Last night,' admitted Matt.

'What did he say?'

Matt paused. 'That he was in pain.'

'So what did you do?'

'I made a small adjustment to his pain relief since his existing dose was having almost no effect.'

The son's eyes narrowed.

'How small was this adjustment?' he demanded. Matt felt like a child clinging to some precious toy which a larger, tougher kid was trying to snatch away from him.

'I can give you all the details of your father's drug regime and how we chose to manage it, but not now. I think that, if you need any further discussion, then your mother would probably want to be present.'

Matt remembered the calm, clear-voiced Mrs Zoy with a rush of affection. She had said, 'If Anthony doesn't want you to do it, if he chooses to wait for death, then he won't ask. But if his pain and distress become unbearable, we hope you'll respond with humanity to his request for help.' A woman who would make a speech like that could be relied upon to protect Matt from the savagery of her son, even in her grief.

'What kind of doctor are you?' demanded Mr Zoy's son. The lines on his face stiffened and his body inflated a little so that he seemed now to loom over the desk.

Matt drew back. He recognized this ability to increase body size at will as, uniquely, the ability of a bully. He recognized it from school recess and from someplace else, way back. There had been a man, huge in frame, dark-haired and dark-eyed who could swell before you, and when he did that you braced yourself because it meant he was going to say something mean and demeaning.

Matt felt suddenly nauseous. He found it hard to address himself to the Zoy son's question. He looked down at the place his feet would be if he were standing up instead of sitting stiffly at a desk.

'Er . . . a good doctor, I hope . . .' he finally replied.

'So you're a pain specialist? Right?'

'Oh,' said Matt, amazed that he had misunderstood the question. 'Oh, I see what you mean. I'm a general surgeon but my specialization is endocrine and oncological surgery. That means —'

'And how long have you been a surgeon?' the man demanded.

'Well, I guess I started during my residency . . . say, nine years ago.'

The man ran his hand through his hair again and looked angrily at Matt, as if he expected him to add something, so Matt went on: 'After that, I moved towards gastrointestinal surgery but I realized I'd made a mistake. I spent three years in field hospitals in Africa, which gave me wide surgical experience. Since I got back I've moved into endocrine and oncological surgery. It's an unusual career path.'

'I'm waiting,' said the man dangerously. 'I'm waiting to hear that at some point in your career you specialized in pain relief. I'm waiting to hear how a guy who's spent years learning how to cut people open can know what drug to put in the arm of an old man in pain, a man who had been given every reason to believe that new treatment would prolong his life.'

Matt rearranged himself in his chair. He remembered how he had thought of calling Mike Salinski last night and decided against it because of the oncologist's drink problem. He tried to make his voice calm and reasonable.

'It happens that I do have very extensive experience in pain relief from my time in Africa. But, in this case, remember I operated on your father twice and have been a key member of his treatment team. We're all trained to deal with pain relief at this hospital, although we refer patients who need long-term palliative care to Red House. In your father's case, we opted for ongoing care here and he and your mother agreed to that. Your mother seemed to have no worries about Mr Zoy's medical team.'

The man stood up suddenly and Matt saw how big he was. He wore a short-sleeved shirt. His arms had the full curves of the overfed. Who was that other overproportioned man in Matt's memory who could bully you effortlessly just by shifting his weight an inch? Matt could not recall a name but thinking about the man made him feel uncomfortable.

Mr Zoy's son was speaking now. His voice was loud, but worse than its volume was its undertone of threat.

'My mother's shocked and very surprised by my father's sudden death. We neither of us thought it was time and neither did Dr Salinski. We're going to demand a full autopsy. I want to reassure myself that the so-called small adjustment to his pain relief, so-called, didn't shorten my father's life. Not by one minute, Dr Seleckis. And my mother's going to be looking for that reassurance also.'

When the man opened the door, Matt could see beyond him to the waiting area shared by all the surgical examining

rooms. It was thronged with patients and most head
turned at the sound of the door, or perhaps at the
voice beyond it. Mr Zoy's son, in his anger, left the
wide open. Matt felt exposed, like an actor on whom the
curtain has been raised prematurely.

He had an intercom he could use for the chaperone to
bring in the next patient but instead he regained his com-
posure by walking into the waiting room and summoning
the patient himself. He did not recognize the middle-aged
woman who leaped up at the sound of her name. She did
not greet him but walked right past him into the examining
room, pulling up her shirt to expose the wound on her belly
before she was inside. She began to exude words as though
they were oozing from her surgical scar.

Matt examined the scar while she talked and then sat
down near her, watching her thyroid, how her eyes darted
then stared, how her face moved as she spoke, the extrava-
gance of her hand gestures. He forgot the Zoy family. He
opened the woman's file and glanced down at her notes as
she talked, talked without stopping. Her story involved a
suggestion of medical negligence and a hint of domestic
violence. She was unable to present her physical condition
separately from her personal problems and, he knew, was
somehow asking him to treat her unhappiness. As with every
new patient, he had rapidly and simultaneously to assimilate
the information delivered in a file, in the patient's own
words, and by his own eyes. Then he had to synthesize this
into a coherent understanding and a proposal for treatment.
All this while showing kindness and sympathy as well as
maintaining the minimum patient consultative turnover
figures for the Department of General Surgery set by the
hospital's management board.

Saturated by the array of human problems placed before

him over the next hour or two, he thought he had eliminated the Zoy case from his mind. But at almost exactly eleven o'clock he found himself checking his watch. He called his secretary and asked if she thought Mrs Zoy had any intention of keeping their original appointment.

His secretary made a low whistling noise. 'Isn't one Zoy enough for you? I mean, the son's phoned three times. He wants an autopsy. The mother's next-of-kin so I've had her calling to confirm. Then she phones to ask when they get the results. Plus she must've talked to the labs because I just had a call requesting the decedent's file.'

'I'll take it down there at lunchtime,' said Matt. 'I need a walk in the bracing spring air.'

'There's lots of bracing spring air in the office,' said the secretary happily.

'Who's the pathologist doing the Zoy autopsy?' asked Matt. One of the hospital pathologists was a sort of friend with whom he occasionally ate lunch.

'R. R. Ringling. Sounds like a telephone company. Know him?'

'No.'

Matt tried calling Mike Salinski but he was unavailable. He looked through the Zoy file to confirm that the oncologist had written nothing about a new course of treatment.

His phone buzzed and a brisk woman announced herself as Rachel Ringling.

'I'm waiting for a patient file from you,' she said. 'I've already requested it once this morning.'

'Are you doing the autopsy on Mr Zoy today?' asked Matt. Usually bodies were lined up on trolleys awaiting autopsy like cars in a gridlocked city.

'Just as soon as I get that file,' she said shortly.

'I was planning to bring it over when I've finished my morning patients. I'd like to discuss it with you.'

'No discussion necessary. I need it right now, I'll send someone.'

Matt checked the file once more for a note from Mike indicating that he planned further treatment for the patient. When he was satisfied there was none, he scribbled an almost indecipherable line on the back confirming, just above the nurse's report of the patient's death, that he had administered 150 mgs of Zornitol at 11.45 p.m. The resident had already signed the file, stating that the primary cause of death was respiratory failure due to metastasis of thyroid cancer to the lung.

Matt squinted at the words and closed his eyes. Immediately he could smell the forest. His heart began to pound and his breathing became laboured. He was surrounded by trees. He could hear the whisper of leaves beneath his feet as he searched for the car. The search had all the familiarity of routine. He suspected that he had been looking for the figure in the red car every night, in his dreams, for many years. This time, however, he could not see the red car, although the smell of the forest's decay, the presence of death and the knowledge of his own role in that death enveloped him again. The knowledge was a burden. It was almost too much for him to carry. He was stumbling between the trees, staggering sometimes with a weight so heavy that it tugged down on his right arm and banged viciously and repeatedly against his right leg. He arrived at a clearing in the woods. There below was the lake, sun bouncing off it so that it looked like a hoop of shining light. And here were his parents. They were sitting with their backs to him on a seat or a log, not the ground. Evidently he was surprised by something because he stopped suddenly. They heard him and turned around to face him. For a moment he glimpsed his mother's face, and then, as usual, she was gone. Matt was left wondering if this was a dream or a memory.

'Got a moment?' said a voice from the door. Matt put the Zoy file rapidly aside as though it were hot.

'Hi, Jon,' he said.

Jon Espersen was the amiable head of General Surgery. It had been Jon's decision to rehire Matt after his long spell in Africa.

'Next week's M and M, we'd like to change it to Monday. Can you do that or would it be a nightmare of re-organization?'

Matt picked up his diary. The two men had known each other for many years. When Matt was a new young resident, Jon had been a senior, and Matt had followed him up through General Surgery and specifically into endocrine and oncological surgery. But when Jon had started to help run the department, seeking to develop its reputation, he had shepherded Matt and others into gatrointestinal work. The new gastric bypass operations came in and Jon founded, at the expense of other areas, the Obesity Unit. Matt remembered himself in those earlier days as too large and too gawky, as though his body and the way he used it was a physical manifestation of some inner awkwardness. Colleagues always detected this about him and interpreted it as an unwillingness to compromise, and it made them uneasy. Matt had alienated many, including many who agreed with him, when he had argued strenuously against the Obesity Unit. Then, after the first time he had cut through the layers of subcutaneous fat on a woman the weight of a large pony, Matt had announced his intention to leave for Africa.

'Come on now, you're overreacting,' Jon had argued right

back at him. 'Africans are needy because they have too little, Americans are needy because they have too much. But they're all needy.'

Matt agreed with this but he knew with certainty that he did not want to spend the rest of his life performing obesity operations.

'I don't want to get fat on fat,' he had said and Jon, who was almost wilfully good-natured, had smiled and eventually accepted his decision to go.

'What time Monday do you want the M and M?' asked Matt. Morbidity and Mortality conferences were compulsory weekly closed-door sessions when surgeons were supposed to confess their mistakes and confide their worries to one another.

'Morning?'

'Well, if it's early . . .'

'How about eight? A lot of people are saying they can do eight o'clock.'

'Fine.'

'Do you have anything you want to discuss?' asked Jon. His tone was relaxed but his eyes were sharp. His good-natured bulkiness and easy manner masked an acute intelligence.

'Well, maybe,' admitted Matt.

'Good. We'll confirm Monday at eight with your secretary,' said Jon. 'How's Denise doing these days? Christine was saying it's a while since they've seen each other.'

Their wives were friends, and it was a friendship which predated Matt's relationship with Denise. It went right back to Denise's first marriage.

'She's fine, just always busy with Austin and workshops. But I'll tell her to call Christine,' Matt promised.

Jon waved and disappeared. There was a small knock at

27

the door and a very young man entered. Matt thought this must be the next patient but the boy said hesitantly, too shy to look into Matt's face, 'Dr Ringling sent me . . .'

'Oh sure, I have what she wanted right here,' said Matt, and he handed the shy boy the Zoy file and buzzed in the next patient.

3

The very next day, Matt experienced once again that strange, stinging sensation behind his eyes. It happened as he watched his father trying to pick up a log in the woodshed. It was like a cloud of small bugs trapped in his head buzzing tirelessly at the windows. After a couple of moments he realized with a start what was happening. He was going to cry.

He stepped out of the woodshed into the feisty sunshine. He took deep breaths. He ran his eye along the distant treeline and up over the jagged white tops of the mountains like a child tracing with his finger a familiar pattern in the rug.

Then he turned around. For a few moments more he watched his father, Hirsh Seleckis, Dr Hirsh Seleckis, aged seventy-five, stiff around the hips, particularly the right, sometimes forgetful, his hair still abundant but now snowy-white, yet certainly recognizable as that same strong and dependable Dr Hirsh Seleckis whom Matt had known all his life . . . he watched this man struggle with a log. As he watched, the cloud of insects came back. They banged fervently against the inside of Matt's face without regard for their own safety or Matt's. His eyes, in what felt like self-defence, began to exude water.

Matt couldn't remember the last time he had cried. His work had brought him into contact with so much human suffering that he believed he was almost immune to tears, his own or others'. When people cried he felt the detachment of a bank clerk counting money (that rustle and thump of bills, efficiently smoothed by rapid fingers, snapped into place, the quantity noted, without reference to, or thought for, the sweat which earned those bills or the goods they might buy). But now he realized that, since he had caused the death of Mr Zoy, he had experienced some grief of his own. He could hardly believe it. His own tears were so unknown to him that he had no recollection, even, of crying at his mother's death. And now, as the sun pierced the holes in the woodshed roof with long, straight spears of light and his father bent over the log, wrestling with it unsuccessfully and breathlessly, as a rip gaped in the old man's plaid work shirt revealing whiteness, thinness, oldness where Matt had only ever known strength, as father and son inhaled the shed's air of still woodiness, Matt was forced to give in to tears.

He wanted to help his father with the log but it was imperative that Hirsh did not see him crying. He stumbled along the path through the woods, not in the direction of the house but down the steep hill towards the road and the lake. When he was out of range of eye or ear he leaned against a tree and allowed his chest to heave painfully into the silence and the tears to run down his face in salty rivers. The smell of the woods, their earthy dampness, enveloped him. He did nothing to dam his tears and they fell on to his chin and then his shirt.

Far below, through the leafless trees, you could catch glimpses of the lake. It was still as an animal waiting to pounce. It was the deep, deep blue of deep, deep mountain water. Matt recalled how it felt to swim it those cold depths, how it seemed to be composed of some other kind of water from his hot tears. Its iciness bit at your limbs while the sun warmed your back and burned your cheeks and made your hair feel like a hot hat. He had spent all his boyhood summers making camps in these woods and swimming in that lake.

Still shuddering a little, but aware that the storm which had hit him was beginning to subside, he darted from the shelter of the tree to the shelter of the next, as though he were expecting another shower imminently. Nearby, between two trees, was what looked like a giant wooden spider's web. Someone had nailed planks and gnarled lumber to the branches of growing trees so many years ago that now the dead and the living wood were twisted up together. In places, sunlight shone through. He recognized this as the remains of one of his mother's sculptures. Hilly, when she had given up her real love, music, had transferred her affections from one art form to another and then another. This had been her sculpture trail. Like almost all her other efforts, it was never finished, although the sculpture trail had been cut short by her illness rather than the usual loss of enthusiasm.

And then he saw it. A wooden seat that Hirsh had made many years ago from logs and which Matt had seen a thousand times since but which he now recognized anew. It was the seat on which his parents had been sitting in his dream, no, in his memory, for that stumbling rush through the forest with some heavy load to find his parents now had all the texture of something remembered.

He felt the excitement of stepping into his own memory. He had been standing right here when he had come upon them. Exactly, right here. In those days, when the trees were lower, you could see down to the lake and the sun had been shining across it so that it had looked like a huge disc of light behind his parents.

He had felt relieved, even surprised at first, to find them. They were sitting close together, their arms around each other. He hadn't wanted to interrupt them but he had something to say, something important he had been hurrying to tell them. His heart was banging against his chest like a bird throwing itself against the wires of a cage. In his hand there was a burden which plucked at his shoulder socket and had bruised his right leg. He put it down now and its contact with the generations of dead leaves on the forest floor released a fresh, pungent odour. He put it down, but the great weight he was carrying did not leave him and he recognized that the weight came from inside him, from a hideous knowledge that there had been a death and he had caused it and he was old enough to understand that, even if you said you were sorry, death remained an irrevocable, irreversible event.

He said something, maybe called to his parents, and they had turned and when he saw their faces he . . . he . . . here the memory became dream-like again because it seemed to him that both their faces were ashen and his mother's tearful.

He longed to chase after the memory, like a dog chasing a rabbit right down into its hole and dragging it out. But as usual, any memory involving his mother was elusive. It had evaporated now, leaving him with its burden.

He sat down on the log seat. He closed his eyes and let emotion lead him back into the past, but now he was not at the log seat, he was standing amid the trees again at a distance away from the red car. He wanted to get closer but something was preventing him, so he had halted and was now staring through the trees, trying to discern the dim shape behind the steering wheel. Once again he was waiting for the shape to move, willing it to open the car door, to get out, to shout, to bellow reassuringly with laughter, but the shape remained motionless.

He was so overcome by nausea that he at once opened

his eyes and the trees all around him in his father's hillside yard listed and leaned for a moment like the bristles of some giant ancient brush.

His tongue felt metallic. He examined the log seat. The curious patterns in its surface had been carved not by Hilly or Hirsh but by armies of insects over the years. Nearby, the evidence of Hilly's sculptures was almost archaeological. When Hilly had died, Matt and Hirsh had, in a small act of homage, tried to finish some of her uncompleted projects: the sculptures, the mosaics, the wall collages, the Christmas decorations, the sewing; they had even considered whether they should find someone to continue the three chapters of the novel she had once started. But gradually their endeavours had been overtaken by a sense of futility. Guiltily, without talking about it, they had dropped the projects, Matt first and then Hirsh.

From this seat you were supposed to be able to see the lake and admire the sculpture trail but the trees had grown right up to smother everything, the sculptures were ruined and he was a man now and not a boy. Below, a car engine hummed as it passed the lake and climbed up the mountain road. He sighed. These days, Matt often reached out for his mother, trying to capture something more substantial than his own elusive memories, but she always slipped away without ever leaving a fragment of herself, not a cell of her skin or the hem of her dress. Matt dated this keen new hunger to know her from the birth of his son.

He got up slowly and began to gather some of the fallen lumber from beneath the crumbling wooden shapes. It was only good for burning now but he felt diffident about burning his mother's sculpture. Hirsh had probably seen the wood and chosen not to take it, but Matt resolutely tucked the damp lumber under his arm and picked his way back up the woody path, feeling the sun, like a rich but capricious relative who bestowed gifts and then kept taking them back, briefly warm his face every time he stepped out from under a tree.

If Hirsh recognized the wood, he made no comment. He made no comment about Matt's absence either, although he looked hard at his son's face, perhaps searching for an explanation. Matt had known he would and had taken care to position himself away from the light. The rip in Hirsh's shirt sleeve gaped as he stacked the wood. Matt tried to ignore the similarity between this thin white arm and the arm of Mr Zoy as the needle had sought a vein. He thought Hirsh looked older than last time and last time was only a month ago. His eyes had sunk a little deeper. Or maybe his face had thinned slightly. It was hard to define aging, to isolate one in that series of small transitions.

Looking around, Matt saw that the struggle between father and log had been lost. His eyes began to sting again at the evidence that Hirsh, once alone, had taken something much smaller on to the sawhorse.

Matt went to the big log which had defeated his father and made a show, yes, he acted, faked, the action of a man picking up an extraordinarily heavy piece of lumber. He gasped at its weight as he hoisted it into the air, staggered with it to the sawhorse and then set it down, leaning against it, breathing deeply. His father watched him from the half-dark, and maybe, just maybe, he raised one eyebrow a little, Matt couldn't be sure because he now felt really breathless. The log had been light enough but the mime show seemed to have some weight of its own.

He dusted off his hands. Hirsh added a piece of rotting lumber to the stack and it made a dull, crumbling noise, then broke.

'Dad, I killed a man,' Matt heard his voice say. The words sounded wooden in the still air. They sounded old and rotten. He could smell decay.

The break in Hirsh's activity was almost imperceptible. He froze, momentarily, and then continued to arrange the lumber so it lay in line with all the rest of the stack. When he had finished, he straightened his body upright, twisting it a little at the right hip. He looked directly at Matt. Even in the dim woodshed you could see how brown his eyes were, how they shone from inside. He was alert. His look was searching.

'I know,' he said at last.

Matt, leaning against the ancient timber walls of the shed, felt his body lurch a little as though the walls had given way. How could Hirsh possibly know about Mr Zoy's thin, unshaven cheeks on the hospital pillow, his insistent, whispered request to die? And then he understood that Hirsh had dealt with similar situations in his time, that he had probably, as a family doctor, faced the requests of the dying more often that Matt. He would never have given in to these requests. His 'I know' indicated that he guessed Matt would.

Matt told the whole story. At the end, Hirsh was silent, then he asked, 'How many milligrams of Zornitol did you give him?'

'Two hundred milligrams.'

'When was his last dose?'

'Two hours before. He was having one hundred milligrams every four hours but it wasn't working for him. Or not enough to make him want to live a little longer.'

Hirsh nodded. His face remained expressionless. He said, 'Supposing the nurse had arrived when you called. Would you have told her to give two hundred milligrams?'

35

Before he thought about that, Matt smiled a little at the way, for a man of Hirsh's generation, nurses would always be female. Then he considered his answer.

'Probably I would have had her give just one hundred and fifty' he said at last.

There was a silence which went on so long that Matt began to feel uncomfortable. He sat down on a log and waited for Hirsh to speak but it seemed he was never going to. Finally Matt asked, 'So, was I wrong?'

Hirsh sighed.

'Probably most people would say you weren't wrong. But you were wrong in the eyes of the law. I think you must have known you were taking a risk. I mean, one hundred and fifty milligrams could just about have qualified as pain relief but two hundred . . .' Hirsh grimaced. 'Why did you do it?'

'I don't know why I gave in,' admitted Matt, remembering how Mr Zoy had looked at him as though he knew him, as though he knew what Matt had done and what he would do, just the way Hirsh was looking at him now.

'Why doesn't Mrs Zoy get the god-awful son off my back?' he asked irritably. 'Why is she calling the path labs and demanding an autopsy when she was the one who asked me to show some humanity if the old guy requested it?'

'Because he's dead and she isn't feeling too good,' said Hirsh. 'Probably he was ready but she wasn't. He might have told her she could be there when he died. Or maybe she's just letting the son blow off his anger for a while.'

'Supposing the hospital investigation board starts to ask questions?'

'Don't tell them any more than you have to. And you should disclose that a senior oncologist is a drunk and can't be called in the evenings for a prognosis.'

'I couldn't say that!' said Matt

'He needs help if he's drinking every night.'

'He can do what he likes when he isn't on call.'

'Does he get drunk when he is on call?'

Matt had twice been phoned in the night recently by apologetic residents who should have been calling Salinski and Matt had guessed why.

'He really is a good doctor. And a nice guy, not one of the prima donnas,' Matt insisted.

'I've seen doctors close ranks on a faltering colleague too many times,' said Hirsh, and Matt shrugged because he didn't see himself as a member of the ranks at St Claudia's and he was pretty sure his colleagues didn't see him that way either. His circuitous career path, combined with his failure to interest himself in a golf handicap, marked him as an outsider.

He said, 'It may even be worse than the hospital investigation board. Rachel Ringling in the path labs sounds like the kind of woman who'll bypass the hospital procedures and just hand Zoy's file right over to the state prosecutor the minute she finishes the autopsy.'

Hirsh thought for a minute, and when he spoke he sounded so serious that Matt felt immediately nervous. 'Yes,' said Hirsh. 'I'm afraid that is possible.'

Matt's voice was very small in the quiet woodshed. 'Do I need a lawyer?' he asked.

Hirsh said, 'Not this time. Not yet, anyway.'

Matt looked at Hirsh. He asked, 'Did you ever kill anyone?'

'Oh yes,' said Hirsh. Matt studied him keenly. Hirsh's definitions were strict. Probably some small oversight had meant he once failed to save a life rather than that he had actually taken it. Matt waited, hoping Hirsh would offer more details, but his father began to stack logs in a decisive way which prevented further questioning.

That night Matt, though tired, slept poorly. He was finally asleep when he heard a gunshot.

He woke up instantly and felt his body temperature drop. Small hairs all over his legs and arms and neck stood upright. He started to sweat and shiver at the same time. He fought an urge to retch. The gunshot was bad enough but, worse, it must have broken into a dream about the car, the red car in the woods, because he was now experiencing the misery and nausea which accompanied the car like a bad smell.

He tried to sit up in bed but there was a burden on his chest, a residue from his dream, which felt too heavy to discard and too painful to carry. A man was dead and it was his fault. He remembered Mr Zoy. He rolled over so that he lay face down into the pillow.

He wanted to lie still under his burden, waiting for it to lift or go away or pass by osmosis back into the fabric of his body, but knowing that he could not leave the gunshot in the air, uninvestigated, unchallenged, he rolled over again and pulled himself on to his elbows with a massive effort and listened into the night. He was straining to hear anything which wasn't silence. It seemed to him that the shot had been unnaturally loud and that its report had echoed on and on as though someone had fired a rifle right outside the house, brutalizing the silence and deafening the inhabitants.

When he had been motionless and alert for long enough, he turned on a light and shuffled towards Hirsh's room. His tongue felt metallic and the smell of the outdoors, of damp trees and rotting leaves, seemed to fill his nostrils.

He knocked on the door.

'Dad? Dad!'

There was no reply and now the silence induced as much

panic as the gunshot. Like Austin looking for comfort in the night, he pushed his way into his father's room.

'Dad!' he said loudly and he heard Hirsh start and gasp for breath. The light went on and Hirsh was sitting upright in bed, staring at him.

'Matt? Is that you? What's happened?' Hirsh began feeling for his eyeglasses on the table beside him.

'Did you hear it?' demanded Matt.

'What?'

'The gun! Someone fired a gun right outside the house!'

Hirsh put on the glasses and blinked for a moment. He looked old, the wrinkles etched deep into his face.

'Right outside?' he demanded.

'Well, it was loud, real loud.'

'Oh . . .' said Hirsh. 'Noise always sounds loud at night. It'll just be Stewart shooting raccoons. Ever since he got a night sight he's been decimating the raccoon population around here.'

'It sounded closer than Stewart's house.'

'Well, the raccoon may have led him over this way. Don't worry about it.'

'A single gunshot in the middle of the night in the middle of nowhere and you don't think we should worry?' demanded Matt. But he was beginning to feel less sure of himself now.

'It happens more often than you'd think. And believe it or not, we don't consider ourselves the middle of nowhere. And it's only just after midnight, not so late. Or . . . you might have dreamed it.'

Matt felt irritable. 'I wasn't dreaming about guns.'

'Well, don't worry, just go back to bed,' Hirsh instructed. His light had clicked off before Matt even closed the door.

Matt returned to his room but he knew he would not

sleep. He opened the window. Cold mountain air rushed in on him. Otherwise, there was nothing. He craned his neck out of the window. More nothing. He could occasionally detect movement up in the treetops, the mass movement of branches in the breeze.

He waited and listened, the cold gradually anaesthetizing his body and his fears. Despite the fact that he had lived in the hunting state of Utah most of his life and, during his years away, had never been far from the thud of battle and the report of firearms, the sound of just one single shot always harried him. A single shot indicated a direct hit, a target awaited, a kill fast and sudden.

When he climbed back into bed the sheets felt cold and unwelcoming. The shot began to echo inside his head as though the muzzle of a rifle had been fired right down into a well, the well where all the memories were. The red car, forgotten for years, now only had to be recalled for an instant for its residue of misery to last for hours. It was like poison ivy: a second's contact could cause weals across the skin which remained for months or even years. He knew that he had done something terrible to the figure in the red car and that this knowledge was protean and could take on many hideous shapes and that probably it would be less harmful to find out the truth than to live with the fears it generated. But, just now, the contact with his past which such an investigation would necessitate was an unbearable prospect.

'It wasn't Stewart, it was John-Jack Perry,' Hirsh informed him at breakfast. 'I just called and he said he fired at a raccoon last night.'

'Was he right outside this house?'

'No, down near the lake, on the road near Stewart's place.'

Hirsh was cooking oatmeal, watching it and stirring it

with a wooden spoon which made soft, tapping noises on the side of the pan. He had placed a bowl of sliced fruit in the middle of the table. Matt sat down and picked up a piece of apple.

'But it was so loud!' he said.

'Sounds are loud at night, especially here, because noise moves up the mountain. He agreed it was anti-social to be shooting after midnight. But John-Jack needs something to shoot outside the hunting season or he gets sort of edgy. He's been that way ever since Anita left him.'

Over the years, since he had become a full-time resident, Hirsh had got to know just about everyone in town and he knew their stories too, as though he had lived here all his life.

'I guess he hit the raccoon,' said Matt, 'as he only fired one shot.'

'No, he missed. One shot's all you get at most beasts. After that they're gone or they're dead. Surely you remember that much about hunting?'

'I don't remember much about hunting,' Matt confessed. 'Except I didn't enjoy trying to kill wild things.'

'We've all got the killer instinct,' said Hirsh, beginning to distribute the oatmeal evenly between two bowls.

'The killer instinct was for cavemen,' Matt said. 'It was bred out of us between the Ice Age and the day someone baked the first Orio cookie.'

Hirsh shook his head. 'We all have a killer instinct and if you think otherwise, I blame myself. We had just that one hunting trip and it wasn't a big success.'

'I don't remember anything much about that, either,' said Matt.

'You must remember something, just a little,' Hirsh told him, and Matt realized that he did. He remembered a whole

crowd of hunters, perhaps too many. They had been instructed to move soundlessly through the undergrowth looking for signs of deer, their scrapings or their footprints or
the marks they left on trees with their antlers. Whenever
you cracked a twig everyone was mad at you but they
couldn't talk so they just glared. He had been wet and cold,
and then it had all ended with a massive and sickening crack
of gunfire, just like last night's.

'Did we kill anything?' he asked Hirsh.

'No,' said Hirsh patiently.

Matt knew he had forgotten the hunting trip because it
had been unpleasant and he had chosen to forget it. Memories were like tiny mammals which you kept in dark cages.
Sometimes you had to open the cage and fetch out the
animal and stroke it and feed it. If you failed to do this, it
would just quietly die of neglect. He was almost certain he
hadn't opened the cage marked Hunting Trip in years because he had wanted whatever was inside it to fade and die.

'I know what would jog your memory,' said Hirsh. 'I'm
pretty sure I have a home movie about it.'

Matt's heart sank. There was nothing wrong with the
word home, or the word movie, but when you put them
together they made a horrible sound.

'I don't think so, Dad,' he said. 'You wouldn't have been
able to take that heavy old cine equipment hunting along
with your gun.'

'Maybe I just filmed the beginning. When we were setting
off or practising. I'm sure there's something about it. We
should take a look . . .'

Matt remembered the home movie ritual with dread. It
took hours to find the reels in their metal cases and then
more hours to erect the screen, then the projector had to
be positioned and repositioned so that the picture fell on

42

the screen and not on the paintings which hung on the wall beyond, making for surreal double images. Finally the projector, which was capricious, had to be persuaded to work, but not so enthusiastically that it burned the film. When it was whirring smoothly and emitting an ominous heat there were a few moments of bright light on the screen before the movie started. Usually Matt and his mother, the movie's only audience, had stretched out their hands and made shadow puppets, their brief contribution to the evening's entertainment. He remembered his mother's fingers making rabbits' ears twitch on screen. He had, in these snatched seconds over the years, perfected a two-handed duck. And then there were numbers flashing by and they dropped their hands back in their laps as the movie began.

What followed was always humiliation and embarrassment. Generally it had taken Hirsh so long to organize the processing of a film and then to edit it that the Matt in the audience was old enough to find the antics of the Matt on the screen hideously juvenile. After the first few minutes he would discover himself watching the screen through splayed fingers as though it were a late-night horror movie. Between his hands he saw a scrawny, strangely half-formed kid in too short or too baggy pants and with too long or too short hair, and Matt denounced him. There could be no relationship between himself and that kid closer than cousin, no, make that second cousin. The young Matt threw himself around energetically but aimlessly in the periphery of shots as though he had rabies. He seemed to want to attract the camera's attention and then, when something especially idiotic achieved this aim, apparently had no idea what to do in the camera's eye and backed off, pulling faces and falling over.

'I could get it all ready for the next time you come. I'll

43

need to find the projector and . . .' Hirsh was saying, but Matt wasn't listening to him.

The last time he had seen Hirsh's home movies was in that period of numb grief which followed soon after Hilly's death and which he now remembered as a months-long silence. Maybe they had already begun to feel the substance of their memories of Hilly slipping away from them, maybe that was why Hirsh had suggested getting out the old movies. But the movies' therapeutic value had been non-existent.

'I may have to ask you to climb up into the roof space . . .' Hirsh had finished his oatmeal and was thinking out loud. 'The reels of film are all up there.'

'Sure,' said Matt heavily. He hoped that Hirsh would forget all about the idea but right after breakfast he heard the unmistakable sound of the ladder being unfolded and the hatch to the roof space being lifted. He sighed and went into the hallway.

'I could do it myself . . .' said Hirsh, seeing Matt's lack of enthusiasm. 'I must have been up there only last year . . .'

'Just tell me what I'm looking for,' said Matt, taking the torch Hirsh handed him and easing his long body through the hatch. The still air seemed to resist his intrusion. It carried the scent of old things which had long lain untouched and unused.

'Well, somewhere over to the left I built in a sort of closet thing . . .'

'When you say left . . .'

'I mean south. Over the living room.'

Matt had to bend double to approach the closet. He also had to tread carefully and only in the places Hirsh had prepared so his foot didn't go through the living-room ceiling. He wiped cobwebs from his hair and kicked aside the corpse of a mouse which looked as though it had been freeze-dried.

'Are you okay?' Hirsh was standing on the ladder and calling into the roof but the air up here seemed to absorb words like a vacuum. He was saying something about a big black bag which contained the old cans of film.

'It'll take me a while,' called Matt. 'Go make more coffee.'

He looked around at the collection of dusty objects. Most of it was broken furniture but there were some of Hilly's mosaics and pictures stacked up against the chimney. He could see a child's crib. It was green and it had a rabbit, maybe the rabbit from *Goodnight Moon*, painted on the inside where a child waking early would open his eyes and perhaps talk to it. The crib must have been his and there must have been a period of his life when he saw the rabbit every day but he had no recollection of this. Nearby was a small, wooden child's chair, also green with a white rabbit. Matt turned away. There must be a memory of this somewhere inside his head but it had long ago grown frail and disinte- grated, while the crib and the chair had remained as sturdy as ever. That was the opposite of most memories, which retained substance long after the remembered – a place, a person – had ceased to exist.

He went to the makeshift closet that Hirsh had built into the wall and when he opened the door he immediately found the thick black plastic bag. He lifted it and could hear the cans of film sliding over one another inside. As he was closing the door he saw that something, a large envelope, had been lying beneath the bag. He put down the films and picked up the envelope. It was big and thick and was addressed to his father.

Afterwards he asked himself why he hadn't so much as stopped to consider whether he should open an en- velope addressed to someone else. He decided that he must have assumed some relationship between the contents of the envelope and the films that had been lying on top of it.

He pulled out the pile of pages and recognized them immediately, from their size and weight, as dating from the era before photos became more throwaway than memories. They were studio pictures, printed on thick, old photographic card, and, as they emerged from the envelope, he saw that the pictures were black and white.

He turned the photos over and shone his flashlight on the top one. His mother. His heart began to beat faster. He was always looking for Hilly and now, unexpectedly, hidden in a loft closet, he had found her. He pulled the picture towards him and turned it around. He almost immediately drew back from it.

In the photo, his mother was naked except for a scarf, draped to half-cover one breast so that the nipple winked from behind it. She thrust her heavy breasts forward provocatively and her smile was a mixture of greed, excitement and invitation. Matt's head began to throb. Suddenly he felt as though he carried on it a great weight: a boulder, or the full load of the roof just above. He stared at the picture. The moody black and white graininess suggested some artistic pretension on the part of the photographer but the content reduced his mother to a cheap pin-up in a cheap men's magazine.

Balancing the other photos and the torch with difficulty, he put his mother face-down on the shelf she had come from. For a ludicrous moment he feared the back of the photo would show Hilly's backside, her rear caught provocatively mid-wriggle, but there was only the blank photographic card, its age lending it a soft, wool-like quality.

The next picture was similar. Although clearly a studio shot, there had been some attempt to simulate a forest floor. Hilly's skin glistened under the photographer's lamps (had she rubbed herself all over with oil?) and this time she lay back, leaves sprinkled across her body as though she had been sleeping in the forest in the fall and the leaves had just blown there. He looked at her finger and saw that she wore her wedding ring. She wore another ring too, on her right hand, which he thought he recognized. It was a single diamond set in the centre of a simple gold flower, the petals of the flower folding inwards towards the diamond. There had been some story attached to the ring. It had been lost and then found, perhaps. Anyway, it had generated some drama of its own. In the pictures, the light which spun off Hilly's body spun off the diamond too and had been trapped by the camera.

He looked at another picture and then another, quickly, without staring too hard. Despite the provocative arrangement of leaves and scarves and scraps of clothing, he searched for and found something beyond the idiotic vacancy of a pin-up. She had a high, intelligent forehead and her smile was half-mocking, perhaps self-mocking. And he had to admit that she was beautiful, not just her face but her breasts and the unfashionable but sensuous curves of her waist. It was hard to say how old she was. In her sexual prime, certainly: anywhere, in fact, between thirty and forty. And didn't most mothers of that age in that era spend their time buying Girl Scout cookies or taking self-improvement courses at college or donning leotards for the new-style work-outs? But Hilly had always been different: she had been noticeably nonchalant about health and beauty, haphazard about cooking and oblivious to lycra. He shuffled the photos and they made a soft, whispering noise between his fingers. If she had been a stranger to him, he might have admired these pictures. But she was Hilly and he wanted to find his mother, not some shameless sexual exhibitionist.

47

'Have you got them?' called Hirsh from the hatch.

'Yep, I'm just coming,' Matt said, stuffing the pictures back into the envelope and replacing it in the closet.

'What are you looking at?' demanded Hirsh's voice. He sounded agitated. It was imperative that his father did not know he had seen the photos and so, as soon as he had replaced them, Matt grabbed one of the half-finished paintings which leaned nearby.

'I'll show you,' he called.

As he climbed down through the hatch, passing the bag of films first to Hirsh, Matt supposed that his father must have taken the pictures. Hirsh had been a keen amateur photographer, although Matt had never known him take pictures in black and white, or in a studio. His mother and father, he acknowledged with filial grudging, were allowed to have fun together in any way they wanted. It was even sort of nice to think that they had still enjoyed themselves after years and years of marriage.

Hirsh took the bag and the painting.

'Where's that?' asked Matt, looking at the painting as though he had just been examining it up in the roof space. It depicted a rocky stream with high mountains behind struggling for space against a deep blue sky. In one corner a small wooden cabin was sketched in but, typically, Hilly hadn't bothered to complete the picture and the cabin, in pencil strokes only, looked faded and ghost-like.

'Well,' said Hirsh. 'Well, I guess that's the Mouth of Nowhere.'

Matt began putting away the ladder and dusting himself off.

'When did Mom go there?'

'Just before she died, that's why she never finished the picture. We took that hike. That magnificent hike. I don't know

48

how she found the strength except that she really wanted to go and when your mother really wanted something . . .'

'The Mouth of Nowhere,' repeated Matt. The phrase had a certain familiarity. 'Where is it?'

Hirsh gestured to the mountains.

'High, real high. It was quite a hike. Hilly had read about a ghost village up there. It was one of the most beautiful places I've ever been. Your mother thought so too.'

'Where was I?' asked Matt. 'When you went on this hike?'

'I think you opted to stay in town.'

'I didn't want to go hiking? With you and Mom?' Matt was shocked. It would have been one last vacation to remember Hilly by, and he had chosen not to take it.

'You didn't want to be with your mother when she was sick. You didn't like seeing her so quiet and fatigued. You didn't want to know that she was dying.'

Matt was silenced by his own lack of compassion.

'It's okay,' said Hirsh. 'It's normal. She understood. It was better for you to grow away from her before she left you. Anyway, you were a teenager, you were supposed to grow away.'

'So . . . what happened? On this hike?'

'We made camp there for a few days and we swam and ate and talked. That's why your mother called it the Mouth of Nowhere. Because we talked and talked and talked. All those words we had to say. Then we hiked home again. When she found the strength for all that, I thought maybe she would find the strength to live. But she died a few months later.'

Matt wanted to ask Hirsh what the words were which he and Hilly had to say. But, of course, that was the kind of question you couldn't ask Hirsh. Nor could Matt ask him about the red car. The idea of doing so was absurd, the sort

49

of crazy thing you thought of in the night. You might as well get in a rubber inflatable raft on Arrow Lake and, instead of steering around the ghetto of sharp rocks which everyone knew inhabited the lake's cooler west side, row right into them.

Later that morning, Matt walked down to the log seat again, but now the place was devoid of memories. The clear air and fine spring light seemed to penetrate the recesses of his mind and clean away the darkness. He could recall his memory of running through the woods to find his parents here, but he could no longer recall the event itself.

He walked around on the hillside like a browsing animal. Maybe he would recognize the place where the red car had stood. But, except for the drive and the house at the top, Hirsh's yard was too steep for any car.

He scrambled right down the hillside to the road. It was a grey strip of little-used blacktop. It was so silent that his footsteps sounded metallic and their echo was metallic too.

If you followed the road around the lake a little way to the right you passed the Minelli house. In Matt's boyhood there had been four brothers and their parents who stayed here on vacation whenever Matt did and they featured in all his memories. The father, Mr Minelli, had been a big, energetic man who had played ballgames and rough-housed enthusiastically with his boys. The youngest son was small for his age, the same age as Matt, and he had preferred to play with Matt. The two had become friends and were, eventually, inseparable. Swimming, riding, playing in the forest, a short-lived fascination with Monopoly, rope swings, tree houses: Steve and Matt had done everything together. Matt never had such a friend down in the city where he went to school; probably Steve didn't either. In winter, Steve had probably hung out with his big, rough brothers and gone to hockey games with his father, whom Matt now recognized as the bully he had recalled when confronted by Mr Zoy. Mr Minelli had been the guy who could swell suddenly to immense proportions before making some particularly belittling remark. He could make himself bigger and make you smaller at the same time. Privately and in secret, Matt remembered hating Mr Minelli.

He looked through the trees for the Minelli house but it was invisible, or maybe it was just the colour of tree trunks. It seemed strange to him now that he and Steve had been such close friends up here without ever making contact when they were away from Arrow Lake and leading their normal lives down in Salt Lake City. Even though they lived in different parts of town they could have seen each other sometimes but the possibility had never even occurred to them.

Then, one summer, the Minellis didn't come to the lake. Matt had hung around every day waiting for Steve, expecting big Mr Minelli to appear suddenly and frighteningly from around the side of the house, but their lot remained silent and the bushes grew up around it and finally it was filled by strangers. It turned out that the house had been sold because Mr Minelli had died. Matt had never seen Steve or any of the Minelli brothers since.

On remembering the Minellis, Matt swung left along the road. He didn't want to think about Mr Minelli or about Steve any more. Summers weren't the same on Arrow Lake after they had gone. Everything had changed. The Minellis had been replaced in Matt's life not by any new friends but by Hilly's cancer. His mother's illness had gradually come to dominate his world until it had felt like an extra member of the family, an extra person in the room who clung tenaciously to Hilly, following her silently whenever she got up to move around the house. When Hilly had died, Matt felt her absence to be doubly acute because her illness had gone with her.

He walked firmly the opposite way around the lake from the Minelli house. There was an old trail near Stewart's place, leading to the lake. He walked back across the road and up the hillside a bit and it seemed to him possible but not certain that the red car had stood between the trees down there. The possibility triggered no further memories; in fact, the red car began to disintegrate a little. The closer he came to it, the further away it moved, like a rainbow.

When, in the afternoon, Matt started out for the city, he initially drove down the road as far as the lake. Then he backed his car on to the trail by Stewart's place, got out and ran up the hillside a little way and peered back at his car through the trees, and for a moment he was pierced by the knowledge that he had found the place where the red car had stood all those years ago and therefore, probably, where the death had occurred. But he had found it by a process of deduction and his memory was still unable to tell him who had died or why or how he had killed this person. If he wanted to know all that, he would have to ask questions and read old newspaper reports. He decided he did not want to know.

4

When Matt got back down to Salt Lake there was a car standing right outside his house. Since drives were broad and ample here almost nobody parked on the street, certainly not outside Matt's house unless they were visiting.

The car was red. He knew its colour was the reason he found its presence so alarming. The car, parked inappropriately, seemed to have jumped right out of his own subconscious. For a moment he wondered if it were there at all and then he tried to laugh at himself. This kaleidoscopic confusion of past and present was absurd. Of course the car was there. Nevertheless, while he waited for the garage door to begin its silent ascent, he looked at the red car. He saw that someone was sitting in the driver's seat. He stared, waiting, from old habit, for reassurance that the figure would move, but the early evening light danced on the windshield and reduced the figure to nothing more than a motionless shadow, and this was even more alarming than the presence of a discernible nose, eyes and mouth.

His own car safely in the garage, and the door beginning its descent, Matt moved into the darkness at the garage's edge and looked out on the red car at the kerbside. Now he could see the figure more clearly. It was almost certainly a man and the man reached up and touched his head, so there was no question, not that there should ever have been a question, that the man was alive. The man was looking right at the house, maybe right at Matt. He seemed familiar and, as the door swung slowly closed between them, Matt thought he recognized the mixture of crags and bulk which belonged to a patient, or anyway someone connected with the hospital.

In the kitchen he did not call Denise or Austin but instead moved swiftly and silently to the window. He could not hear the red car's engine start so he was surprised when it glided away. He stood looking out of the window for a few moments more but the car did not come back.

In the living room, oblivious to his presence, Denise and Austin were lying on their bellies on the floor doing something with pieces of wood and plastic which was alternately constructive (Denise) and destructive (Austin). He watched them, loving them. Their faces were framed by hair of the same warm chestnut colour and in the evening light their cheeks had such rosy beauty that he sighed, and his sigh alerted Austin to his presence.

The little boy rushed over to him, yelling ecstatically. Matt scooped him up in his arms the way he did every evening. Their reunions were always joyful. There was almost no other daily activity to which this word could properly be applied and, when Matt looked back on the days before he had met Denise, he regarded them as joyless. Now, he was aware that not only did he receive great happiness, but he sometimes actually spread it. When his reunions with Austin had occasionally taken place in public places, a restaurant or a shopping mall or a park, the boy's happiness, his uncomplicated delight at being reunited with his father, brought joy even to complete strangers. Matt knew this because if he looked up he saw smiling faces all around him.

Denise kissed Matt. She said, 'It won't be so cold next time. We'll definitely come with you,' and her words made Matt feel warm, as though he had taken a gulp of whisky, until he remembered that next time there would be the home movies and he couldn't let Denise see those.

'There was a car outside,' he said. 'Do you know who it was?'

Denise shook her head.

'No one rang the bell,' she told him. Matt could not stop himself going back to the window and Austin ran to check too, but the car was gone.

Denise asked about Hirsh and then she said, 'We went to see Grandaddy Clem. You know, Austin really is beginning to look a little like him.'

Matt did not like Denise's folksy use of the word Grandaddy and he wanted Austin to look like his father, not his grandfather, but he was still feeling happy enough to overlook this.

'How is Clem?' he asked.

Denise's brow furrowed. Austin climbed on to Matt's shoulders.

'I think I may have to go back tonight when Austin's in bed,' she said cautiously.

'Why?' demanded Matt with a flash of irritation. He had come home to spend the evening with Denise, but Clem, as so often, had intervened. The old man's nursing care at Mason House was second to none, so why did he always call Denise to plump up his pillows? She was generally exhausted when she got home and Matt suspected her father made unreasonable emotional demands on her although he could not imagine what these might be. Denise was open and generous, but Matt had discovered early in their relationship that she had private areas as well. He had learned not to ask too much about some things: specifically, Denise's father, or her first husband.

'Daddy's sort of agitated at the moment. I just have to sit and talk with him until he calms down.'

'What's he agitated about?'

'He gets thinking about the past, reformatting it a little the way we all do. When you near the end of your life you reassess. And it's not always easy.'

'There are psychiatrists who specialize in that kind of thing,' Matt offered. 'I'll bet that Mason House . . .'

Denise's voice was soft. 'I don't think Daddy needs a shrink. This reassessment is a perfectly natural, normal process and he's coping with it pretty well.'

Matt thought of his own father. Hirsh had given no indication that he recognized death's proximity but maybe he underwent the uncomfortable process Denise had described at night, alone and unhappy. What stopped him from calling Matt the way Clem called Denise whenever he was anguished? Compared to Hirsh, Clem was very good at growing old. To relieve his daughters of any concern he had selected Mason House because it provided a high standard of meals, care and support. There was a gym and a pool and a hairdresser and a choice of restaurants and the facility had won awards for the variety and quality of its community activities and for its success in maintaining the independence of its clients. And, most important of all, Clem, who was in such constant and debilitating pain that he required a lot of care, reported that the nurses were both skilled and courteous. Once he had suggested to Matt that Hirsh took a look around. Clem thought that anyone who saw Mason House must want to live there and when Hirsh did not visit he did not take Hirsh's absence personally but indicated that he regarded this as evidence of Hirsh's refusal to contemplate the future realistically.

'Actually . . .' Denise said shyly, looking up at him with bright eyes, 'I had a sort of idea . . .'

Matt smiled at her. She looked excited.

'I think it would do Daddy good to take a vacation,' she said.

Matt had scarcely known the sickly Clem go any further than the barber's on the second storey of Mason House, and mostly the barber came to him these days. He opened his mouth to ask any of the obvious questions, but Denise waved her hand to silence him.

'Don't give me the objections, sweetheart. I know all the reasons he shouldn't. But there are overriding reasons why he should.' She started to count off reasons on her fingers. Her hair had fallen from its clasp and framed her face, looking golden in the evening light.

'First, he never goes out these days and I think he's lacking stimulation. Second, all this worrying. A holiday might at least ease that for a while. Third, he's talking about Mom a lot and the nicest thing would be to take him somewhere they went together. Best of all would be back to the place they honeymooned. It's right by the beach, it's warm and sunny and healthy, the food's sure to be good . . .'

'By what beach?' demanded Matt. Which side of the continent had Clem honeymooned all those years ago? California would be far enough, Florida or South Carolina disastrous.

'Liguria!' she said, and although he couldn't think for a moment where, on this vast planet, Liguria might be, the accented way Denise delivered the word, rolling down into the 'u' and then up on to the 'r' like a surfer gave him an uncomfortable indication that Liguria might not be in North America at all. And something in the precise lilt of her accent did not suggest Hawaii. He was hoping for Mexico when she said, 'Liguria, Italy.'

'Liguria, Italy!' shrieked Austin, who was occasionally a good mimic. 'Liguria, Italy!'

'Would that be . . . ?' Matt began slowly. 'Italy, Europe?'

Denise nodded. 'Listen, I know it sounds crazy. But, if you fly first-class, airlines can accommodate disability these days. Especially when there's an accompanying doctor.'

Matt swallowed. 'Does that mean I'm also going to Liguria, Italy, Europe?'

Denise looked hurt. 'Not if you don't want to,' she said quickly. 'I mean, it's just an idea . . .'

And although Austin, rearranging himself frontwards across Matt's face, had temporarily blocked Denise from view, Matt could feel her turning from him, sense her back and shoulders retreating.

'But,' he called over Austin's body, as though Denise were already out of the room, 'would you go too?'

She laughed nearby and he realized that she hadn't turned or gone anywhere.

'Of course. Austin and I would go. It would be a family trip. And we'd take a nurse along for Daddy so it would be a vacation for us, too. You'd only have to get medically involved if something went wrong.'

'You know . . .' said Matt carefully. Of course he didn't want to take a vacation that was entirely designed to accommodate the needs of a sick man. His whole working life was spent accommodating the sick. But he knew that to sound the smallest bit reluctant would be to hurt Denise, and that was impossible. Denise, who had brought tranquillity and music and joy into his life, Denise, who in her quiet way gave everything and asked nothing. 'You know that Italy isn't air-conditioned . . .' He remembered a lot of things about a long-ago trip to Venice and the most prosaic was the way he had sweated there.

'You're not going to tell me that there's no air-conditioned hotel in the whole of Liguria!' she said energetically, making Liguria sound big, bigger than Texas.

'But maybe not Clem's honeymoon hotel.'

She smiled at him. 'I'm going to find out about all that. But only if you'll say yes, that you want to, that you'll help make it a great vacation.'

He somehow secured Austin with one arm and then put the other around Denise.

'I want to go to Liguria, Italy, Europe and will do my best to make it a great vacation,' he pledged. She knew she was asking a lot. Probably she wouldn't ask it for herself but Matt had learned a long time ago that she would do almost anything for her father.

Later, when Austin was asleep, Denise looked at Matt apologetically.

'I should go see Daddy. I'm sorry. I don't feel we spend enough time together as it is. This weekend our fathers are really coming between us. Then next weekend I have a course . . .'

Denise was a music therapist. She worked with epileptics, depressives and an impressive assortment of other neurological and psychiatric problems and was so highly regarded that she now ran weekend courses for other therapists. Since having Austin, she had gradually ceased to work with patients and had increased the number of courses she ran. Matt had watched her once and admired the way she chaired workshops, encouraging the participants while maintaining her own firmness and clarity.

He was in bed but not asleep when she came home. He sensed her fatigue from the way she sank on to the bed and under the covers, gracefully, like a big ship going down.

'Hi,' he said into the darkness, and she stretched a leg across him.

'Daddy thinks Liguria is a great idea,' she announced softly. 'Now tell me about what happened with Hirsh this weekend.'

'Nothing much,' said Matt.

'Something did. I could see it in your face when you came in. Did you try to talk to him about moving house?'

Matt groaned a little. How could he have forgotten that the whole point of going up the mountain to see Hirsh had been to discuss moving? To play the clear-thinking son who gently steers the confused, elderly parent towards a more suitable lifestyle, a lifestyle with a push-button garage and air conditioning in summer and an untemperamental furnace in winter and a careline. But he had failed even to mention the subject of moving.

'I arrive meaning to talk to him about things and then I just can't,' he admitted.

They had, of course, discussed the Zoy case and that had opened the door to more intimate discussion. But Matt was aware that both he and Hirsh had failed to walk through the door.

'So what did you talk about?' persisted Denise.

'You're too tired to hear about all this.'

'I'm not. I want to hear.'

'Well . . . I cried.'

He couldn't hear Denise's breath. Then into the silence she said, 'Cried? Tears? You cried tears?'

Haltingly, Matt told her how he had watched Hirsh struggling with the log and found himself sobbing. She listened so quietly that he thought she might have fallen asleep. In the next room their son breathed. Somewhere in the seams of the house something – ducts, vents, pipes, wires – hummed soothingly. Matt felt the insects stir behind his eyes again, as though woken by a sudden rise in temperature.

She took his hand and moved her body close to his.

'Maybe you realized,' she said, 'that you were sawing logs for winter firewood, acting like Hirsh for sure has another winter. And then it occurred to you that from now on you can't count on him being there. Next winter. Or any winter.'

'Maybe,' said Matt, although he seldom if ever thought about Hirsh dying. His father's non-existence was a concept too massive to embrace.

'Or,' said Denise, 'maybe it's simpler. Maybe it's just that you were sawing logs for next winter when you know you really want to have him move house before then.'

But Matt was sure that, deep down, he didn't want Hirsh to move. The house, until Hirsh's retirement, had only been a vacation home but it felt like his main boyhood home. He and his parents would drive out of the city and through the mountains for summers and many weekends and when they arrived Hirsh and Hilly would sit in the hot, purring car watching through the windshield as Matt jumped out and ran ahead of them and fought with the rusty bolt on the garage until it slid back and the doors swung open. He could feel the way the air changed as he stepped into the darkness. It had been sleeping, its molecules sluggish, and now, startled, it rearranged itself into vacation air. He would stand back triumphantly, holding the door, while his parents drove slowly into the wakening dark.

For the rest of the summer, Matt and Hilly became joined to the Minellis so that the two families, their meals, arguments and games, were all woven from the same cloth. Hirsh joined them from the dusty city for a few weeks and whenever else he could and his presence at first caused an unravelling and reworking of threads. By the time he left the families were woven differently but still woven together.

Then in September they all packed up. Matt's goodbyes

to the Minelli family were swift and awkward and his heart ached at the way the house's air would atrophy without the life and noise he brought to it, as he thought of all those molecules sinking into an unhappy slumber without him.

The two families would travel back down the mountain on the same road but never at the same time. Matt would always look for the Minelli car but he never once saw it on those trips down to the city. School started and they resumed their city lives. But when Matt looked back at his childhood it was the summers he recalled, summers with the Minellis. His own life seemed to have been wrapped up in the wooden house in the mountains. If Hirsh left the old place, Matt feared he would lose a part of himself. As for Hilly, she would be gone for ever. It occurred to him as he fell asleep that she might be recovered at the Mouth of Nowhere. He thought of her sitting on a rock by the stream under one of the improbably towering mountain peaks she had painted. She was talking, talking, talking. If Hirsh sold the old house, Matt would have to climb up into the mountains to try to catch the echo of her voice.

5

Matt was able to dismiss his concern about the car he had seen outside the house. It was ludicrous to feel your hands getting clammier every time a red car touched the perimeter of your life. Probably whoever was inside had just pulled over to take a call on their cellphone.

But as he left the garage on Monday morning, thinking about the day ahead and wondering if the Zoy file would show up on his desk with a letter from the path labs or, worse, the medical ethics officer, a red car passed at an abnormally slow speed. Instantly, Matt's fears returned. His heart thudded. His hands felt damp. The car was travelling so slowly that it might have been pulling away from the kerb outside the house. Matt was able to catch sight of three of the letters on the plate: MMV.

He debated whether to follow the car, which was travelling south and not north towards the hospital. By the time he had decided to do so, even if it meant arriving late for work, the car was already out of sight. He accelerated around the long, lazy bend but there was still no sign of the car. He had driven, far too fast, to the end of the street before he realized that the driver must have taken a side turning. He flung the car dangerously around and then cruised back towards the house, slowing to check every turning on the right and left. The driver behind was getting annoyed. When Matt glimpsed red at the end of a long straight road to his right and swung the car suddenly towards it, the driver behind honked angrily.

Matt sped down the quiet residential street, overtaking slower early-morning drivers. But once again he was too late. The red car had turned at the end into the gathering rush-hour traffic which was already clogging the major routes downtown. Even if it were still close enough to see, it would be impossible to find it among the other cars and trucks.

He turned into the soup of vehicles and then began to cut in zigzags across town towards the hospital where the roads were wider and the traffic faster. Then, when he was nearing the hospital parking lot, a car came up too close behind him. He glanced in his mirror with annoyance because there were two lanes other cars could use. He saw red and looked right back into the mirror. The car was following behind him at a dangerously close distance, so close that he should have been able to see the driver's face. But the windshield was just a dark, blank screen.

Matt slowed his own car so that the other driver would be forced to overtake but the driver, slowing too, remained glued to Matt's fender. Behind him, other traffic was bunching. Several drivers pulled out angrily, hooting or glaring, but Matt did not speed up. He was trying to recognize the car's make or see its number but the car was too close to ascertain either.

Then, as they approached an amber light, the car suddenly fell back, overtook and zoomed ahead. As it accelerated past him, Matt stared in at the windows and realized that the driver's anonymity was protected by darkened glass. Nevertheless, there was an intimation of his shape and it seemed to Matt that this conformed, in mass and outline, with the shape of the Zoy son. The traffic light turned red, arresting Matt while the car disappeared far ahead of him, He had time only to confirm that the letters MMV were on the plate.

Although the car was almost certainly far away by now, when Matt parked at the hospital he nevertheless found himself looking anxiously all round before opening his door. When he saw nothing to disturb him, he tried to laugh at himself. Was his subconscious so haunted by a red car that he had paranoiacally begun to mistake bad driving for malevolent behaviour?

He walked more purposefully than usual into the building, holding his body upright and his head straight, the way a totally sane person should walk. Before going inside the building, he permitted himself just one furtive glance around the parking lot.

There was no mention of Mr Zoy among the files and letters on his desk. However, the rescheduled Morbidity and Mortality conference had already started and his secretary shooed him right out of the office. Matt knew he should probably say something about the Zoy case at the meeting.

As a resident, Matt had found M and Ms invaluable but now he was more senior it seemed to him that doctors used the sessions for career advancement or to undermine the careers of others, staying quiet rather than admitting their mistakes unless it was strategic to do so.

Today the atmosphere was amiable as foolhardy new residents admitted the difficulties they had inserting central lines. A senior surgeon smiled at them kindly and admitted to puncturing the lung of a famous patient while putting in a central line. Everyone looked at him in surprise. 'It was thirty-two years ago,' he added hastily.

'Well,' said Matt, 'I did something worse last week. A terminal patient begged me to increase his pain relief. He'd been receiving one hundred milligrams of Zornitol at four-hourly intervals. I estimated that the patient had only days left to live, a week at the outside. I was reluctant to disturb the team oncologist, Mike Salinski, to confirm this prognosis – after all, it was around midnight.'

A few heads nodded. Most people knew about Salinski's drink problem.

'It seemed to me that there was a clinical need to increase pain relief and I therefore gave the patient one hundred and fifty milligrams of Zornitol. This was about two hours after his last dose.'

Matt paused.

'I signed out the Zornitol but because it comes in hundred-milligram phials I had to check out two hundred milligrams. I then signed to say I had disposed of fifty milligrams.'

He did not sound convincing, even to himself. But probably nobody here needed convincing. They had all understood. He knew that from the room's silence, from the way that nobody moved.

'The patient died forty minutes later. The family have demanded an autopsy. The patient's son is angry and behaving in a threatening way.'

He wished he could say for sure that the figure in the red car was Mr Zoy's son. If he could accuse the man of stalking him he might gain instant sympathy. But the possibility that he, Matt, had somehow produced the red car himself from some old well of guilt had not left him.

He looked around. Everyone in the room remained motionless. Still nobody spoke. Matt felt himself reddening. He wanted to hear another human voice, a reassuring one. He noticed that the Mormon surgeons, who always sat together, were looking at him fixedly.

When Jon Espersen spoke, his tone was relaxed and kind.

'Matt, you can assume the hospital will give you full back-up on this one,' he said. 'Probably most of us would have chosen to increase the patient's pain relief.'

There were murmurs of agreement. Matt guessed that at one time or another many of them had given in to the pleas of a dying patient and crossed the line between relieving pain and relieving life itself.

'However, since this case is already on my desk,' Jon continued pleasantly, 'I do know it has one problem area. Your assumption that the patient only had days to live.'

Matt was surprised. 'You think he had longer?'

'The oncologist had told the patient and his family that he was considering including the patient in a new trial of a radioactive targeted drug. Preliminary clinical trials indicated that it could give another six months of life. Although the patient might have been assigned to the arm receiving the placebo, not the drug.'

Matt exhaled loudly. There were protests from some of the other surgeons. Jon Espersen held up a hand.

'Mike Salinski's notes are notoriously cryptic and since all he wrote was "Try 782?" at the bottom of a page, none of us can blame Matt for missing it. Mike failed to record the discussion he had about drug 782 with the family, although both he and the nurse remember it. He did stress that the patient wasn't guaranteed a place in the trial and, of course, he might not have responded to the treatment at all. However, it's one reason that the family's making such a big noise about the death now.'

Everyone spoke sympathetically on Matt's behalf. It was not the first time he had confessed at an M and M to mishandling a situation but now he was surprised by the level of support he received and the comfort he drew from the reassurances of his colleagues. You were supposed to be able to say anything at M and Ms but, since over half the department was Mormon, one thing you couldn't say was that you had deliberately brought the life of a terminally ill patient to an early conclusion. The Mormon group kept silent throughout the discussion but watched hawkishly.

'I understand,' said one of them to Matt just as the meeting was about to break up, 'I understand that your action may have significant consequences. I mean, beyond any moral consequences which may be troubling you, doctor.' He did not use Matt's name. Matt had almost never heard this man speak before.

'I have a cousin in Autopsies,' said the man, making Matt want to groan. Mormons had cousins everywhere. 'I think there's going to be some detailed questions asked about the exact Zornitol dosage.'

Matt's whole body, including his face, felt as though it were caving in.

'We know there'll be a high concentration of Zornitol in the patient's blood. Matt's told us that. The exact dosage cannot be determined at autopsy,' said Jon smoothly. 'We understand that Matt used one hundred and fifty milligrams and disposed of the rest. I think we all support Matt on that one.'

A number of people murmured agreement.

'Clearly the patient put Matt under immense pressure to provide this relief,' snapped a woman. 'And that should be taken into account.'

'So should the unavailability of the oncologist,' said someone else.

There was muted assent. As they left the room, a number of people walked by Matt and expressed further support. It was the first time Matt had felt in any way integrated into the department or accepted by colleagues. Without anyone mentioning Mike Salinski's drink problem, they had all understood Matt's dilemma and sympathized with it. As he left the room, it occurred to Matt that all he had to do to gather other doctors around him was to kill someone. He recalled something his father had said about doctors closing ranks on a faltering colleague.

'Don't worry, Matt,' said Jon Espersen, finding Matt in his office afterwards. He stood near the window and smiled as he breathed in the fresh air from the missing panel. 'In fact, there is going to be a meeting about the Zoy death. It's scheduled for a couple of weeks' time . . . The Zoys won't be there.'

Matt felt immediate relief at the Zoys' absence, and Jon saw this and smiled at him. Despite their differences, they had always liked each other. When Matt had returned from Africa, Jon had initially offered him gastrointestinal work, which he had refused. He was waiting for one of the few new vacancies which were arising in Salt Lake in endocrine and oncological surgery and, when other offers came from St Louis and Boston, he did not accept them. When Jon became head of the whole General Surgery Department he was able to offer Matt the first vacancy which arose in Matt's chosen specialization.

'Who's going to be at the meeting?' Matt asked.

'You, me, Mike Salinski, two people from the Ethics and Medicine Board and a couple of managers. It's just a review of the evidence so we can make some kind of decision about how the hospital's going to handle the Zoy family. The son's quite a troublemaker.'

Matt nodded, but his throat felt lumpen and his tongue metallic.

'It's not a witch hunt,' Jon said. Way back in their residency days, the much slimmer Jon had been regarded by some of the junior staff as impossibly handsome. Now, although he was not fat, his shape had become amorphous. He had no time for exercise these days. He was completely

69

bald. His face was broader and he had jowls. He looked as though the old Jon had been connected to some kind of pumping machine and inflated.

'Hear about the Case du Jour down in the Emergency Room? Guy admitted after eating fish from his freezer. Kept saying he'd caught the fish himself and frozen it fresh so he thought it would be all right. But guess when he caught the fish? Twenty-five years ago. Can you believe it?'

Jon walked off down the corridor chuckling to himself. Matt chuckled too. He made a note to tell Hirsh about the fish which had been in the freezer for twenty-five years. Hirsh was legendary for keeping things in the freezer three times longer than he should. Denise had some meat in the freezer which had been there ever since Matt could remember, he should tell her the fish story too. But mostly Matt chuckled with pleasure because this was the kind of anecdote he often overheard others trading in the hallways and the cafeteria but in which he was seldom included, probably because colleagues felt they could never predict his response. Now, however, he was beginning to feel liked for the first time in his career and he suspected that this was because of Denise. She was changing him, smoothing him. Her love, yielding but ceaselessly generous, reminded him of a river flowing over rough rocks, rounding their jagged edges.

That night, Matt and Denise had tickets to a piano recital at the concert hall downtown. This was not unusual. Music was a part of Denise's life. When Matt looked at her long, lean body, with its flowing grace, he thought that probably she had music inside her, so that if a surgeon ever opened her he would be surprised by a burst of harmony. She played the flute to a standard which seemed professional to Matt although she assured him it wasn't.

'That meat which is lining the bottom of the freezer . . .' he said in a snatched moment as they prepared to go out. He was shaving. He could not see Denise but he was aware of her reflection in the bathroom mirror to his right. Without even looking, he sensed her slow, precise hand movements and felt her leaning in towards the mirror as she put on her makeup.

'Oh darn,' she said and began rubbing vigorously at her face.

'Is it deer meat or did I imagine that?' he asked.

She said, 'Uuuuu.' She was running a fine pen around the edge of her lips.

'How old is it?'

'Darn, darn,' she said again and there was more rubbing. She was already dressed for the concert in the long, loose layers she favoured. The colours were autumn colours but no two layers were exactly the same, like a leaf fall. Her hair, under the burning bathroom lights, looked golden.

'Stop distracting me,' she instructed him. 'This is art. No one ever made great art while thinking about the contents of the freezer.'

He guffawed. Her beauty required no art at all, let alone great art. He decided to tell her later Jon's story about the twenty-five-year-old fish in the freezer.

Later, when the babysitter had already appeared and was renewing her friendship with Austin, as Matt waited for Denise to appear in the kitchen looking effortlessly ready, he rummaged in the freezer for the meat. The freezer had been Denise's and when it had arrived the big slabs of frozen meat had been at the bottom of it. He found one of them and saw that it was indeed deer meat and that the date on it came from more than three years back. So it originated from Denise's previous marriage. That was why she hadn't

71

answered his questions. Like anything to do with Weslake, her first husband, it had been treated as a hallowed relic.

As he shut the freezer, Denise appeared, her presence announced by the swish of the fabric which hung around her slim figure and floated a little behind her when she walked. She smiled. Her face was bright with anticipation.

Before a concert Matt, arriving home tired from the hospital, would secretly resent the whole event: the extra shower, the extra shave, the less comfortable clothes, the hurried early meal, the preparations for leaving Austin, the arrival of the babysitter and the way his son would not meet the eye of either parent when they said goodbye. But when they took their seats in the concert hall, Denise would make small gestures of excitement, as though composing herself to receive the music like a lover. She would arrange and rearrange her clothes around her and Matt would smell again the perfume she had worn on their early dates together, smell her long, golden chestnut hair, and he would feel the sudden beat of sexual excitement. When the music began he would reach for her hand, glad he was here.

The pianist, a famous Russian touring the US, was barely fifteen minutes into his repertoire when Matt became aware, to his astonishment, that his face felt both hot and wet. He put a disbelieving finger to his skin and it slid across the dampness of his cheek. He was crying. Tears were cascading down his face and dropping on to his shirt. His heart beat hard and his head throbbed as though the music had somehow penetrated it and become amplified. Denise had not noticed. The elderly woman on his left had not noticed.

Matt calculated that if he kept very still and did not sniff, despite the fact that tears now seemed to be also running down the inside of his nose, it was possible that no one would see. He was unable, however, to stop crying. He knew without even thinking about it that if he allowed his thoughts to wander they would lead him to the boy who had stood, anguished, on a woody hillside one day many years ago, witnessing his parents' sadness and affection, or to the same boy who had watched a red car by the lake hoping to see movement within it but already knowing there would be none.

He did not move his tongue even to swallow so that he could avoid its metal edges and, to limit his inhalation of the forest smells which lay in the air around him, he scarcely breathed. He devoted his concentration to suppressing the sobs which tried to shake his torso. But this iron will could not clasp back the tears. They streamed down his face in rivulets.

Matt braced his body, staring rigidly at the tiny model piano below on the stage and the little wind-up toy which appeared to be playing it. Without moving his own head he glanced around at the thousands of other heads. Many were grey and had exposed their owners when sleep came by slumping forward or sideways. Matt's senses seemed suddenly heightened. He could smell new carpet. He could smell hair spray. Right next to him the old woman's dress had the betrayed odour of clothes which had been brought out after a long spell at the back of the closet. The scene was entirely prosaic. Except for the music, which now seemed to have entered his bloodstream. It was being pumped around inside him, subjugating his entire body to its flow and rhythms. His breathing rose when the music swelled and fell away with the last bar of the movement.

Without looking at him, and barely seeming to move, Denise passed him a tissue. He accepted it gratefully, damming his nose and eyes.

'Shit, why did that happen?' he asked when they were

sitting inside the car in a long line of concert-goers, waiting to leave the parking lot. 'I mean, it just sort of sneaked up on me.'

'Music does that,' said Denise simply. 'Chopin does that.'

'Was it Chopin?'

'Second Piano Concerto. Didn't you recognize it from the Death March in the third movement?'

But by the time the pianist had reached the third movement Matt had been devoting every ounce of his attention to bodily control. He had been concentrating on each muscle, guarding corporeal exit routes until it had seemed all the sphincters in his body had closed and there was a ring of steel in his penis, anus, ears, mouth and nose. When eventually he managed to turn his whole body into metal he was satisfied that even his pores were closed. Nothing could exit and nothing, not even music, could enter. Except that his eyes continued to weep.

'That piece of music must have some kind of emotional significance for you,' said Denise, 'which your heart recognized long before your head. Can you remember hearing Chopin's Second before somewhere? Does it have some connection with your mother, maybe?'

And he knew at once that she was right. As usual. She was not just ballpark right, generally, approximately right the way doctors like Matt often were when they made a professional judgement. No, when Denise was right she had the precision of a swift, silent bullet aimed directly at the heart.

'My mother played it,' Matt heard himself say. His voice shook. He felt tears again and this made him so mad he cut right across a merging car and turned away from the surprised, angry faces of its occupants. 'I didn't even cry at her funeral and now just look at me. I don't get it. I keep crying for reasons I don't understand at all.'

As though looking at a series of snapshots which had fluttered out of different and unrelated albums, he remembered Mr Zoy's thin, white arm. He remembered the needle, the way it had finally slid through the flesh and the way Hirsh's white arm had flashed at him through the rip in his shirt. He remembered a red car standing among trees and a woman naked in a black and white picture and a painting of some mountainous place his mother had called the Mouth of Nowhere.

They were filtering out on to the street now. Blue lights flashed at the top of the Walker Building. The Rosebay Building lights shone pink. When Matt had first returned to Salt Lake, one of the comforting, small-town touches he had enjoyed about the city was the way the names and coloured lights of these downtown buildings always remained the same.

Denise said, 'Matt, I know your mother was a concert pianist but I thought she never played the piano again after she married. Ever. You told me that you never heard her play, not even when you were learning.'

'Shit,' said Matt. 'I thought it was true. But now I do recall her playing once. Just once. That Chopin.'

Denise studied him and seemed about to speak. Matt hoped she wouldn't and maybe she sensed this because she said nothing more. They drove home in silence. Once, Matt started when he saw a red car. It glided right up behind him as though it wasn't going to stop and then the driver stood on his brakes at the last minute. He believed once again that he recognized the bulky figure of Mr Zoy's son and, as if to confirm his fears, he thought he saw a movement within the dark car which could have been the driver running his fingers though his hair in a gesture Matt remembered from their meeting. Then he reminded himself that the strange

75

sodium of the downtown lights made cars look colours other than their own and at the next set of lights saw that the car wasn't even red and its number plate did not contain the letters MMV. Once again, he found himself doubting his mental stability. Maybe, every time he was upset or just feeling vulnerable, his subconscious was producing a red car from out of the traffic which gave him a few unpleasant moments but which could be relied upon finally to drive away with his feelings on board. He wondered if he should discuss this suspicion with a shrink.

At home, Matt and Denise took their silence to bed with them. It seemed to lie between them. Matt was remembering Hilly playing the piano that day. It must have been summer because they were at the vacation house in the mountains and she was wearing a sleeveless dress. Matt could recall how long and beautiful her arms looked, swelling from her shoulders with a soft fluidity. Her fingers, moving rapidly over the keys, were pure liquid. When he had glimpsed her face he had been transfixed by her unfamiliar range of expressions. The movements of her body, though practised, were all new to him and there was a violence, a passion, which had frightened him a little.

'Is that when you stopped learning the piano? After you heard your mother play Chopin?' Denise asked suddenly into the silence as though she knew his thoughts. She reached for his hand and it rested lifelessly in her own.

'I'm not sure,' said Matt. Then he realized she was probably right. He had struggled on for years with his lessons, his mother refusing to help in any way, not even when he first started.

'Mom, how many counts in a quaver when it has a dot right after it?'

Hilly turned to him without smiling. Often she stooped

a little when she spoke with him so he wouldn't feel small but she didn't stoop this time.

'I don't remember,' she said coolly. 'Don't ask me any more questions.'

'But Mrs Moran's giving me a test on Wednesday . . .'

'If you don't know the answers then I guess you'll fail,' said Hilly in a tone which indicated that it was immaterial to her whether he passed or failed. She had shown her disapproval and disagreement with his piano lessons in every way she could without actually forbidding them. He walked the two blocks to Mrs Moran's house and back alone. He took sole responsibility for practising and for finding his piano books before each lesson. Hilly had refused to have a piano in the house so Hirsh had bought Matt a small electric organ which he was obliged to play in his bedroom with the sound turned down. When he became a little more advanced, Hirsh had produced some headphones which plugged into the organ and apologetically asked Matt to use them so that Hilly didn't have to hear him practise, even distantly.

'It's difficult for your mother to listen to a beginner . . . after playing at her level,' Hirsh had explained apologetically.

Matt knew – it was information he seemed always to have possessed – that Hilly's level was high, the highest. She had once been a colossus in the world of music. She had been asked to play at Carnegie Hall where the greatest players in the world could be heard. She had been invited to study under a Latvian who was famous for taking only the best pupils and who in turn always became famous. She had won prizes, received awards. And she had given it all up to come to Salt Lake City to marry Hirsh and have Matt. She never, to Matt's knowledge, touched a piano again. Except just that once.

77

'So why did she play the Chopin for you?' asked Denise.

Matt shrugged in the dark. He was sure that, when Hilly had played, it wasn't for him.

'We were with these friends who we saw on holidays. They owned a cottage near ours, up in the mountains, a little nearer Arrow Lake than us. I think they persuaded Mom to play one evening. She said no, no, no. And then, I couldn't believe it, suddenly she must have said yes. I guess they kept asking until she gave in.'

He thought about the Minelli family again. He remembered them in the lake, their torsos above water level barbecued by a long summer's sun. Big, noisy Mr Minelli and his four boys were playing some kind of ballgame in the water which involved a lot of shouting and splashing. Hilly was playing too because she liked that sort of thing and hardly hid her disappointment that Matt didn't. In this memory, Matt was sitting on the shore with Mrs Minelli, a small, round, dark-haired woman, and the pair of them were watching the ballgame. Matt was waiting for Steve to fall victim to some underwater attack by his father or brothers, at which point he would usually pull out and play with Matt. He had assumed that Mrs Minelli found the spectacle as unengrossing as he did but he was wrong because sometimes, suddenly and surprisingly, she yelled support for one of her sons.

'Go, Steve, go! Attaboy, Jo-Jo!'

Where had Hirsh been? Probably still down in the city, working. His vacation was weeks, not months, but he would get up the mountain whatever evenings he could, usually joining them on Friday nights and leaving early Monday morning.

'Were they very close friends?' asked Denise, and Matt knew she had detected through the darkness some change

78

in his tone when he mentioned the Minelli family. He had heard it himself, that small constriction of his throat.

'I guess so. They were always doing fun things. Mr Minelli used to think up games and stuff and we generally joined in.'

'The whole family? I mean, your parents too?'

'Well, not Dad so much because he wasn't always around.'

He heard Mr Minelli's voice suddenly in his ear, smelled the smoke of his cigarette and the odour of past cigarettes on the man's clothes. 'Don't tell your father,' Mr Minelli said. Matt felt dislike for Mr Minelli engulf him but from old habit this feeling remained unspoken.

'So your parents were friends?'

'The whole family. There were four boys and the youngest was my age. Steve. Steve Minelli. We were the best of friends, did everything together all summer.' They had been more than playmates. They had shielded each other from the antagonisms of the older boys or Mr Minelli, called each other on the telephone when they woke up, or just appeared in each other's houses as an unannounced and unquestioned presence. They had swum in the lake, tried white-water rafting for the first time, nearly broken their necks climbing up to a deserted and rotten tree house to replace its timbers, hidden in forest camps from Steve's older brothers and especially from his terrifying father, for hours on end . . . they'd even, Matt remembered now, gone on that hunting trip together.

'Did you lose touch with him?' asked Denise.

'His dad died,' said Matt. His voice rasped and his throat hurt as though something he couldn't see was tightening around it in the darkness. He had to force the words out and they sounded wearied by their tough journey when they were finally spoken. It was Mr Minelli's death which had divided his childhood. There had been the summers before the Minellis left Arrow Lake, and the summers afterwards: quieter, less remarkable, less memorable, like the day after the party.

'So . . . ?'

'So the Minellis didn't come back up the mountain after that.'

'But the whole family was friends with your family? That's how they persuaded your mom to play the piano? I guess you had a piano up at Arrow Lake in those days.'

Matt made a guffawing sound to show the impossibility of this.

'No piano there. No piano down in the city. Strictly no pianos allowed.'

So where had Hilly played Chopin with long, brown liquid limbs and her whole body participating in the performance? It could only have been Arrow Lake as that was the only place they ever saw the Minellis and they were a fixture of this memory, the three elder boys entangled in a motionless sprawl across the sofa, Steve's back leaning against Matt's chair, Mr Minelli's huge frame sitting in silence for once and with an almost transcendental stillness as Hilly played. And Matt had surely been sitting in the little brown armchair in the living room at Arrow Lake.

He remembered how the music had bound him to the chair. At first it had bounced off the walls but gradually it had generated a heat of its own which seemed to give the room and anything solid a kind of elasticity so that the only certainty was Mom and the music and everything else – the chair, the walls, the Minellis – had the consistency of butter. But since there was no piano at Dad's house and there certainly had never been one during his mother's lifetime when it was just a vacation home, this memory must be faulty. He must have dreamt or imagined Hilly playing. Except he knew from his own tears tonight that he had not.

6

Just a short while after crying at his father's house and crying at the concert, something else happened which seemed to be connected. In Matt's memory it happened the very next day, although in reality the events were probably a few weeks apart. Strangely, it happened at the hospital.

The day started well, with the review of the Zoy case. Matt had entered the meeting nervously but was treated warmly by everyone. He found he enjoyed unanimous support, including that of the medical ethics officer. Of course, he did not tell them that Mr Zoy had asked to die, just that the patient had requested stronger pain relief. He repeated that he had injected only 150 mgs of Zornitol and disposed of the rest of the phial.

Mike Salinski confirmed that he had mooted the idea of the radioactive-targeted drug and apologized for not making this note clearer in the patient's file. He said that he remembered having strong doubts that the patient would respond to the new treatment and that the patient had confided he did not wish his life to be prolonged by the drug if there was no corresponding alleviation in his pain.

The meeting concluded by giving Matt its full support. The medical ethics officer said she would compose a letter to Mrs Zoy and her son confirming what had happened the night of Mr Zoy's death and stressing that the hospital did not believe further investigation or action was appropriate.

When they came out, Jon Espersen clapped Matt on the

back. 'I think you can put that one behind you,' he said cheerfully.

'Is there anything more the Zoys can do?'

That very morning Matt had seen the red car again, this time in the hospital parking lot. It had been driverless. Empty, it had seemed even more of a threat. Matt had circled it warily, in case the driver jumped out from behind the darkened windows. Then he had driven anxiously around the parking lot looking for Mr Zoy's son but there had been no one. He found the position of the car particularly worrying. Matt usually arrived early enough to choose his parking place and he had got into the habit of parking in C section, somewhere around rows 9 and 10 where he could gallop down the nearby stairs and enter the hospital by the doors nearest his office. The red car was standing at the end of row 9, section C, right by the stairs. Matt, not one hundred per cent sure that there was no one hiding behind the darkened windows, rapidly committed the car's exact make and number to memory and then nervously took the elevator.

'Well,' said Jon, 'I guess they can pursue their case, but, without the support of the medical ethics officer, they're on weak ground.'

Matt, though almost certain that the Zoy son would pursue the case, thanked Jon for his support and was just considering whether he should now mention the red car when Jon said, 'Glad Denise and Christine finally got together the other day.'

Jon and his family knew Denise through Denise's first husband. Jon and Weslake had been friends, so far as a devout Mormon like Weslake could ever be friends with a serious Protestant. But they had certainly played golf and perhaps even gone hunting together. And it happened that

83

Jon and Christine, whose house was in the wooded outskirts of the city, lived near the spot where Weslake had died in Yellow Creek Forest.

'They did? Denise forgot to mention it,' said Matt.

'Christine said how good Denise is looking these days.'

'She's very well,' agreed Matt. 'Must be something to do with all that yoga.'

'She took up yoga again?' asked Jon in a voice of surprise. 'I thought she had to give up. Didn't it cause her some problems at one time?'

Matt shook his head. 'She doesn't look to me like she has any problems with yoga. She looks to me like her body's made of rubber bands.'

'I remember Denise going to Christine's Iyengar class for a while, but she stopped because of joint problems or something.'

Matt shook his head again. 'No joint problems that I know of.'

'She's not too upset by this scandal, I hope,' said Jon, pausing in the hallway and dropping his voice. Matt was shocked that Jon saw the Zoy death as a scandal. He opened his mouth to reply when Jon added, 'I'm talking about Dr Smith's Slimtime. Christine didn't even like to mention it to her.'

Matt halted. Dr Smith's Slimtime had been Weslake's company. Weslake had been otherwise known as Dr Smith and his company marketed slimming products which Weslake himself had formulated.

Matt had no idea what scandal at Slimtime Jon was talking about. It was probably some employee dismissal case that had nothing to do with Denise anyway but he had no way of knowing because Denise hardly ever mentioned Weslake, let alone Slimtime. It felt to Matt that she guarded the purity of her first husband's memory, as though talking about him with her second husband would somehow dilute that memory, but Matt didn't want to admit any of this to Jon so he said non-committally, 'She seems fine about it.'

'If Weslake was around he'd have been able to put things back in order in no time,' remarked Jon before turning in to his office.

The irritation Matt felt at this mention of Weslake's name, at Jon's casual confirmation of his old friendship, penetrated his thoughts. He remembered that once Denise and Christine had visited Weslake's grave together, and he had learned this through Jon and not through Denise. Probably they had done so again and this was the reason Denise had not mentioned her meeting with Christine. Matt suspected that Denise often visited Weslake's grave. Whenever he found discarded wrappings in the car he thought they might come from small floral bouquets and he felt suspicious and annoyed, as though Denise were visiting a living lover instead of a dead husband. He hoped that she did not take Austin with her on these pilgrimages to the cemetery. It would be too bad if he grew up with a wholly unsuitable sense of loss for a man to whom he was unrelated and whom his father secretly hated.

Matt spent the afternoon in the operating theatre. The work was routine except for one surprise: a patient who, once opened, proved to have not one tumour on his liver but tumours seeded like chickenpox all over his abdomen.

'Jesus Christ, is there anything we can do here?' asked Matt's junior. 'Is there any point doing anything?'

'No,' said Matt. 'I guess we'll just close him back up.'

'I mean, how long do you think he's got?' asked the assistant, an Australian whose every remark, even his questions, sounded like an exclamation.

'How long,' Matt replied evenly, stitching the patient while the image of Mr Zoy, begging him to hasten death, came unbidden into his mind, 'has any of us got?'

He hadn't wanted to discuss the patient's impending death with the patient lying right there and possibly a part of his anaesthetized brain capable of hearing and understanding speech. He half-believed that the same was true of the recently dead. A few years ago an Eritrean nurse had asked him to be silent and remain still after a death. He had assumed her to be religious but later she had explained she believed it possible that patients can not only hear but assimilate for at least moments after their clinical death.

'Human body don't close down fast like the doctor's computer,' she had said. 'He come into this world slow, he go out slow, too. Senses drain away and hearing is last to go.'

Matt had thought of his computer, the way shutdown required at least three decisive moves by the operator before the screen's image began its gradual disintegration. There was no way of knowing whether the nurse was right but her theory was plausible enough to ensure that Matt no longer treated the recently deceased like a file which had snapped shut.

After theatre Matt was about to wash and change out of his scrubs when he remembered he had left his notes behind. He returned to theatre to find an orderly cleaning up. The orderly, like all hospital cleaning staff, wore loose green scrubs and Matt, barely looking at him, was already leaving the room when he recognized the man. At first, there was nothing to which he could anchor this recognition. He wondered if the man had once been a patient; he even suspected, fleetingly, that he recognized this figure as the one he kept encountering in the red car. He was half out of the operating theatre when the man spoke.

'Don't you recognize me, Matt?'

Matt, who was wearing blue scrubs, stopped in surprise. Someone wearing green scrubs had called him by his first name. Green scrubs and blue scrubs did not mix at the hospital and it was almost impossible that they should be on first-name terms. And when he was through being surprised, Matt felt shocked at how he, too, had unquestioningly taken his place in this colour hierarchy. Without even realizing it. All the other doctors treated cleaners as though they were invisible and after only three years back in his home country, three years in which he had tried to retain something of his different experience and values, here he was acting just like every other medic.

He thought all this before he even began to wonder how the orderly might know him, but he nevertheless stepped forward and held out his hand. It was still gloved in tight, white plastic. The orderly's hand was wrapped in some similar material, but looser and clearer, which squeaked and crackled when the two plastics met in a handshake. Only the top half of the orderly's face was visible because he wore protective masking to clean the theatre.

Matt noted simultaneously the weakness of the man's handshake and the pinched look of his brow. He had big, brown eyes which were thickly ringed by darkened skin and which wore a look of constant near-surprise which Matt had learned to associate with a history of drug abuse. Matt estimated the man was about his own age.

'You really don't recognize me,' said the man. 'I knew you wouldn't remember.'

He sounded forlorn. He pulled his mask down and Matt studied the thin, pale face. The lines running from nose to mouth were etched deep. The echo, maybe of chickenpox, was faintly visible on his cheeks.

The man smiled a thin smile and Matt overlaid images from his ancient past on to this gaunt face until recognition came suddenly, astonishingly. This was one of the Minelli brothers.

'Oh!' Matt said. 'Oh, I was thinking about you guys just the other day! Isn't that weird?' The Minellis had been absent from his mind for many years, so it was hard not to feel, ridiculously, that by thinking about them in recent weeks he had somehow conjured one of them up.

'You're Steve,' he said. 'You're Steve Minelli!'

Before him stood the ghost of his oldest and best friend, pale-faced and drawn. Irrationally, Matt wanted him to take off this mask and reveal the healthy, round-cheeked Steve he remembered.

Then Steve smiled, and his smile hadn't changed, and Matt realized that probably Steve had been thinking all the same things about him. A lot had happened since summers on Arrow Lake but now they faced each other again with a frankness of stare acknowledging that each knew something of his past, of his boyhood self, was locked up inside the other. Matt felt a surge of excitement.

They shook hands again but this time with their gloves off so that the warm flesh of their palms touched.

'Steve!' Matt repeated enthusiastically. 'I'm so pleased to see you.'

'I've worked here for a while,' said Steve. 'And I've seen you around. But I was never sure whether to . . . I mean, with you being a doctor here and everything, I wasn't sure if you'd . . .'

'You should have told me! I don't respect that hierarchy stuff,' Matt assured him, although he was aware that the reason he had not noticed Steve before was something to do with hierarchy stuff.

'How are you, Matt?' asked Steve warmly.

'Well, I don't know how many years it's been . . .' began Matt.

'Twenty-six,' said Steve. 'I calculate twenty-six years.'

'Twenty-six years!' echoed Matt, his tone lending to this passage of time the incredulity which Steve's own delivery had lacked.

'That's when my dad died, twenty-six years ago,' said Steve. 'That's when my mom sold the place at Arrow Lake.'

'Why did she sell?' Matt blurted out. He knew he sounded eleven years old again, protesting against some adult unfairness, and he knew that this protest had been waiting for twenty-six years. 'I mean, couldn't you guys have come up the mountain for vacations without your dad?'

Steve stared at him. His eyes were dark and bright and wide.

He said, 'We couldn't go back to Arrow Lake after Dad died there. We couldn't, Matt.'

Matt's heart began to thud. He felt the weight of the acute anxiety which he had carried down the hillside the day he found his parents sitting on the log bench. There had been a death, and he had been running to tell them, and his heart had felt heavy and his throat tight and he had been so nauseous that the trees had seemed to list all around him.

'Oh,' said Matt. 'Of course. Of course, he died right there by Arrow Lake.'

He caught his own breath now, as though he had been running around the operating theatre, although it was fear and guilt which squeezed the air from his lungs. The man in the red car was Steve's father. Mr Minelli. The big bully, hated by Matt, sat behind the steering wheel, his motion, his thoughts, his breath all halted by death.

Steve was looking at him curiously. 'Did you forget?' he asked. His voice was soft.

'No! No, no,' Matt assured him. 'How could I forget a thing like that?'

He had chosen not to think about it for twenty-six years but pieces of the memory had anyway somehow seeped in under the door or through the mail slot. Mr Minelli had sat lifelessly in the red car and Matt had felt a mixture of relief and horror at what he had done.

Steve was talking now, asking Matt questions. Finding answers required the same effort as waking himself for work when he had just spent a long night at the hospital.

'My mom died when I was in high school,' Matt heard himself explaining. 'Breast cancer.' He thought his own voice sounded as though a metal tongue was clanging in a metal mouth. 'Dad's still up in the mountains. It's not just a summer place now. He sold the house in town and retired up there.'

'In the same house?' asked Steve. 'The same little wooden house? How about the other guys? Sheriff Turner, is he still around? And that tall, thin guy who lived down by the lake, I think his name was Stewart . . .'

Matt said, 'We have a lot to catch up on. What time do you finish work?'

'In about an hour. I'm not working the night shift this week.'

'Let's go for a beer.'

Steve looked pink and pleased. 'Oh, sure,' he said. 'I'd sure like that. If you've got time.'

'I'll soon be through,' Matt assured him. 'I just have to check on a few patients and do some reports.'

But up in his office, Matt was unable to concentrate on the residents' annual assessment folders he was supposed to be completing by tomorrow.

Mr Minelli had died up at Arrow Lake. He had been in his car at the side of the road and Matt had seen him through the trees. He had half-expected Mr Minelli to get out of the car and make oversized gestures, shouting at Matt for peeking, calling him a yellerchicken or one of the other names he reserved for kids who weren't joining in the game with enough noisy enthusiasm. But he had not moved or spoken or climbed out of the car because he was dead. He had, of course, been shot. As everyone who had been around Arrow Lake at the time must recall, as Matt now recalled with intense clarity, the close-up clarity of a shaving mirror which makes everything ugly, the man was found dead in his car from a gunshot wound. Matt, of course, had not actually pulled the trigger and so everyone must have assumed he was innocent. Only he knew that the death was, nevertheless, his responsibility.

Steve had suggested they meet in a university bar. Matt arrived to find it dark and thronged with students. Steve was waiting for him by the door and led him at once to a gloomy corner. As they sat down with their beer, Steve smiled, and it now seemed to Matt, in the half-light, that he hadn't changed at all. His frame was so slight that he might not have grown since they were both eleven, as though time had stopped for him when that awful thing had happened at Arrow Lake. Matt, on the other hand, seemed to have been devouring life, growing disproportionately and stopping only when he had become improbably tall. Even sitting down, he had to stoop a little to hear Steve.

'I really appreciate this,' Steve said. He looked shyly at his beer. 'I know how busy you docs are.'

Matt, studying Steve's unnatural pallor, wondered if he might be unwell. He seemed reluctant to talk about himself. Matt coaxed him and then Steve explained that he had studied at the U but had flunked out with a drug habit. He had travelled the country, sometimes working and sometimes not. He had settled in Seattle where he had finally taken some courses in fine arts, kicked his habit, and was gradually establishing a reputation for himself as an artist when he had decided to come home to Salt Lake.

'It just kept raining in Seattle,' he said. 'I mean, sometimes for weeks at a time. I found myself longing for Salt Lake, for some dry heat and the sun on my face. So about a year ago I came back here. I had to start all over again, new reviewers, new galleries. It hasn't been easy. You lose faith in yourself. You ask questions you never asked before.'

'I know just what you mean!' agreed Matt. 'I came back here too. About three years ago. And I had to start all over.' They looked at each other frankly, acknowledging the similarities in their lives.

'I was already a surgeon when I went away,' explained Matt, 'but I wanted to change my specialization. In Africa I did just about everything, and when I came back I was sure what kind of a surgeon I wanted to be but it took a long time to convince everyone else. People just don't want you to change.'

'What did you do in Africa?' asked Steve. Few people had asked Matt that question. At best, others treated his time away as a sort of hole in his life. At worst, they steered widely around the subject, as though he'd been in jail for four years after doing something unmentionable. Matt found himself grateful for Steve's obvious interest now. He talked about Africa, about his work with the dying and the diseased and the undernourished. He realized as he spoke that he had begun to regard his experiences in that other continent the way his colleagues regarded them: as a career blip. Now it was a relief, even a pleasure, to speak freely.

Steve listened with admiration until Matt finally checked himself.

Steve said, 'I'd be happy if I'd made a fraction of the difference to just a fraction of the people you've helped.' His face looked pale and sad. 'Your life has been worthwhile,' he added.

'It stopped feeling worthwhile when I got back here,' said Matt. He described how hard it had been to return to the opulence of his native country, how angry he had felt at the over-consumption and conspicuous wealth, how his anger had perhaps discouraged other doctors from employing him. How depressed he had felt working as a locum for almost a year, waiting for an opening here in oncological and endocrine surgery, studying and offering help on departmental research projects just to keep up with professional developments.

'Did you meet your wife here at the hospital? Is she a doctor?' asked Steve.

'She's a music therapist. I was doing locum work, quite soon after I got back. Denise's father is LDS, bigtime. He lives in a mostly Mormon rest facility called Mason House and I was on call one night. I met Denise at his bedside. I was really miserable. My home country still seemed sort of insane, fixated on frenzied acquisition and consumption. Then she walked into the room and she just radiated. I mean, radiated this calm. She didn't seem to suffer from an insatiable hunger to accumulate material goods the way everyone else did. She was like a lifebelt.'

'She sounds wonderful,' said Steve. He smiled widely, and once again the smile afforded a glimpse of the boy Matt had known.

'Remember the broken glass?' asked Matt, who hadn't himself thought of it in years but had now been ambushed by a memory of his parents' vast porch window with cracks radiating across it like a giant spider. 'We used to play ballgames around by the porch even though Mom told us not to, and when we saw the glass was cracked we just knew they'd blame us. We were so sure they'd think we did it that after a while we began to think we had.'

'We went skulking away in the woods, we were so sure we'd done it,' said Steve, laughing.

'Up in the tree house,' said Matt.

'And when our dads came asking who broke the glass we looked guilty . . .'

'So of course they thought we must have broken it!'

'And in the end, so did we!'

They were laughing now but the porch glass had been important enough at the time. Since the window had been broken by a sharp impact that might have been caused by a ball, and since they often did play too near the porch, and since he and Steve were the most likely culprits, he had come to understand that he and Steve really must have broken the window. Even now he thought that, given the balance of evidence, they had probably done it.

'And remember that hunting trip?' Steve said. 'Remember how we all went into the wilderness? The others had real rifles but you and I were so small we had air rifles and we were determined to show the others what we could do with them. I guess that hunting trip's one of the biggest memories of my childhood. I mean, one I'll really treasure.'

Matt tried to look enthusiastic but mostly what he remembered about the hunting trip was that he hadn't enjoyed it. To hide this, he asked, 'Do you still hunt?'

'Oh, sure. Most years. There's a big wilderness out there, it's important to experience it.'

There were other ways of experiencing the wilderness apart from killing the animals who live in it, thought Matt, but he knew his was a minority view in Utah and that most men here, sometimes even his father, exercised their inalienable right to hunt.

'I don't,' he said.

'You don't hunt!' exclaimed Steve. 'Boy, you're really missing something.'

'I don't have the killer instinct,' said Matt.

Steve smiled. He looked right at Matt. 'We all have it,' he said.

'Not me.'

Steve watched him unblinkingly, his smile fixed. 'Oh no?'

'No.'

'We all have the killer instinct,' Steve insisted. Matt remembered Hirsh using the same words. Steve continued, 'We all have that instinct, it's just some of us don't want to admit it. I mean, don't you remember that first hunting trip? How we stalked the buck? Didn't you want it to end in a kill?'

'I can't remember much about that trip,' admitted Matt.

Steve looked amazed. 'You don't remember how close we got to that muley buck? Five kids, two adults, and we followed his trail and sneaked right up on him without one of us making a sound. Matt, that sure was an achievement. And it was thanks to your dad. He was a good hunter and could find a deer anywhere.'

Matt was pleased. Involuntarily, he smiled.

'It sure was a shame he didn't hit it,' added Steve ruefully, and then Matt remembered. He remembered why the hunting trip had been an unwelcome memory. Hirsh had missed. The hunting trip had happened twenty-something years ago but Matt found himself reddening still. Hirsh had aimed, fired and missed. The mule deer had been turned side-on like some cardboard cut-out stationed for easy target practice. A clear shot through the trees. Mr Minelli had indicated for Hirsh, who, as scout, was a little ahead of the others, to take him. The sound of the shot brutalized the silence they had observed for so long. Immediately the deer turned and started to run. It had bounded, unhurt, from sight, the crash of undergrowth still audible long after the animal had disappeared. After that they lost heart and lost the trail. The fall skies turned colder and darker. They made the long journey back to the lodge in single file, seldom speaking. The Minelli boys occasionally joked or argued together but no one, not even Steve, had said a word to Hirsh or Matt and the two of them had remained silent all the way home. Matt's face, his cheeks, his mouth and his nose had all felt frozen by the temperature and that silence. Later, Mr Minelli, telling his wife and Hilly what had happened, had, unforgivably in Matt's view, laughed at Hirsh. His laughter always seemed to have one blunt edge and one sharp edge, like a knife. Sometimes it showed when he joshed with his boys, that sharp edge of cruelty.

Steve talked, unprompted by Matt, about that trip. About how they had learned to build hides up trees, how he believed he had seen the retreating back of a brown bear but no one, least of all his father, would believe him, how the hunting lodge where they had stayed became later a luxury hotel where he had worked one summer as a student. He recalled the boxy wooden bunk beds at the hunting lodge, the argument with his big brother over where the guns should rest for the night, the discovery that Flip had left his weapon loaded.

'Do you remember our house?' Matt asked cautiously.

'Real well,' said Steve. 'I always liked your house.'

'Do you recall that it ever had a piano?'

Steve's face screwed itself up under his dark hair while

he thought. The hair was cut so short that you didn't at first notice that it was receding.

'I guess I don't,' he said at last. 'I don't think I recall any piano out there . . .'

'I have a memory,' Matt said, 'of my mother playing the piano in our house.' He coughed. He could hear his own tone, cautious, studied, betraying the importance, to him, of his words. He tried to lighten his voice but only succeeded in exposing his feelings still further. He closed his eyes and briefly saw again her fingers on the keys, her body in motion, the musical liquidity of her movements. 'I recall her playing Chopin there. Which is weird. Because I'm sure we didn't have a piano.'

'Your mom could play the piano?' asked Steve politely, and Matt almost gasped at this innocent betrayal of such an immense piece of family history.

'She used to be a concert pianist,' he said shortly.

'I didn't know that,' said Steve. 'I remember your mom laughing, always laughing. I remember her laugh.'

'Always laughing?' echoed Matt.

'Sure. She liked a good time,' insisted Steve.

'I guess so,' admitted Matt. 'But there was another side to her as well.'

'There's another side to us all,' said Steve.

Matt asked him about his painting and Steve corrected him.

'At the moment I'm a photographic artist,' he said. Then, stretching his back and with unnecessarily strenuous arm movements which indicated a certain shyness, he fished in the pocket of his jeans and produced a small card. 'I'm having an exhibition at the Big White Space. I sure wish you'd come, I'd be honoured if you could make it. You and your wife. I mean, the opening night is Tuesday next week.

Think you can come?' There was something urgent in his tone.

Matt nodded at once. 'I'll do my best. I know Denise would love to come too if we can find a babysitter. If not, maybe I could check out a couple of friends. One of them loves art. He travels all over and tries to see exhibitions wherever he goes . . .'

'Bring him!' said Steve. 'But Matt, I have to warn you, since you work at the hospital. You're going to see a lot of stuff that will be familiar. You'll probably think it isn't art at all. But . . . well . . .' He looked shyly down at his beer. 'That's what artists do. They refine the everyday and re-present it.'

'What kind of familiar?' asked Matt cautiously.

'Well, sort of familiar and mysterious at the same time,' said Steve. 'That's what I aim for, anyway. My work is an attempt to refine reality. Experiencing it should be like picking up someone else's eyeglasses and looking at the world through extra-strong lenses. It's very intense and it can be unsettling. Art should be that way. Do I sound pretentious? I sure hope not.'

Matt assured him that he did not but he decided that, at home tonight, he would repeat as much of the conversation as he could remember and Denise would bring to it her usual clarity. He tried to memorize some of Steve's words but they darted away from him like little fish. Refine. Familiar. Extra-strong lenses. Hesitantly, as though he didn't do it often, Steve talked on, and the more he talked the faster the fish swam away.

When they had finished their beer Matt said he should go home. He knew he had already missed that moment when Austin came hurtling towards him on his small, thick legs, face alight with pleasure. Austin would be in bed now, but at least he could spend a few hours with Denise. He got up and, as if both men had become suddenly aware that their time together had been unsatisfactory, they began to talk rapidly, reminiscing with a new urgency. The lake, their parents, the Minelli brothers (Flip, Danny and Jo-Jo), that hunting trip, the forest camps, swings they rigged up between trees, wheelbarrow races and bikes and Sheriff Turner and the guy at the store with no hair and no teeth.

'I sure wish there were a few pictures,' said Matt as they left the bar. 'My dad has these terrible home movies but I'd like some pictures. Especially of my mother.'

He remembered the photos he had found up in Hirsh's roof space. When he said he'd like some pictures of his mother, he didn't mean that kind of picture.

'Oh, we have pictures,' Steve said. 'I mean, we used to have a lot, including of your family. Probably my mom still has them. I'll ask her.'

His eyes looked into Matt's. Those dark eyes in that distinctively shaped forehead (not round but curiously angular) were so unmistakably Steve's that Matt wondered how, even masked, he had failed to recognize his old friend at first.

Steve said, hesitantly, 'Maybe it would be real nice for your dad and my mom to get together some time.'

'Dad doesn't often come down to the city . . . but, of course, he might make an exception for Mrs Minelli.'

'She's just the same,' said Steve. 'Except when you knew her she wasn't LDS.'

'She became a Mormon?'

'After Dad died she went back into the Church. Grief takes some people that way. I guess you'd call her devout. But the Latter Day Saints look after widows and she's in a great community. Nice people. Especially now they've given up trying to convert me.'

Matt, who had already been having serious doubts that Hirsh would make the trip down the mountain to see Mrs Minelli, was now certain that he wouldn't.

Outside the false dark of the bar, real dark had fallen. It felt cool and refreshing. Variations in its density gave it the complexity of something handwoven. The two men stood with the evening's blackness between them.

'Matt . . . you said you remembered my father's death,' said Steve. Matt swallowed.

'Do you really remember the accident?' Steve crunched the word 'accident' as though it was something small lying in the road which he had driven right over.

Matt nodded, very slightly. So that was how he had escaped justice. There had not been a full investigation into Mr Minelli's death because the official version of events was that there had been an accident.

'Well,' said Steve, 'we never really understood it. I mean, how Pa's own gun could have gone off and killed him like that. I was just a kid of course, but I grew up not understanding it. I think that uncertainty got to all of us in different ways. Mom turned devout. Flip kept marrying different girls. I used too many bad-for-me substances. And Danny . . . he couldn't handle it at all. One day he went away and he didn't come back. And I think it's because we've just never understood.'

He had moved a step closer to Matt and had dropped his voice. Other people on the sidewalk sounded much louder, even when they had passed and were being swallowed by the night.

'What don't you understand?' asked Matt. He heard his own voice, low like Steve's, so low it seemed to tremble a little.

'I don't usually talk about this but since . . . well, since we go way back and since you were sort of there . . .' Steve's black eyes studied the sidewalk and then looked directly into Matt's own. 'I believe . . . we all believe . . . that someone killed our father.'

Matt felt something in him recoil. When Matt and Steve were boys they had enjoyed scaring each other with ghost stories. They had agreed that, if they ever saw a ghost, they would look away and then look back and, if the ghost was still there, they would know it was real. And when Steve said these words, when Matt heard him say that someone had killed Mr Minelli, he looked away, just as though he had seen a ghost. Then he looked back. And when he saw Steve's face, distressed, staring at the sidewalk, biting his lip, he knew this ghost was real enough.

Matt wanted to say something but no words came. Instead Steve spoke: 'I've been trying to understand my father's death for twenty-six years. I guess I never will.'

His compact body seemed to droop like a plant which needed water. He extended an arm to Matt and for a moment they grasped each other's hands. Steve's felt small wrapped inside Matt's big palm.

'So, are you going to come to my exhibition?' asked Steve in a louder voice with forced joviality. Matt promised him, with a similarly forced enthusiasm, that he would. Steve nodded and with a last, darting smile he disappeared into the evening. Matt was left standing on the sidewalk. His flesh seemed to crawl with small, biting insects and his arms and legs ached as though Steve had walked away leaving him with something too heavy to hold.

7

Matt told Denise about Steve's exhibition.

'I'd sure like to see it but Tuesday is Rosetta's Jazz Dance night,' she said. Rosetta was their regular babysitter. 'Anyway, I'd prefer to slip in later when Steve isn't around. It's always awkward looking at work with the artist right there.'

Denise was doing headstands. She practised yoga each night right after Austin went to sleep. She had never asked Matt not to talk to her while she pulled her legs and arms into impossible and beautiful shapes, but when he watched her, admiringly and sometimes aroused, he usually did so in respectful silence unless she spoke to him.

'Did you ever have to give up yoga because of joint pain?' he asked her suddenly, forgetting to be silent. Her body wavered. Matt thought she might remain in the headstand but she returned to vertical with her head uppermost.

'No, why?' Her face was pinker than usual.

'Jon Espersen mentioned it today. He said you started going to classes with Christine and then left because of joint pain.'

'Oh, that.' Denise's cheeks were red, probably because she had just turned through 180 degrees. 'It was the teacher. Too vigorous. I just found another class.'

She stood on her head again. Her face looked different now gravity pulled it in a new direction. It looked like someone else's face, fuller and less contented. Matt knelt down and then bent his body so the top of his head pressed against the floor. He peered at her between his knees. Now they were both upside-down but even this still did not make Denise's face look the same as it did rightways up. Their eyes met and her mouth turned down. She was smiling at him.

'Where is this exhibition?' she asked.

'The Big White Space. Where's that?'

'It's a very good space in a strange location, a small shopping mall. I think it's right out on Thirty-third.' Her voice was different. An upside-down voice. 'They have a lot of exhibitions there.'

'What kind of exhibitions?'

'All kinds. Painting, ceramics, installation art, sometimes it's used for theatre . . .'

Matt was uncomfortable. He righted his body and for a moment felt light-headed. 'I mean, good painting, good theatre?'

'Sometimes very good. But certainly mixed.'

He tried to remember some of the things Steve had said about his work but the fish kept swimming right away.

He grasped at a few of them. 'Steve thinks the artist should . . . erm . . . redefine the everyday . . . so it feels familiar and mysterious at the same time.'

Denise spluttered with laughter and toppled right over. She sat up and her face's normal lines, strong and vertical, returned. Some wild chestnut hair had escaped from its clasp and was clinging to her cheeks.

'It can't be good,' she gasped, 'to laugh when you're standing on your head.'

Matt smiled back and kissed her.

'You smell of beer,' she told him. They went into the kitchen and Denise began to fix a meal while Matt opened the freezer.

'Was I talking garbage about art?' he asked. 'I think that's what Steve said but I may have got it wrong.'

She laughed again. 'Nothing wrong with what you said. It's the way you said it. What are you looking for in the freezer?'

'I'm thinking to myself,' said Matt, pulling out one of the big bags of deer meat from the bottom layer, 'that maybe we shouldn't keep this stuff any longer.'

Denise, predictably, said nothing. Matt realized that he still hadn't told her about the case of the twenty-five-year-old fish. He told her now but all she said was, 'Well, that deer meat isn't twenty-five years old.'

Matt took a closer look at the date on one of the packs. Mid-October, three years ago. That meant the deer's demise had preceded Weslake's, and perhaps only by a few days. Probably Weslake himself, a keen hunter, had actually shot it. Sentiment alone was keeping the meat in the freezer.

He felt annoyed, as usual, at the way Denise posted Keep Off signs up all around Weslake as though he were a sacred statue.

'We should eat it or throw it out,' he said harshly.

Denise was silent, just as though she hadn't heard him.

'Actually, I don't think anyone should eat it,' continued Matt, as though this were a normal conversation 'But if you don't want to throw it out, probably Dad would take it.'

Denise still did not reply. She was chopping something and the movements of one smooth shoulder were as small and rhythmic as a machine's. Matt felt his belly tighten. Any question, anything at all, which touched on the life and death of Weslake, even the mention of some goddam deer meat, had this effect on Denise. She seemed to disappear inside her own body and no conversation was possible. Her silence on the subject, her guardianship of his shrine, irritated Matt and had fostered in him a sort of hatred. Who could fail to hate the man whom Denise had loved and, plainly, still loved? Of course she loved Matt, she had married him, but it sometimes seemed that their marriage had been moulded and honed by her grief for handsome, successful Weslake Smith instead of her feelings for Matt. He slammed the freezer shut.

Denise paused at the chopping board and said, as though the subject of Weslake's venison had never even come up, 'If you want to know whether your friend Steve's any good, you really should take Jarvis to that exhibition.'

'Jarvis probably won't be around for the opening night. Anyway, I can invite Troy.'

But, by a stroke of luck, Jarvis, who had an exceptional knowledge of art, did happen to be in town on Tuesday night. He was a truck driver who hauled liquids, many of them dangerous, right around the country but that week he was doing some short-hauls and going home every night. He had three children and often only returned to Salt Lake on weekends, not always in time for a Friday night beer. Matt and Jarvis and Troy had been meeting on Fridays since they had graduated from high school together when Troy had been heading for law school and Matt had intended to study medicine and Jarvis had started saving for the deposit on his first truck.

'So what kind of thing are we going to see here?' Jarvis asked as they headed towards the suburb where the Big White Space was housed. Troy was driving and had told Jarvis to sit in the back seat, since he was a notoriously bad passenger.

Matt said, 'Photos, I guess. He said his work would be mysterious and familiar at the same time. I think he meant familiar to me so maybe it's something to do with the hospital.'

'Oh, boy. It's gonna be like brains and kidneys and stuff floating in formaldehyde,' groaned Jarvis. 'Watch that dishevelled old guy in the beat-up brown Chevy on your left, Troy, he's driving erratically.'

'I know,' said Troy.

'He's driving erratically and he has that kind of face. So watch him,' insisted Jarvis.

'What kind of face?' Matt asked. He made his voice sound calm but he felt nervous sitting in the front seat. Troy generally drove so fast and distractedly that if there were any obstacle in the road, Matt felt sure Troy would be unable to avoid it.

Jarvis said, 'He's got a bad driver face. I can tell them a mile away.'

'What is it? The nose? The chin?'

'It's a kind of scowl. And they often sit way back, like they have an extra windshield the wrong side of the steering wheel.'

Matt turned to look at the bad driver but he melted from sight.

'See!' roared Jarvis. 'He did it again! He pulls past for no discernible gain and then, also for no reason, he falls back.'

'I know,' said Troy. Matt wished he would slow down.

'And he's all over the road. He could be drunk. Or he needs eyeglasses but he has an overdeveloped ego which won't allow him to embrace the possibility of physical decline and its inevitable culmination, death.'

'Uh huh,' said Troy with resignation. The years that Matt had been away, Troy and Jarvis had hardly met. Then, when Matt came back, the three of them had resumed their Friday nights. When Matt, alone with one or other of them, had asked why they had dropped Fridays during his absence, Troy had said, simply and quickly, 'I can't take that guy undiluted.' Jarvis, however, had gulped beer for a full minute before answering and this silence, from a man who was rarely without words, had felt long. But finally he had sighed and said, 'It's to do with workable group dynamics. Can three people play chess? Nope. Can seventeen people play basketball? Nope. Can two people drive a car? No. No, they cannot, not to the satisfaction of any of the participants.'

'Is it because deep down you don't like him?' Matt had boldly asked each of them, and they had each stared back at him, too shocked at the idea even to issue a denial. And it was true that, when a runaway truck had crashed, hideously, into Jarvis on a steep downhill stretch of Interstate near Salt Lake, Troy, white-faced, his brow furrowed with worry, had visited Jarvis at the hospital every day, usually dragging Matt from his duties to visit with him.

'Burn him off,' Jarvis advised Troy now. Matt hoped that Troy would ignore this advice. They were already too close to the car in front 'Get that foot hard on the gas, Troy, and leave this bad-faced guy behind. He's dangerous, believe me.'

'I have pains down my right leg which make rally-driving kind of difficult right now,' said Troy with a glance at Matt. He was a notorious hypochondriac.

'It's that grumbling appendix,' roared Jarvis, referring to one of Troy's most frequent worries. Troy almost never met Matt without asking him to feel his appendix. 'It's started slippin' down your leg. Hey, watch the Chevy, Troy!'

'Maybe you should close your eyes and let me drive, Jarvis,' said Troy wearily. 'I mean, just this once.'

Jarvis was unoffended. 'So, this artist friend, Matt. What's his name again? Steve what?'

'Minelli. I knew him when we were kids. I haven't seen him for over twenty years.'

'Never heard of him. If he had any kind of a following in Salt Lake I'd probably know about him.'

'Well, he's been living in Seattle. But if he's exhibiting his work in the Big White Space, doesn't that mean anything?'

'Nope. Anyone can rent that place. I could exhibit Arnie there if I wanted to.' Arnie was Jarvis's new truck, a monster of gleaming paintwork and chrome and pipes and valves.

The Big White Space shared a parking lot with Hal's Mufflers, a small religious bookshop called the Spirit Level and the vegetarian Osiris café. When they had parked the car, they could hear relaxation music behind the chatter of soft voices from the café's courtyard.

'That kind of place makes me throw up,' said Jarvis. 'I'd like to get drunk and misbehave in there.'

'Good idea, Jarvis,' said Troy. 'And when you're through doing truck driver, come make like the art critic with me and Matt.'

Jarvis did not leap to the defence of truck drivers. He said, 'I mean, no one in that place would so much as get out of their ergonomically designed, renewably resourced wooden chairs. Let alone punch me out. And you know why? Because they're all vegetarians.'

'They might punch you out but they wouldn't eat you,' said Troy as Matt steered Jarvis's large body out of the path of a moving car.

'Am I walking normally?' asked Troy. 'Watch me walk, Matt, and tell me if I'm limping on my right side.'

He hobbled across the street ahead of them.

'You're not limping. It's just your wallet's too heavy,' Matt told him.

The Big White Space was anonymous, like a library, from the outside. Inside, they were handed a leaflet giving them brief biographies of the six artists who were exhibiting. Jarvis grasped it in one plump hand and tugged at his hair with his other hand as he read Steve Minelli's paragraph out loud to the others: 'Steve has travelled extensively on highways throughout the USA where the many scenes of accident and carnage he encountered forced him to refine his ideas about death.'

Troy snorted with laughter and Jarvis kneaded his doughy face into a ball. 'Jeez, why the carnage? Did he drive on the wrong side of the road?'

'Shhhhh,' said Matt. People were standing singly and in groups nearby drinking some kind of fruit punch and a few heads had turned towards them. But, too loudly, Jarvis read on: 'Steve's first exhibit, at the Seattle Sand House, shared some of these scenes. His examination of death and its impact on life—' Jarvis and Troy both laughed simultaneously.

'Death has certainly been known, on occasion, to have an impact on life,' said Troy wisely.

'Why, in extreme cases death's even been known to end it completely,' agreed Jarvis.

'Shhh, here comes Steve,' hissed Matt.

'". . . its impact on life,"' read Jarvis, '"has been furthered by his contact with one of the main hospitals here in SLC, where death is a routine occurrence."'

Matt groaned and Troy guffawed again. 'So that's how come you earned that merit award?' he said to Matt. 'It must have been for patient turnaround. All these routine deaths are improving your figures.'

'Er, let's see here . . .' continued Jarvis. '"Steve's interest in death's sting has been heightened this year because he has now reached the same age at which his father, Arthur A. Minelli, died."'

Matt felt a curious sensation in his neck as though someone had stepped close behind him, very close, as close as they might stand in a crowded elevator. He swung around but there was no one. He became aware that the hairs on his neck were erect but he didn't know if this was caused by the reference to Mr Minelli or to his death. I believe, we all believe, that our father was killed.

'Hi, Matt, I'm glad you could come.' Steve held out a gaunt hand.

Matt introduced Troy and Jarvis.

'We just read your biog. You're sure dressed appropriately for your pictures,' Jarvis said.

Steve looked down at his black clothes and his face seemed to weaken a little as though he might cry. Matt glared angrily at Jarvis but suddenly Steve's face broke into an angular smile.

'Isn't the programme terrible? The manager of the Big White Space wrote it and I'm really embarrassed. Did you read the bit about death and its impact on life?'

Troy guffawed again.

'Just so long as you don't believe your own publicity,' said Jarvis.

'I think it's shit,' said Steve and Jarvis grinned at him warmly. Steve looked directly at Matt and said, more confidentially, 'My work is very influenced by my father's death, of course.'

He looked at Matt, as though expecting him to say something.

'You know all about that,' he prompted. But Matt still only nodded speechlessly.

'Let me get you some punch,' offered Steve, 'and then you can take a look at the work. My pictures are way over there at the end.'

Steve led them to a table and then poured them each a drink from the leafy punch bowl. The ice in it had melted down to ghost ice which slipped soundlessly from the ladle but the rustle and thud of fruit and leaves in liquid could be heard distantly, like someone giggling.

'I'm sorry your wife couldn't come,' said Steve to Matt. 'But if you want to renew an old friendship, my mom's right over there.'

He gestured with the punch ladle and Matt recognized Mrs Minelli at once. She was the same short, round shape, perhaps shorter and rounder. Her hair was grey now. She held a glass of water and although she stood alone in the gallery, she had an air of self-containment which Matt recognized. She saw Steve waving with the punch ladle and she walked right over and shook hands with Matt as though they had seen each other only last week. She made no comment on his height, or how many years had passed since their last meeting, or how similar or dissimilar he looked to either of his parents.

'Hello, Matt,' she said. 'Steve told me you'd be here.'

Her face was unmistakable. Big eyes, small mouth. The effect had been triangular in her youth, but age had softened its angles.

Jarvis and Troy melted off in the direction of the pictures while Matt held a halting conversation with her. Had she always been so difficult to talk to? He asked about Flip ('Now very successful in real estate, just like his father was,' said Mrs Minelli), Danny ('We believe he's living in California somewhere') and Jo-Jo (a practitioner of alternative medicine, Matt did not request further information). She did not return his interest by asking anything about his own family but he furnished her with details anyway, of his mother's death and his father's retirement and move to live full-time in the mountains. She received the information politely.

'Steve says you have some photos,' Matt added. 'Old pictures of the lake and our families . . .'

For a moment she looked surprised.

'Well, I think I threw most of them out,' she said slowly. 'But I can take a look for you . . . would you want to borrow them?'

'Anyway, look at them . . . maybe take copies . . .' he said. He thought of Hirsh's house and its carefully stored memories of Hilly and the past. The home movies in their metal cases, the sculptures which had been left respectfully to crumble in situ, the projects which Hirsh had attempted to finish and display. 'But . . . why would you throw them out?'

Mrs Minelli's shoulders stiffened a little but her tone was unvarying.

'Well, of course, not all my memories from that period are happy ones. However, give me your phone number and I'll call you if I find anything.'

She was searching through her purse now. He watched her. She wore two rings. One was a plain wedding ring. The other was a single diamond. He leaned forward a little to look at it more closely. It was a single diamond set in a small, simple gold flower.

He recognized it at once. He wanted to ask, 'Why are you wearing my mother's ring?' but the question was too bald. While he tried to rephrase it in his head Mrs Minelli was saying, 'I've seen Steve's photos and I have to get back for a ward meeting now, Matt.' She was holding out a pen and a notebook. He stared at the ring and failed to take the pen.

'Give me your phone number,' he heard her say with the forced clarity of someone speaking to a foreigner, as though she might be repeating the words a second or even a third time. 'Although, really, I think I threw all those pictures into the trash.'

Matt scribbled his number and then clumsily shook hands. As he did so, he felt the diamond, his mother's diamond, press against the inside of his hand. When Mrs Minelli withdrew her fingers, he continued to stare at the ring. It was the same one, he was sure of it, from the way the petals of the flower curved in slightly as though trying to capture the light which radiated from the gem.

She was turning now. Before she could go he asked, maybe too abruptly, 'Mrs Minelli . . . your ring. Did my mother give it to you?'

She looked down at the ring as though noticing it for the first time.

'No, Matt,' she said, after a pause. 'My husband did.'

She was so small that she made him feel immense: not in a dignified, towering way but in a way that suggested there really was too much of him. He began to apologize, explaining that he remembered his mother had a ring very like it. She was already gone before he had finished.

He looked around for Steve. He was busy talking to guests. By now, Troy and Jarvis had seen all the other displays and were approaching Steve's work at the end of the building. They looked comical, Matt thought with affection, Jarvis the size and shape of a mattress, his thick hair sprouting in all directions, Troy small and bald and wiry at his side. When he reached them, Jarvis was not looking at Steve's photos. He was staring at his punch and jabbing a finger at the fruit and leaves in his glass.

'I know there's punch underneath, I know because I saw him pour it but I'm damned if I can get to it through the jungle canopy.' He threw back his head and bent the top half of his torso backwards. His glass hovered, base-up, over his mouth.

Troy said, 'In a minute someone's going to think you're a sculpture and buy you.'

'Hopefully,' said Jarvis, still waiting for the punch to arrive, 'a wealthy heiress.'

'Could we just look at the goddam pictures as though we're a little bit interested?' pleaded Matt in an undertone.

'I already looked at them,' said Jarvis.

'I've been watching you and you only just got here.'

'A glance was enough. They're sensation-seeking crap. I don't want to discuss his work with him except to say: go get yourself a proper job.'

Troy and Matt looked at each other, shrugged and turned towards the pictures. They studied them in a silence occasionally punctuated by exclamations from Jarvis: 'One drop. Two drops. Three drops. Incredible, this rain forest is so dense that no liquid can penetrate and the punch is defying gravity's great force.'

'Wow,' muttered Troy to Matt without taking his eyes off the pictures. 'Doesn't it feel like someone just stuck a camera in your trash can and called it art?'

Matt remembered how he had met Steve when he had gone back into the operating theatre to retrieve his notes. It had seemed to him then that Steve must be cleaning the theatre but now he realized that Steve might have been photographing it. There were about eight pictures of theatres right after messy operations. The shrouded operating table, the blood smeared down its side and pooling on the floor, the knives and other instruments lying askew, the machines with valves hanging, some wads of sterile packaging stuck to puddles of water and blood and, in a metal bowl, some kind of human offal.

Matt hoped this wasn't one of his theatres. Surely his scrub nurse wouldn't let him leave his work spaces looking like the scene of some terrible crime?

'I mean,' said Troy, somehow managing to wrinkle skin that was stretched tightly over his face, 'is this art?'

'Nope,' said Jarvis, who had left his punch glass upside down on the floor and joined them. 'Like I said, it's crap. Did you see these?'

Troy and Matt studied the pictures Jarvis indicated.

'Shit, are they dead?' asked Troy.

Matt found his voice. 'No, they're under anaesthetic. That's the recovery room. Patients go there after theatre to wake up. Sometimes it gets pretty busy . . .' There had in fact been many complaints from the hospital's nursing staff about the inadequacy of the recovery room. Sited in the centre of a ring of operating theatres, it could hold up to ten patients but sometimes it held more, trolleys rammed into one another at acute angles like a pile-up on the Interstate.

'Looks like some kind of mass suicide,' said Troy, standing closer to the photos and staring.

'I told you,' Matt repeated testily, 'they're under anaesthetic.'

'Think he woke them up to ask if he could take their picture?' muttered Jarvis. 'I mean, isn't there some sort of law against it?'

Troy creased his small, hard face into a thinking position.

'I'm sure I could find one,' he said. 'If any of those guys wanted legal representation . . .'

'Now, there just has to be a law against this,' said Jarvis, indicating the final photos. 'Don't try telling me these guys are under anaesthetic.'

'No,' said Matt quietly. 'No, that's the morgue.'

The photos were in stark black and white. They showed a row of bodies from which life had been extinguished at various stages of aging and illness. The bodies were mostly naked. A few were covered by light sheets which emphasized rather than hid their human form. Not all the pictures showed the faces of the dead but some of them did.

Afterwards, they stood in the parking lot while Troy and Jarvis smoked. Jarvis had positioned himself right by the courtyard of the Osiris café and he faced the sky when he exhaled so that his smoke would waft over the wall to the vegetarian diners.

'So is your Steve pal sick or what?' Troy asked.

'Well, he always was a nice guy and he still seems like one . . .' said Matt.

Troy agreed. 'He's nice. But he may be sick as well.'

'He makes you nervous,' observed Jarvis.

'Shit, that's not true,' protested Matt.

'I didn't say you're scared of him. I said he makes you nervous. Like you owe him something or you're trying to make up for something.'

Just because Jarvis looked like his truck these days, it was too easy to think the man must have lost that sharp perceptiveness which had always been so startling. Matt wanted to blurt out, 'I think I killed Steve's father.' Discussing it with the other guys would feel good. It would bring back something like normality to his inner life. He could tell them how Mr Minelli's body had sat, motionless, behind the driver seat of the red car and how these days he sometimes felt stalked by red cars, both the one in his memory and another one. It might belong to a man whose father had died at the hospital, or Matt might be imagining its very existence, and neither of these possibilities was pleasant. He opened his mouth to speak but, as though an invisible hand had slipped right across his face, no words were audible.

'Maybe,' suggested Jarvis cunningly, aware that his arrows were hitting their target, 'you're so damn egalitarian that you're overcompensating? I mean, because you're a big-shot doc and he's just a lowly cleaner who mops up after one of those deaths which happen so routinely to your patients?'

Matt, assaulted again by the truth, was still unable to reply. Not that it was worth arguing with Jarvis, since he always had to have the last word. Particularly when he was right.

'We played together every summer for years and years . . .' Matt began.

'Oh,' said Jarvis witheringly. 'So, this friendship, it's a memory-sharing thing.'

He exhaled aggressively in the direction of the Osiris café but there was no wind tonight and the smoke seemed to disintegrate in the air right over his head. Troy inhaled, slowly and deeply. Matt saw how Troy's face showed his pleasure. Matt never smoked but he was the kind of doctor who did not criticize those patients who did. His own mother had smoked, sometimes heavily. And he acknowl-edged, maybe even envied a little, the satisfaction smoking gave his friends. That quiet, fraternal act of communion as they passed one another cigarettes, the way the slow rhythm of inhalation and exhalation seemed to amplify res-piration and fill silences. He sometimes saw hospital staff taking cigarette breaks behind the kitchens and it seemed that smoking meant they were doing something together while they were doing nothing and this heightened their camaraderie.

'Steve Minelli,' breathed Jarvis, smoke wafting from his mouth as though it were forming Steve's name. 'I can tell you one thing about him. When he seems like he's pouring you punch, he isn't. You try to drink it and there's only leaves and twigs and stuff in your glass. Bear that in mind, Matt.' He drew on his cigarette again, inhaling deeply. 'So, all those years ago, were you big pals?'

'I don't recall ever drinking punch with him, Jarvis. But we were big pals in the summer vacations: his folk had a cottage near ours. We spent every summer together up to the age of . . . about eleven'

'So was it a kid thing or a whole family thing?'

'Oh, definitely a family thing.'

They ate, fought and played together like one family. They were so close-woven that sometimes the cloth snagged, leaving frayed strands or even a hole.

'Don't tell your father,' Mr Minelli said to Matt one day. He had placed an arm around Matt's back and it was heavy like a yoke or some other unwelcome burden. They were standing silently together staring out of a window at the lake.

'Don't tell your father. Okay, Matt?'

Matt had been unsure what he should not tell but he had agreed anyway and, whatever it was, he had never told. At the time, and now, he had hated himself for making this promise to Mr Minelli. It felt as though he had betrayed Hirsh.

Jarvis said, 'Kids and parents, all pals? Everyone friends like in *The Bobbsey Twins*?'

Matt remembered the two families eating together at the Minellis' picnic table by the lake. His mother was a little distance from the rest of the group, her back turned. She was sitting by the water, smoking slowly. She held her cigarette so still for so long that in the breathless summer evening the smoke rose in a straight line.

There was one other smoker in the group. Mr Minelli.

Their mutual habit sometimes made Hilly and Mr Minelli seem like members of an exclusive club. They passed each other cigarettes or lighters and sometimes sat apart from everyone else, smoking together. But in this memory, although Hilly sat at the water's edge, Mr Minelli was seated at the picnic table right next to Matt. He was telling a story in a voice which was confident of the laughter which must follow. He handled his cigarette differently from Hilly, creating small clouds of smoke all around him which made Matt cough. And he tugged on his cigarette with his mouth, tapping the ash to the ground with a restless finger so that Matt was aware of his movement even without looking at him. After a while, Matt had wondered if the man's voice or his smoke was more choking.

The memory was so potent that Matt was only dimly aware of the strains of 'Waltzing Matilda' vibrating in his pocket and he did not associate this with his own cellphone until Troy actually took it, opened it, said briskly, 'Hold the line, please, caller, Dr Seleckis is right on hand to save your life . . .' and then held it to Matt's face.

'It's probably the hospital,' said Jarvis gravely. 'Calling about another routine death.'

Matt realized his Australian colleague must have stolen his cellphone and reprogrammed its ring to play 'Waltzing Matilda.' He had done this to almost everyone in the department. The double row of General Surgery offices sometimes echoed with an eerie cacophony of 'Waltzing Matilda's.

'Honey, it's me. Are you okay?' Denise's voice was crisper than usual as though the phone had grilled its soft edges.

'Sure, why?'

'That cough sounds terrible!'

Matt was startled. He thought he had been remembering coughing, not actually doing it.

119

He swallowed. 'I'm fine,' he said.

'Matt, Daddy's not feeling too good and . . . well, I should probably go over there . . . I waited as long as I could before calling you . . .'

'That's okay.' Matt tried to hide the irritation that he felt whenever Clem took Denise away. 'I'm probably closer to Mason House, want me to go instead?' he offered, knowing he would be refused.

'I think it's just one of those times when he wants me. I tried for a sitter for Austin but of course . . .'

'It's okay, we've finished in the exhibition anyway.'

'Are you sure?'

Across the road, groups of people were leaving the Big White Space.

'Looks like the exhibition's closing now,' said Matt. 'I guess we were the last to arrive.'

'Apologize to the guys for me,' Denise said. She liked Troy and Jarvis, although she seldom saw them. 'Maybe you could invite them home here for a beer? I'm leaving right away. Belinda Lampeter said she'd cover until you arrive but she can't stay longer then about thirty minutes.'

Matt did not invite Troy and Jarvis for a beer. He had visited Troy in his apartment sometimes and had once or twice stopped by in the suburbs to pick up Jarvis, waiting in the hallway with the handlebars of small tricycles and the wheels of small trucks sticking into his shins while Jarvis extricated himself from the sticky embraces of his kids. But the three men never met in one another's houses.

As he pulled off the busy streets into the quieter residential areas on the way home, Matt became aware of a car behind him that was taking just the same route he was. This was unusual, since from habit he cut diagonally around the city, taking a left on Harvard then a right on Yale, then a left followed by another right. By the time he turned into his own street, he was sure the car must be following him. Before reaching his house he slowed up until he had almost stopped, but instead of pulling impatiently past him the way any normal driver would do, the car slowed too. Matt's heart beat faster. The car, he was almost certain despite the deception of the street lights, was red. He could stop right here and see just what the driver would do next.

But now Belinda Lampeter, who must have been waiting at the window for him, appeared in the drive and he was forced to turn in. The car behind swished on by, its engine almost noiseless.

'Sorry to rush right off,' said Belinda. 'But I'm expecting a call from Judy in New York.'

Belinda's daughter was a busy and successful magazine editor and Belinda was always expecting a call from her.

'Austin's fast asleep,' she told him.

'Thanks, Belinda, we really appreciate this,' said Matt. And just as Belinda was about to dart off to her own house, he said, 'Did you just see that car? The one which pulled in right behind me?'

Belinda shook her head. 'I didn't really notice a car . . .' she said absently.

'You didn't see it?'

So the car which he thought had followed him on a zigzag trail across the city had been entirely a figment of his imagination. Probably the other cars had too. Matt felt blood drain from the smaller tubes of his body, as though the tide had just gone out. He would have to call a shrink.

'Oh, wait, now I think about it, there was a car behind you . . .' she said.

Relief. The tide came back in like a flash flood.

'Did you think it was acting sort of strangely?' he

demanded. 'I mean, it pulled in behind me just before I turned . . .'

Belinda looked vague.

'Um, well, no, Matt, not really. I mean, he was waiting for you to turn. That's polite, I guess. Too many drivers are impatient these days. There's too much pushing past people.'

Matt nodded and thanked her again. At least someone else had seen the car. He might be paranoically misinterpreting the car's actions but at least he wasn't imagining its existence.

He watched as she walked down the path and then along the sidewalk a few paces and then back up her own path. Matt would have cut across the grass.

As he put the car away, he wondered if Belinda Lampeter was the kind of woman who never cut corners or if she just didn't like the neighbours to see her doing it. In the Mormon neighbourhood where Denise had lived with Weslake, people watched one another all the time and when the windows were open they could hear you too. Neighbours made no secret of their interest. As a Latter Day Saint it was your duty to report to the ward the failings of other Saints. And when Denise and Weslake had been trying for a child, everyone had prayed for them. Everyone in the ward, everyone in the stake, for all Matt knew, everyone in the Tabernacle Choir. There was no privacy in a Mormon neighbourhood, so it had been hard enough for Denise when she met Matt. She had finally slid away from the Latter Day Saints like a snake leaving a skin behind. And there had been no question but that leaving the Church had inevitably meant leaving the neighbourhood.

Matt went to Austin's room. He gently disentangled the twisted bedcovers and rearranged them over the sleeping child. Then he watched Austin. He swelled with love at the sight of the boy's small fingers on the pillow, the roundness of his cheeks. There were times when he felt irritated by Austin's demands, his irrationality, his incomprehension of others' needs and life's limits, but in the presence of the sleeping child he felt only love's ache. Whatever complex structure Matt had built in his life, personally, professionally, could be melted away in an instant by his tiny son to expose raw, gaping emotions.

Austin was their miracle child. Denise had been previously unable to conceive. Despite all those prayers and a little help from the infertility clinic, she and Weslake had not managed to produce a baby. And then, astonishingly, to their immense joy, quite soon after meeting Matt and perhaps too soon after Weslake's death, she had discovered she was pregnant. Matt had never experienced one moment's doubt that this was the right thing. Indeed, he sometimes felt that this was the only thing he had ever succeeded in doing better than Weslake.

He waited up for Denise but still she did not come home. He thought of calling Mason House to ask pointedly whether some emergency had detained her but he knew that both Denise and Clem would resent the intrusion. There were private areas of Denise's life and Weslake was certainly one but Clem was another.

Finally Matt went to bed. He did not sleep. He lay in the silence, waiting for Denise. Had the driver of the red car been following him tonight or had he just happened to take the same route, hanging back politely when Matt turned into his own house? The way Belinda Lampeter wrinkled her nose in confusion when he had questioned the driver's motives made him once again suspect himself of paranoia. He realized he was more afraid of the possibility of his own paranoia than he was of the driver of the red car.

He thought about his conversation with Mrs Minelli tonight. I believe, we all believe, that our father was killed.

Matt strained to remember Mr Minelli's death. He strained so hard he didn't know where his mind stopped and his body began, he strained his arm and neck and leg muscles as though he could physically reach out and grab the memory.

He could smell tobacco. Smoke from Jarvis's and Troy's cigarettes had insinuated itself into his hair and on to his skin but the smell had the mustiness and familiarity of something accumulated over years, as though Matt was a heavy smoker and nicotine clung to his every cell.

'Don't tell your father,' Mr Minelli said, breathing smoke over him, the stench of tobacco oozing from his pores. The skin on his face was smooth, as though he had just shaved. They had been looking at the lake, but not through a window as Matt had supposed earlier. No, they had been on the terrace, standing together. Mr Minelli had been smoking and then suddenly, surprisingly, no, shockingly, he had offered Matt a cigarette. Matt had stared at it, not knowing what to do.

'C'mon,' said Mr Minelli. His voice was charming, cajoling. 'Don't think I don't know what you guys get up to in school these days.'

Matt was not yet even a sixth grader. It had not occurred to him to smoke in school or anywhere else. He knew how much Hirsh hated Hilly to smoke and he knew that he shouldn't and he had no intention of doing so. And now Mr Minelli was offering him a cigarette.

'No,' he said. It was frightening to refuse an offer that this big, insistent man wanted him to accept. And Mr Minelli took this as a no to his previous request, about not telling Hirsh something. That's when he had made himself bigger just by shifting his weight around. Now when he spoke he didn't sound so nice. He said, 'It will be real bad for you if you start shooting your mouth off, kid.'

'I won't tell anything,' Matt promised, and Mr Minelli had nodded and stood on the terrace as long as it took to finish his cigarette. He did not hurry. Matt thought he would never finish it but finally he crushed its stump underfoot and went back inside the house without saying a word.

Matt was relieved to be left alone but he felt nauseous. He was a small boat which was being pitched violently by the vast and stormy adult world. He was nauseated by his own promise to guard one of Mr Minelli's secrets. He should have stood up to him, told him that he didn't keep secrets from Hirsh, thrown that big bully's cigarettes back in his face. Except that Mr Minelli had made a mistake. He thought Matt knew a secret but he was wrong. Matt had no idea what he was supposed to keep from his father.

And later (weeks? Days? Months? It didn't matter because they were all the same now, they were all the past), Mr Minelli had died. And at his death, as he stood in the woods staring down at the red car, Matt had guessed that this was the final event in a chain which he might have broken if he had understood the secret and stood up to Mr Minelli that day on the terrace by telling his father. His promise to Mr Minelli had been the beginning of his culpability.

He wished he could remember what the secret was. Even if he hadn't understood it at the time, he might understand it now. And had he alone known the secret? A man was found shot in his car; hadn't there been accusations, investigations, a team of policemen combing the mountainside for tiny forensic clues? Had they questioned him and suspected his guilt? Who had decided that the death was an 'accident'?

Last time he had visited Hirsh, when he had been telling his father about Mr Zoy's death, he had started by saying that he'd killed a man and Hirsh had looked right at him in that firm, omniscient way and he had said, 'I know.' Possibly, Hirsh had thought Matt at last was going to confess something about the Minelli death. And when Matt had asked if he needed a lawyer for the Zoy case, Hirsh's reply was: 'Not this time.' As if he knew all about that other time.

Matt turned over in bed and then over again. If, that day on the hillside (evening, he now believed. The memory, as though it had emerged cleaner from the wash, was becoming clearer. He was able even to examine the light which fell in shafts across his parents and know that there was a trickle of low sun through the trees from the west), he had been finding his parents to announce Mr Minelli's death, why had they already been crying? Did they already know of the death and, worse, guess his involvement in it? He sighed and turned again. The memory could, of course, be faulty. Memory was like that. It was polluted water, full of the flotsam and jetsam of a thousand other shipwrecks. It could never be pure, but the emotions it evoked were reliable.

Matt was sweating now. He was sweating and twisting his body between the sheets to avoid a truth which was unwelcome and uncomfortable but which he knew was right. He wished he could slam the lid back on the well and once again persuade himself to forget all about Mr Minelli's death. But this was impossible. The childhood past had forced its way into the adult present and now he would have to deal with it in an adult way. And as a constant reminder there was now Steve, haunting him in hospital hallways. His father's death had ruined Steve's life and that of his mother and brothers while Matt enjoyed a stable relationship with his own father, a good career and a happy marriage. There was only one right thing to do. Matt would have to find out exactly how Mr Minelli had died and what his own role and responsibilities had been in this death. And when he knew the truth, then he would have to try making amends to Steve and his family.

He started to relax a little, now that he had confronted this conclusion at last.

He heard Denise's key in the lock and shortly afterwards he felt her weight gently enter the bed. It seemed she was heavier than usual from fatigue. He heard her stifle a yawn.

'I'm awake,' he told her softly and she rearranged her body so that it pushed up against his.

'How was the exhibition?'

'You're too tired for that stuff now.'

'I'm not. I want to hear about it.'

So Matt described the Big White Space and quoted Steve's biography at her and then he told her about the pictures, first the operating theatre, then the recovery room and finally the morgue. She listened with evident interest.

'Did his work ennoble death or the human body in any way?'

Matt thought about this but could produce no reply.

Denise waited a moment and then rolled over on to her elbow so she could watch him more closely in the dark. She seemed vital and alert now, like someone who had just woken and was leaving sleep's periphery instead of someone about to enter it.

'I mean, what did you feel when you looked at them? And what do you think he intended you to feel? Shock? Revulsion? Fear? Loss? Respect for human kind?'

Matt sighed. 'You're asking the wrong guy. For me there have been a lot of bodies so probably I react differently from other people. But Steve's such a nice guy. Quiet and sort of meek. I just can't imagine him taking those photos.'

'What did Troy and Jarvis say?'

'Troy was shocked, I think. He asked me if Steve was sick and Jarvis said it was all attention-seeking crap and someone should sue because he didn't get permission to play paparazzo to the dead, except they shouldn't because Steve probably was doing it just for publicity.'

Denise sounded thoughtful. She had occasionally accompanied Jarvis to exhibitions in the past. 'Well, I have to respect Jarvis's opinion . . .'

'If you want to know how I felt,' said Matt slowly, 'I felt the way I did in Eritrea when some guy from a British newspaper showed up and began taking pictures of my field hospital. When I say hospital I mean two bloodstained tents and a lot of wounded people and some of them had already crossed the line between wounded and dead. I told him to get out but he wouldn't go and I was too busy to make him. He kept saying that people needed to know what was happening in Eritrea and these pictures would help them understand. I was mad at the time but afterwards I thought maybe if he published his pictures and they shocked people then maybe, just maybe, someone might do something to help end that stupid war. Or some more aid might filter through.' Matt could hear his heart beating harder as he spoke and his breath grow a little shorter as the anger he had felt that day, like a sleeping dog, jumped up and started to bark. 'But of course, he was boosting his own career, that British guy. He was probably going to get payment and recognition for those pictures. They certainly didn't result in any new aid money flowing in.'

Denise was silent for a moment.

'Okay, you can't justify Steve's pictures that way, there's no senseless war at St Claudia's for him to expose.'

'Jarvis thinks it's all about self-advancement,' said Matt. 'But Steve just isn't like that. He had this intimidating father and he's always been quiet and sensitive, not pushy at all. I guess maybe he was a little weak sometimes . . .'

A memory of Steve had alighted on him, unbidden and unwelcome. It still had the power to sting through the thick layer of years. One day, when he was perhaps nine and not such a strong swimmer as the Minellis, they had rigged up a rope swing on a branch overhanging the lake. The rope had swung far out over the water and the bigger boys would fling themselves with a great splash when it reached its most distant arc. Steve had been using it when the rope had snapped and he had been thrown prematurely and awkwardly into the water. Matt had waited, biting his lip, for Steve to surface but he had not done so. The Minelli brothers were all far away by the lake rocks, yelling and swimming. No one else had noticed. Alarmed, Matt waded in, then swam out to where Steve had fallen. He could not find Steve or any evidence of him, only the broken seat of the swing. He began to panic. Then he heard laughter. Steve had surfaced far off, over by his brothers, and they had all witnessed his panic and were finding it hilarious. Steve had swum over. He wasn't laughing any more but he was smiling. He said, 'I didn't mean to scare you, Matt.' But Matt had swum back to the lake shore, angry and red-faced. Steve had been a nice guy but, ultimately, he had been allied to his brothers and not to Matt. Once Hirsh had found Matt tearful after some such betrayal and had explained that it wasn't a betrayal, it was just that blood was thicker than water. That was the first time Matt had heard the phrase and it had fascinated him.

Denise was still thinking about the exhibition. 'Well, he might have entirely artistic motives.'

Matt faltered. 'Or . . .' he hesitated. 'Or, he has some emotional need which he uses the pictures to express. Some trauma, some shock, something terrible which happened . . .'

'Do you know of anything?'

'Um . . . well, I guess his father died. I don't exactly remember the details.'

His words felt weighty with their own significance, so weighty that he could hardly say them, barely mumble them. Amazingly, Denise did not seem to notice.

'Well, I should go to the exhibition so I can make up my own mind,' she said. 'I'd really like to. I'll try to get there this week.'

Matt was surprised. Why would Denise, whose most recent contact with death had been brutal, want to see Steve's pictures? He rolled over so he faced her. He touched her cheek lightly.

'They might upset you.'

'We all have to learn to look death right in the face,' she insisted and for a moment it seemed to Matt that the night and the silence intensified a little. There was no sound. No distant traffic, no plane overhead, no furnace or fridge rumbling.

'You already did that,' whispered Matt into the darkness at last. 'Denise. You already looked death in the face.'

He could see the outline of her chin and cheeks but not their fine details. There were points of light where her eyes shone.

'Maybe . . .' She hesitated. She drew an uneven breath. 'Maybe it's pulling me back. I mean, until I come to terms with it.'

Matt knew how trauma pulled you back until you tamed it. He understood how the human mind heals itself by returning to the unbearable, reaching out to the untouchable, caressing the repugnant. That was probably why Steve was drawn to the hospital morgue. And Matt remembered how, the first time he had worked in a war zone and quantities of casualties had been dragged into his dressing station with their limbs and heads hanging like rag dolls', he had vowed never to return. But somehow he had, again and again, until he could operate on any body, no matter how dehumanized by gaping wounds, dangling joints, pulverized organs.

'You don't need to see these pictures,' he whispered to Denise. 'It's been more than three years. And now you have me. Now you have Austin.'

He started to hate Weslake again. He could feel his body stretched thin by jealousy until it felt like a long, straight line. Denise still loved Weslake. She had just admitted that she still couldn't come to terms with his death. She had probably been visiting his grave recently with Christine. Matt's skin was taut with hatred. Then she reached out for him, and his muscles softened as he smelled her and as she pushed herself sensuously against him.

'Thank God I have you,' she whispered, running her hands down his flesh. He felt the first, familiar small tugs of arousal. As she rolled on to him and lay along his body like some basking animal, his skin softened again and all traces of his hatred for Weslake disappeared, swallowed up by love and desire for Denise.

Later, when he was feeling quiet and happy and satisfied, when he had begun to experience that deep relaxation which gathers like darkness in the brief pause between sex and sleep, when Denise's breaths had lengthened slowly and the small movements of her body indicated that she was already dreaming, Matt reminded himself of his decision to determine his involvement in Mr Minelli's death and to make amends, in any way possible, to the Minelli family. The knowledge that this was the right, although the hardest, thing to do released him into sleep.

'Weslake!' screamed a voice, eerie with pain. 'Weeeees-laaaake!'

Matt tried to sit upright and take hold of Denise but sleep seemed to have given her an unnatural strength and she was clutching at him, pinning him to the bed.

'Weslake!' she screamed. The room vibrated with her misery. She held on to him as though he were falling over a terrible precipice. She was crying now. Her body was shaking with the deep sobs of undiluted pain.

Matt overpowered her. He pulled himself upright and took her in his arms and whispered in her ear.

'It's all right,' he said. 'I'm okay, Denise. Everything's going to be all right.'

Gradually her grip loosened and her body relaxed and her breathing regained its rhythm. Matt sat in the dark. Denise had thought that he was Weslake and he had experienced her suffering first-hand. As if that wasn't bad enough, he had actually comforted her by pretending to be Weslake. He fell into a miserable sleep. His dreams were pale and unsatisfactory and the sleep itself had a thin, light quality like a blanket full of holes.

8

It was Clem's birthday and Matt had, at Denise's request, taken time off work to join in the small celebration she planned. Anxious to fit all he could into the short day that was left to him, Matt saw with a sinking heart that he had an appointment with Mrs Zoy after his clinic. Somehow he had known that one letter from the medical ethics officer wouldn't close the case.

'Sorry about Mrs Zoy,' said his secretary, coming in with her screwdriver. 'But I warned Mike Salinski's secretary and Jon Espersen's secretary to keep thirty minutes free in case you need them.'

Matt was embarrassed that she had understood the problem so well.

'And,' she added, 'Mrs Zoy promised not to bring her son.'

'What are you doing with that screwdriver?' he asked.

She smiled at him. 'Complaint from Buildings Admin.'

'The bald moron?' he asked sympathetically, getting up from his chair.

'Well, he's sure bald but I guess he's not so moronic as I thought,' she admitted. Her face, as she climbed on to the chair, was flushed.

'No? He's taking away all our fresh air and you've decided you like him?'

She pulled a face and signalled for Matt to pass her the missing window panel. He held it in position while she screwed.

'I wouldn't go that far. However, the heating's off at last

and the air conditioning's going on today, so I said I'd put the panel back. He offered to help but of course I wouldn't let him.'

Matt studied her face as she studied the screw. 'You like him,' he said.

'Turns out he's from Ellensburg, which is only a few miles from where my grandma lives,' she admitted.

'He's from Washington State too?'

'My cousin went to school in Ellensburg! My aunt Jessica got married there! It's such a coincidence, we just have to go on a date to talk about it.'

Her face was a deep pink now. 'But if the air conditioning doesn't go on, no dice. I've made that clear.'

After clinic, Matt made his way back upstairs and immediately noticed the comfortable, uniform temperature of his office.

'Hear that humming and whirring?' asked his secretary. 'Feel that cool air? One bald guy just got himself a date. Can't decide whether to wear my tight pink top with the grey pants or my sleeveless electric-blue dress.'

'Wear both,' Matt advised her. He was preparing himself for his meeting with Mrs Zoy when his secretary informed him it was cancelled. He was relieved but his secretary, noting this, shook her head.

'Unfortunately, this is the reason it's cancelled.' She handed him a letter from the medical ethics officer. It stated that the patient's relatives had not accepted her advice to drop the case and that they planned to challenge Matt's version of events. They had indicated that they now wished the matter to move through the hospital's formal complaints system, which required Matt to submit written evidence and then attend a tribunal, the date for which was already set in early October.

Matt read the letter twice. The words danced on the page and the paper seemed to bulge malevolently in his hand.

'You don't have anything to worry about, you didn't do anything wrong,' said his secretary. Her voice was high. She was protesting. He looked at her and saw that her eyes were glassy and her cheeks red. Her mouth was turned down like an unfunny clown's. Was she mirroring his expression or was she experiencing her own dismay?

Jon Espersen appeared in the office suddenly, as though they had called him. Matt handed him the letter but it was clear Jon already knew of its contents.

'I'm sorry about this, Matt. That son is a pain in the butt. It's easy enough to calm down the situation when we talk with the bereaved wife but as soon as the son gets involved the whole thing's inflamed again.'

Matt wondered how many calls Jon had made to the Zoys on his behalf.

'Thanks for supporting me,' he mumbled.

'Not so many of these things get to tribunal stage,' said Jon. 'But we had the big renal failure case a few years ago. And I do recall that we took legal advice before going into tribunal.'

Matt sighed.

'Technically, you don't need to, but if the Zoys aren't satisfied with the hospital tribunal then they can take the case into the civil courts and the judge is entitled to examine the tribunal report in some detail. So it's better to get a lawyer involved at this stage.'

Matt nodded. His body felt numb. He could imagine a long corridor of litigation stretching ahead of him, litigation which would require him to reiterate under oath the small untruths he had scribbled on the patient's file and in the dispensary drug book. In a foolish moment of weakness he had risked his whole career for Mr Zoy and now Mr Zoy wasn't even around to thank him.

'I wasn't head of department then but I know we used a good lawyer for the renal failure case,' Jon was saying. 'I'll get the guy's name. We have got a lot of time for all this since the tribunal isn't until the fall.'

There was silence in the office for a few moments. Matt knew he was supposed to say something but the silence continued. Despite the air conditioning his secretary's cheeks had turned to a deep, hot red. Then Jon, studying Matt's face gravely, announced he was taking him downstairs for lunch.

In the cafeteria, Matt sat in front of food he could not eat.

'Listen, Matt,' said Jon. 'You look like a guy who's done something wrong and knows he'll be found out. That is not the right attitude.'

Matt tried to look innocent.

'You acted in a wholly humane, generous fashion towards a helpless, dying old man and now his family is beating up on you,' said Jon. 'This tribunal thing is nonsense. It's a charade. You know that. I can guarantee you are going to walk away from this affair with everyone saying you're a great doctor. So calm down, for heaven's sake.'

Matt told Austin to calm down when he yelled or screamed. He didn't know how you could calm down if you were already sitting very still and silent.

'The Zoy son's a bully. I've seen his type before. He wants you to feel crushed, Matt. So don't give him the satisfaction. Try to avoid seeing him or talking to him but, if he makes contact with you, don't let him feel he's getting the better of you.'

Matt told Jon of his suspicion that he was being followed by the Zoy son.

'How sure are you?' demanded Jon, watching him closely.

Aware that he was in danger of sounding paranoid, Matt said, 'I'm one hundred per cent sure that someone's following me in their car. Not every day but often enough for me to notice. But they never get out of the car and I can't see who's behind the wheel because the windows are darkened.'

'Have you taken the make and number?'

'I got to work one morning and found that he'd beaten me to my normal space. The lot was almost empty except for this red car parked just where I always park. So I finally got the details.'

Jon sighed thoughtfully. 'But there was no sign of Zoy himself?'

'None at all. Although I did take the elevator that day instead of the stairs.'

'And you're sure . . .' Jon was still watching him, 'that it's always the same car?'

'Well, most of the time,' said Matt firmly. He could not afford to air his doubts in front of Jon. 'When I've briefly glimpsed the driver it seems to me it could be Zoy.'

Jon sighed. 'This sounds serious. How far do you want to take it?'

'I don't think we can do anything until he gets out of the car or anyway goes one step further. Actually threatens me, threatens my family . . .' Matt swallowed. He thought of Denise and Austin and felt his eyes fog with anxiety.

'Somehow I don't see him doing that. It sounds like classic bullying stuff to me. He wants to threaten and intimidate you without actually placing himself in danger of reprisals. I think you should make a note of the date, time and place whenever you see him. And take my advice, act cool. Don't let him see that he's rattling your cage,' said Jon. Matt nodded. When he got up to go he was aware that Jon was looking at him with concern.

'This whole Zoy thing is placing you under a lot of pressure,' Jon commented. 'Try to forget about it between now and the tribunal or it'll ruin your summer.'

Matt turned to face Jon. 'I'm not paranoid and I'm not imagining it.' He hoped he sounded convincing.

'I believe you,' said Jon. 'We need to think how to deal with this guy.'

As they walked back upstairs together, Jon said, 'Tell Denise I'm sorry about what's happening right now at Slimtime. Christine showed me the *Tribune* article. I'm sort of glad Weslake isn't here to see it.'

Matt bent to tie his shoelace so Jon couldn't see his face. He tried to make his tone bluff as he said, 'Oh, Denise seems okay about it all.' He determined to trawl the Internet one night when Denise was asleep to find out what was happening at Slimtime.

Matt arrived at four o'clock in Clem's apartment, breathless because he had rushed to be on time. Clem buzzed him in. The old man was arranged neatly in his enormous armchair, looking small as a doll in the lavishly furnished room. There was no sign of Denise and Austin.

'We said four-thirty, not four,' Clem told him.

The old man looked more shrunken than Matt remembered. His clothes hung on him loosely with an unfamiliarity which Matt knew meant he spent most days in bed. However, Clem greeted him warmly and when they shook hands Matt found his grip as vicelike as ever.

'I'm so pleased you're coming to Liguria with us,' he told Matt, as though Clem and Denise were married and Matt the lucky gooseberry whom they were allowing to holiday along with them.

Matt wondered if Weslake had ever felt similarly annoyed by Clem. But Weslake, like Clem, had been a high-ranking member of the Mormon Church and father and son-in-law had enjoyed a relationship which was independent of Denise. Weslake had frequently visited Mason House alone to hold intimate talks about Church matters. Matt, however, had rarely if ever been here by himself and he wondered what he would now find to say. He had always felt Clem's religiosity a barrier to all communication.

Clem came from a wealthy Chicago family and Denise's childhood had been privileged and cultured. Then Clem and his wife had been converted. When Denise had told Matt about the conversion he had imagined the impact of the Mormon Church on the family like a huge cartoon fly swat, flattening Clem and his wife and all their daughters with an immense force. They had moved to Salt Lake and integrated apparently seamlessly into Mormon society but they weren't and never could be the same as the Utah Mormons. They knew too much of that other world outside the Church.

'Well, Matt,' said Clem now, leaning back in his chair and surveying his son-in-law. 'I'm glad we have these few minutes alone together because I'd like to say how grateful I am to you for making Denise so happy. I never thought she could be happy again when Weslake died but, thanks to you, she is.'

Matt was surprised and embarrassed and he felt his cheeks redden a little. He said, 'When I met her right here in this room, it was the luckiest day of my life.'

Clem smiled. 'Good thing I was sick that day, eh?'

'Good thing I was just back from Africa. Good thing I was doing locum duty. Good thing I was working that shift . . .' Matt's voice trailed away. He hadn't been watching where he was going and now he had a horrible feeling he had driven right up to the gates of the Church. And sure enough, Clem's smile had turned pious.

'The Lord was working His purpose out for you, Matt,' he said solemnly, stroking his small white beard. Matt braced himself for a religious lecture but instead Clem's eyes kept moving in an alert, worldly way. Although now faded, it was easy to believe that once he had been an estimable figure in Salt Lake property. His body was still but his hazel eyes, exactly the same colour as Denise's, made him look like an old fox.

'There's no doubt, you're a lucky fellow, Matt. She always had many suitors. Right up until the day she married Weslake, there was still some guy trying to make her change her mind. But I told her to turn all others away and she took my advice. Weslake was a handsome, charming fellow from a good family. When she married him she married within our Church. I believed that was what the Lord must want.'

Matt shuffled his feet. He was aware that Clem had initially not supported his marriage to Denise because he had not wanted his daughter to marry out, correctly predicting that she would leave the Church.

'But, you know, I sometimes wonder if I did the right thing, telling her to marry Weslake,' said Clem carefully. 'In the light of what eventually happened.'

Matt was going to make an anodyne comment about the benefit of hindsight but Clem interrupted him. 'She did love him so darn much and she was such a good wife and she wanted a baby a lot and it was awful to see her suffer when she couldn't have one and then when the Lord took her man away. As for Weslake, he worked all the time. Worked in his clinic. Worked on his slimming products which, incidentally, are now having a few problems. Gave any free time to the Church. No wonder that, despite all our prayers, no children ever came along. You have to be in the same room sometimes if you want to make a child.' Clem chuckled.

Matt, who had detected something like a criticism of the sainted Weslake, sat very still. This was a more astringent Clem than usual. When Denise was around, the old guy was saccharine.

'Denise still suffers,' Matt said. 'She dreams about him at night and calls out his name.'

Clem looked hard at Matt. The old guy's tie was knotted into his collar. It looked grotesquely large on his tiny neck.

'That must be pretty irritating for you,' he observed. 'I forget, did you ever know him? Weslake wasn't exactly a doctor but he worked in that field, so I guess you might have come across him.'

Matt shook his head. 'No, but of course, I saw him on TV.'

Weslake had been a doctor of biochemistry with medical pretensions. He had set up, at an absurdly young age, a thriving clinic for patients with weight problems and his treatments had been based on a mixture of common sense and his own formulations. When Jon Espersen had brought the new, safer gastric bypass surgery to Salt Lake and patients were still wary, Weslake Smith had frequently referred clients, hence the two men's friendship. By then, Weslake had already started marketing a range of slimming products as Dr Smith's Slimtime. Matt remembered, before he left for Africa, the local TV commercials which featured Weslake, clad misleadingly in a medical white coat, a winning smile on his face, endorsing his own Slimtime. Recently Matt had found, among Denise's collection of old videos, a compilation tape of all Weslake's commercials. He had watched it with Austin while Denise was on a music therapy weekend. Weslake's mixture of handsome, reassuring medical presence and quack salesman had alarmed him. Worst of all, Austin had sat in fascinated silence throughout, riveted to the commercials as though Weslake had some kind of charisma.

Matt had gone to the drug store and examined one of the Dr Smith's Slimtime blue and white cans. It claimed you could lose ten pounds in two weeks just by eating Slimtime before each meal. Matt doubted that. He disapproved of Weslake's promises, which he saw as endorsement and exploitation of the poor eating habits of the overweight. He suspected that Weslake's referral of patients to Jon Espersen was an attempt to gain credibility with the local medical community.

'Denise never talks about him,' said Matt.

'Too painful,' said Clem wisely.

'Everything to do with Weslake is sacred. For example, there's this deer meat in the freezer which he must have shot just before he died and she doesn't want to eat it and she doesn't want to throw it out and she doesn't want to talk about it.'

'Ah,' said Clem, settling himself into his chair. 'It wasn't shot, it was roadkill. You know what happened when Weslake died?'

'I know he was running in Yellow Creek Forest when he got hit by a car . . .'

'Running to keep fit for the hunting season. I'm no hunter myself but I understand that fitness is important. He was running after work in the dark and he got hit by a car and there was scarcely a mark on him. They think he was killed almost instantly. Not that the driver stopped to find out. The police made a lot of inquiries. They had roadblocks up for a while, stopping all the regular drivers who came that way, looking at their cars. They even made investigations into Weslake's life which, of course, as he was a Saint, they found to be blameless.'

Matt was accustomed to Mormons referring to themselves as Saints, although it still sometimes irritated him.

'And, of course,' said Clem, 'they had to investigate Denise. Take a look at the car. Only a few days before, Weslake had been driving it when he hit this deer. He'd been hunting and shot nothing but, on the way home, he'd run over a deer and he'd taken it home for the freezer. Sort of a consolation prize. Personally, I never can understand why people get cold and wet shooting deer when you can run them down without even trying. Anyway, you can imagine the crazy thoughts the police had when they found traces of that accident on the fender. That is, until they matched it up with the dead deer in the freezer. So that was sort of an important deer for Denise. I mean, Weslake killed the deer just the way someone killed him only a week or so later.'

For a moment Matt thought he could smell the forest. He thought he could smell his father's hillside. Weslake had died in a forest, the scent of pungent woodiness in his nostrils.

'I can understand why the venison was important at the time,' said Matt. 'But I don't know why Denise won't deal with it now.'

'Women!' said Clem, rolling his eyes. 'They're impossible, but don't we love them? If you want my advice, you should just quietly remove that roadkill. I think she wants it gone but she doesn't want to sanction its going, if you see what I mean.'

'My dad might eat it, even if it is three years old,' said Matt.

'Waste not, want not,' said Clem, assuming his habitual expression of religious virtue and devotion. 'Give it to Hirsh.'

Matt was relieved that Denise was arriving now.

'We've been having such a nice talk,' Clem told her, smiling foxily at Matt.

'Four-thirty, darling, not four,' Denise said, kissing Matt. Austin ignored his grandfather and to Matt's delight gave his father a full-force greeting. Clem watched tensely as though he expected them to topple an ornament or a photo. It seemed to Matt that Clem always expected Austin to behave like a grown-up. He looked pained when the child climbed over his armchairs or grabbed another cookie, and her father's disapproval sometimes made Denise, in Matt's opinion, unusually severe with Austin.

A wide, uniformed woman appeared with a birthday cake and some kind of herb tea which contained no caffeine and which Mormons were allowed to drink.

'Let us pray,' said Clem now. Denise bowed her head and Matt tried unsuccessfully to scoop Austin on to his lap and hold him still.

Clem prayed for all of them, for their holiday in Liguria, and for the President to find a way through the internationally awkward situation which now dominated the headlines. Matt, who had not voted for the President and disapproved of the international situation, allowed Austin to spring from his arms during this last part and the little boy disappeared, giggling, under the sofa between his grandfather's legs.

'Amen,' said Clem and Denise solemnly.

Matt did not like the way that Denise observed her father's faith so submissively when Clem was around. However, she was always serene when challenged. She said it was acceptable to observe and obey while keeping her own heart independent: she had done this all her life.

'I don't object to the Church. I don't have any argument with it,' she had explained simply. 'I just always knew I wasn't truly one of them. If that's hypocrisy then I guess I'm a hypocrite.'

Matt did not think Denise was a hypocrite, but he suspected Clem was. Troy said it was possible but hard to get rich in property development around here without indulging in occasionally dubious business practices. Troy was always telling Jarvis and Matt about the white-collar crime in Salt Lake City and Matt was almost certain that Clem was capable of reconciling his religious beliefs with unethical business behaviour.

He was thinking just this when he suddenly experienced the near-shock of creativity. His brain had linked two previously entirely unconnected sides of his life. Clem and Mr Minelli. During Clem's years as one of the biggest movers in Salt Lake property he must surely have encountered Mr Minelli. Hadn't someone, Mrs Minelli or Steve, said that he had been in real estate?

Matt waited patiently as Clem kept up a conversation with Denise about Liguria. She was cutting the cake with an enormous knife. Matt tried to tempt Austin down from her back, where he seemed to have taken up residence, like a bear up a tree, but the little boy clung on, grinning.

Only Denise could remain graceful under these circumstances. Today she wore shades of red and brown. Her clothes flowed around her simply in a way that did not draw attention to themselves but made Denise noticeable in any room. Matt believed she had the enviable ability to free her life from complication and this ability showed in her clothes. Other women Matt had known would agonize in front of their mirror in the morning, frantically trying on first a dress and then a skirt and then another so that by the time they finally rushed out to work the floor would be a patchwork of rejected garments. And they would nearly always leave complaining that their clothes were the wrong colour or didn't match or were too bright or too loose or showed too many bulges. Denise slipped into her clothes each morning without indecision and then seemed to forget that she was wearing them for the rest of the day.

Matt waited for the discussion about Liguria to flag but Denise and her father did not stop talking. He tried unsuccessfully to bribe Austin down to the table with small pieces of cake but Austin refused to budge and his presence on Denise's back did nothing to suppress the conversation. The right moment to speak never seemed to come. Finally, Matt cut in with his question.

'Clem, did you ever come across a guy called Minelli?'

Even Matt was surprised by his interruption but the old man reacted smoothly. 'Would that be Arthur Minelli?'

Matt remembered his mother calling Mr Minelli one day. She had been standing on the hillside and yelling, 'Arthu-uuur!' Why had she been calling him? Where had Mr Minelli been? Like most of his memories of his mother it was without context. It was a fragment which floated through space like debris hurled from a rocket by an early space mission.

'Arthur Minelli,' he confirmed.

'Oh yes,' said Clem, 'I remember him well.'

Matt sat up and his whole body was suddenly alert. The bright, light clarity which the past brings to the blurred present of the elderly was going to shine for him.

Matt said, 'He had a vacation home near ours at Arrow Lake. He and his wife were big friends with my parents.'

Don't tell your father. It will be real bad for you if you start shooting your mouth off, kid.

Clem nodded. 'He died very tragically.'

The smell of the forest, dense, rotting, growing. A glimpse

146

of a car, a red one, parked through the trees, a motionless shadow within it.

'He was a nice enough man. Excellent company. I remember his laugh.'

Someone else had remembered a laugh. Steve Minelli had recalled laughter but it hadn't been his father's. It had been Hilly's.

'It was a sort of loud laugh, I think,' suggested Matt. The laughter had always been sudden and unexpected, the joke generally aimed at humiliating someone, and more than once, unforgivably (at this Matt felt a stabbing pain high in his belly), that someone was Hirsh.

'Yes, yes,' said Clem, passing Denise his empty plate. She anticipated this move almost before he made it and her hand was ready and waiting.

'He was such a big guy, he was sure to have a big laugh. Now, as a matter of fact, it's thanks to Arthur Minelli that we did so well on the Rosebay Building deal. He got into trouble over it. In way too deep. I mean, he'd started off as a residential realtor and, although he'd done quite well on some small commercial ventures, I believe he'd been in partnership then. With Rosebay he was in it alone and he didn't really know enough about the commercial game for that. Completely overstretched himself all round and might actually have faced some problems with the law if he'd lived.'

Remembering the Rosebay deal made Clem's face sharpen and grow younger. His eyes looked hawkish.

'We could all see he was going wrong. I remember that summer. A few of us tried to indicate to him that he'd taken some wrong turnings along the way but Arthur wasn't having it. He'd been vacationing and he was relaxed and brown and he had this new confidence, he was sure of himself. He probably thought we had some other motive in offering assistance. He would have had to let us help him eventually, of course. But then summer ended and the Lord intervened.'

Matt had lived in Utah long enough not to be surprised by the alliance of business and piety.

'He died in the fall?'

'At summer's end.'

Summer's end. When the air felt newly harsh in the mornings and your stomach rearranged itself into a knot as you started to pack, and the molecules up in the mountains reorganized themselves to fill all the spaces you left behind when you started the long trip back to the city.

'Yes,' repeated Clem, 'the Lord intervened at summer's end.' It was clear from Clem's tone which side of the Rosebay deal the Lord had been on.

'Must have been early September because we cleaned up on the deal in October, November: it took them a few months to sort out his estate. And there was a police investigation into his death, of course.'

Matt felt tiny hairs stand up all over his body. His forearms, the back of his neck. He smelled bruised leaves. He was standing on the hillside and across the road, parked in the belt of tangled trees which lined the lake, was a red car. The car did not move, the shadow in it did not move, but there was movement. Someone was running towards the car. Someone was following more slowly and there were voices, shouting, their pitch alone communicating, the way birds communicate through notes without words, an acute alarm. There was a car engine too, but it was not the engine of the red car. It was another car, roaring along the road.

'Why did the police investigate?' he asked, hearing a penetration in his own voice which suggested he was speaking in a silent room instead of one where a mother was trying to persuade a reluctant child to try peppermint infusion and two staff members were calling to each other out in the hallway.

Clem paused. He closed his bright, hazel eyes to think. Matt waited, his breath shallow so that he would inhale as little of the forest as possible in this room filled with the smells of cake and carpet and cleaning aids. At last, Clem opened his eyes.

'There was an accident and it was a strange one. But I can't now remember the details. Certainly there was an automobile involved.'

People were around the red car now. They were staring in through the windows and one of them was opening the driver's door, slowly, slowly, slowly. It was Hirsh. His slowness was agonizing. Why was he so slow?

'I don't recall exactly what happened . . .' said Clem. 'But I think he made some stupid mistake with a gun. Not that Arthur Minelli was an idiot: he was a clever guy and he had many talents. I remember, for example, that he was a wonderful photographer.'

Matt felt himself swallow.

'A photographer? What kind of photographer?'

'Portraits, I think. If I remember rightly, he specialized in black and white.'

If Matt had thought at all about who had taken those pictures of his mother, he had assumed the photographer to have been Hirsh. They were of a more professional quality than Hirsh's usual snaps but Matt had chosen to ignore this. The possibility that Mr Minelli had taken them, that his mother had posed for Mr Minelli, darted into his mind. 'Arthuuuur!' It was an ugly, unacceptable possibility and it darted right out again. It was a bird which had flown into glass, the way birds flew into the big porch window which

Matt and Steve had broken, and now the bird had bounced off and was flying rapidly in the other direction.

'This was at a time,' Clem was saying 'that everyone else was doing colour. People thought black and white was sort of old-fashioned. But I remember Arthur showing me some of his pictures and in my opinion he got wonderful results with black and white.'

There was a tap, tap at the window which sounded like a bird's beak on the glass but might have been rain.

'It was a hobby but he could have been professional. He was good. Oh, I guess he was a good man. But he was lax about details, a little slapdash. And that's what finished Rosebay for him and, if memory serves, that's what finished his life.'

9

A little while later, in early summer, it was time for Matt to go back up the mountain to Hirsh for the weekend. Denise reminded him that she and Austin were to go too. 'It'll be warmer up there now and it's a long time since Hirsh has seen Austin. He'll be amazed by the changes,' she said.

But Matt had remembered it was home movie weekend.

'Not this time,' he told her firmly. 'Too dangerous for Austin. Dad has a big squirrel problem and there's bait everywhere. We'll make a definite date for later in the summer.'

The ease and alacrity of his lie astonished him. He seemed to lie as though he'd had a lifetime of practice. He even managed to extract the frozen deer meat from the freezer and stow it in the trunk of the car without Denise knowing and that was sort of a lie too.

He headed out of town with the mountains to his left, far beyond the city's sprawl. Although rows of cars in dealers' yards and cut-price shopping malls flashed past him close by, if he measured his progress against the distant mountains then it seemed he travelled no distance at all. Their immense, flat faces gazed out across the plain towards the Great Salt Lake. He thought of the early Mormon settlers, arriving from the other side of the continent with their handcarts, walking for days across endless plains towards unmoving mountains, feeling they would never near their destination.

His own impatience to be changing altitude made his

fingertips tingle against the steering wheel. When he was a boy, the journey to Arrow Lake had seemed interminable, so anxious was he to arrive. Now he changed lane more often than was necessary, oozing in and out of the evening traffic just to feel the reassurance of the car's constant motion. Then he was out of town, off the Interstate, and beginning his ascent and descent of the first pass. He saw the empty chairlift, sweeping slowly and silently up the mountainside.

The drive was not strenuous. Matt was relaxed by the regular rhythm of hairpin bend and curving road, along with the knowledge that an undemanding time with Hirsh lay ahead. He knew Hirsh was waiting for him. The lake, still and silent and black like the evening sky, was waiting, the wooden house was waiting, the hillside yard with its big trees and its ruined sculptures, it was all waiting for him. His thoughts fixed on where he was going; he forgot, for once, to miss Denise and Austin and to hope that they were missing him.

And then, in his rear-view mirror, he saw a red car.

It was so far behind that the car was only glimpsed and the glimpse was so rapid that he immediately suspected he had imagined it. He drove now with his eyes fixed on his mirror. The car did not reappear for a few minutes but then, on one unusually long, straight stretch, he saw a pinpoint of red just before he cornered. He slowed and on the next long stretch caught sight of it again as he was starting to swing the car around the next bend.

His heart beat faster. There were plenty of red cars around, it didn't have to be that one. But he knew traffic was scarce on this road, and it was particularly unusual for anyone else to ascend the pass this late in the afternoon.

He lost sight of it for a while but as he gained altitude

and the turns got tighter he was able to look down and see, not far below him, a red car making its way up the ribbon of asphalt like a determined ant heading for food. Three corners later, it appeared once more. Matt saw a rare pull-in ahead and made the sudden decision to stop and let the car pass.

He sat in a silence broken only by the occasional ticking of the hot engine. Then, just before he thought the red car could appear, he remembered Jon's admonition to seem unworried and he reached for his cellphone, pretending to make a call.

His mime show went unnoticed. The red car did not pass.

Matt waited. He knew that it must appear soon. There was nowhere it could have turned to right or left and there was nowhere it could have stopped except on the blacktop itself.

All Matt's senses were trained on the rocky corner behind him, from which he knew the car must emerge. The blacktop was so old and weatherbeaten that it had turned grey and the yellow lines had almost faded to white. The asphalt emitted some of the heat it had taken in during the day so that it seemed to tremble a little. The road's emptiness glared at him.

Matt's body was rigid. He let the cellphone drop. He strained to hear the car, preparing himself constantly for its appearance. And, as each moment passed and there was nothing to see and only the deep silence of the mountain to hear, his tension grew. He rolled down his window as though to get some scent of the red car but the silence of this wild place engulfed him. His skin tingled in the new coolness.

The pull-in was nestled against the sheer ascent of the mountain's face. Overhead, bald patches of thin mountain soil were sometimes exposed between the boulders and the green masses of plants. Across the blacktop was a drop of thousands of feet, so sheer it could make your head spin to stand over it. The red car could not have gone down or up the mountainside offroad and turning would be a difficult manoeuvre on this narrow ledge. So where was it? Even travelling very slowly in a very low gear, it should have arrived by now. Why didn't it appear?

The heightened state of anticipation made his nerves buzz until they seemed to protest at the ends of his fingers and deep in his belly. When the noise came it made his whole body jump.

Someone was drumming on the roof of his car. Matt's heart somersaulted. His nerves throbbed. His blood drained. That part of his mind which was still thinking recognized the noise as rocks and he understood that someone had thrown a handful of pebbles at him. The noise had stopped now but it was replaced by a more distant rumble. Was the red car, impossibly, driving down the steep mountainside towards the roof of Matt's car? He ducked and craned his neck up in time to see a boulder flattening a path high above the pull-in. It bounced over plants and across rocks, sending small shards of them showering ahead of its own trajectory. Another smattering arrived now on the top of the car.

Matt started the engine and moved off with such rapidity that afterwards he had no memory of doing it, like the time he had found himself outside the house and later learned there had been an earthquake.

When he looked back he saw the boulder crash down to the pull-in and smash the ground with force, sending large rocks skimming across the road like marbles. The boulder would probably have missed his car. Matt had known that by instinct when he saw it rumbling down the steep slope but instinct also told him that he would take some of the fall-out.

Breathless, his heart still throbbing like something bruised, he continued his journey. He drove as quickly as he could, swinging the car around each bend and choosing to ignore the possibility that other traffic might be coming in the opposite direction. He looked frequently in his mirror and once slowed for a good view of the ribbon of road behind him. It was empty. For the first time in many years he paid attention to the periodic signs, BEWARE FALLING ROCK.

When he reached Arrow Lake, the daylight had turned dusky. The outskirts of the little town were a collection of small, wooden roadside houses. Some were old and had been painted bright colours to make them look newer while the newer houses, in sombre colours, tried to look old. A few houses didn't try anything. They were engulfed by plants or by goods. Their porches were overrun by hardware and soft toys long disused, there were old pans which someone had placed by the steps two years ago and hadn't noticed since, and there were last year's Christmas lights winking from behind the clutter. Hirsh's friend Lonnie lived in one of those houses. Matt glanced at Lonnie's place as he passed. The porch was piled high with old furniture, defunct fridges and pieces of broken air conditioning which Lonnie passed without seeing each day on her way to the home where Robert lay in his coma.

Matt wound down the window. The air had a thin, mountain quality which he immediately craved. He stopped the car in the parking lot on the town side of the lake and climbed right out, watching the road behind him. Inhaling here seemed to clean inside his lungs. He took deep, satisfying breaths, like a smoker. It seemed to him that the mountain oxygen was druggish, so that the more he gulped the more he wanted. Evening was insinuating itself: the mountains were beginning to absorb it, the unmelted snow which hung on the highest slopes was beginning to absorb it, the lake was beginning to reflect its darkness. When he turned around he saw that the old-style lamps in the main street were lit and the stores were bright.

He watched the road, half-waiting for the red car to pass, knowing that it wouldn't, not sure if the car had ever been there. He had seen the suspicion of paranoia flit across Jon's face more than once when they had talked about the car and the suspicion might be well grounded. By definition, he would be unable to diagnose his own paranoia. How long would the red car, real or imagined, keep following him? Until he had somehow penetrated the past's thick barrier to understand his role in Mr Minelli's death? Until the Zoy tribunal in the fall? At the thought of the tribunal he felt his heartbeat grow a little fainter.

No traffic passed except for a pick-up which turned out from one of the drives nearby. After ten minutes he got back in the car.

Hirsh's house was isolated on a wooded slope a little above the town and the lake but well below the late snow-line. It had been designed by an architect as his own summer home about fifty years ago. It was long and low and had the distinctive right-angles of the period but by now its wide stretches of wood and glass had been pummelled by the same weather which sculpted the mountains and battered the trees and the house looked organic, as though it had been seeded there long ago and grown slowly over the years.

He swung into the drive which led through the woods and as he neared the house he glimpsed Hirsh's car in its shack and then saw two other cars parked near the porch. One was big and shiny and old. The other was old too but no one had taken such good care of it. A fender was twisted, there was a history of bad parking and poor manoeuvring etched into its sides, and in places patches of paintwork were missing. It could only be Lonnie's.

For a few moments Matt stood still, breathing the smell of wood and leaves which was the smell of Hirsh's yard. On the ground by the porch window, the window Matt and Steve had once broken in a ballgame, was the small corpse of a bird which, on some urgent mission to find food or build a nest, had crashed right into the glass. He picked up the bird's cold body and laid it respectfully in the under-growth.

He opened the porch door and yelled a greeting. There were no lights on in the house but he heard an answering shout from the living room. In the half-light he could discern three figures seated around the fireplace. Hirsh grinned at him and started to speak, but his words were eclipsed by a louder voice.

'Well, hi there, young Doctor Matt!' exclaimed Sheriff Turner. He sat next to Lonnie with one leg stretched out straight and motionless in front of him. He made getting-up movements but Matt recognized this as a gesture: the sheriff did not actually intend to stand. Matt played along with the fiction, coming right over to shake hands as if to prevent the old man leaping from his seat. He felt his own hand crushed by the sheriff's just as he had when a boy.

'How're you doing, Sheriff?' he asked. The title had stuck, although Sheriff Turner had retired many years ago.

'I got more damn problems with that knee. I mean, it's the cartilage or something. Your pa did explain it to me one time but he don't make much sense since he turned senile.'

Hirsh continued to grin at Matt and it gave Matt pleasure that his father was glad to see him, glad that he was here.

'I mailed off the subscription to my hunting magazine twice because I forgot I did it the first time,' Hirsh explained. 'Elmer says that's dementia.'

'Sorry to be the bearer of bad news, Hirsh, but anybody who parts with his cash twice over is definitely missing a screw or a sprocket,' insisted Sheriff Turner.

'Hi, Lonnie,' said Matt quietly. Lonnie had not moved her large, round body when he walked in although she watched him with her eyes. She did not meet his outstretched hand with her own so instead he squeezed her shoulder. Hirsh had already told Matt that ever since Robert had been in a coma, Lonnie had been getting gradually more comatose herself. Hirsh said there were days when Lonnie seemed to be denying that her body even existed, she sat so still.

Elmer Turner resumed his mission to prove Hirsh's senility. 'Tell me this, Hirsh . . . did you ever walk into rooms and forget why you're there? Eh? Ever failed to complete a crossword 'cause you can't get that word and then find the answer's something simple like, say, skunk or raccoon? Ever go to the store for milk and come back with sugar?'

'I've been doing all those things for forty years,' Hirsh said, chuckling.

'Ever sat in the dark because you didn't notice it's practically night?' asked Matt. 'Ever forgot to light the fire because you didn't feel the temperature drop? Ever fail to offer your son a beer after he just drove all the way around the mountain?'

Hirsh chuckled some more and started to get up stiffly but Matt stopped him.

'I'll do it,' he said. 'And I have some stuff I should put in your freezer right away. Anyone else want a beer?'

'I must be going,' sighed Sheriff Turner but he made no move. 'I guess I'll have a beer first.'

'Don't do the light,' said a hoarse voice. 'Do the fire and the beer but don't do the light.'

'Sure, Lonnie,' said Matt easily but he felt saddened by the way Lonnie spoke, as though her voice had become rusty with disuse and it hurt now to speak.

He first of all fetched the deer meat, noting with surprise that the freezer's walls were thick with ice. When he returned with the beer, Matt looked closely at Lonnie's face. In the darkness it seemed broader and maybe flatter than it used to. Her hair was greyer but her skin was unlined.

It was easy to light the fire. Hirsh kept it laid ready, with newspaper that he had rolled neatly and then tied into knots. There were twigs on top of the newspaper and bigger sticks on top of the twigs and the whole was arranged inside a structure of logs.

Matt struck a match and the fire spread hungrily from the newspaper outwards. It sulked a little when it reached the logs but then it regained its strength and began biting at the logs like a rabid dog. They watched this display in silence. When the flames were big, Matt sneaked a look at the old faces around the fire and saw how the glowing light seemed to smooth them into a sort of youthfulness.

'You're looking sad tonight, Lonnie,' he said. 'Are things just the same?'

Lonnie sighed and rolled her eyes at him.

She said, 'It's coming up to the anniversary.' Her voice was without expression.

'Your ... er ... wedding anniversary?' asked Matt,

knowing he was saying the wrong thing but unable to find the right thing.

'No,' said Hirsh rapidly when Lonnie looked pained. 'The anniversary of Robert's accident.'

Matt jumped reflexively. Of course that was the anniversary Lonnie meant, there was no other kind for her now.

'How many years is it . . . three?'

'Five.'

'Five. Five!' Matt hesitated because he was reluctant to ask the question every friend, every neighbour, every shopkeeper in town had asked Lonnie a thousand times. 'And there's been no change in his condition?'

'Nope,' said Lonnie. 'He's still the same as he was that day five years ago. Even looks just the same. Hasn't aged. He's like the Sleeping Beauty. I don't dare age either or he'll wake up and think I'm his grandma.'

'You still truly believe that he will wake up?' asked Matt. He tried not to sound doubtful or sceptical. He tried to sound like one detached doctor asking another professional their opinion.

'Totally,' said Lonnie in a tone of steely conviction. 'There was a guy in Florida only recently who woke up after nine years.'

Matt wished the guy in Florida had stayed in his coma instead of giving false hope to thousands of families who faced decisions about prolonging or withdrawing life support. He wanted to tell Lonnie that the Florida patient was one in a million but there was no point: those odds were good enough for Lonnie.

'You still visit every day?' he asked.

'Sure. And I still speak to him. I tell him everything. I believe he can hear me and understand me. He just can't reply.'

'You're doing the right thing, Lonnie,' said Hirsh kindly. 'Talking to him, playing him music, telling him what's happening out there, it's the right thing to do.'

'She don't tell him everything, Matt,' said Sheriff Turner significantly. 'Ain't that right, Lonnie?'

Lonnie sighed and looked at Matt. 'I don't buy that much but I can't tell him when I do. He'd just be worrying I was spending too much.'

'You still haven't mentioned that you won the state lottery?' asked Matt incredulously and, with a minimum of movement, Lonnie shook her head. In one of fate's cruel knife-twists, Lonnie had won the lottery right after Robert, while lopping trees, had fallen from the ladder in his own yard. Lonnie had not moved house or even renovated. She wanted everything to be just the same for Robert when he woke up and so she had permitted herself to buy only the kind of consumer goods that Robert wouldn't remember or care about. She was always changing her fridge and her microwave and her TV and her kitchen pans.

'Hurts me to think of all that money mouldering away at Wells Fargo doing nothing,' said the old sheriff. 'Makes my cartilage throb with pain.'

'I give some every year for coma research,' Lonnie told him defensively. 'And I told you boys you can have anything you want.'

'Lonnie, we don't want your money,' said Hirsh patiently, in the tone of one who had turned down many prior offers.

'Can it buy me back my youth?' said the sheriff. 'That's all I want and money don't buy it. To be young as Matt and wise as me. Tell me, Matt, what do young folks like you do with yourselves to have fun these days?'

The sheriff spoke as though Matt was unmarried and clubbing every night. In fact, Matt didn't see himself as young any more. Ever since he had came back from Africa he had felt significantly older than the peers he had left behind.

He shrugged. 'Mostly I just relax with Denise and Austin. But I go out for a beer about once a week with the guys. This week we went to an art exhibition. In fact . . .' His heart suddenly began to beat with a new force. The Minellis. Certainly the sheriff, and perhaps Lonnie too, had known them and would remember everything about the strange accident which had killed Mr Minelli.

'In fact . . .' He caught his breath again. 'Well, I bumped into someone at the hospital who maybe you guys recall. Steve Minelli. The Minelli family used to live a little ways around the lake in summer, remember?'

He thought he detected movement, that all three of them had moved simultaneously and involuntarily. But, since a log was rearranging itself in the fire, maybe only the light had changed. However, he noted that all their faces were turned to him now, even Lonnie's. Their expressions were informed but uninformative. They were waiting.

'We remember,' said Hirsh hoarsely, and it seemed to Matt that his father's body was rigid like the logs in the fire and some instinct told him that if he loved his father he would stop right there. He loved his father and he didn't stop.

'They had four boys and Steve was the fourth. He was a good friend of mine, we used to play together all the time when we were kids. I was delighted to run into him again. And guess what, he works at the hospital now and he's an . . .' Matt hesitated. He thought of how Jarvis would be swerving across blacktop right now, applying screaming brakes, leaning on the wheel, if he could hear Matt call Steve an artist. 'And he also has an exhibition of photos in town right now and he invited me.'

'He works at the same hospital you do!' exclaimed Elmer Turner. The sheriff used his hands to rearrange his straight leg so it pointed in a different direction. Then he looked around at the others before remarking. 'That's quite a coincidence.'

'Do you think he's changed much?' asked Lonnie.

'Of course, in twenty-six years he's changed but ... I think he's probably the same old Steve underneath. I think we still have a lot in common.'

'What job does he do?' she asked.

'Well, he's a cleaner. He cleans the operating theatres, for example.' And probably the recovery room and the morgue but Matt decided not to mention them. He watched the fire but it seemed to him that his father and Lonnie and the sheriff were all looking at one another.

'What did you think,' asked Hirsh, in the same gruff voice, 'of his exhibition?'

Matt paused. 'I'm not the guy to ask about art. Denise is going soon and her opinion's worth having. But didn't his father take pictures too? I mean, wasn't Mr Minelli also a photographer?' He heard his own voice. There was a note of animation which was too loud or too eager or too something, as though hinting at the presence of the pictures up in the roof space.

'I thought he was in real estate,' said the sheriff.

'Well,' said Hirsh, watching Matt closely, 'he wasn't a professional photographer but he was a serious amateur. Had his own darkroom. I believe he used to rig up a little studio even here at Arrow Lake. He had lights and stuff. But his day job was definitely real estate.'

A little studio with lights. Matt caught himself hoping that his mother wasn't the stuff. He turned to the fire so that its glow would disguise his reddening face.

'I recall Steve very well,' said the sheriff. 'How do you think he's managed under the wheels of life's big truck, Matt?'

'If life's a truck,' Lonnie corrected him rapidly, 'we are not underneath it, Elmer, we are at the wheel.'

'Speak for yourself, Lonnie. Kid lost his daddy early,' said the sheriff, raising an eyebrow. He looked at Matt, waiting for his reply. 'And if I recall it turned out there were debts and other money problems. They had to sell up here, any-ways. So, how do you think he's doing, Matt?'

Matt said, 'Okay I guess. He's had a drug habit in the past but I get the feeling his life's more stable now.'

'Did he say where he's been all these years?' asked Hirsh. 'Seattle.'

There was a silence. 'Oh,' echoed Elmer Turner without expression. 'Seattle.'

Matt asked, 'Elmer, were you sheriff when Mr Minelli died?' He remembered the figures which had been moving around the red car parked in the woods. Hirsh had opened the driver's door slowly, slowly, too slowly. There had been someone else, voices, and the sound of a car on the road.

The old sheriff nodded and then took a rapid gulp of beer, somehow engulfing the nod so that Matt wasn't sure if he'd seen it or not. He knew that he had already received a number of tiny hints and warnings, in the register of a voice or the movement of a hand, to stop asking questions about the Minellis, but he was compelled to do so because the lid was off the well now.

'I remember he died from a gunshot wound. Do you recall exactly what happened?' he asked.

And it seemed to Matt that there was a current suddenly in the room, as though electricity had jumped from the wall sockets and was buzzing between them. He guessed that the current actually came from inside himself, from the anxiety generated by talk of Mr Minelli and from his need to understand more about his own role in the man's death. Maybe, though, Matt's electricity had touched his father because Hirsh suddenly rose and reached for the fire tongs.

'That log's going to fall,' he said, poking at the blazing beast until he had pushed it into the heart of the fire. And now Elmer was easing himself out of his chair, grabbing at Matt and Lonnie for support.

'Oh, it was so long ago I can't recall the details but I remember it was an ugly sort of accident,' he said. 'And a terrible shock for the family.' He gasped as his legs took on the burden of his weight. Lopsided, he was considerably shorter than Matt. 'Move your arm under my elbow, would you, Lonnie?'

Matt and Hirsh stood on the porch watching the two cars slide slowly away from the house into the darkness. Lonnie, behind, had forgotten to put her lights on so that the cars seemed to evaporate into the night. Matt and Hirsh were silent for a moment and in that moment they could hear the engines of the cars as they turned on to the road and headed down the hill, past Stewart's place and the lake and on towards town.

10

'I guess Lonnie doesn't ever give up hope,' remarked Matt as they walked back into the house.

'She can't ever give up hope,' said Hirsh, 'or she'll sort of cave in on herself like John-Jack Perry's outbuildings when he set dynamite under them.'

Inside, Hirsh began to cook their meal. Matt sat down at the table and picked up a magazine.

'Why did John-Jack dynamite his outbuildings?' he asked.

'To show Anita how mad he was when she moved out,' said Hirsh, as if this was sufficient explanation for a ton of wood and metal caving in on itself. 'When John-Jack moved all the rubble away, underneath he had the only flat area for miles around and he made that little shooting range.'

Matt looked down at the magazine in his hands and saw it was the hunting magazine Hirsh had subscribed to twice. 'Why do you still take this?' he asked. 'You don't hunt any more.'

'Sure I do,' said Hirsh, 'just a little, to keep my hand in.'

'You still shoot?'

'Mostly pests. Elmer had a skunk around the place and he's a bit shaky these days so I shot it. Otherwise I just shoot for something to eat.' He was chopping things and putting them into a hot pan and the room hissed with smoke and steam as if it had a mouth of its own somewhere.

'You shoot to eat!' Matt was both surprised and annoyed. The only time Hirsh irritated him was when he affected poverty. 'Can't you afford the Seven Eleven any more?'

'Game's the best meat there is, lean and healthy. And it tastes good, too. There was this deer around which was lame and it was kinder to kill it. I hung the meat a long time and then I cooked it real low and real slow and at the last minute I added some low-fat cream and herbs and the guys came over . . .' The guys were Elmer, Stewart and Lonnie. Strictly speaking, Lonnie wasn't a guy but she liked to be included. Before she had started participating in Robert's coma she had boasted that she could outdrink and outswear any guy in town, although she never noticeably did much of either, and once she had claimed that she could piss higher up the wall but she had failed to demonstrate this also.

'Did the venison taste good?' Matt asked.

'Though I say it myself, it was delicious.'

'I put some deer meat in your freezer tonight,' said Matt. 'It's three years old. Eat it at your own risk.'

'They say you shouldn't freeze deer meat longer than a year but you can. In fact, if you do it right you can freeze it for ever.'

'Well we just had a guy in the emergency room who ate a fish that had been frozen twenty-five years.'

'Would have been fine if he'd frozen it right,' chuckled Hirsh. 'How much of this three-years-old venison did you bring?'

'If you put the bits together it would probably make most of a deer. There wasn't much room for it, though, because your old freezer's all ice.'

Hirsh groaned. 'I know, I know. It's fuzzy around the edges. I mean to defrost it but I never get around to it because you have to race to get the freezer melted without all the food that was in it melting too. Then water gets everywhere and you have to mop it up . . .'

He was talking like an old man. An old man who for the

first time was confounded by the difficulties of a routine chore. Matt remembered how he had struggled with the log in the woodshed.

'You could buy a new one which self-defrosts,' he suggested but he already knew what the response to this idea would be.

'There's nothing wrong with the old one!' exclaimed Hirsh.

Matt smiled. He said, 'I'll defrost it for you tomorrow.' He expected Hirsh to object. He waited for Hirsh to say that he had all the time in the world and would get around to defrosting the freezer one day but to his surprise Hirsh accepted the offer. Were there other things around the house he should start doing, Matt wondered. Before now almost any offer of help would have insulted the capable Hirsh. Was this the beginning of a gradual transfer of responsibility, with Matt finally doing everything for a helpless old man, the way Denise did for Clem?

Hirsh was asking him about the venison he had put in the freezer.

'Where did it come from, anyway?'

Matt explained that the deer had been Weslake's last victim. Hirsh listened closely.

'Matt . . .' he said quietly. Matt looked up in surprise because his father rarely used his name. Hirsh had lowered the heat under the pan and was looking back at him. 'Let me ask you something. Did you ever meet Weslake?'

Clem had asked just the same question.

'Well, I knew about him, naturally, he was such a big noise in town with his weight clinic and his TV commercials. And when we were first starting on gastric bypasses he supplied the department with a lot of patients.'

'But did you two ever actually meet?'

'No.'

'Even though you were both in gastrointestinal?'

'He had a clinic of sorts but he wasn't a doctor. I'm not sure anyone but Jon Espersen took him seriously, and that was mostly because Weslake was supplying guinea-pigs for our stomach bypass operations. So there would have been no reason for me to meet him professionally.'

Matt heard his own voice and it sounded defensive. Hirsh was watching him with the focus of a hunter in the forest. He seemed to have forgotten the pan. Its contents didn't smell right any more. Matt got up and made to lift it from the heat but Hirsh reached for it first with a spry movement. Matt sat back down silently and opened the hunting magazine without really looking at its pages.

'So, Jon Espersen and Weslake knew each other but you two never actually met.' It was probably a statement but it might have been a question, the same question for a third time.

'Jon and Weslake were friends. Denise and Christine were friends and still are. They used to do yoga together or something,' said Matt, getting up. He felt large and hot and awkward when Hirsh questioned him this way. He wanted to get out of the room. 'But that was all before I met Denise,' he added over his shoulder.

He left the kitchen purposefully like a man who had forgotten something and was going to fetch it. In the hallway he paused. He was aimless.

He went into the living room. He switched on the lamp and stood watching the room as though it might move. The shadows lining its edges seemed to mask a wealth of memories, distant memories from the hot summers when he and Hilly had stayed here together while Hirsh worked down in the city and sometimes appeared looking worn in the dusky evenings. Matt opened a drawer somewhere inside his head and slid out the memory of his mother playing the piano. He unfolded it carefully. Its colours were not completely faded. It had the very quality of low light and shadow which existed in the living room right now. Had it been night-time when she played?

The memory was just beginning to take shape when he noted, drearily, the movie projector and screen tucked discreetly against the back wall in readiness for a long evening's entertainment.

'Dinner's ready!' yelled Hirsh. Matt returned to the steamy kitchen. He moved the hunting magazine to clear a space for his plate. He said, 'Steve Minelli kept talking about that hunting trip we took with Mr Minelli and the boys.'

Hirsh's reaction to the mention of the Minellis was calm enough this time.

'Did he happen to mention how I missed the mule buck?' he asked, distributing food unequally between their two plates so there was more on Matt's.

'He's a very nice guy. He didn't actually put it that way.'

'They never let me hear the end of it. The truth is that I'm not a good shot but if I hadn't been pretty sound at scouting and still-hunting and stalking we wouldn't have got within a mile of that buck. And actually I still am pretty good at still-hunting and stalking.'

'You still are? How long ago did you shoot the lame deer in the yard?'

'It wasn't in the yard when I shot it,' said Hirsh patiently. 'I saw it in the yard but I followed it about five miles around the mountain before I could get it. I mean, it wasn't that lame.'

'Five miles!'

Hirsh looked as though he was trying not to smile but the smile forced itself out anyway. 'Not all of it was uphill,' he said, mildly.

'But your hip . . .'

'It hurt afterwards but I was so intent on hunting the beast I almost forgot about it when I was out on the mountain. Just proves how much of pain is in the mind.'

'How did you get the meat back here?'

'Aren't you going to eat this nice meal I cooked for you?' sighed Hirsh. Matt hastily ate a forkful as if this was a trade-off for Hirsh answering the question.

'Good,' he said. 'Delicious.'

'Well,' said Hirsh, 'I dragged it near to a road and then took the car up there for it.'

'But when?'

'The fall before last. I did a bit of hunting this fall, too. I covered some ground. A few miles at a time. I guess I did okay.'

'Did you shoot anything?'

'I missed a few times. Mostly I'd get the beast in my sights and then I'd ask myself a question.' Hirsh paused to eat. Matt thought his father's face had thinned since the last time he was here, or maybe his eyes had sunk a little deeper, but they were still the sort of brown that made them seem to shine all the time.

'I'd get the beast in my sights and then I'd say to myself, Hirsh, you're about to kill a living thing, take its life clean away. It doesn't matter that it's an animal, do you have a good reason for committing this act? You scouted it, you followed it and you stalked it. Now, do you need to eat it? And if I'm not hungry, the answer might be no.'

Matt looked back boldly at his father.

'Maybe it's because you're scared you'll miss.'

Hirsh shrugged. 'I know I'll probably miss. I'm not scared of it. No, when you get older the urge to kill definitely diminishes. I believe that it's quite strong in childhood. It can still be powerful at your age. By the time you get to my age, it's weak but it's still there. The killer instinct. All sorts of things can ignite it, not just hunger.'

Matt, shaken by Hirsh's reference to the killer instinct in children, said firmly, 'I don't feel any urge to kill at all.'

Hirsh looked at him, his eyes shining like flashlights. Matt leaned back in his chair a little. 'I mean,' he added, 'I've never really understood why you wanted to hunt.'

Hirsh smiled again, a fuller, more generous smile now. His teeth were small and strong.

'You have to get out into that wilderness to understand. You have to get out there on a real hunting trip, not the kind guys do nowadays with luxury trailers and cellphones and pants with heating in the pockets. Not the kind of thing I do, which is walking out of my house and then walking back to it before darkness falls. Nope, you have to be out there with the silence. You have to work with the elements, understand the natural world and become a part of it. And, if you feel hungry and know there's only one way to get fed, well, that's how to find the killer instinct inside of you.'

This was a long speech for Hirsh. When they had cleared away the dishes and Matt was waiting for the coffee to brew, he glanced at the hunting magazine and thought that the advertisements for clothing and equipment didn't seem to have anything to do with the experience in the wilderness that Hirsh had been describing.

After dinner, without discussing it, they went into the living room for the home movies just the way they used to when Hilly was alive. Hilly had liked the movies and there had always been an air of expectation as she led the way, coffee in hand. But Matt's whole body, now as then, drooped at the prospect of what lay ahead.

Hirsh threw some logs on to the slumbering fire and poked it until it hissed and spit angrily at him, then burst suddenly into flame. Matt was successful pulling up the screen on his third attempt and then he helped Hirsh move the heavy projector and table into position. Hirsh bent over it. He was threading a reel of film but it looked as though he was nursing the old machine in his arms.

Matt sat in the armchair waiting tensely for the movie to begin and suddenly, unexpectedly, recollection and reality coincided. This room, as it was the night it became filled with Chopin, and this room as it was right now. The two of them clicked together like one of Austin's plastic toys, and he realized that he had sat in this very chair but it had been turned around, turned around to face the glass doors which opened on to the terrace. Minellis had sprawled on the sofa as though they were watching a ballgame on TV, except the sofa had been the other way around, with its back to the hearth as well. And Hirsh's worn old armchair? Mr Minelli had sat in it motionless. Everyone had been motionless, all the movement in the room belonged to Hilly. And there had been someone to his right, their body rigid. And hadn't he looked up while Hilly played and been startled to see yet another person here, a latecomer standing in the doorway? He turned now, suddenly, trying to capture that person's ghost in the corner of his eye.

He stared around the room as though seeing it for the first time. The furniture gave a new shape and substance to his memory. But, the piano? He looked around wildly, foolishly, for the piano. Then he realized. Of course! Obviously! The piano had been on the terrace. It had been just outside the room and the glass doors had been flung open.

The piano had intercepted the light, which was why the room of his memories was so dark. It had not been night, but perhaps evening, and the great shape of the piano, his mother seated at it, had blocked the room's main light source.

'Dad,' Matt said before he could stop himself. He was almost breathless with delight at his discovery, at the process of deduction which had led him to the truth. 'Didn't Mom play the piano out on the terrace once?'

Hirsh looked up at him over the projector.

'What?' he said. There was hostility in his voice, but you had to know him well to detect it.

'Did we ever have a piano which we kept out on the terrace?'

Matt imagined Chopin's Second Piano Concerto flowing from Hilly's fingers, wafting out across the terrace and filtering down through the thin air on to the woods and the lake and even the little town where grains would fall on people's noses and eyelids and they would stop and look up for a moment although they might not be sure exactly why.

'A piano? Left out on the terrace? It would have been ruined in no time,' said Hirsh.

'Maybe we just had it for one summer or something.'

'A piano!' echoed Hirsh in a tone which reminded Matt of the great importance of pianos in this family, reminded him that they were significant for their absence.

'We could have kept it covered in tarpaulin out there maybe,' said Matt, his voice losing substance along with his memory.

'But Hilly would never have had a piano, you know that. It was hard enough to persuade her to let you have that little electric thing in your room.'

'I thought I remembered Mom playing the piano. Just

once. And it was out on the terrace here. I went to a concert with Denise and I recognized the music and then I remembered Mom playing it.' And as he spoke, recalling but not mentioning his tears at the concert, the memory came back again forcibly, like a log falling into the heart of the fire and springing into flame. Hilly's long, brown arms (So! It must have been summer!), her fingers, her hands, her whole body possessed by the music, her face pulling itself into strange shapes of violent emotions. And Matt, mesmerized and strangely frightened, had not moved as her body swayed over the piano like a snake hypnotizing the keys, until suddenly he had looked around and there in the doorway had stood his father.

Matt had been shocked by the look on his father's strong face. He saw how all the straight lines were crooked as though Hirsh was being melted by a great and painful heat. He had been frightened. His parents were both different that night, different from their familiar selves.

'But,' he cried now, 'you were there! You must remember! The piano was on the terrace and you came in late and no one noticed, I mean, except me. You arrived and you just stood in the doorway watching . . .'

He was gripped suddenly by the ridiculous and fanciful possibility that his father, way, way down in the city, had heard the notes of the piano, the knock of wood on wood carried somehow from tree to tree until it reached Salt Lake. Hirsh would have heard it and left his surgery abruptly, responding to the call as though to an emergency, taking the fast route to the house, winding up the mountainside and arriving just in time to witness the end of Hilly's performance. But Hirsh, this calm Hirsh, whose face had been set so strong in his old age that the twisting, melting face Matt remembered must belong to some other Hirsh, this

Hirsh was speaking. It was only with a supreme effort that Matt could listen, so much more real did this same room almost thirty years ago now seem than the present. Hirsh was saying, '. . . nearly ready and I sure hope the old lady doesn't burn up the film . . .'

The phone rang and Hirsh reached for it. He greeted the caller warmly.

'Squirrels?' he said. 'Well, there are always squirrels around here . . . come to think of it, I did get one in the roof . . . Oh sure, sure, I have to bait them. Certainly. Er, Matt's right here, I'll pass you over to him. We're about to watch some home movies and it takes the projector a while to warm up.'

Matt winced. 'Hi,' he said sheepishly.

'There are home movies!' came Denise's gentle voice. She sounded breathless as though winded a little. She hadn't even greeted him. 'Home movies and you never told me!'

'Just a few,' allowed Matt.

'But how fascinating! Is your mom in them?'

'I guess so.'

'And you? When you were small?'

'Not that small. I was at least eight, maybe older. Someone gave Dad this old camera . . .' But he had already guessed what was coming next.

'I'd really love to see them.'

'Nope.'

'Oh, come on, Matt.'

'No way, absolutely not.'

'Did you know Hirsh was going to show them today?'

'Yes.'

'Is that why you wouldn't let us come with you?'

'Yes.'

There was a pause. 'Oh, Matt.' He waited for her to be angry, as she had a right to be, but her voice was soft and kind. 'Are you ashamed of them?'

'Maybe.'

'Of yourself when you were a kid? Or someone in your family?'

'Probably. But I haven't looked at them in years. I'll answer that question when I've seen them again.'

He heard his own voice. It had risen a few notes and was stubborn and unyielding, like a sulky boy's. He tried to resume his usual self, his usual way of speaking.

'Is everything all right with you and Austin?' he asked.

Denise told him about the words Austin had said today and how he made friends with another kid at Liberty Park, just walked right up to the other boy and said, 'Hi, let's play.' Matt smiled at this story.

'Okay, sweetheart,' said Denise kindly. 'Go watch the movies and try not to suffer too much.'

'Did I manage to cover for your little white lie?' asked Hirsh, grinning but not looking at him as Matt took his seat, the same seat he always sat in for movie night. The lights snapped off. 'Squirrel bait! I mean, why don't you want her to see these movies?'

But Matt did not have to answer because the projector was hissing like a steam engine and the bright white light which preceded the pictures was shining directly on the screen. Matt did not jump up and do the two-handed duck, nor did he attempt his mother's twitchy-eared rabbit. He waited and then there she was. Hilly. She was tall and upright. She was walking down the drive and she waved and then approached the camera, swaying a little at the hips, smiling broadly, looking absurdly young and beautiful. Behind her was a lot of space and a lot of sky because the trees around the drive were small and twiggy back then. How much darker the world had become since her death. When Hilly walked down the drive there was sunlight everywhere as though she pushed back shadows.

Way behind her, at the far end of the drive, refusing to cooperate with the shot, was a small figure, hands thrust stubbornly into the pockets of cut-off jeans, hair shaggy.

'You were nine,' supplied Hirsh. 'You decided that you didn't like your picture being taken.'

'Mom sure did,' said a voice hoarsely.

'What's that?' Hirsh called over the whirr of the old projector.

'Mom loved having her picture taken,' said Matt more loudly.

Hirsh did not reply.

When, fifteen minutes later, the film rolled off the edge of the spool and was clicking frantically until Hirsh could stop the projector to rethread and rewind it, Matt knew why he had always hated these movies so much. It wasn't his own antics. It seemed to him now that his idiocy was just the kinesis of a normal boy and although not endearing it was inoffensive enough. No, his mother was the problem. He had just watched her soundlessly running, jumping for balls, swimming, singing, dancing. There were other people in the pictures with her, of course, the Minelli boys or himself, but they were just extras, there to throw a ball to Hilly or swim alongside her. She took a starring role in every shot. She was a show-off and an exhibitionist and maybe Hirsh had even bought the camera to meet this need. There was no sense in which the movies were a record of family life. They were movies about Hilly.

The projector made hot noises. Hirsh was putting another reel on.

'Now then, this is a few years later,' called Hirsh over the wheezing projector.

A ragged line of boys with guns on their shoulders, as though they were just off to war, suddenly flickered into sight.

'Ah, here it is, this is us setting off on our hunting trip . . .' Hirsh said.

The hunting trip. Had it taken place in the summer of the Rosebay deal, the summer when, according to Clem, Mr Minelli had been tanned and over-confident? The summer which had ended in his death? Matt cleared his throat and watched the screen intently.

The boys, four Minellis and himself, turned in response to some silent order and marched towards the camera, led by the immense figure of Mr Minelli. Matt watched the man's grin, his cartoonish marching, and experienced a displeasure so profound that he could actually taste it in his mouth. He ran his tongue over his teeth but his mouth felt dirty. Mr Minelli had been dislikeable, with his vast, knowing smile, his loud voice and his orders. And there had been that laugh. His laughter had always opened up suddenly. It was a monster which appeared when there was a secret or a weakness or a mistake. It was treacherous laughter, like falling into a huge, echoing canyon.

Here was Steve. He looked cute because he was being serious and important with his gun. He had always been dwarfed by his brothers, as if their continual teasing and bullying had physically belittled him.

The mighty Mr Minelli roared an order for the boys to turn. The movie was silent but you could nevertheless feel your seat vibrate at the great sound he made. On screen, Steve jumped a little. Matt wondered what it had been like for Steve to have a father who shouted and bullied and always got what he wanted. He felt the satisfaction of an anger defined. That was why he had disliked Mr Minelli, disliked him so much that his stomach now felt as though he had eaten rocks for dinner, it was because Mr Minelli always got what he wanted.

'Don't tell your father,' Mr Minelli had said to Matt out on the terrace and the young Matt had agreed. His anger at his own easy acquiescence was alleviated only slightly by the pleasure of turning down Mr Minelli's offer of a cigarette. The offer had been a double mistake on Mr Minelli's part. Mr Minelli had assumed that, because Matt was tall, he was mature. He had assumed that Matt had understood whatever adult information of importance in the adult world he should keep secret. And he had assumed that Matt was old enough to smoke at school behind the bike sheds. He was wrong on both counts.

The line of boys turned raggedly and marched off the screen and into the forest. At its end came Matt, too tall and too gangling. He was trying unsuccessfully to march in time with the others and he carried his gun as though it might explode any minute.

'I thought the hunting season was in the fall,' said Matt. His voice seemed to have swelled inside his throat and it was an effort to speak.

'There's limited buck-hunting in the summer,' said Hirsh. 'Although it's nothing like as good as fall hunting.'

I believe, we all believe, that our father was killed. He had been killed shortly after these pictures were taken. The embarrassed boy at the end of the line who couldn't march in time or hold his gun properly had killed the fleshy monster at the head of the line and everyone on the screen appeared wholly ignorant of this earthquake which awaited them, although it lay just weeks ahead. Matt stared at the screen, searching for some indication, perhaps encoded, of the future. But, if there was information encrypted here, he could neither find nor decipher it.

The boys marched off on their hunting trip and then suddenly it was over and the scene had changed. Mr Minelli was driving towards the house, waving. There were boys hanging out of the windows and Mrs Minelli was sitting stiffly in the front seat. Matt swallowed. He remembered the occasion. Mr Minelli had arrived up the mountain with a new car and they had all piled inside and come over to the Seleckis' house to show everyone. This was the car. The car was red.

Now there was some kind of go-kart, built on an old set of wheels. Mr Minelli stood aboard it while, slave-like, his sons dragged it along and Mr Minelli played the Roman emperor, cracking an imaginary whip magisterially. Another exhibitionist, thought Matt grimly. It seemed to him that, in this movie, Mr Minelli and Hilly competed against each other to dominate every frame. Bird-like, Mrs Minelli, arms crossed, head nodding, sometimes appeared to the side.

There was no doubt that this was Mr Minelli's summer. He swam, he raced, he hunted, he climbed trees, he bought a new car, he rowed a raft, he was a Roman emperor. By the end of the movie he had begun to eclipse even Hilly.

Twice, Matt thought he glimpsed the diamond ring on his mother's finger which Mrs Minelli had worn at the exhibition. As Hilly sat smoking dreamily in the yard, for once unaware of the camera, he studied her fingers but discerned enough only to fuel his suspicions, not to confirm them as fact. He tried to recall the story of that ring. He knew Hilly had told it a number of times, always to the listener's surprise. If he could remember it, he might be able to explain why Mrs Minelli and his mother had identical rings. But the story escaped him. He resolved to get back into the roof space somehow, without Hirsh knowing, to look at the ring Hilly wore in the pictures.

The movie, thankfully, featured few shots of Matt. There was only one sequence of him alone in the frame. He was playing a piano. Hirsh had focused on his hands and then cut to his face. The boy's concentration was acute, so acute that it gave his face a shadowy, bruised look. If the movie hadn't been silent and you could hear the music, thought Matt, then the child's immense effort wouldn't be so noticcable, but the weird noiselessness of the piano emphasized it. He felt sorry for the boy, he was obviously the kind who let things matter a lot. And then he remembered that he had been that boy.

The camera pulled back. You could see how old the piano was: its surface had the patina of great age and it even had candleholders on either side of the music stand. And, when the camera pulled back still further, you could see that it was actually outside.

'See!' cried Matt now. 'I told you so, Dad! There was a piano on the terrace!'

'Not our terrace,' said Hirsh. 'Millicent and Elmer used to pull their piano out back sometimes so Millicent could play where it was cooler.'

Matt felt no relief when the pictures ended. The home movies, though painful, were interesting. He'd forgotten that makeshift go-kart he used to play in with the Minellis, it had dropped right out of his memory like a piece of meteor breaking off and floating into space. And he'd forgotten the raft races, too. And it was good to see himself goofing around with his friend, Steve.

'Are we going to see some more?' he asked, turning to Hirsh. His father was rewinding the film. He did not reply but shook his head. He stood behind the projector. The light which burned from within the machine lit his face and Matt could see that his expression had mellowed in the last hour or so. The facial lines were darker, as though someone had come along with a thick pencil and shaded them in. Hirsh's face had a fine, firm bone structure which he had retained despite his age. But now the skin seemed to sag. His eyes reflected the projector's light too brightly.

Matt rapidly turned away. Although he had never, ever heard Hirsh criticize Hilly for anything except smoking, he had been bracing himself to ask a question. Was Hilly always such an embarrassing exhibitionist or did she just perform for cameras? But now it seemed that to speak at all would intrude on Hirsh's private sadness. Matt watched the blank screen in silence. He hoped that by the time he turned around Hirsh would have maintained his usual equilibrium. To give his father extra time, Matt began rearranging the furniture and taking down the screen – guaranteed now, as in the past, to collapse suddenly on your fingers – before turning around.

When he did so, the reels of film were back in their metal cases. The projector's wooden box had been lowered on top of it. Hirsh was busy winding the cord. Matt could see that he looked more composed now. Matt said, his voice gruff as though he had not spoken for a long time, 'Was I good at the piano?'

It seemed a safe subject.

'Well,' began Hirsh, and his voice also had the same roughness of disuse, 'I'm no judge but I believe you were. Your teacher certainly thought so.'

'I wish I hadn't stopped. I'd sure like to be able to play now.'

Hirsh busied himself with the cord. It ran through a slot to a pocket on the side of the box. Hirsh had made the box.

It was designed so you never had to lift the projector off its base, you just had to raise and lower the box.

'Well, you know how your mother felt about the piano. It was hard for her to give it up and I guess she didn't encourage you to start.'

Outside, moonlight fell on to the terrace like a spotlight on to a stage. Hirsh quietly wound the cord. Matt looked at the moonlight. The past once again synthesized into the present. His mother, playing the piano, Mrs Minelli, straight-backed, to his right, Mr Minelli motionless and, in the door-way, finally, Hirsh. The scene was so real that if he closed his eyes he could feel the music creeping over his body and the deep breath of Mr Minelli nearby. Matt sat without moving, hardly breathing, not wanting to break the thin membrane between now and then.

Hirsh spoke, indicating that Matt could carry the heavy old projector back to its shelf, and Matt returned to the present thinking that nothing in the movies his father had shown him tonight could take him so close to that membrane.

He realized later, in bed, that Hirsh must remember Hilly playing the piano on the terrace. Matt recalled his father's face as it had been all those years ago, twisted and maybe even damp, and the way his father had leaned on the door-frame because he seemed too weak to support his own weight. Sure, Hirsh remembered the piano. He just didn't want to remember out loud. His was the face you couldn't quite see by the firelight, the back turned to you in the kitchen, the long silence. Hirsh wasn't going to share his memories and if Matt wanted to know more about his mother, about their summers up here in the wooden house, about Mr Minelli's death and his own part in it, he would have to find out about it without Hirsh's help.

11

The following morning, Matt defrosted Hirsh's freezer. Hirsh helped at first, then he hung around not helping but bringing cups of coffee and chatting a little. He fetched Matt some old towels to mop up all the water from the freezer and finally he went outside to start work on some falling branches.

Matt spread the towels around the freezer. Their woven faces had no significance and had not been thought of for years, yet he recognized them as though they were old friends. They were worn and faded, of course, not just with age but with sun. They had seen many summers by the lake, where they had lain waiting for him to emerge from the water, unnoticed until they were needed. There was one in the shape of a huge fish that had a knowing, even lascivious, expression. Matt had particularly liked it because it was big and covered him all over when he came out of the cold water. He used to wrap it around himself and walk up through the woods to the house, the towel snaring on branches as he passed. He examined it for snags and snarls now, and it was full of them and the patina pleased him. It told his summer story.

When the Minellis had gone, it wasn't so easy to cut home through the woods. Their land lay between the best lake beach and the hillside and, when they weren't there any more, when their house had been bought by tall, blond strangers, Matt hadn't enjoyed those moments of trespass, had felt vulnerable as he crossed the strangers' yard wrapped in his big blue fish towel. A couple of times he might have walked home along the road but that had felt uncomfortably formal. He could recall little about those later summers. His memories seemed to stop when the Minellis left.

Matt scraped the last ice on to newspaper and then poured the slivers into the big sink in the utility room. By now the sink was filled with ice shelves like a small continent. It cracked at him as though it were angry with him for melting it. Some of the ice was smooth and clear and thick and might have the corpses of prehistoric animals preserved inside it. Some of it was covered with a soft surface like snow in a Christmas movie. Some sparkled like diamonds and it was right then that Matt remembered the story of his mother's diamond ring.

She had found it in a freezer. She had found it in a freezer at the supermarket, sparkling up at her, camouflaged by ice. But she had sharp eyes and did not mistake it for ice. She had scooped it up and held it between her thumb and forefinger. Matt, trailing reluctantly in her wake – he had probably only come into the supermarket to select his break-fast cereal, his sole opportunity to wield power over his diet – had started at his mother's sudden cry. He had watched her staring at the diamond, holding it to the light, and he had thought it was ice and had sighed to himself in resig-nation. She was going to do something loud and embarrass-ing, like making a big fuss over some funny-shaped piece of ice. But when he had taken the tiny gem in his hand and seen its smooth, even facets, he, too, saw that it was a diamond.

Hilly had told the store manager about the diamond and the man had taken her name and address and phone number and said that he would call if anyone tried to claim it but he was sure no one would. Someone had lost that diamond but they didn't know where. If he didn't call within a month she was to consider it hers.

Hilly had placed the diamond in cotton wool in a small box on the table by her bed. She had waited a month to the day. When no one called, she had the diamond set in a simple ring. Hirsh wanted to do it for her but something about the way she had found the diamond when tens or maybe hundreds of other shoppers had missed it made her possessive and she had organized the setting herself. She wore the ring with what had seemed to Matt a special affection. And then, many years later, the same ring, or an identical one, had reappeared on the finger of Mrs Minelli, who had, in a swift, single sentence, excised the ring from its history.

When he had cleaned the freezer and switched it on again and placed all the food back inside its humming interior, Matt threw the dirty towels into the washing machine. The big blue fish gave him its lazy wink as he closed the door on it. Then Matt went out to find Hirsh.

His father was surrounded by sappy, tangled branches as though he had just this morning grown a magic hedge around himself. He was cutting them back from the garage where they threatened to entwine any car left there too long.

Hirsh didn't hear him and for a moment Matt stood quietly, watching his father working. His movements were slow and deliberate but, faced with a recalcitrant branch, the old man seemed strong enough. He stopped when he caught sight of Matt from the corner of his eye.

'The freezer's done,' said Matt.

'Well, thank you for that,' said Hirsh, and their eyes met through the magic hedge and in that moment there was a recognition between them both that Hirsh couldn't do everything any more. Probably they already knew this but

Matt, anyway, had been reluctant to assent to the knowledge. Now they marked this milestone in silence. There was
nothing to say.

Matt broke the silence at last.

'While I was doing it, I remembered about Mom's ring.'

'Hilly's ring?' asked Hirsh slowly and without comprehen-
sion. Finally he looked at Matt for an explanation.

'The diamond she found in the freezer. Remember? At
the store?'

Hirsh suddenly seemed invisible through the tangle of
stems and foliage.

'The diamond ring,' Hirsh echoed flatly. He spoke without enthusiasm, which was not what you were supposed to
do when someone mentioned the remarkable find. You were
supposed to smile or say how extraordinary it was or shake
your head at how strange and wonderful life could be. And
Hirsh wasn't doing any of those things.

'I remember how she shrieked and held it up to the light
and I thought it was a piece of ice. You know how she'd
get sort of excited about things which didn't seem so special
to anyone else? I thought maybe she'd found some ice. I
had to hold it myself to believe it really was a diamond,' said
Matt. He thought that maybe if he could re-create the scene,
Hirsh might react the way he should.

'Where?' demanded Hirsh, his voice harsh.

Matt began to feel lost. So, he had defrosted the freezer
for his father. That didn't mean he had given Hirsh permission to plummet towards senility just five minutes later.

'In the store, Dad,' he said patiently. 'In the store. Mom
found the diamond in the freezer and she had someone
make it into a ring. Remember?'

Hirsh, with a movement of great impatience, perhaps a
stamped foot or a wave of the hand which held his cutters,

anyway, a hasty gesture that was not typical of him, said, 'But you weren't there.'

'In the store? When she found it? Sure I was there.'

'No, Matt. No, you weren't. I mean, why would you go to the supermarket with her?'

'To choose my breakfast cereal. I was allowed to choose my breakfast cereal.'

'Not this time.'

'Dad—'

'You weren't with her, no one was.'

'But—'

Hirsh said, 'She told us at home after dinner one night. We'd finished eating and she said, "I found something interesting at the store. I found it a month ago, but I didn't want to show you until I knew it was mine." Then she fetched this box. It had cotton wool in and she lifted up one piece and there was a diamond sitting there. She passed it around to us and she said, "How much do you think I paid for it?" Then she told us the whole story. You weren't with her when she found it, Matt.'

Hirsh's magic hedge seemed to have grown while he was talking, not just higher, but thicker, its fronds and branches shooting leaves, stalks, even thorns, so it was getting harder and harder to see through it.

Matt glared at his father's form. If Hirsh hadn't been wearing a red plaid shirt it would have been impossible to locate him.

'I remember being at the store,' he said in a small voice like a boy's.

'No, Hilly told the story so many times to so many different people that you absorbed it. That can happen, ask any shrink. The past we think we had, that we think we remember, it's all woven together with the pasts of others

189

and dreams we once had and stories we overheard or read or saw on TV.'

Matt felt bewildered and affronted. There was anger in his father's voice. He recognized it but he hadn't heard it for years. He tried to recall when Hirsh had last been angry. He could only remember that incident when Hilly was supposed to have stopped smoking and Hirsh had found her secret supply of cigarettes.

The yard was silent. In the forest, a bird called to another bird and it answered. Way down by the lake, a dog barked.

If your past consisted of the pasts of others and dreams and stories from books and TV then maybe nothing he remembered about Hilly was true. Whatever wraith appeared when he thought of her was entirely fictional. And the hillside, the day he had stumbled down it to find his parents and saw them sitting on the log seat? The red car, parked amid the trees at the roadside? Were these memories taken from some third-rate TV comedy from his childhood? He felt bruised and crushed. And then he remembered the piano. He had remembered the piano on the terrace and then he had seen it in the movie last night, seen it with his own eyes, right there on the terrace no matter what Hirsh said. It was Hirsh who was fictionalizing the past, not Matt. He felt angry for a moment but then he remembered his father's eyes last night, how they had been wet at the end of the movie.

'I guess it doesn't matter,' he said at last. 'It doesn't matter whether I was there in the store with her when she found the diamond or not.'

And now the magic hedge was on the move. Hirsh was lifting one whole section of it, effortlessly, with a pitchfork, the section which lay between them and which was just sappy twigs and air anyway.

When Matt put the movies back up in the roof it was an easy matter to remove the envelope containing Hilly's pictures from the shelf. Deftly, and without opening the envelope, Matt closed the hatch to the roof space. Hirsh was still busy in the yard and did not notice Matt stowing them under the driver's seat of his car.

Soon afterwards, Hirsh came into the kitchen to find that Matt had made a plate of sandwiches and salad. He pulled off his yard gloves and sat down. He did not make reference to his earlier anger but said, 'I've been thinking a lot about our conversation last night. About hunting. I realize I've been remiss. Every father should introduce his son to the pleasures of the sport and I failed.'

'Why does every father have to teach his son to kill things?' asked Matt testily.

Hirsh paused. He always responded thoughtfully to Matt's challenges. At last he said, 'I guess it's a sort of becoming-a-man thing.'

Matt felt his pulse quicken with irritation. 'I became a man anyway.'

'Sure, sure. But you've never had one of life's great experiences. Being alone, in the wilderness, with only your wits and your physical abilities to feed you. I know you saw and experienced hardship in Africa but now you drive around in air-conditioned cars and eat pre-wrapped meat from the supermarket. As a matter of fact, I was thinking to myself that it may not be too late to put things right.'

'Put what right? Do I have to switch off the air conditioning in the car or what?'

Very carefully, Hirsh said, 'I was thinking it's not too late for us to take a trip.'

'A trip!' The word brought to mind only Liguria.

'A hunting trip,' said Hirsh.

'Are you kidding?'

'No.'

'We go out and kill things?'

'Then we eat them. You eat meat from the supermarket, Matt, which someone else killed, and probably less humanely.'

'But I mean, a trip? A hunting trip? Like with the Minellis? In a lodge? With a load of guys who smell of wood and beer and gunpowder?'

'No lodge, and no other guys. Just us. In the wild for three or four days. I could show you what it's all about. We should have done it years ago.'

Matt munched on his sandwich. He could think of nothing to say. The sheer absurdity of the idea made him want to laugh but he knew that Hirsh was serious. His father, who never asked him to visit but was delighted when he did, who never made a single demand, who had not even raised an eyebrow but been entirely supportive when Matt had apparently thrown away a promising career to work in Africa, who never intruded into his life but only offered help when it was needed, this father was now inviting Matt to take a trip. Not just any trip but a hunting trip into the untamed wilderness of the Rocky Mountains. What was it about old age and arduous trips? There was Clem and Liguria and now there was Hirsh and hunting.

Finally, Matt said, his voice soft, 'Aw, Dad, you can't go stumbling around in the wilderness for days and days at your age.'

'Not by myself, I couldn't.'

This silenced Matt again. So Hirsh was more than inviting him. In fact, he seemed to be telling Matt that he needed him. Something in Matt's throat tightened painfully.

He heard his own voice, oddly deep. 'When?'

'When the season opens in the fall,' said Hirsh quickly. 'I can plan it over the summer. We have to get you a licence and we're late but with Elmer's help that shouldn't be too difficult. And before they give you the licence you may have to attend a short course on gun safety. In Salt Lake those courses run all the time, I'll give you a number to call. You'll need some suitable clothing, warm and waterproof and quiet, and of course, you'll need a gun. Probably you can borrow one.'

'What kind of supplies would we take?' asked Matt, his tone cautious to indicate that Hirsh should not mistake any questions for acceptance. He took another sandwich. It was so easy to make a sandwich that the idea of stalking and killing your dinner before you could eat it seemed perverse to the point of insanity.

'Minimal supplies because food weighs a lot. Carbo-hydrates and water, basically. The mountains supply the protein.'

'Peanut butter sandwiches? And how about cans of beer?'

'No. Powdered potato, oatmeal, maybe rice. Sandwiches for the first day only.'

'Supposing we don't kill anything on the first day? What do we eat for dinner apart from instant potato?' asked Matt, thinking how good his sandwich tasted.

'Well, in those circumstances you generally do find some-thing to eat because you need to,' said Hirsh, chuckling.

'Generally? How? Do we turn into hunter-gatherers and pick nuts and berries and things?'

Hirsh laughed out loud. He seemed to become cheerful when he talked about the hunting trip and that alone made the subject tolerable.

'That's one possibility. There's a surprising amount to eat in the mountains.'

'Let's get real,' said Matt. 'We have to take along enough food to keep us going for the whole trip. Because we probably aren't going to kill anything.' He realized too late that he had moved out of the conditional tense. He was talking as though he really was going to spend the valued vacation time he had left, after Clem had taken his bite out of it, freezing on a snowy mountaintop while he waited for a deer to walk his way.

'Sure we are,' said Hirsh. 'That's the whole idea. We're going out there to live on our wits and our skills. And that means killing, by snaring or shooting or fishing.'

Matt groaned.

'No lodges or luxury trailers for us,' Hirsh said enthusiastically. 'We're going to hunt for our food. That's the way hunting's always been. That's the way my father taught me.'

'Grandpa Flint used to hunt?'

Matt remembered Grandpa Flint as a very sick man who could not move without help. Maybe there had been a grizzled old muzzle-loader hidden in his walking stick.

'Sure. In his youth most men did.'

'When he was still a Mormon?'

'He hunted before they excommunicated him and he hunted afterwards.'

Matt could not recall why Grandpa Flint had been excommunicated from the Mormon Church; he could only recall that the reason wasn't shameful and interesting like sex or drink. It was something boring like doctrinal differences. After that Grandpa, a popular doctor in the city, had been outspoken against the Latter Day Saints. Hirsh had spent only his earliest years inside the Church.

'And,' added Hirsh, 'I will never forget my first hunting trip with him. When he taught me to hunt.'

'What happened?'

'Well, I tried to shoot an elk and missed. That won't surprise you. Except I just half-missed. So we had to track it in case it was wounded. And then my father did shoot it dead. That's how I learned to hunt. And we certainly didn't have three days' supplies of peanut butter sandwiches with us.'

So this trip was about the past, the family's past. Was Matt supposed to continue the tradition and take Austin hunting one day? Like a lot of family traditions, this one was going to stop when it reached him.

'How old were you?'

Hirsh guffawed.

'Well, you're probably almost as old now as Pa was when he took me on that trip. So to say we've left it a little late would be an understatement.'

'So why didn't we do it before?'

Hirsh looked at his sandwich as though it might offer the right answer. Then he took a bite out of it and ate meditatively.

'I did try. But, like an idiot, I tried with Arthur Minelli and all four of his boys. Of course it didn't work, there were too many of us and Arthur was the kind of guy who needed to entertain. He was always onstage. You can't hunt a beast and be the centre of attention. It doesn't work.'

Arthur Minelli, a massive presence, blustering through the forest, walking into branches, snapping twigs, cracking jokes. Taking pictures.

'Was that the summer he died?' asked Matt.

Hirsh was busy eating. It took a long time for him to finish, so long that he seemed to have forgotten the question. But finally he said, 'Yes, it was that summer.'

That summer, the one they had seen in the movie last night. It had been the summer of the Rosebay deal, the summer of brown limbs and confidence, the summer of the piano on the terrace and his mother playing it, the summer of go-karts and chariots and swimming, the summer of hunting, the summer of a diamond ring, the summer of death.

Matt said, 'I remember you getting real mad at Mr Minelli on our hunting trip. When we stayed at the lodge.'

'I felt mad at him most of the time on that trip. He ignored all the basic principles of gun safety. He made way too much noise and he wanted to spend too much time at the lodge.'

'There was some girl at the lodge!' Matt remembered. 'A waitress? He kept talking to her and it got sort of embarrassing.'

Hirsh grimaced. 'Probably,' he said. He rose and crossed the room to fetch the fruit bowl. 'That's the kind of guy he was.'

'I thought you were friends!' protested Matt. He had personally disliked Mr Minelli but hadn't the two families seemed like one by the end of each summer?

'We got along well enough,' said Hirsh. 'But we never should have hunted with him. Never. I mean, you didn't ask to go again.'

'I guess I never wanted to,' confessed Matt.

'Well, things were so different from my boyhood. You had non-stop kids' shows on TV and pre-packaged meat from the supermarket. You never could have understood the pride I used to feel at coming home with some prime cuts for the family.'

Matt began to think of objections to the hunting trip which he could reasonably offer. In October he would only recently have returned from Clem's Liguria trip. He didn't want to leave Denise and Austin. Maybe he could attend some important professional development course: he could probably find one if he looked hard enough. Then he remembered the Zoy tribunal. Maybe its date would conflict with the hunting season.

'You have to train for a hunting trip,' continued Hirsh. 'I mean, we'll need to do a lot of shooting practice. And we'll need to be at our fittest, that's something we should start now. A fitness programme.'

Matt knew that the moment had come to voice his objections but, unable to deflate his father's enthusiasm, he remained silent. Hirsh looked pleased. Taking Matt's silence for acquiescence, he made various references to their trip all day.

They ate an early meal so Matt could get back down to the city in time to see Austin before bed. They ate hungrily after their day outside. Hirsh was a good cook. For years this was a necessity because Hilly, although she enjoyed cooking, tended to get distracted by other things while a meal was in progress: a phone call, a TV programme which arrested her as she passed the set, a sewing project in another room. Hirsh would usually arrive just in time to transform semi-raw or overcooked messes into meals. Hilly generally took the credit for the dishes which Hirsh had saved (this had become a private joke between Matt and Hirsh). Very often, when Hirsh was late home or had been called out, she became so involved in whatever else she was doing that she forgot to cook at all, which was how Matt had turned into a virtuoso sandwich-maker.

'Next time you come we'll have some of that venison you brought,' said Hirsh. 'I'll be eating it over the summer. I intend to have my freezer clear by October for all the meat we'll be bringing back from our hunting trip.'

Matt sighed at yet another mention of the trip.

'Will we be hunting right around here?' he asked hopefully.

'Oh, no. We're going to a place I once went. I've wanted to go back for years.'

'Somewhere we hunted with the Minellis?'

'No, no. Much further and higher. Real high, too high for most hunters. I've only been there in summer and I didn't have a rifle. But I could see it would be a great place for hunting when the fall came.'

'Were you hiking in summer?' asked Matt, but before he had even finished asking the question he knew the answer.

'With your mother,' said Hirsh. 'To the place she named the Mouth of Nowhere.'

1 2

When Matt left Hirsh's he was aware that under his car seat, along with toys thrown and crackers dropped, were the photos of Hilly. He felt as though he were sitting on something corrosive. He would have to leave them under the seat, emitting their noxious gases, until he could examine them closely enough to confirm that the ring Hilly wore in them, the ring made from the diamond she had found in the freezer, was the same as the ring Mrs Minelli had worn at the exhibition. In addition, Matt was hoping for some indication that Hirsh had been the photographer.

The chance to examine them came unexpectedly early. Although he had left the mountain in plenty of time to see Austin and Denise before the child's bedtime, when he arrived home he found Denise's car absent. In the house was a thin silence and on the kitchen table a note in Denise's clear, sweeping hand: Gone to Daddy's, back around seven-thirty, Dxxxx.

Matt put on a sweater and went back out to the garage, not because the evening was cool but because the garage had an unwelcoming cold all of its own, like someone's back turned. He switched on the lights and paused and looked around. The snow shovel. The leaf rake. The lawn mower. All neatly arranged along one wall. None of it was his. Denise had brought Weslake's seasonal equipment to their marriage and even though Weslake was dead the snow shovel still seemed to be Weslake-and-Denise's snow shovel and not Matt-and-Denise's.

He slid the large envelope of his mother's photos out from under the car seat. It appeared mysteriously untarnished by the glutinous debris of Austin's snacks. It was clearly postmarked. The envelope had been sent to Hirsh, correctly addressed, about a year ago. His name was printed in neat capitals by a tidy hand. There had been no attempt to hide the sender's address. Thirty-three sixteen, E. Craig, SLC.

Matt, who had travelled over much of the city as a locum in the miserable year after his return from Africa, was unable to recall East Craig. It was irrelevant anyway as this was probably an envelope which Hirsh had chosen randomly for storing the pictures.

He decided to approach the pictures clinically. He would look not only for the ring but for any other information about his mother which the photos might expose.

He began to examine the pictures with the same degree of concentration with which he might a scan or an x-ray with a radiologist. He knew that some doctors used looking at this kind of information as a way of not looking at the patient. He had done so himself when he had very bad news to deliver.

First he scrutinized the backs of the pictures, searching for dates or a scribbled note or initials. But there was nothing, just a few faint pencil marks which time had robbed of their meaning.

When he began to look at the photos themselves, he avoided his mother and examined only the backgrounds. He looked over them slowly, painstakingly. There was no hint of any location but the photos were unmistakably studio shots with the same drapes behind each. The arrangement of the drapes, however, differed. He guessed that the pictures might have been taken over several sessions.

Finally, he minutely scrutinized his mother's body. He

tried to look at each photo afresh, as though she were a new patient in each of them. He examined her body and her hair and her fingernails.

In five photos, the patient wore the same small, stud earrings. The drapes behind her in these pictures were also identically positioned. That was one studio session. From slight differences in her hair and the drapes he could discern another session. The remainder probably dated from a third occasion.

The pictures had been taken in summer, probably over just one summer, the summer of the hunting trip, the summer his mother had worn the diamond ring in the home movies, the summer which had ended suddenly with Mr Minelli's death. That summer.

It was not difficult to place them in chronological order. The best guide was his mother's suntan. In the earliest pictures her body glowed, newly discovered by the sun. Gradually, she darkened, remaining pale, but not white, within the lines of her swimsuit. Matt remembered his confusion and embarrassment when, as an almost-teenager, he had discovered her sunbathing nude one morning on the terrace. He had retreated rapidly inside the house and, when they saw each other later, neither had mentioned the incident.

In only four pictures was the patient's left hand visible and on it she wore her wedding ring. No nicotine stains. In the photos taken at the third session, she wore, in addition to her wedding ring, the diamond ring. It was on her right hand. The golden flower petals pointed towards the diamond in their midst. The diamond's sparkle was captured as a cross of light by the camera. It was identical to the ring Matt had seen on Mrs Minelli's finger. It was the same ring. My husband gave it to me.

His final deduction concerned her left breast. In the lower

outer quadrant, third quartile, well below the nipple, the oil which she had used to make her body shine revealed a slight puckering of the skin in one picture. Although this quadrant was not visible from all the angles the photographer had chosen, and although the puckering was slight or even non-existent in the earliest pictures, he could, in the latest pictures, discern a tiny but distinctive disarray of the skin, a wrinkling on the breast's surface which, to the trained eye, suggested the likely presence of a tumour.

He put the photos away now, stuffing them back in their envelope under the car seat. He went into the kitchen to pour himself a beer. He thought about that small nugget of skin, puckered on his mother's breast. Everyone was always telling Matt what a good doctor Hirsh had been. Salt Lake City had practically declared a day of mourning when Hirsh had retired. He still received cards and phone calls from grateful patients and invitations to family events from patients whom Hirsh had delivered miraculously as babies or saved from some rare, life-threatening disease in childhood. Matt had entered medicine knowing that he could never be loved and respected the way Hirsh had been. And all the time Hirsh had failed even to notice his wife's cancer. Except, of course, Hirsh probably hadn't seen her breasts or maybe any part of her body because, during that period, it had been reserved for another man. Matt took another gulp of beer.

'We're so late!' said Denise. She entered the house with a sleeping Austin in her arms. Matt got up to help her. He hadn't heard the garage door or even the car.

'I came home early specially for to see you,' Matt told her reproachfully. She looked at him and frowned.

'I'm sorry. I'm really sorry. Some of Daddy's old pals showed up and we got talking and . . .'

Matt took Austin from her and she somehow managed

to kiss him during this manoeuvre. He inhaled her scent, warm, flowery, slightly musky. Austin, on the other hand, smelled distinctively of the Mason House rugs, a chemical smell which pervaded all the rooms and corridors.

'I'll put him right to bed,' Matt said, and when he returned she was fishing some paper from her purse.

'What's that?'

'Something for you to sign.'

'Have you drawn up my will for me?'

'No, honey, it's from the insurance company.'

'I already have insurance, Denise.'

'This is from Daddy's insurance company. For the Liguria trip.'

'Oh, that,' said Matt. He was always forgetting about the Liguria trip.

'I said that we'll be accompanied by our own personal doctor and so they need you to fill in this form. You have to sign and send it when you've read Daddy's medical records.'

'Are you kidding?' said Matt. 'All his records? Going back for ever? It would take me a month.'

'Just for the last five years. I rang the Medical Center at Wasatch Panoramica and they have a form for Daddy to sign which will give you access. I'll sort all that out.'

Matt picked up the insurance papers, which were thick and closely typed. He put them down again and picked up his beer instead. Denise was telling him about Liguria, about hotels and air conditioning and beaches and prices.

'My dad wants to go on a trip, too,' said Matt. 'With me.'

Denise looked surprised. 'He does?'

Hirsh never went anywhere very much these days, hardly even down into Salt Lake.

'It's a hunting trip.'

'A hunting trip with you?' Denise looked even more surprised. Matt noticed her cheeks turn a shade pinker. Hunting had been Weslake's sport.

'It's completely insane,' Matt assured her, 'but you know what these old guys are like when they're determined. I have to dissuade him slowly and subtly.'

'Don't dissuade him,' said Denise. 'I think it's a wonderful idea.'

Matt groaned. 'What's good about getting wet and miserable so you can kill some poor dumb animal?'

'Weslake used to say a few days in the wilderness changed people,' said Denise, and Matt immediately felt anger plucking at the small tubes inside him, at the nerves and blood vessels and arteries, as though his body were a discordant instrument and anger were strumming at it. Weslake's name alone had not provoked this reaction. It was the way his words had been cited by Denise, as though even from the grave Weslake had some special wisdom to offer.

'Do you want me to change?' he asked.

'No!' She smiled. She put her hands on his shoulders. 'But I know the mountains are a great experience. I mean, being out there, concentrating hard on finding your deer and killing it, well, that can sort of liberate you. Liberate your mind. It gets cleared of all the little things which you think matter when you're down in the city.'

Since Denise had never herself hunted, Matt assumed she was still quoting Weslake. He did not look at her.

'And,' she continued, 'it would be a wonderful thing to do with your father. He has the knowledge and you have the strength. Plus, round a campfire you might be able to say all those things you've been meaning to say.'

'You mean, while we're dying of overexposure, I might talk him into moving down to the city next year?'

Denise turned his face towards her and made him look at her. 'Stop deliberately misunderstanding me. I think this would be a wonderful trip for you both and you should definitely go. And . . .' she added softly, 'you and me, we've had some good times in the wilderness together. Right?'

She pushed her body closer to his. Just thinking about the hiking trips he had taken with Denise excited him. Their first summer together, the summer of Denise's pregnancy, they had walked in the mountains for a week. The live silence of the empty landscape seemed to wrap itself around them like a blanket, and this had liberated them from the city's myriad small restrictions. The hikes had been sexually charged. They had stopped in forests and by lakes and under rocks to make love. Now, as they remembered this together, Denise got up and pulled him towards the bedroom, ignoring the small Sunday-night chores and forgetting even to switch off the kitchen lights.

'This isn't the kind of wilderness experience I expect to have with my father . . .' murmured Matt as he felt the smooth slimness of her body slide along him. He told himself that it didn't matter about Hirsh's stupid hunting trip or those pictures of his mother or the dark well of Mr Minelli's distant death or even, yes, it didn't even matter about Weslake when he could feel Denise's body so receptive to his own. He seemed to swell and harden on the outside while inside his heart softened. For so much of his time he could not allow himself to feel. He had to experience the traumas of others with the necessary detachment of the clinician. Denise's fluidity, that rolling sensation of her warm body around his as though he were bathing in a stream, could soften the rock he had become.

Afterwards, when she was falling asleep, he remembered her sighs of satisfaction and thought that, every time he and

Denise had good sex, Weslake was diminished, just a little bit. Another miracle pregnancy would diminish him still more, of course.

Then, the following day at the hospital, Jon Espersen informed Matt that there were rumours Dr Smith's Slimtime would be closed within a week. Matt gleaned, without revealing his own ignorance, that the FDA had tightened up the rules on slimming products and, after a full investigation, they had declared Slimtime did not comply with regulations. Slimtime had to decide whether to limp along on its old reputation or to close. It seemed to Matt that somehow last night's lovemaking had played a role in the announcement, as though, by satisfying Denise, he had routed Weslake.

Matt was pleased that, with Slimtime closed, another constant reminder of Weslake would be gone. Maybe Denise would start to forget that terrible day when the police knocked at her door to tell her that her husband wouldn't be coming back from training in the forest that night or any night. Maybe her memories of Weslake, her memory of her love, would be papered over by newer, shinier memories of Matt and Austin.

He walked the hospital corridors humming cheerfully under his breath. Then, just before lunchtime, he passed a green-clad man smelling of antiseptic and saw it was Steve Minelli.

'I have some reviews of my exhibition,' Steve told him in answer to his inquiries. 'It's been pretty controversial but on the whole they're good. I guess . . .' He hesitated. 'Probably you're too busy for a sandwich in the cafeteria? I could show them to you.'

Matt was aware that having lunch publicly with a man in green scrubs could compromise the department's new warmth towards him. Then, immediately, the knowledge that he had even considered this shamed him into agreeing to lunch at once.

Steve produced cuttings from the *Deseret News* and the *Salt Lake City Tribune* as well as some of the alternative weekly newspapers. Matt scanned them. A cancer on the face of St Claudia's. Undermining our trust in health-care workers to treat our dead with dignity. Insidious sensationalism which tries successfully to shock and upset. No bereaved person should visit. Immediate closure of exhibition called for.

'That should get them lining up around the block,' said Matt.

'It has, actually,' admitted Steve shyly. His hair was freshly cut, very short, giving him a skull-like appearance. He handed over a review by a critic praising the exhibition.

'The guy who wrote this, Sylvester Suzuki, he's a highly respected art critic in the city who sometimes reviews exhibitions in New York . . .'

Sylvester Suzuki said that the pictures were a major contribution to the debate between art and taboo. They challenged our assumptions and aired our fears.

'I've had inquiries from galleries in Boston and New Mexico,' said Steve, and Matt congratulated him and felt pleased for him even though he had to admit to himself that he found the pictures repugnant.

'What did your mom say about the exhibition?' he asked.

'Well, nothing much,' said Steve. 'Art isn't really her thing. She's a real practical sort of person. She's into functionality.'

'She hasn't changed at all, not after all those years,' said Matt. 'I even sort of remembered the ring she was wearing.'

'A little gold flower? With a diamond in the middle?'

Matt nodded.

Steve was unwrapping his sandwich cellophane, but without much interest in its contents. All around them was the clatter and chatter of the cafeteria but Matt felt his ears filter out these noises, as though Steve's voice was getting louder, as though Matt knew just what Steve was going to say next.

'There was quite a story behind that diamond. Don't you remember? My dad found it in the supermarket and had it made into a ring for Mom. He found it in the little supermarket we used at the road junction towards Goat Bend. Mom must have sent Dad and me over there to buy a frozen chicken and the diamond was just sort of lying in the freezer along with all the ice. That's why no one else noticed it. But Dad had eyes like a hawk. I couldn't believe it. He kind of shouted and held it up to the light and I thought, what's so exciting about a piece of ice? And then I looked at it and I realized it was a diamond. A diamond! In the freezer of the supermarket! Jeez. You could see from the way it sparkled that it wasn't glass or anything fake like that.'

Steve smiled at Matt. Matt recalled how he had smiled that day by the lake when the Minellis had all laughed at Matt and Matt had first learned that blood was thicker than water. He watched Steve, who was beginning now to tear at his sandwich as though it were a big piece of meat that he held in his hands.

So Hirsh, as usual, had been right. Memory was woven from our dreams, from stories overheard, from old television shows, from things you'd read once and thought you'd forgotten. You even raided other people's memories and made them your own. Steve had been with his father when Mr Minelli had found the diamond and somehow Matt had stolen the diamond and deposited it inside his own memory.

Except . . . if Mr Minelli had found the diamond and

given the ring to his wife, how had Hilly been wearing it both in the photos and the home movies of that summer?

'I guess you don't remember the story,' Steve was saying. 'I guess you just remembered the ring. Dad had it made up into this flower shape for Mom. It wasn't to my taste but Mom sure liked it.'

Matt said: 'I half-remember it.'

He told Steve how he had watched Hirsh's home movies and how they had been filmed setting off on the hunting trip. Once again, Steve enthused about that trip in particular and hunting in general.

'As a matter of fact,' Matt said, 'Dad wants the two of us to go on a hunting trip this season.'

Steve stopped eating for a moment and stared at Matt.

'A hunting trip together! What a great idea! Father and son in the wilderness, that's always cool.'

Everybody but Matt seemed to think the trip was a great idea.

'Who wants a wilderness experience,' he asked, 'with a man not so far off eighty years old?'

'But you said the old guy's fit. And he'll have his own personal doctor with him.'

Now the hunting trip was starting to sound like the Liguria trip, only colder.

'Yeah,' agreed Matt mournfully. 'I'll get to save his life.'

'Lighten up! It's going to be a real bonding experience. I mean, you're so lucky you've got a dad to do this with,' said Steve. There was a moment's silence between them which Steve broke.

'Soon as you tell people you're going hunting, they'll give you their number one tip. I'll give you mine. It's about scent. Those critters have a sense of smell that's sharper than a dog's. Get out in the woods beforehand with a knife and scrape up all the pine sap you can and put it in a ziplock bag. When you need to cover your scent, there it is, all ready and waiting. Some guys use deer shit but if I'm going to get all covered in something, I go for pine myself.'

'Right,' said Matt. 'Thanks.'

'Listen, you're going to need a lot of equipment. A lot of the right kind of clothing. Do you have it?'

'No.'

'Well, I have everything you need. Except I may not be able to loan you my gun because . . . well, because guys don't loan their guns. But your dad can find you one of those. My stuff is stored at Mom's house on East Craig. All you have to do is tell me, and we'll go over there and you can try things . . . I'm smaller than you so maybe everything won't fit, but I'll bet some of it does.'

It seemed to Matt that Steve's voice was echoing a little.

'Your mom. Where did you say she lives?'

'You go up Riverdale for miles and miles and when you get to the big mall there, turn left.'

'What's the address?'

'Thirty-three sixteen, East Craig.'

'Oh,' said Matt, slumping back in his seat and putting his hands on the table as though Steve had just passed him something too heavy to hold.

'You know it?' asked Steve.

'I recognize it . . . um, did you say up Riverdale . . . ?'

And that zone behind Riverdale did come to mind now. Small houses, yards bounded by wire dog-fencing, kids galore and their bikes on the wide, open street, and, at the corner, almost swamped by a huge parking lot, a Mormon church, its acute angles and low spire borrowed from some other place, some other religion, some other culture, but distinctively Mormon.

'I think I recall visiting the area when I was a locum,' said Matt at last.

'It's very LDS,' said Steve.

'Yep,' agreed Matt miserably. He longed for his afternoon clinic to start. When you were in clinic you received information like scans or x-rays and you felt the patient's body and you listened to their symptoms and you read their notes, and it was like sight-reading a piece of music for Mrs Moran's piano classes: however strange the individual notes, when you played them all together they usually created something recognizable as a tune. But all the information he had received about his mother lately, her ring, the pictures, when you put it together, it was endlessly, formlessly dissonant.

On the way back to the elevator, Steve said, 'My mom never really got over Dad's death. He gave her that ring just before he died and that's why she always wears it.'

'It must have been a terrible shock,' Matt said. His heart had started to beat faster.

'Oh yes,' agreed Steve. 'It was a shock. Like I said before, we never really could understand it. He died in this accident but folk, I mean, folk like Sheriff Turner, they never much wanted us to know the details. And it was kind of a weird accident.'

Matt felt his stomach tighten and panic rise as Steve spoke. He had difficulty not reaching out with one hand at the drab wall of the hospital hallway to prevent himself from falling right into the dark well which suddenly gaped before him.

'He was in a car when he died, right?' he asked.

'He was shot in the car. Down near the lake. They said he died because he kept the rifle loaded and it fell and fired once but . . . well, you try that. It's sort of difficult.'

There had been a single shot.

The smell of the forest was asphyxiating, more pungent than it ever could be in reality. His parents were sitting together on the log on the hillside. In his hand was something heavy, so heavy that he was unable to prevent it touching the leaves at his feet and, provoked by it, the leaves were releasing their ancient, rotting odour. It must be a gun. A gun was weighty, a gun would bang against your legs, a gun might explain something of his parents' horror as they turned to face him.

'Like I told you, we don't think it was an accident. We all think someone killed Dad. But who? Why?'

Matt swallowed. 'Did he have any secrets?' he asked. 'Stuff he didn't want people to know?'

Steve shook his head vigorously.

'He wasn't a secretive kind of a guy. He couldn't keep a secret and he just didn't have any.'

'Don't you have any suspicions?' asked Matt. 'About who killed him? Could it have been connected to his business activities at the time?'

Steve shook his head. 'He was involved in a very important building project downtown. The Rosebay Building. You know it? Big, solid, fine block in the heart of downtown. But I don't think . . . I don't know. Of course, Mom asked questions at the time and we've probably asked some questions since. Jo-Jo and me once even went to a psychic medium but . . . well, we've never gotten any answers. And that's made it harder to grieve.'

Matt said, 'Most patients will tell you that uncertainty's worse than knowing. Even if what you know isn't good.'

Steve halted now and Matt halted too, so that people behind them were forced to make rapid diversions. Steve looked at Matt anxiously. He spoke in a low, urgent voice.

'Can you help me, Matt? Maybe we can do something with all this uncertainty I've lived with for so long.'

'Well ... of course, I'll help you if I can. But I don't see—'

'You could ask some questions ... get some information.'

'What kind of information?'

'Anything. Anything people up at Arrow Lake might remember, anything they say, about the way Dad died.'

Matt breathed heavily. He felt a net closing on him, the past's net.

Jon Espersen passed with three colleagues. On seeing Matt and Steve they were silent, until Jon said, 'See you in clinic in five minutes, Matt.'

When they were out of earshot, Matt said, 'Steve, why don't you go up to Arrow Lake and talk to people your-self ... ?' He thought he was speaking quietly but heads turned. They detected a tone which was out of place here in the hospital hallway. He moved to the side and flattened himself against a wall but Steve seemed oblivious to the passing staff.

'I'm his son, they're not going to tell me anything. But they might sort of ... let something slip to you.'

Matt coughed. He wanted to take a step back but couldn't. He could only remain wedged against the wall.

'Of course I'll pass on anything I hear about your father's death, but people don't talk about it much.'

'You could ask them,' urged Steve. 'You could just ask a few questions and see what they say.'

Matt was silent. He already knew he had to find out about Arthur Minelli's death and what his own role had been. He already knew that, when he understood all this, he should tell the Minelli family. He should confess. They could decide what action they wanted to take, what action would best ease their load. At the very least, a resolution might give them a kind of relief. At worst, they would instigate some kind of retrospective prosecution.

Steve's tone was pleading now. 'I feel that if we could just know a little more, things would be different. It would change everything for us. When Dad died, it all went wrong. Your life carried right on and now you're a doctor but for us it was all different after Dad died. For twenty-six years we've lived with grief and uncertainty. If that changed then maybe . . . maybe other things would change too.' His face seemed to collapse a little. He might have been close to tears. He looked like someone whose elder brothers had just been teasing him.

Matt said, 'I'll do everything that I can.'

A light suddenly seemed to have been switched on over Steve's head. His face shone. He radiated pleasure. He seized Matt's hand.

'Thanks, Matt,' he said. 'I feel so lucky I met you again. I feel like now the past is going to get sorted out.' He was smiling broadly. He was smiling like the Steve who had been laughing at Matt with his brothers in the lake that day, when Hirsh had first explained to Matt that blood was thicker than water. Matt turned towards his clinic.

He arrived feeling almost light-headed, as though he and Steve had been drinking strong beer all through lunch.

'That guy causing you any problems?' asked Jon Espersen, intercepting Matt as he hurried towards the examining rooms. Outside there was a throng of patients.

'What guy?' asked Matt, looking around, knowing, as soon as he had asked the question, that Jon meant Steve.

'That cleaner you were talking to. Is he causing you any problems?'

'Well . . .' Matt hesitated. 'No.'

'He's a troublemaker,' said Jon. His amiable face was serious. 'Seems he's been photographing theatres before he cleans them, snapping pictures of patients in the recovery room, there's even a rumour he's been taking pictures in the morgue, for heaven's sake. Human Resources have been reviewing a disciplinary action against him but when they saw the pictures they couldn't decide whether to send him to a tribunal or a shrink. Is he hassling you about something?'

Matt could see both curiosity and anticipation on Jon's face. He was hoping Matt would offer some revelation which would help Human Resources to nail Steve.

'I knew him when I was a kid is all,' said Matt.

'You mean he's a friend of yours?' demanded Jon.

'He was when we were boys.'

'And now he wants to rekindle the friendship? I'll bet he does. Well, that guy's caused the hospital a lot of trouble with his pictures, and General Surgery has come in for criticism for the way we leave the theatres. So be careful around him, Matt.'

Matt nodded. The idea that Steve, small, shy and suffering for his art, could be perceived as a real threat by the juggernaut which was the General Surgery Department seemed ludicrous.

Jon was already turning to go. Then he paused.

'By the way, do you still see that red car?' he asked.

Matt nodded wearily.

Jon looked concerned. 'Has Denise ever seen it, too?'

'Well, no,' admitted Matt. 'I mean, I've never asked her because I don't want to worry her, but she hasn't mentioned anything like that. But one night a neighbour saw it.'

Belinda Lampeter had thought its behaviour polite, but she had nevertheless seen it, and that alone gave the red car a credibility, or at least a life outside Matt's imagination.

'Hmmm. When do you have your appointment with the lawyer?'

'Soon.' Matt preferred not to think about the lawyer or the Zoy tribunal.

'Ask the lawyer for advice on this one,' said Jon. 'Zoy hasn't gotten out of his car yet but if this is still going on then it may be time to call the police.'

13

Matt had not anticipated returning up the mountain to see Hirsh for another month but now that they were going hunting, everything seemed to have changed. Hirsh phoned often – to tell Matt whom to call about Hunter Education courses in town, to check his sock size, to discuss fitness programmes.

'We're not going until October,' said Matt, who hated gyms and knew he would have to get up very early in the morning to run before the day grew too hot.

'Start now,' Hirsh advised him. 'You won't regret it. I am personally walking every morning and it's important that your regime includes a gradient.'

'There aren't any gradients in Salt Lake,' said Matt.

'Sure there are, behind the temple, up to the State Capitol Building. That whole area's steep. It's right by City Creek Canyon, you could run around there a few times. You should do that every day.'

On Denise's birthday the San Francisco Opera happened to be in town. Unfortunately, Matt was on call and so had to keep his cellphone switched to vibrate. During the opera's most moving aria he felt the unmistakable beat of 'Waltzing Matilda' against his thigh. Edging out of his seat, he disturbed at least fifteen people, only to find when he reached the lobby that his caller was Hirsh.

'Good news! That outdoor clothing store on Fortieth is starting its summer sale tomorrow with boots. John-Jack says boots are down by fifty per cent! You should get there as soon as you can tomorrow before all the good ones go.'

'I have boots, Dad.'

'They're too noisy, I've heard them.'

'Noisy? They're waterproof and they're comfortable . . .'

'But they've got a kind of a squeak. I noticed it last time you were here. Too many hunters let their boots give them away, Matt. If you can get crêpe-soled, that's ideal. Now, apparently the rest of the sale starts in a couple of weeks. So you need to get up here as soon as you can because the guys are placing all their clothing and equipment at your disposal. You need to try it so you'll know by the time the sale starts what you have left to buy.'

Matt was anxious to get back to the opera.

'I could try to come this weekend,' he offered. 'But Denise was planning to bring Austin on the next visit . . .' He had even agreed to let her watch the home movies.

'This is a working weekend,' said Hirsh. 'I'd sure like to see them but they should come next time. Get here on Friday night and you could leave after lunch on Sunday . . .'

Afterwards, when Matt told Denise, she reminded him: 'I've arranged for you to go to the Medical Center on Friday to read Daddy's notes right after work. Then you can sign the form. As soon as the insurance company gives the okay I can start confirming all the bookings.'

She was talking about Liguria of course. These days, she was nearly always talking about Liguria. She sometimes dropped yoga in the evenings now and instead, as soon as Austin was asleep, went straight to the computer to find out more about north-west Italy. In the daytime, Austin's new favourite toy was travel brochures, which he liked to rearrange across the living-room floor.

'I guess I'll have to read the notes and sign the forms

and then head off to Dad's,' said Matt. These trips, which were supposed to be taking place in the fall, were making unwelcome inroads into the summer.

On Friday afternoon he drove to the Wasatch Panoramica Medical Center where a secretary had prepared a small room for him. The computer was not switched on. There was a glass of water and a reading lamp and what looked like a coffin on the floor.

Denise's doctor, Dan Murvitz, put his head around the door. He had been at medical school with Matt, where they had been in the same ethics group, found they generally agreed with each other, and become friends. When Dan became a family doctor and Matt a surgeon they had lost touch, only rediscovering each other when Matt had visited the clinic with Denise during her pregnancy.

'Jeez,' said Dan, 'I heard all about this trip, and you're a model husband and son-in-law is all I can say.'

'Is Clem your patient?' asked Matt.

'Nope,' said Dan, pulling a face which might have indicated relief. 'He's on Barbara van Essen's list. So, Italy, eh? We stayed near Venice a couple of years ago and you know something? It was May and they had this heatwave. No goddam air conditioning anywhere. And they don't heat the swimming pools. You headed for the pool to cool down and it was like slipping south into the Antarctic. We tried to immerse ourselves in culture instead but . . . well, you know. We were glad to get back to Salt Lake.'

'We're going to Liguria,' said Matt gloomily. 'It's by the sea, which I gather is also unheated.'

'You want the sea? Hey, fly to California. Takes one hour and they even air-condition the beach huts.'

'Clem honeymooned in Liguria,' explained Matt. 'We're all going to be walking down Memory Lane with him.'

The secretary had switched on the computer now and clicked the keys which took her to Clem's file.

'So, what's this stuff?' asked Matt, pointing at the coffin.

'The patient notes,' said the secretary.

'They're not onscreen?'

Matt looked at Dan for an explanation and Dan guffawed and came into the room and fiddled with the lid of the box. He looked much older. It wasn't that he had lost hair and gained weight like Jon Espersen. If anything, it was the thinning of his face which had aged him, the loss of any hint of childish roundness. He wore glasses now but these did not hide the myriad of pencil lines criss-crossing the area around his eyes. Maybe he was just tired. Maybe aging was tiring, thought Matt. Probably he had those tiny lines too.

Dan pulled the lid off the box. It was filled with a long line of papers, thickly packed.

'Way back in the twentieth century,' said Dan, 'when we introduced computers and, here in the United States, even air conditioning, we put all the patient notes on computer. But we only went back to 1945 because it was costing us a fortune.'

'These are Clem's notes pre-1945?' asked Matt. 'I thought I only had to go back five years.'

'Clem's insurers have contacted us to specify that you have to read the whole caboodle,' the secretary informed him. Matt made late-night horror movie noises and Dan grinned at him.

'Just tap Enter when you get to 1945 to read the rest on-screen.' The secretary got up. 'I'll fix you a coffee so you don't go to sleep.'

'Gotta read them if you want the insurance clearance,' Dan said, handing Matt the first browning folder from one end of the box.

'If you were me, would you bother?' asked Matt, employing the argumentative tone which he recalled from ethics group.

Dan sighed and wrinkled up his face seriously, the same way he used to.

'Hmm, well, never, of course, forgetting Prof. Blake and *Ethics for Doctors*, I guess I would. I'd speed-read but, if I had to sign to say I'd read them, then I probably would do that.'

Matt still felt grudging. He had hoped to get up the mountain before dark. 'Do I really need to know he had his tonsils out aged five?'

'At least you won't be diagnosing tonsillitis if you do,' said Dan, getting up to go. 'Happy reading, Matt. Is Denise okay?'

'Ridiculously healthy. Must be all that yoga,' said Matt, giving his routine response to inquiries about Denise.

'No bruising these days, then?'

'Bruising? From yoga?' Matt had opened the first of Clem's files but now he looked up. 'Actually, I believe she did have a joint problem for a while when she overdid it . . .' Had Denise told him that? No, it had been Jon Espersen. Denise had pulled out of Christine Espersen's yoga class.

'I recall it as bruising. Unusual but not impossible with some of these demanding yoga positions,' said Dan. He was looking closely at Matt. 'So, what's she saying about Dr Smith's Slimtime? Was it all a terrible surprise or was she expecting it?'

Matt did not like to admit that he and Denise did not discuss Weslake and he had no idea how she felt about the collapse of Slimtime.

'Doesn't seem too upset. She's immersed right now in Liguria, its people, language and culture.'

From the door, Dan guffawed again.

'Remember to pack deodorant!' he yelled over his shoulder.

Matt rapidly skimmed through Clem's childhood medical notes. They had a historical interest. Doctors in Clem's youth seemed to have been more cryptic but Matt spent no time deciphering their words or agonizing over their abbreviations. He barely looked at some pages. However, he noted that Clem had been sent to a psychiatrist when he was only ten years old, a surprising referral in that early era. Incredibly, a letter from the psychiatrist was still attached. It was typed with a manual typewriter which gave it the texture and variability (a faint S, a C which was always a little above the line, a B below it) of something handwritten.

Clement's parents have been divorced for a year now and Clement continues to feel guilt-ridden. Typically for a child of a broken family, Clement believes that he alone is responsible for his parents' separation. In Clement's case both parties have unwisely confided in him the peccadilloes of the other. Whatever the criticism, Clement always takes it upon himself to defend the accused party by claiming a role in, or even full responsibility for, their action. This is an attempt by a child to exercise some degree of control over tumultuous events which are taking place outside his control and beyond his understanding in the adult world. This case therefore endorses this doctor's view that divorce has a pernicious and debilitating effect on our children . . .

A pedant! So shrinks hadn't changed much in seventy years. However, his comments were interesting. Matt had not known that Clem's parents were divorced. It was hard to imagine Clem as a small, guilt-ridden child, but it came as no surprise that he had learned early to be controlling.

Matt flicked through the rest of the notes rapidly and was just about to move onscreen when he was interrupted by 'Waltzing Matilda'.

'Hi, honey, it's me,' said Denise. 'Daddy just called. He wanted you to go over to Mason House when you've finished reading his notes. But I guess you won't have time . . .'

Matt paused. He was going to be Clem's doctor for the trip, just for the trip, which was in September. He had no inclination now to answer medical questions which Clem should be asking Dr van Essen.

'What does he want?' he asked warily. 'Is it urgent? I was hoping to get up the mountain before night.'

'I don't know exactly but I doubt it's urgent. Can I tell him you'll go on Sunday when you get back?'

'Okay,' agreed Matt. He did not trouble to hide his reluctance. 'But I'm not going to take over the role of his regular doctor except on vacation.'

'Thanks, darling,' said Denise, and he knew from her voice that she was smiling at him. 'I'm going to miss you tonight.'

It was still a bright evening as Matt's car crawled around the side of the first mountain. BEWARE FALLING ROCKS. From habit he scanned his mirror for the red car. Even if he didn't see it for a while, its absence afforded little respite because Matt was always looking for it now. He had determined to follow Jon's advice, never looking directly at the driver or reacting in any way to the car's presence. He had also written down the approximate date and place of every encounter or suspected encounter he could remember.

Now he checked his mirror at the end of each straight stretch of road, before dragging the wheel around the next bend, and, as he travelled further and no car appeared, he began to feel liberated from a tension which he now realized was a constant presence in his life. He had often wanted to tell Denise about the car, asking her if she had seen it. But he knew that doing so would introduce the stress of continual vigilance to her life also.

As he gained altitude, he saw that summer had crept high up the mountains now. It wasn't just that the white places had become green. There were tourists' cars rolling slowly around the hairpin bends, bare legs dangling from the chair-lift and, when he looked up, he could occasionally see rock climbers, their bodies flat against verticals as though the whole world had been rotated through ninety degrees.

He thought about Clem's medical notes. The most recent, and relevant to the trip, had held no surprises. But the notes which were a little older had been startling. They confirmed Clem to be, as Matt had always suspected, capable of breath-taking hypocrisy. All the time he had been a pillar of the city's religious life he had been afflicted by repeated sexually transmitted infections ('I wish he would keep out of whorehouses or at least pay more for a cleaner whore!' his desperate doctor of the time had scribbled) and, while publicly following the Mormon prohibition on alcohol, he had managed to hide a drink problem.

It was astonishing to Matt that Clem had allowed him to read the notes. Since it was the insurance company's condition of the trip, the old guy must want to go to Liguria a lot. Matt, for his part, would have preferred not to know so much about Denise's father which he could not tell her. He imagined how shocked and hurt Denise would be by the truth. Much as he resented Clem's position in Denise's life, he did not want to dislodge the old guy from his pedestal, even though it would be easy to do so now.

As usual, the relentless twists of the mountain roads had

a lulling effect on Matt. He found the scraps of the report by Clem's psychiatrist, a man who was practising a science in its infancy, recurring in his head as though they had a rhythm or a rhyme.

Guilt-ridden. Peccadilloes. Responsibility. Clement believes that he alone is responsible for his parents' separation.

Gradually the light changed. It shone red. The mountains turned pink and rosy like something from childhood. Soon their innocence deepened to something darker and then they were colourless, drained to a grainy grey.

Accused party. Tumultuous events of the adult world outside his control or understanding. When Matt had read the words at the clinic no particular significance had been apparent but here, where the failing light brought a new chill and clarity to the high air, they seemed to have some special but elusive importance.

The mountains turned black and disappeared.

He reached Arrow Lake. He passed Lonnie's house. There was a light on over the cluttered porch and, inside, a single light downstairs. He pictured Lonnie at her computer, finding medical websites or sitting motionless in front of the TV. His father's friends didn't go out much after dark. They all stayed alone in their houses.

By now the moon was rising. He passed the lake. He passed Main Street. He passed the little Mormon church. He climbed up the hill to Hirsh's house. He turned in to the drive. He had made this trip so many times in his life that each return now assumed epic qualities, as though every journey up the mountain was part of some much larger, longer journey. He switched off the car lights and the engine and let the car roll towards the house by moonlight.

Despite this noiseless approach, Hirsh appeared at the door as he drew up outside.

'Good timing! Dinner's ready,' he said, without any greeting, as though Matt had just stepped down to the store for five minutes. 'We're having venison.'

'Not that old deer meat? Weslake's roadkill?'

'It's fine,' said Hirsh. 'If you know how to freeze a beast it'll keep just fine and Weslake evidently knew how to freeze.'

Matt made no comment. He carried his bag into the house.

'Doesn't it smell delicious?' said Hirsh, serving the venison in a creamy sauce with mushrooms.

'So long as you can forget it's three years old,' Matt said gloomily. But the venison tasted as good as it smelled. After the first mouthful, Matt, who had first started feeling hungry way back in the clinic, didn't care how old it was.

'Trust Weslake to run down only the best deer,' he said.

'He knew how to butcher it, that's for sure,' agreed Hirsh. 'Most people leave in too much fat and bone marrow and then it gets real gamey when you freeze it.'

'There was nothing,' Matt said, 'that Weslake could not do. Perfectly.'

Hirsh gave Matt one of his searching, bright-eyed looks.

'I don't understand,' he said. 'If you never even met the guy, how come you dislike him so much?'

'Because Denise thought he was wonderful and she still does. She won't allow his name to be sullied by mentioning it out loud and she's always visiting his grave. It's tough to feel warm towards him in the circumstances.'

'So,' said Hirsh, watching Matt cutting a piece of meat, 'you're jealous.'

'Yes,' admitted Matt. 'Apparently Slimtime's in trouble with the FDA for making false claims, and I feel nothing but delight.'

Hirsh shook his head. He said, 'Maybe you're mad

because she married him the first time around instead of you.'

Matt stopped eating and stared at his father. 'What does that mean?'

'You tell people that you two met right after you got back from Africa,' observed Hirsh, 'but I know it's not true.'

Matt felt as though his face had swollen. His cheeks seemed to be in front of his eyes now, distorting his vision so that there were two or even three Hirshes across the table, eating calmly.

'I saw her at the airport,' explained Hirsh.

'What airport? When?'

'Don't act so indignant, I saw her with my own eyes. When you left for Africa. I went to the airport to see you off.'

'But . . . we'd already said goodbye, Dad! I drove up here the day before I left. You didn't come to the airport!'

'After you'd gone down the mountain I got to thinking and I decided that I didn't want you just walking through the airport alone with no one to wave you into Departures. I went down there and I saw you, but there was a girl with you. I watched the way you two were saying goodbye and I realized that I'd made a mistake, a terrible mistake. So I didn't intrude. I just turned around and came home again.'

The venison in Matt's mouth suddenly tasted of nothing at all. Its texture was dry, like cardboard. Around it, his mouth was dry too.

'When you got back from Africa,' Hirsh continued, 'it wasn't so long before you introduced me to the girl I'd seen at the airport. You were going to marry her. I was delighted, Matt, and, by the way, I think Denise is the best wife in the world to you. But I don't understand why you had to tell everyone you'd only just met. Unless maybe you'd been having an affair with her when she was married to Weslake? That's one possible explanation.'

Matt felt as though Hirsh had been punching him. He sat back in his seat and pushed his meal away. It was uneatable now.

'Oh, c'mon,' said Hirsh. 'Don't be dramatic about the simple truth.'

Steady, sturdy Hirsh. Shifting your chair around and not finishing your dinner was his idea of drama. He should spend some time with a few of the prima donnas in General Surgery.

'Why are you saying this now?' asked Matt. 'If you've known all along?'

'When I see you being mean about Weslake, taking delight because his company's in trouble, it's so unlike you that I have to ask myself why. Plus I think you're usually honest, so I'd like to know why you've been dishonest about such a small, simple thing as when you met your wife. I mean, it's just not true that you met her when you were a locum at Clem's bedside.'

'It's true that we remet at Clem's bedside. That's when our relationship really began,' said Matt. He could feel his face was hot and his voice low.

'Don't try telling me that the relationship I saw at the airport was only just beginning.'

'No, it was ending. I originally met Denise at Jon and Christine Espersen's. They had a party and Weslake was sick or something and Denise came without him.'

Although Matt had been instantly attracted to that younger Denise, he now suspected that she had been less beautiful. She may have had the rosy roundness of youth and a cascade of chestnut hair but the Denise of today, with her slim face and high cheekbones and the more restrained hair, had a sort of dignity and fragility which made her beauty heart-stopping.

'She wasn't married but she was already engaged to Weslake. I wanted her to leave him and marry me and she nearly did.' Matt looked up and found Hirsh's deep brown eyes fixed on him. 'She nearly did. Then her father and the Mormon Church prevailed and she decided she just had to go through with it.'

'And you went to nurse your broken heart in Africa,' said Hirsh.

'I wasn't expecting to see her at the airport,' said Matt. 'When she came to say goodbye it was harder to go. Terrible, in fact, because we both still felt ... we ... well, we knew that if her marriage was going to work we'd have to agree not to see each other again or speak or have any contact. So we agreed right there. And we kept to it.'

'You must have just about got back here when Weslake died. Didn't she try to contact you to tell you what had happened?'

'I was back here but she didn't know I was back and she didn't tell me anything.'

Hirsh nodded. 'So you didn't want people to know that the first time around, she chose Weslake? That's why you lie about it?'

'In my view, the first time she let her father and the Church choose Weslake. But, yes, that's why we lie about it.'

'Did she love him?' The words came out awkwardly. This wasn't Hirsh's usual kind of talk.

'Evidently,' said Matt grimly. 'Since she's never really gotten over his death.'

There was a silence. Matt looked at the remains of his meal, drying on his plate. How could he ever have eaten that stuff? How could Hirsh eat it now? He did not look at Hirsh but knew, nevertheless, that he was being watched.

'Good,' said Hirsh at last, 'I'm glad we've got that one cleared up. It's been bothering me for a while and I guess I needed to know. I mean, I have to trust a man before I head off to the wilderness with him.'

Matt wasn't sure if this last remark was a joke, but Hirsh carried on eating until suddenly he let out a cry of pain so loud and so unexpected that Matt jumped to his feet.

'Dad! Are you okay?'

Hirsh was tenderly removing something small and hard from his mouth.

'Nearly broke my tooth,' he said, rolling his tongue and grimacing.

'Weslake left his penknife in the meat?' suggested Matt.

'I'm not exactly certain what it is.' Hirsh examined the small scrap of metal which rolled beneath his fingers. 'Metal, no doubt about that . . . Are you sure this is roadkill?'

'According to Clem.'

'You do find shot in roadkill sometimes, because there are a lot of idiots around trying to take down deer with unsuitable guns or unsuitable ammo. Probably it was wounded already when it wandered in front of Weslake's car.'

Hirsh put the metal on the table beside his plate. He seemed to have forgotten their earlier conversation. He made no further allusion to Weslake. He told Matt that tomorrow they were to have lunch with Elmer and select from the equipment which people were offering to loan Matt.

'I suggest we do some serious exercise in the morning,' said Hirsh. 'Have you started training yet?'

Matt admitted that he hadn't.

'We'll be hunting over long distances at high altitudes and steep gradients,' Hirsh warned. 'Fitness is the difference between success and failure for a hunter.'

'Last week you said that boots are the difference between success and failure,' Matt reminded him.

'Well, that's true too,' said Hirsh. 'Have you got your new boots? Good. You can put them on and we'll walk over Tungsten Head and then down to the lake for a swim.'

Before bed, Matt went out to look at the stars. In the clean air here you could see them with astonishing clarity. You could see that there were not just the big constellations visible from the city but millions more stars peppered around and beyond them, more stars and galaxies of stars, forming an endless and unfathomable series of constellations. When you looked at them you were looking back in time, sometimes right back to the youth of the universe.

The stars seemed perplexing but they could tell you things. If you understood them, if your trained eye could navigate its way through the dense and beautiful necklaces of light, then a chronology would be revealed. Until now, every man, all through history, had admired the night sky without knowing anything of its secrets. Only modern man could unravel the necklaces and understand the story they told.

14

Hirsh woke Matt early the following morning.

'We should walk while it's still cool,' he said.

'This is like the army,' groaned Matt but, once they had started walking, the sense of loss of sleep fell off him like old mud from his boots. He was pleased by the morning light's fresh and shadowless quality. The distant peaks stood out against the sky like a child's cut-outs. As they moved up the hillside through the forest they startled a number of animals and birds, including a doe and her young.

Although Matt was faster at first, as they neared the end of their walk he was forced to admit his father was probably the fitter.

'Okay,' Matt said breathlessly, as though Hirsh had been arguing with him. 'You win. I'll start running again next week.'

'And don't forget your Hunter Education course,' Hirsh reminded him.

They finished their walk at the lake. They approached from the road, coming out of the forest and joining the asphalt near Stewart's place. On the left the lake was visible through the trees. Their boots drummed on the blacktop. They passed the small track which led down to the water, the track where Matt believed Mr Minelli's red car had stood with Mr Minelli dead inside it. Hirsh did not look at the track or turn down it but continued in silence along the road. On their right was their own land, climbing steeply up to the house. They had almost reached the Minelli lot when

Hirsh finally led them off the road and through the woods to the lake.

'Did Mr Minelli die somewhere around here?' asked Matt. It was easier to ask questions if you didn't think about it first, if you just plunged in like plunging into the lake's cold water.

'Oh,' said Hirsh carelessly, apparently without thought, 'I guess it was somewhere around here.'

'What happened?' asked Matt. 'What happened when he died?'

'It happens to a few people every year. He did that thing you should never do, he drove with a loaded gun. That's how he became a statistic. If the car goes over a jolt or the gun falls over or you grab it too carelessly, then the gun fires and sometimes it fires right through a human being.'

It was warm now. A couple of swimmers were visible on the other side of the lake near the rocks, otherwise there was no one around. Hirsh started to change into his swimsuit.

'Was it anyone's fault?' asked Matt.

Hirsh was irritable. 'Only Arthur's, of course. No one else was around when it happened. His family was all at home except for Steve, who was playing with you up at our house.'

The words seemed to echo in the air around Hirsh's head. They rose high up the slopes and reverberated around the mountains.

'I was playing with Steve when it happened?'

'Up at our house.'

Matt began to change into his swimsuit. His whole body was rearranging itself, as though a big stone inside it was rolling around. He had been playing with Steve Minelli at the time of Mr Minelli's death. He had not been in the woods or near the lake or the red car.

He heard his own voice, sensible, rational: 'Maybe Mr Minelli didn't know that the gun was loaded. Maybe some-one else loaded it and didn't tell him.'

Hirsh shook his head vigorously. He was walking towards the water now.

'Has Steve Minelli been getting at you?' he asked without turning around.

Matt did not reply because his father was entering the water, striding right in as though he couldn't feel the cold and didn't know he was walking into melted glacier. When he began to swim his movements looked unhurried. His strokes were even. His body cut cleanly through the water, leaving behind it a V-shape in the water's smooth surface. He looked fit enough, even sinewy, but his body showed the hollows of age. Matt looked down at his own smooth body. Maybe aging was just the accumulation of shadows.

He followed his father into the water. He remembered the way the rocks stubbed your toes and bit the soles of your feet. He walked gingerly through the shallows, feeling the lake's icy fingers wrapping themselves around him, reclaiming him as they had each summer of his boyhood. Once again he had the strange sensation that nothing which happened between his summer swims in this lake was real: reality was restricted to the bite of the water.

He swam and his thoughts became simple like the thoughts of a water animal. When his head was beneath the surface he felt the strange sounds of the water's world, the whisper of its thousand hidden voices. When he was above the water he sensed the trees, the sky, the mountains, without seeing them. His eyes discerned only the refraction of the sun on the surface.

The world was simple when it was reduced to the rhythm of your stroke. Clement feels guilt-ridden at the divorce of his parents and believes he alone is responsible for their separation. When each parent confides in him the peccadilloes of the other, Clement always takes it upon himself to defend the accused party by claiming a role in, or even full responsibility for, their action.

Matt flipped over on to his back and floated in the water with his eyes closed.

This is an attempt by a child to exercise some degree of control over tumultuous events which are taking place, outside his control and beyond his understanding, in the adult world.

He saw Hirsh lying on a towel at the shore, drying himself in the sun. Matt turned and swam hard. He breathed every third stroke, and the sensation of water, then air, on his face, the filling and draining of his lungs, gave a regularity to his thoughts.

This guilt, this sense of responsibility that he felt for Mr Minelli's death . . . he twisted on to his back and thought of throwing it, like an enormous rock, one he had been carrying around too long, to a waiting Hirsh, standing at the shoreline with arms outstretched to catch it. His body immediately felt liberated and more lithe. He floated freely on the lake's surface like a boat without an anchor.

Mr Minelli was on the terrace right next to him. He said, 'Don't tell your father.' The heavy arm he placed on Matt's shoulders felt oppressive, too weighty to shrug off. When he pushed at Matt the cigarettes in their pale packet, KENT printed in gold letters right across it, Matt shrank back beneath Mr Minelli's arm as though the packet contained a weapon.

'C'mon, don't think I don't know what you guys get up to in school these days.'

But Matt had continued to resist the offer. Mr Minelli

finished his cigarette and crushed it underfoot. Then he went back into the living room. Hilly was in there. She had been there all along, waiting while Mr Minelli had steered Matt out to the terrace to talk to him.

Matt had been looking for her and he had run into the living room and found Mr Minelli on his knees on the floor. Hilly sat on the sofa right by him, laughing, laughing so hard she had tears in her eyes. She had explained to Matt that Mr Minelli was looking for her contact lens. Matt had glanced at Mr Minelli, who was now lighting a cigarette, and he had been irritated by the idiocy, the foolishness of the man's smile. Hilly was forever getting people to look for her contact lenses. There had been occasions when whole roomfuls of people had helped her search. And if it wasn't her lenses it was her glasses, which she was always taking off and leaving places. It was one of her irritating habits, but Mr Minelli did not seem to be irritated by it.

Mr Minelli handed Hilly a cigarette. Then she leaned forward, bending her long neck down to him because he was still on the floor. His body inclined towards hers. Their heads were close together. Their cigarettes touched. You could see the small circle glow orange at the tip of his mother's cigarette and then Hilly drew away and inhaled deeply. She put her head back and blew smoke up to the ceiling. It came out of her mouth in a thick tunnel which became a spiral and, before it reached the ceiling, a whisper. Matt stood staring at them. There was silence in the room. Then Mr Minelli sprang to his feet and put an arm around Matt and pulled him out to the terrace.

To an older boy, to a more perceptive boy, maybe to any boy in America apart from Matt, it would have been obvious that Mr Minelli had not been searching for a contact lens and that he was on the floor because, on Matt's entrance, he had thrown himself off the sofa where he had been lying with Hilly. But the possibility of his mother's deceit had not then occurred to Matt, nor that she was laughing at her own lie and his gullibility in believing it. Or maybe, he thought now, she was just laughing because she was happy.

Matt had agreed to keep a secret he didn't know or understand but he had assumed that the secret had something to do with cigarettes, with that careful joining of two filter tips and the unnatural circle of orange light which passed between them. Smoking kills, he knew that much from Hirsh, and within a few weeks Mr Minelli had died. Matt had always believed that his pact with the man had given him some grave responsibility but it was clear now – it had the icy clarity of a melted glacier – that the secret was not after all connected with Mr Minelli's death, or not in any way which would have enabled Matt to prevent that death. If he had wanted to.

He approached the shore now. As he touched the lake bottom, for the few moments before he had fully adjusted to being a land animal again, his body felt cumbersome. But when he emerged from the lake he felt lighter. He felt cleaner.

He sat down on a towel next to Hirsh. Hirsh was silent, the way Hirsh was invariably silent, but now his silences seemed to have a new significance. There were things he had done that he could not talk about. He was carrying a rock around which he had wrapped in silence.

They basked for a while and then they changed and walked back up to the house, skirting the Minelli property.

Matt cleared his throat. 'Who lives there now?' he asked.

'Summer folk,' Hirsh told him shortly. 'The last family was Swedish. I don't know the new people but they see me walk through here and they don't try to stop me.'

They climbed back up the steep hill through their own woods, past Hilly's rotting sculpture trail, past the log seat where Hilly and Hirsh had sat the day Mr Minelli died, past the woodshed. It would soon be time to meet Elmer Turner for lunch.

'Do you remember when Steve and I broke that window?' asked Matt, as they went into the house through the porch.

'I was never so sure,' said Hirsh over his shoulder, heading straight for the shower, 'that you did.'

Mr Minelli had stood over them like some downtown building which you couldn't see to the top and he had said, 'Come on, kids. I don't like yellerchickens. I don't like kids who don't own up.' He was standing in front of the porch. The cracks in the porch glass radiated out from behind him as though he had just stepped right through it. 'I'm gonna get mean. I'm gonna get real mean if you guys don't tell me you broke that glass.'

And the consequences of saying you hadn't broken the glass now seemed far worse than the consequences of saying you had. Matt, fighting the sensation that he was shrinking before Mr Minelli, said, 'I did it. With the baseball. I broke it.' And Mr Minelli's face split into an unwelcome smile which radiated all over his face in big cracks.

While Hirsh showered, Matt opened up the roof space and fetched the envelope of Hilly's pictures from the car. He glanced at the address as he replaced them in the closet. Thirty-three sixteen, East Craig. They would, of course, have been in Mrs Minelli's possession if her husband had taken the pictures. They would have been left among his effects at his death. Had she sent them to Hirsh twenty-five years later in anger or disgust or sadness? He hoped that they weren't an accusation.

Then he went outside and ran down the hillside to the place where Mr Minelli had died.

He stood on the track by the lake where the red car had stood, looked at his watch and then turned and ran across the road and up the hill, taking the shortest route to Hirsh's log seat. He sprinted until the gradient was too much, then he slowed to a walk until he reached the seat. He threw himself down on it and looked at his watch. Three and a half minutes. He added ninety seconds to get his breath back. Five minutes. Five minutes after shooting a man you could position yourself next to your wife on your own seat in your own yard and appear genuinely startled when your son appeared to tell you about the accident. You could say, 'I know,' and your son might think you must have meant that you'd heard the shot. But in fact, you had inflicted it yourself.

Matt looked out across the place where the lake would be if it weren't obscured. Calm, phlegmatic, sensible Hirsh. The Hirsh he knew never could have killed a man, even a man he hated for loving Hilly. But the Hirsh who had stood in the doorway that night Hilly had played the piano, that summer, the summer of the Rosebay deal and the hunting trip, that Hirsh who had been near melting with his load of misery and emotion, that Hirsh was capable of anything.

Hirsh appeared from the shower with tousled hair. Matt watched him walk, without his eyeglasses but with an easy familiarity, to his room. Then Matt showered, weaving his body in and out of the warm water, wondering at his new knowledge and the new silences that must now lie between him and his father.

He tried to sound normal and cheerful as they walked out to the car. 'Are we going to Elmer's house?' he asked.

'No. The Lion's Paw Café.'

Hirsh looked tired after the morning's exercise. His walk was stiff on his right side.

'What do people eat at the Lion's Paw Café?'

Matt wanted a bowl of chilli. Probably the Lion's Paw didn't offer chilli.

'Most days I believe Elmer eats either steak with French fries or macaroni cheese from the kids' menu with salad.'

'He's a regular there?'

'He eats there daily. The staff are like family to him.'

Elmer's wife Millicent was dead but there were children, seldom mentioned, never visiting.

'They do a nice onion soup, I think,' said Hirsh. 'And, of course, the Lion's Paw is famous for pies.'

'What kind of pies?'

'Every kind of pie you can think of as long as it's high-fat and high-sugar.'

They had paused next to Matt's car.

'We'll take mine,' said Hirsh gruffly, walking on towards the garage.

Matt stared at him. He put his hands on his hips.

'Oh-oh,' he said. This question of who drove was a sore which had run through his adult relationship with Hirsh like a canker through an apple. Hirsh didn't like, had never liked, the way Matt drove.

'Dad. I'm a father. I'm a doctor. I do major operations all the time. Legions of patients thank me for saving their lives. Somehow I drive myself and my family around town safely. For heaven's sake, trust me to get us a mile down a country road to the Lion's Paw Café.'

He heard his voice rise. Not in volume or even in pitch. What was that dangerous note? Anger? Frustration?

Hirsh halted by his own car and looked back at Matt. There was a moment which Matt recognized afterwards as potentially terrible, when both men stood rooted to the spot by their cars, glaring at each other. Then, surprisingly, Hirsh burst out laughing and walked back to Matt's car.

'It's not as if,' Hirsh said, opening the passenger door, 'I'm such valuable cargo.'

Matt climbed in too. The car had absorbed the morning's sun. It felt steamy in here, like a glasshouse.

'Sure you are,' he said, 'that's why I'm going to drive carefully.'

He put the car into gear and it slid forward into a young tree which had seeded itself right by the drive. The tree bent accommodatingly.

'Shit, shit, shit,' said Matt. Hirsh laughed again, a surprising, deep roar of a laugh. So, finally, did Matt.

'I don't usually do that!' he said. 'I usually put it in reverse when I want to go backwards.'

'Nothing wrong,' observed Hirsh, 'with trying something new.' And he guffawed again.

The truth was that Matt didn't have a good driving record. His car had a couple of small knocks and scrapes on it where he had touched gateways and kerbs. Jarvis, a notoriously bad passenger, generally refused to travel with him.

Now he turned out of Hirsh's gateway and down towards the lake. Hirsh craned his neck to right and left as though he were driving and they were emerging on to a busy Interstate.

'How far did we walk this morning?' asked Matt. 'Ten miles? Twelve?'

'About six,' said Hirsh. They were approaching a bend and, although the car was crawling, Hirsh's right leg was straightening up on to an imaginary brake.

'Are you a really terrible passenger with everyone or just with me?' asked Matt irritably.

'I guess I'm just a nervous passenger. I certainly never wanted your mother to drive me,' admitted Hirsh.

Matt was about to speak again when Hirsh cried, 'Slow down!' as though there were a large mammal blocking the road.

'I'm only doing twenty,' protested Matt.

'See if the parking lot behind the Lion's Paw's full. If it is, then you can park on the street outside Macintyre's. This may involve parallel-parking which may require the car to go backwards, so remember to use your reverse gear.'

Matt didn't laugh. Through the glass of the Lion's Paw Café he could see Elmer, leg supported by a low chair, waving enthusiastically to them.

'Both hands on the wheel, don't attempt to wave back at him,' warned Hirsh. As they parallel-parked outside Macintyre's there was a deathly hush in the car. Matt, who could usually fit the car into a tight space without really thinking about it, felt anxious and was relieved when he pulled the car neatly in at the kerb.

'You drove! You were driving, I saw you,' bawled the old sheriff at Matt when they joined him in the café. 'I can't believe your dad let you. What an honour! What trust!'

Matt shook hands with Elmer. Hirsh greeted his friend by rolling his eyes.

'It was kind of stressful,' Matt admitted.

'I once drove him home when his car was getting repaired. It was about fifteen years ago. It was so stressful my cartilage's hurt ever since,' Elmer told Matt in a tone that was both confiding and loud enough for Hirsh to hear. 'I mean, would you say he's the kind of guy who needs to stay in control all the time?'

Matt considered this. 'Well, no, I wouldn't. He's not controlling in other ways.'

Hirsh said, 'A car is a lethal weapon. The consequences of a very small mistake can be immense when you're behind the wheel.'

'True,' said Elmer. 'We give young kids licences along with their candy. Most of them don't realize the damage they can do, leastways not until they've done it.'

'Not only to those they hurt,' said Hirsh. 'It's a fact that, if you kill someone, you never can be the same person you were before.'

Matt stared at him. He waited for his father to say more but Hirsh was busy with the menu now. Elmer was pointing out today's special to them on a blackboard in the corner and recommending the macaroni cheese from the kids' list. The waitress was standing by for their order, licking her fingers to move faster through her notebook.

You can't ever be the same again, Matt repeated to himself, when you've killed someone.

Since there was no chilli on the menu, he heard himself agreeing to an adult-sized macaroni with mixed side salad. Then the waitress was going and the old men were discussing driving again. Hirsh was saying, 'Just as soon as Matt got his driver's licence I made him sit down with me to hear about the accidents I've seen.'

It was true. Hirsh had given factual accounts of a number of car crashes in hideous detail. The head-on while overtaking was bad, the decapitation of the girl who swerved in front of a truck as she turned the dial on her radio was awful, and the car hitting the pedestrian and then driving on was the worst. Had Hirsh described the horrified face of the victim, visible through the windshield, as his body started its trajectory off the car's hood, or had Matt later supplied that detail?

'If you were the driver of that car,' Hirsh had said, 'you'd dream about it every night for the rest of your life. There are at least two victims of most crashes. The guy who didn't cause it and the guy who did. Everyone should remember that and drive carefully.'

Their food arrived.

'Looks great, Marcie!' Elmer told the waitress.

'It's your lucky day, we got Nat in the kitchen,' she said, skilfully dodging around Elmer's straight leg.

'How is that boy?'

'Aw, he had another bust-up with Michelle and Tiff's just lappin' it all up,' said Marcie. She dematerialized and reappeared across the room.

'Those kids!' said Elmer affectionately. Matt thought about Elmer's life alone, apparently forgotten by his faraway family, restricted by poor mobility, entertained by the TV and the love-life of the kids at the café.

'Is it good?' Elmer asked Matt anxiously. The macaroni cheese was still too hot to taste but Matt assured him it was.

'We're not taking our coffee here. We're going home for coffee so you guys can take a look at my hunting gear. I got it all laid out ready for you.'

'Thanks, Elmer,' said Matt.

'You just choose what you want, Doctor Matt. We're all tickled pink you're walking the old guy through the wilderness.'

'So long as I don't have to carry him through the wilderness,' said Matt.

'I got a rope stretcher you can have but it'll take up a lot of room in your pack,' offered Elmer.

'No,' said Hirsh. 'We're carrying the minimum.'

'Well, I got everything you might need, even hunter underwear if you ain't too fastidious,' said Elmer, eating his steak.

'Matt might draw the line at underwear,' said Hirsh.

'Don't be so snooty!' Elmer admonished him. 'You go see what it costs to buy brand new long underwear in wool and then maybe you'll change your mind.'

'Will it fit?' asked Matt.

Elmer grinned steakily at him. 'I wasn't always this shape, young Matt. I didn't always have a cartilage, you know. You forgotten I used to be sheriff here? You forgotten I was a pretty trim guy?'

Matt could mostly remember Elmer driving around the district in his car, his belly spread wide beneath the steering wheel.

'I just meant that you're a couple of inches shorter,' he said.

'Well, we noticed that and, as a precautionary measure, I invited Stewart over for coffee since he's your height, and he's bringing his stuff and maybe Lonnie too.'

Matt hadn't seen Stewart for a few years. He remembered that, the last time they met, Stewart's heart had been almost brand-new and he had talked compulsively, obsessively, about the transplant. He had spoken glibly the names of obscure drugs and their side effects, discussed the emotional impact of carrying someone else's heart, and asked Matt for advice on his eating and exercise regime.

'So everyone by Arrow Lake's bringing all their hunting gear over to your house this afternoon?' said Matt. 'I thought the season didn't start for months.'

But now he had given the old men an opportunity to lecture him on the importance of summer preparation for fall hunting and they seized it enthusiastically, often competing to speak. Matt guessed there were many more hunting lectures to come.

'What about a gun?' he asked at last. For the first time there was a moment's silence.

'Okay, what kind of pies are you guys having?' said Marcie, appearing at their side, notepad at the ready.

'Just the usual for me,' Elmer told her. He looked at Matt and Hirsh apologetically. 'I nearly always have the apple and cinnamon. Millicent used to make the best apple and cinnamon.'

Matt could remember Millicent Turner. The whole time he had known her she had been a small, scurrying, grey-haired woman. She had seemed not to change or age at all from Matt's childhood until her death about five years ago.

When they had eaten their pies and said they were delicious, just as if Millicent had cooked them and was sitting right there, they set off in convoy towards Elmer's house, Hirsh tense in the passenger seat.

'Now, be careful,' he warned. 'The danger at this time of year is tourists. Tourists who don't know where they're going. They're looking for the inn or somewhere to buy postcards and they're not looking at the road.'

'The danger in the winter is ice or skiers rushing through to the resorts,' retorted Matt. 'There's always danger.'

'Well,' agreed Hirsh, 'it's good to be aware of it.'

'Do I really have to hunt in Sheriff Turner's old underwear?' asked Matt as they turned into Elmer's drive. He lived near Lonnie in one of the wooden houses on the edge of town.

'You can wear your own underneath. You should have the sort which wicks moisture right next to your skin, then a layer or two of wool on top of that.'

'Why isn't Elmer offering to loan me a gun?'

Matt switched off the engine. They sat in the silent car. Ahead of them, Elmer was negotiating with his cartilage to lever himself from the driver's seat.

'Should we help?' asked Matt, watching him.

'Nope, he'll be insulted. Matt, it's difficult for a man to loan another man his gun. Elmer loves his gun and he looks after it real well, even if he doesn't really use it any more.'

'Does he think I won't take care of it?'

'It isn't that. Over the years you kind of get to feel that your gun has moulded itself to your body and your strengths and weaknesses as a hunter. It becomes an old friend. It's hard to let someone else fire it, especially if that means admitting to yourself that you won't ever use it again.'

'Maybe,' suggested Matt, suddenly cheerful, 'I won't carry a gun. I'll carry all the supplies and equipment and you can do the shooting.'

Hirsh gave one of his small chuckles. 'No, Matt,' he said. 'You're going to hunt, not play sherpa.'

'But where do we get a gun for me?'

'We'll find you one.'

'Where did I get one when we hunted with the Minellis?'

Hirsh thought for a while. He stroked the firm base of his chin. 'I think you borrowed that air gun from Jason.'

Jason Turner was Elmer and Millicent's son. He went east when he was eighteen and his name had been mentioned less and less and now Elmer didn't mention him at all.

'C'mon, guys!' roared the old sheriff. He was out of his car and leaning on it for support as he closed the door. 'Are you going to sit there chatting all day? We've got long underwear to look at!'

Stewart and Lonnie arrived. Stewart was tall and lean like Matt. He had been a power engineer in town, but he had long ago come to the mountains to work at the hydro-electric station when he had fallen in love with Mara. His love had remained unrequited for many years and finally Mara had moved to Colorado to be nearer her grandchildren. Stewart had announced his heart broken, and it happened

247

he was on the transplant list, and it happened that at about that time a donor was found for him. Right after he had a new heart, he met Mona.

Stewart shook hands with Matt and they spent a few minutes calculating when they had last seen each other.

'So, the old guy's got you hunting, eh? Or is it the other ways around?'

'No, this whole trip,' said Matt rapidly, 'is definitely Dad's idea.'

Stewart nodded. He took off his glasses and put them back on. 'Hirsh is brave. Even with this great new heart I wouldn't sleep in a tent in the fall the way you guys are.'

He tapped his chest proudly. You couldn't be with Stewart for long before there was some mention of his new heart.

'Do we get to take a tent?' asked Matt, looking hopefully at Hirsh.

'Probably,' conceded Hirsh. 'Or maybe just a tarpaulin.'

'You're going to need a packhorse,' said Lonnie, 'if you want all the stuff we've brought from Stewart's. It fills the trunk.'

They carried the clothes and equipment from Stewart's car up the steps on to Elmer's porch.

'It sure is nice of you to loan us your gear,' said Matt.

'We'll expect some fine venison in exchange,' Elmer assured him, searching his pocket for keys.

'We're not hunting deer,' said Hirsh quietly, so quietly that no one seemed to hear him at first. 'We're hunting elk.'

There was a silence and then Elmer roared, 'Are you serious?'

'Elk, eh?' said Stewart, taking off his glasses.

'Well,' said Lonnie, 'it sure tastes good.'

'That's if you shoot one,' added Elmer.

'I never have shot an elk. I've hunted them but they've

always slipped away from me. Once, when I was with my father, I injured one, and another time I missed and we tracked that elk for hours. When we found it there was another hunter field-dressing it. That's the closest I've come to taking an elk,' said Hirsh. 'I guess this is my last chance.'

The sheriff was still grinning. 'You don't think elk's a little ambitious at your age and in your tragically declining condition, Hirsh?'

Hirsh looked right back and smiled. 'Got to have ambitions, Elmer.'

Matt said, 'Will someone tell me about elk? Are they even harder to hunt than deer?'

'Well, they're bigger,' explained Stewart.

'Makes them easier to hit,' said Hirsh cheerfully.

Elmer rearranged his stiff leg with his hands while he spoke. Matt had never seen him do that from a standing position before. 'The elk. Average weight: seven hundred and fifty pounds. Average height: five foot to the shoulder. Average speed: thirty-five miles per hour when running but this critter can lollop along at twenty miles per hour all day if it has a mind to. Habitat: way deep in the forest, way high up the mountains, far from roads or houses or hunting lodges. Chances of a guy Hirsh's age tracking an elk and killing it: zero.'

Matt looked from one face to another. They all wore a certain expression, as if they expected him to say something. Finally he said, 'Oh.'

'He's old,' said Elmer, gesturing at Hirsh, who was grinning broadly. 'Humour him, Matt. And just make sure you have an airlift standing by.'

Lonnie gave Hirsh's arm a squeeze. 'I think Hirsh knows what he's doing,' she said. 'I admire him for taking on a challenge like this.'

Stewart put on his glasses and looked through them at Matt.

'Thank heavens he has you with him, Matt. We won't worry if you're there.'

Matt did not share Stewart's confidence in his ability to prevent his stubborn father from wilfully dying of exposure, but now Elmer was throwing open the door like a show-man. The small living room was draped with clothing and equipment.

'Okay,' said Elmer, 'we'll start with your outerwear. I don't care what Stewart's offering on the porch, you won't find a better hunting jacket than this one. Purchased com-paratively recently down in town, Gore-tex for water-proofing and wool covering for noise reduction, warm as toast.'

'If you take his coat, take my lined jeans,' said Stewart, thrusting forward a pair of jeans with plaid fleece lining inside them.

'Oh boy, it's going to be a long afternoon,' said Lonnie, and she glided slowly into the kitchen to make coffee.

Hirsh spent most of the next few hours refusing things.

'Elk bugle, no thank you very much, I've never much cared for bugling. I'll take the nylon line since I can't find mine, but I already have enough flashlights and a couple of very good knives and a great compass and we aren't going to be able to carry that axe, although I can see it's a good axe, Elmer. Now let's be realistic, those socks have shrunk sometime and are not going to fit Matt. And as for hats . . .'

In the corner of the room, out by the back porch, Matt could discern a piano through all the hunting equipment. He wandered over to it. It was the same one he had seen in the home movie, the one the young Matt had been playing with such concentration. It was the piano which had sat out on their terrace one summer's evening and on which Hilly had played the Chopin. He knew it from the candleholders.

When they had finally finished it seemed to Matt he had everything he needed and more to spend all winter in the wilderness. Except a gun. He folded the clothing and carried it out to his car. He made two trips. Somehow in the mountains in the fall, he was going to be wearing it all simultaneously.

He helped Stewart load the rejected goods back into his trunk.

'I sure envy you guys,' said Stewart. 'What a great experience you're going to have out there chasing elk. I'd ask to come with you but I don't want to make too many demands of this heart. My donor didn't die just so I could mess up her heart for her like I messed up my own. I'm following a very precise exercise regime and a hunting trip would be asking too much.'

'You look in good shape, Stewart,' said Matt.

'I think,' said Stewart, leaning forward and speaking confidentially, 'I'm getting closer. Did Hirsh tell you about my search?'

Matt shook his head.

'My donor. At least her family.'

'Your heart donor?'

'Female. Lived somewhere in Utah, maybe even Salt Lake. Deceased aged thirty-nine. Fatal accident at work. I don't even know what her work was. But I'm getting there.'

'Didn't they tell you not to contact your donor's family?'

'They don't give you direct contact. They send you a few details: the age, the sex. And they think that's enough, but it's not. And they give you this postcard. You write your thanks on these few square inches and then they pass it on to the family and that's not enough either.'

'Not enough for the family? Or not enough for you?'

'She may have had kids, Matt. They may be teenagers now. They may be at an age when they need my help.'

Matt said, 'There may be kids and they may need help but not necessarily from you. Not everyone wants to meet the guy who's walking around with their mother's heart inside of him.'

'I have to know,' repeated Stewart. 'If I can give something back, I should do it. She gave me her heart and I'm going to follow it. I always follow my heart. I followed my heart to these mountains in the first place when I met Mara. Now this heart's for Mona.'

He was lifting a gun case out of the trunk. They walked slowly back to the house, Stewart carrying the case carefully as if the guns inside it were loaded.

'How is Mona?' asked Matt.

'She's everything,' said Stewart wholeheartedly.

Lonnie was waiting for them at the door with unusual eagerness.

'And what have we here?' asked Elmer, breaking off from an elk-hunting story.

Lonnie indicated for Stewart to set the big metal case down on the table and they watched in silence as she took a key from her pocket.

'All this equipment you got,' she said. Her voice sounded shaky, as if the small drama she was creating had begun to frighten her, 'but no gun. What's Matt going to do out there without a gun?'

'Well, I thought we'd find him one sooner or later,' Hirsh began, but Lonnie had swung open the lid of the case. There were two rifles inside. Everyone drew a little closer. Lonnie touched the worn wooden stock of one. Her movements were gentle. She stroked it a little.

'This one's Robert's,' she said.

'I recognize it,' Elmer told her.

'Me too,' said Hirsh. 'I've used it. A Winchester with a lovely action.'

'I can't let you take this one, Matt,' said Lonnie looking not at Matt but at the gun, affectionately, 'just in case Robert wakes up and decides he needs it. That's the kind of thing he would do. He would wake up, realize it's the hunting season and just reach for his gun.'

Elmer and Stewart nodded. 'That's just the kind of thing Robert would do,' they agreed.

Lonnie gently unbuckled the other rifle from its holder and lifted it out of the case. 'But you can take this one, if Hirsh reckons it's suitable. Robert did use it sometimes and sometimes he loaned it out. I've used it myself and, so far as I can tell, it's a good gun. He bought it years and years back, in fact, I think he bought it from Elmer.'

She glanced at Elmer but Elmer was staring at the gun. Everyone was staring at it. The room was oppressively silent. Nobody moved to take the rifle from Lonnie. Matt saw that Elmer's eyes bulged a little. His face was reddening. He stole a glance at Hirsh but Hirsh, chalk-white now, did not look back. His jawline had tightened so that his whole face flattened, distorted as though he were pressing it up against glass.

Lonnie, usually so still, looked confused by the silence. Her eyes moved rapidly from one face to the next like an anxious bird's. And, when no one said anything or took the gun, she handed it to Matt.

Then a voice said, 'Put that down, Matt.' Hirsh, rasping, a quiver audible in his throat. 'Put it right back in its case now.'

Matt was too startled to do anything but obey his father. Lonnie looked at Hirsh for an explanation but Hirsh, like the other men, was watching as Matt, handling the gun inexpertly, returned it to its holder. They watched as if the rifle had some life of its own, as if it couldn't be trusted to go back into its case without a struggle.

'Thank you, Lonnie, for offering to loan it. I appreciate that,' barked Hirsh's new voice. 'But this rifle isn't a suitable weapon for Matt to use. It's too advanced for a beginner and it isn't heavy enough for elk.'

Lonnie was silent. She looked at Elmer and Stewart as though something more should be said, but no one said anything.

'Shame it's no good for elk, Lonnie, it certainly seems a nice gun,' Matt assured her as if he really believed there could be such a thing as a nice gun. Its wood and metal had felt alien in his fingers.

Lonnie's face was reddening now. It was possible she was going to cry. The silence continued.

At last Elmer spoke. 'Well,' he said hoarsely, 'it was a kind thought, Lonnie, but unfortunately it just ain't heavy enough for elk. Deer, yes. Elk, no.'

Lonnie closed the gun case. The metal fasteners rang a little in the quiet room.

'I could have sworn Robert gave it to someone for elk hunting,' she muttered.

'We have to be going now,' said Hirsh. His voice had not recovered its usual fullness. It sounded as though some sharp-beaked bird had been pecking away at his throat and left his voice full of holes.

'I'd like to thank you all for the stuff you're loaning and for the stuff you've offered . . .' Hirsh glanced at Lonnie and, seeing her red face, looked rapidly away. 'We really appreciate it. I'm not sure we could manage this trip without your help.'

Then Hirsh left. Matt, after thanking everyone again and squeezing Lonnie's broad shoulders, had no choice but to follow him. When he said goodbye to the sheriff, he saw that his face still had the bulging redness of great discomfort. The old man barely spoke.

15

It was growing dark outside, the dark of early evening when a storm is coming. The skies overhead were clear and the air was deathly still but you could see the storm approaching over the mountains like an angry, waving fist.

Hirsh was already sitting stiffly in the car. Matt climbed in and started the engine. As they drove slowly up the road, Matt said, 'Are you going to tell me what was wrong with that gun?'

'I've already told you. That's no beginner's gun. And there's not enough gun in it for elk.'

'That's all?'

'That's all.'

Matt knew it wasn't all but Hirsh remained silent.

'I think Lonnie was kind of offended,' Matt observed at last.

Hirsh growled a little in reply. 'I'll call her tonight.'

Matt paused the car to admire the moon on the lake. It glittered at them from above and below, the reflection as still as the original so you could get confused about which way up you were.

Matt persisted: 'I got the feeling you recognized it.'

There was a long pause and then Hirsh, very quietly, said, 'It was Arthur Minelli's gun. Now don't ask me any more questions.'

During dinner, a storm hit. First the wind and then the rain and then the hail. It seemed to be trying to break down the roof. It ceased and there was silence for a few moments.

Matt felt relief but immediately the hail started once again, with more ferocity this time, as though a giant were throwing rocks at the house. The room was constantly and freakishly illuminated by lightning. Thunder made conversation almost impossible. Matt thought how it would be out in the wilderness in winter when one of these merciless mountain storms hit. As the storm subsided, he said this to Hirsh, who seemed to relish the idea.

'That's what hunting's all about, Matt,' he said. 'It's about learning the elements are a whole lot bigger than we are.'

'I already know that,' protested Matt. 'I don't need to endanger my life to find it out.' But Hirsh just smiled and, when dinner was over, fetched the maps.

He showed Matt on a small-scale map where they were going. Matt didn't recognize any of the landmarks, nor could he understand where their destination was in relation to Arrow Lake. The map looked like wallpaper. It was covered by the swirls of steep gradients. When Matt asked for clarification, Hirsh said, 'Arrow Lake? Way over there!' and he pointed off the edge of the page.

Hirsh pulled out another, larger-scale map.

'This is a US Forestry Service map. When you're scouting elk, these topographical maps are the most useful by far. Day one we head north up here, and we'll be climbing most of the way. Then we head east. This route takes us through deep forest with meadows where there could be elk.'

'But where are we starting from?' asked Matt.

Hirsh took off his glasses and rubbed the place where they had sat on his nose.

'I wanted to start from home so we did the whole trip on foot. Unfortunately, after a lot of thought, I've had to accept that isn't going to get us where we want to go fast enough. So I'll have Elmer or Stewart drive us up the road to the forest and leave us on the way to Goat Bend. It's called Knee Heights.'

So Sheriff Turner was going to drive them into the forest and leave them there.

'Are we heading for somewhere? I thought we were just wandering around looking for moose to shoot at.'

'May I remind you that we're hunting elk, Matt, not moose.'

Matt hoped he knew the difference. He thought maybe he should buy a book about this when he got back down to Salt Lake.

'If we sense elk are around, we should track them, I agree,' Hirsh was saying, 'but it's good to have an aim. We need to head for somewhere way out back, far away from all those lazy hunters who bugle from their cars and scare all the elk away. We need somewhere we can make a camp. Then we'll use that as a base for scouting.'

'But where?'

Hirsh reached for the topographical map. He pulled it across the table on top of the other maps. They both placed their elbows on it, so that it felt as though the world was flat and Matt was leaning on its thick pile of places. And then he remembered that Hirsh had already told him, weeks ago, where they were heading for.

'The Mouth of Nowhere,' Matt said before Hirsh could. He peered at the spot where Hirsh's finger had been. At first it seemed to have no distinguishing features, just more contour lines which crouched together like the eye wrinkles of someone very old. But when he looked more closely he found that it was a topographical representation of Hilly's painting in the roof upstairs. It was a valley which was surrounded by high mountains.

'This peak's shaped oddly,' said Hirsh. 'It's called the

School Marm. Sort of looks down her nose at the Mouth of Nowhere.'

The valley, by the standards of local contours, was relatively flat. There was a creek or a river running right through it, along to the side, and, at one end, a few straight lines and dots which suggested some human habitation.

'Are these houses?'

'Mineshafts, mostly. There were some log cabins, a long, long time ago, but these lines indicate there isn't much left of them. Last time I went they were in ruins and that was when your mother was still alive. They must be in pretty bad shape by now.'

'A ghost town.'

'Just a few shacks where Mormon Fundamentalists once set up home so they could observe their polygamous practices in peace along with all the other things they considered their holy right.'

'What happened to them?'

Hirsh shrugged. 'Who knows?'

'The Mouth of Nowhere,' said Matt, not much liking his mother's fanciful name for the place.

'I scouted the place for elk all those years ago. I knew that, come the fall, there had to be a lot of them nearby. It has all the features they like: steep mountains, grazing, forest, water. I decided then that I'd bring you back one day to hunt elk. I can't imagine why I've waited so long.'

But Matt suspected that the Mouth of Nowhere was Hilly's place as much as it was an elk place and they were going there so that they could try to capture her one last time.

'If it's such a great place for elk, won't there be other hunters around?'

Hirsh shook his head. 'There are no roads, no tracks wide

enough for their heated SUVs, no campsites for luxury RVs, no cosy little lodges costing hundreds of dollars a night where you eat meat other men killed. So, no other hunters.'

That night Matt dreamed that he and Hirsh were scouting through the forest, tracking not an elk but Hilly, and not the quiet Hilly but the brash, flirtatious pin-up she had become during her probable affair with Mr Minelli. They rarely caught a glimpse of their quarry but they found evidence of her: a scarf draped over a tree, a diamond ring sparkling in an icy river, an occasional sound which might have been elk or might have been her laughter. Either the dream ended or he woke up before they had found her.

The following day, after another strenuous walk, Matt had an early sandwich with Hirsh and then started off down the drive.

He went as far as the Lion's Paw Café, parallel-parked with ease outside Macintyre's, and found Sheriff Turner sitting at his table with a bowl of macaroni cheese in front of him.

'Matt, it's great to see you!' bellowed Elmer, so loudly that the Lion's Paw came to a temporary halt. 'You just couldn't resist another bowl of macaroni, eh? Doesn't the old guy keep you fed up there?'

Matt explained that he was joining the sheriff for a coffee on his way home and Elmer immediately ordered him coffee with a slice of apple and cinnamon pie.

'I'd like for you to taste this. It's very similar to the pie Millicent used to make,' he said. Elmer had told him that yesterday but Matt nodded as though hearing it for the first time.

'Yessir, very like. She died only five years ago and I'm not sure I can remember the differences between Millicent's pie and the Lion's Paw pie any more. That's how we really lose our loved ones, Matt. We gradually forget all their little details. But you know that. You must have forgotten a lot about your mom.'

'Yes,' agreed Matt. 'I'm always trying to remember more things about her. And when I do remember something, I'm not sure it's true.'

It was Hirsh who had told him not to trust his memories, that they were made up of old stories and other people's lives and scraps of TV programmes. It was Hirsh who, no sooner had Matt remembered Hilly finding the diamond in the freezer, told him that he hadn't even been there.

'Well, let me inform you, Matt. Here's a few things you can be sure of. Your mom was beautiful and gracious. I was scared of her, she was so beautiful, but she was always real friendly. She had this laugh . . . I used to think that's what was starting the forest fires around here, her laugh.'

Matt recalled how Steve Minelli had remembered her laugh.

'Look, she was special,' continued Elmer. 'Of course! She was a famous pianist, she performed at the Carnegie Hall, of course she was special. Did a lot of things with you, Matt. Probably wasn't the most patient mom in the world but she sure took time and trouble with you. Had energy, it just cascaded out of her. Most people got a sort of monotonous, deadpan way of speaking, but your mom, well, when she talked it sounded as though someone just lit a match right under her.'

Matt nodded. He knew that was how his mother had been with other people. When he was alone with Hilly, or with both his parents, she would often be silent for long periods. Then a visitor would show up and her lights would go on and she would explode into sound. Matt remembered watching this transformation, enthralled. He had always known that this animated creation was just the public Hilly. That gentle, quiet other person was his mother.

Elmer finished up the macaroni. Pie and coffee appeared in front of them. Matt did not notice the waitress's movements although at one point it seemed to him that a bird might be fluttering nearby.

'I saw the piano in your house yesterday,' said Matt.

'Hasn't hardly been touched for five years. Millicent played it. I should get rid of it but I just can't. It belonged to her grandma and it's even got the old candleholders on it still.'

'I've seen it before . . .' said Matt. 'I think my mother played it.'

Elmer shot Matt a keen glance. 'Well, I do believe that there was some sort of surprise concert your mother gave . . .' He spoke carefully and less loudly than usual.

'Surprise? Who for?'

'I don't remember the details now,' said Elmer. He was stirring his coffee for the third time. 'Millicent agreed to it, not me. Some guys came and took the piano away for the evening and the next day after lunch they brought it back and thank the Lord it didn't get rained on because I believe it was an outdoor concert of sorts since the piano wouldn't go into the house.'

'She was outside. We were inside and Mom played on the terrace. I was there with the Minellis and Dad showed up halfway through.'

'That's because we called him,' said Elmer. 'We took it upon ourselves, Millicent and me, to call him down in the town. We told him to get right up here.'

So Matt's idea that Hirsh had been summoned by the piano itself hadn't been so crazy.

'Why?' he asked. 'Why did you call Dad?'

'Well … because we thought … we sort of felt …' Elmer's large voice faltered. 'Well, something didn't feel right.'

Matt stated: 'My mother had an affair with Arthur Minelli.' The words, once spoken, seemed to carry the shock of nudity, as though someone in the restaurant had just ripped off their clothes. Elmer looked uncomfortable. His face reddened a little.

'Probably it was Arthur who persuaded her to play and who organized the piano, but that doesn't mean … Matt, she was a darn attractive woman and Arthur sure as hell was attracted to her. A lot of men were and I think she enjoyed that. But I don't know what went on between them. I couldn't say.'

Mr Minelli was kneeling on the floor and he leaned forward and his mother inclined her head and their cigarettes touched and where they touched there was a tiny disc of orange light.

'I think they had an affair,' Matt said stubbornly.

'Maybe,' concurred the old sheriff. 'Arthur was probably a womanizer. I remember after he died there were rumours about him and some woman down in the town.'

'Some other woman apart from Mom?'

'Well, it was just rumour. But there had been rumours all summer about Arthur and your mom. I guess she was the kind of gal to like some excitement in her life.'

'Yes,' said Matt, his tone bitter. 'I wonder how Dad felt about her getting some excitement in her life.'

'He didn't show anything, nothing at all. With Hirsh, things don't show. You know that. But probably we can both guess how he felt.'

Jealous, thought Matt. Jealous, just the way I feel about Weslake, even though Weslake's dead.

'Listen,' said Elmer. 'Whatever she did with Arthur, doesn't mean she loved your daddy any the less.'

'That rifle, the one Lonnie got out of the case yesterday. The one you all said is too light to shoot an elk . . .'

'Nah, it's not too light for elk,' said Elmer. 'Good shot at his lungs with a Remington 700 Mountain and he's down.'

He picked up his spoon but did not start on his pie.

'It was Arthur Minelli's rifle,' Matt stated.

'Yes. It was the very same rifle that killed him. Not the kind of history you need in a gun. I paid his widow a good price for it because she never wanted to see it again and who can blame her, and then Robert bought it from me a few years later. He never even knew Arthur Minelli.'

'Would you tell me precisely how Mr Minelli died? And exactly where?' asked Matt, swallowing. He felt his clothes grow tighter and his breath shorten.

'Arthur Minelli gets in his car. He takes his gun and it's loaded, which is a dumb fool thing to do but dumb fools do it all the time and get away with it. Why does he take his gun? Well, he told one of his sons, Jo-Jo I think it was, that he'd seen the old coyote heading up towards John-Jack Perry's place and this was his last chance to get it that summer. Coyote had been causing some bother. Getting at the garbage, killing the neighbour's cat, that kind of thing. Now he pulls the car over, into that trail which goes a little ways through the trees to the lake, right near Stewart's place.'

Matt nodded.

'We'll never know why Arthur pulled the car over. Maybe because he's seen the coyote or he wants to take a look for it. Goes to get out of car, foot hits gun, safety's off for heaven's sake, and it's pointing at his heart. Bang.'

Elmer put some pie in his mouth and chewed it thoughtfully. 'That's all, really. Eat your pie, Matt, it's probably cold by now.'

'Was there something wrong with the gun?' asked Matt. His voice sounded far away, as though he were sitting across the restaurant overhearing this conversation.

'It's a good gun. A very light trigger pull. Said that in the report. But there was nothing technically wrong with it.'

'Who found him?'

'Stewart. So, all three of us who saw that gun in the car with Arthur, we all three of us watched Lonnie pull it out of the case again yesterday, I guess that's why there was something of a silence. Poor Lonnie, when you'd gone we explained everything.'

'But how did Stewart find Mr Minelli?'

'Stewart was at home and he heard the shot and he noticed it was sort of muffled in a not-quite-right way. So out he goes. Sees inside the car and doesn't even open the door, just runs straight back inside and phones Hirsh.'

'Why didn't he phone the emergency services?'

Elmer smiled his big-toothed smile. 'You must remember, Matt, that Hirsh *was* the emergency services. He could always get there faster than some ambulance from Goat Bend and he was a lot more skilled than your average paramedic. 'Course Stewart did call 911, and 'course he called me, but first it was always Hirsh.'

'Who answered the phone?'

'You did. I'm not sure where your mom was.'

Matt tried to remember. There had been various occasions when emergency phone calls had come for Hirsh. He remembered dashing out into the yard, down the hill, up the hill, yelling his father's name.

'In fact, I seem to recall that Hirsh told me you brought him his medical bag. That was quick-thinking, Matt, you were quick. You took the call and grabbed the bag and found your father down the hill with it so he could get to Arthur fast through the yard.'

'I grabbed the bag,' echoed Matt mechanically. Of course it had not been a gun which weighed him down that day but its very opposite, emergency medical supplies. The bag had been difficult to carry. It was made of peeling old leather and it hurt his shins as it banged against them. As he ran through the woods, he had to shift its weight from right hand to left and back to right again. And there was someone else in the woods, someone else running down the hill, far over to the right.

'Now, when I come to think of it, you showed even more presence of mind,' added Elmer. 'Because I do believe one of the Minelli boys was over at your house when it happened. The littlest one, Steve, the one you were telling us was such a good friend. You took the call and you then sent him right home, making sure he didn't go down the yard by any route where he'd see Arthur's car. That was good thinking. A lot of kids would have blurted out everything before a single fact was known, but you didn't do that.'

Steve had been at the house. Matt and Steve had been playing inside together, and the phone had rung and then Matt had said, very carefully although he was looking all around for the medical bag, 'I have to go help my Dad right now, I'll see you later.' And later had turned out to be twenty-six years.

He had told Steve to take the short trail home and then he had dashed down the hillside at an acute angle to Steve's departure so that for a while they could see each other through the trees, and when Steve was lost from sight Matt could sense him a short distance away in the forest. Matt had headed down towards the log seat and found Hirsh and he had been surprised that Hirsh was not alone. Hilly was there. She had been out all day and Matt had not known she was back.

He had felt momentarily pleased to see his mother and pleased to see his parents sitting locked together, lovingly, on the seat, and he had experienced a brief reluctance to interrupt them. Then he had called his father and both parents had turned and he had seen sadness etched on their faces, even tears, and he wondered if they already knew what he was going to tell them.

He had blurted out his news and Hirsh had said something which Matt now remembered as 'I know'. And then Hirsh had got up slowly, taken the bag and moved off down the hillside. Matt had followed him. He had walked right past his mother without looking at her and without speaking to her. He had followed Hirsh towards the scene of the accident.

'You came too,' said Elmer. 'But your daddy sent you right back.'

Hirsh had told Matt to turn back but Matt had gone up the hillside only a little way, then he had peered through the trees at the red car, waiting, hoping to perceive some movement inside it. Stewart and Hirsh had walked up to the car and Hirsh had opened the door slowly, slowly. There had been the noise of an engine sometime, too, because suddenly there were voices and shouting and Elmer was there. Someone, maybe Elmer, perhaps Stewart, had looked up and seen Matt and yelled at him to go away and, sickened by what he had seen, he had been both reluctant and relieved to go.

'Arthur wasn't actually dead,' said Elmer. 'He'd lost consciousness, though. Your father almost saved him. I mean, almost. He did amazing work to keep him alive.'

'What did he do?' asked Matt. His own voice sounded far off. His stomach felt as though there were continents inside it rearranging themselves, mighty slabs of land rubbing against one another. He remembered the woodshed, when the fine spring light had filtered through the roof in arrows and illuminated the dust and he had told Hirsh about the Zoy case. He had asked, 'Did you ever kill anyone?' And Hirsh had said, 'Oh yes,' then he had turned and continued stacking wood.

'Well, I believe cardiac massage to start with. There was a lot of blood but I understand that he'd already established the bullet had gone right the ways through Arthur. Forensic found it afterwards in the back of the car. Now I do believe that your daddy put some kind of tube down Arthur's throat. I'm not sure because I was doing other things too, like shooing you away and turning around some traffic. Anyway, I knew Arthur was in capable hands but when I looked at him it was obvious from one glance he was sliding fast. Hirsh said he was stopping with the massage as it was making things worse. He said he thought the bullet had just skimmed the heart and then he sent Stewart for his kitchen knife and, Matt, I haven't seen anything like what your father did, not before or since.'

Matt felt nauseous, as though he and the old sheriff were floating together on some vast expanse of water, as though the wide wooden floor of the Lion's Paw Café was a raft riding the waves of a rough sea.

'He plunged the kitchen knife right into Arthur! He plunged it right in! God, Matt, if I'd been quicker and if it had been anyone but Hirsh, I would have arrested him. I never actually watched one man stab another right between the ribs before. Then he twisted the knife. Can you believe it?'

'No,' said Matt so quietly that probably Elmer didn't hear him.

'Blood came squirting out like a big red fountain and your dad stuck his finger right into the wound and I swear to God that within a minute, no less than a minute, I thought Arthur Minelli was going to live. He lost that bulgy look around his face and I was feeling his pulse and it came right back and I shouted, "You've saved him, Hirsh, dammit! I thought you were killin' him and you saved him!" Would you believe it took Goat Bend another forty-five minutes to arrive? By that time Arthur was fading again. Hirsh went with him in the ambulance. He said he died about halfway over there.'

People at other tables were listening openly now.

'Wasn't he a great doctor?' beamed Elmer. 'I mean, wasn't he just the best?'

Matt was silent. All his life he had heard what a wonderful doctor Hirsh was. When he had started to study medicine himself, it was with the knowledge that he could never, ever, be such a good doctor as Hirsh. But Mr Minelli had died. Hilly had died.

'If we'd been one mountain nearer to Goat Bend I'm prepared to bet that Arthur Minelli would have lived,' boomed Sheriff Turner. Matt wanted to reply but some great weight was anchoring his voice inside his body so it couldn't get to the surface.

'Well, of course, there was a police report into the death,' continued the old sheriff. 'It said what your daddy did was an incredible, even a foolhardy, thing for a family doctor to attempt. Is there some long medical word for it, Matt?'

Matt said, his voice husky, 'Mr Minelli's condition was an acute situation known as tamponade. If the bullet had grazed the heart it would have caused bleeding, so that every time

269

his heart beat, it squeezed more blood into the pericardial cavity. The cavity was filling up with blood and this was pressing against the heart. Dad was trying to release it by making a hole in the membrane around the constricting cavity.'

'Is that such a crazy thing for a family doctor to try?'

Matt winced. 'Because you could very easily stick the knife in too far. You could penetrate the heart and kill the patient. And most people would be so scared of cutting into the heart that they wouldn't push the knife in far enough. I can't believe that Dad got it right first time.'

'That's Hirsh,' said Elmer loudly 'That's Hirsh for you, the best doc around. Ever had to deal with it, Matt, this pericardial tam-thingummy?'

'Tamponade. Yes,' said Matt. 'At dressing stations during conflicts, I've done it once or twice.'

In war zones, where death stalked the wounded, it felt as though you had nothing to lose by trying pericardial relief, by trying anything. It was also something a cardiac surgeon might expect to do in a pristine operating theatre with anaesthetists and nurses and life-saving equipment to help him. But Hirsh, surgically inexperienced, with only a kitchen knife, had successfully tried it one September day by the still, silent waters of Arrow Lake.

'You manage it all right?' demanded Elmer.

Matt nodded.

'I managed but it's nerve-racking . . .' The first time, the scalpel had not been deep enough, although he had been successful at his second attempt. The next time he had tried it, months later, he had missed the pericardial cavity completely although once again he was subsequently successful.

'It was my job,' Elmer said, 'to break the news to the

family that, in spite of everything, Arthur had passed away. What a job. Who'd be sheriff? Matt, you haven't touched that pie.'

'You eat it, Sheriff,' said Matt. 'I just can't any more.'

When he had left the café he still did not head down the mountain. Instead he turned outside Macintyre's and slowly drove back on the road to Hirsh's house. Once again he stopped just before Stewart's place, swinging the car on to the trail where Arthur Minelli had died. The foliage had thickened as summer had deepened and now he saw that there was barely space for one car's length.

Matt sat still. He wound down the windows. He could see a hint of bright light through the trees: the lake, shining back at the sun. The afternoon's warmth had silenced the world. Even in the shade of the branches, no bird flew, no insect squeaked. No sound, no movement.

If Arthur Minelli had turned his car in here to shoot the coyote, he would probably have switched off the engine and opened the door before grabbing his gun. The gun must have been lying against the passenger seat in some way, the barrel pointing up, because Elmer had said that the bullet was later found in the back of the car. Maybe Mr Minelli had propped it against the gears.

Matt fetched a stick about the size of a rifle and tried, unsuccessfully, to prop the stick against the transmission. He moved the stick in a number of different positions. He sat in the driver's seat and leaned forward, like a man reaching for his gun, and found that it was almost impossible to position the stick so it pointed at his heart. Only if the driver laid the stick along the dashboard could the rifle shoot you convincingly in the heart, for instance if it fell. It was hard to imagine anyone driving with a loaded weapon lying along the dashboard. And that's what Steve had said. Steve had said being shot in the heart by mistake was sort of a difficult thing to do.

Matt got out of the car. Stewart would probably have arrived within two minutes of hearing the shot. He would have appeared from the corner of his land, right by the entrance to the track. He would have looked through the car windows and then run home to call Hirsh. It may only have been five minutes, ten at most, after the shot was fired, that Matt found Hirsh and Hilly sitting on the log seat. And Matt had proved that within five minutes of firing the shot, Hirsh could be up the hill and no longer gasping for breath.

The branches of the trees which overhung the trail seemed to engulf him. He pulled some leaves out of his hair. Twigs snagged at his clothes. As he tried to disentangle himself his movements were slow because sadness felt heavy and it limited him like joint pain. He turned back to the car and found a figure was standing right by it, a tall, lean figure which, for a crazy moment, Matt mistook for Arthur Minelli.

'Oh, hi. Matt, hi,' said Stewart with obvious relief when Matt emerged at his side. 'Is this your car?'

'I just parked here for a few minutes, Stewart, I hope that's okay.'

'Fine, fine. I get a little exercised about people parking here normally but I don't mind if it's you, Matt.'

'Stewart, this is the place where Arthur Minelli died? Right?' demanded Matt.

Stewart stared at Matt hard. His eyeglasses magnified his pale eyes. 'Well, yes it is,' he admitted. 'That's why cars here sort of spook me.'

'Why do you think he pulled the car over in this spot? I mean, there's almost no traffic on that road. He could have just left the car on the blacktop.'

Stewart sighed and looked thoughtful. He took off his

glasses. He had come from the present while, for the last fifteen minutes, Matt had been living twenty-six years ago. Matt's thoughts, his senses, had been in that other place, the past.

'Well . . .' said Stewart slowly. 'He saw something, I guess. Maybe a skunk or a coyote, because I know he was hoping to shoot the old coyote before he left for the town. I heard the rifle's report and came right out here and to this day I don't know how I could tell something was wrong. It was sort of muffled but only sort of. I guess it was just instinct brought me out. Couldn't right away work out where it had come from because the report went on for ever, ricocheting against the mountains. Took me a couple of minutes to find him.'

'Was the car about where mine is?'

'Just about.'

'How was he positioned, Stewart? Was he leaning over? Leaning as though he'd been reaching down for his gun?'

Stewart put on his glasses, swallowed and scratched his head.

'Hmm, well, no, he was slumped over the steering wheel, sideways against the door, as I remember it.' Stewart made not-remembering faces but Matt knew that he did remember, that this kindly man had probably relived the events of that day in his thoughts and dreams a thousand times.

'Was the car door open?' he asked.

'What?' Stewart took a step back. He took off his glasses again and began to clean them on his shirt.

'The car door, was it open? I thought he was getting out of the car when he set the gun off.'

'Well, no,' said Stewart. 'Everyone assumed he was shot reaching for his gun. But it must have been before he opened the car door.'

'Did you call my dad right away?'

'I didn't touch Arthur, I didn't open the door, I just turned and ran back to the phone. I knew that touching him could do more harm than good and I knew that if Hirsh could come right away, that was Arthur's best chance. You could always count on Hirsh, he was such a good doctor.'

Matt nodded mechanically at this mantra.

'So when Dad appeared . . . ?'

'The first thing he did was tell you to go back. You were behind him, you'd just got to the road, I think. We went up to the car and opened the door real slowly. Arthur fell a little and I held him while Hirsh moved the gun. He had to do it very, very carefully, in case it went off again. Actually, I later opened the gun and found there was no more ammo. It had done its work.'

'What was the position of the gun?'

Stewart shook his head. 'I don't remember that, Matt. I think it was leaning against him. I just remember I held Arthur while Hirsh ran around to the passenger side to get the gun and make it safe. Then he came back and we pulled Arthur out of the car and we laid him down, about where you're standing. Hirsh turned him over and said he reckoned the bullet had gone through the heart, he thought it had gone clean through and out the other side. And, if the bullet wasn't still inside Arthur, that meant there was hope. Then Hirsh began working. He worked real hard, kept the heart pumping, tried something terrifying with my kitchen knife, which, incidentally, I never used again. Elmer showed up during all this, I don't remember when, but I remember he thought Hirsh had saved him. I mean, at one point it looked like a miracle had happened. But I could see Arthur was a dying man. He died on the way to hospital.'

Matt stared at the ground where Hirsh had worked hard

to save the life of a man whom ten minutes before he might have tried to kill. It didn't make sense.

'Matt? Matt?' Stewart was saying. Matt looked at Stewart unseeingly. 'Matt, why are you asking all these questions?'

'I wanted to know what happened,' said Matt.

'It was such a terrible thing. You see, Arthur not only lost his life but he ruined a perfectly good heart. If he had been shot fatally in some other part of the body, well then, his heart could have been saved. It could have given a new life to some other person. So, in a way, being shot through the heart took two lives away.'

'Heart transplants were barely happening twenty-six years ago,' Matt pointed out. He wanted to get in the car now. He must have stepped backwards into the forest while Stewart had been talking because twigs were puncturing his earlobes and pulling at his hair and a big branch pummelled his leg. But Stewart wanted to talk hearts.

'That's true,' admitted Stewart thoughtfully. 'I guess what I'm saying, Matt, is that I just object on principle to people wasting good hearts.'

He started to talk excitedly about his research into his heart donor's identity.

'I think I've found her, Matt. Just this morning. After weeks of Internet research, I believe I've really discovered who she was. Soon I'll know all about her, all about her life.'

Matt shook his head. Twigs broke around his ears. 'She may not have wanted you to know all about her.'

Stewart's body looked rigid, locked into position. 'If you take someone's heart, you have to take the responsibilities which go with it.'

'Would you feel that way if they'd given you her kidney or her cornea? I mean, the heart's a big mass of pumping muscle, nothing more. Aren't you getting confused by all that extra emotional significance people give it?'

'Don't tell me,' muttered Stewart, 'that there's no such thing as a broken heart. It exists, believe me. Of course the emotional significance of the heart counts for something, Matt.'

'What about the secrets of the heart?' asked Matt.

Stewart shrugged. 'Love has no secrets,' he said.

Matt shook off the leaves and branches and twigs which seemed to be pinning him to the spot. He thanked Stewart for his help and got back into the car. Stewart stood in the still afternoon shadows at the roadside and watched Matt drive back towards the town. When he was around the corner, Matt reached for the stick he had used as a rifle and threw it from the car.

16

'You look tired,' said Denise, surveying Matt closely. 'And you've got leaves and twigs and things in your hair.'

Matt knelt down and let Austin destroy the evidence of his lakeside conversation with Stewart. When nature was all out of his hair, the child started to arrange the twigs in small piles on the living-room rug. He was wearing his pyjamas, which had tiny boats and trains all over them, and he looked cute. Whenever Matt saw him after even the briefest of absences, he was amazed by the bigness and roundness of Austin. When Austin wasn't there, Matt remembered him as a baby.

'I know something which used to relax you,' said Denise.

'So do I,' said Matt, looking at her hungrily. Denise laughed and went out of the room. Matt lay down on the rug and closed his eyes. He had been thinking so hard today that his head hurt and there were numb patches behind his eyes. Plus he felt the ache of unfamiliar exercise.

Austin murmured softly to himself. Matt could hear Denise opening the closet in the bedroom. Without her, the living room felt different, as though its molecules had been displaced by her absence. Each absence of a loved one has this effect, Matt thought, no matter how temporary the absence or how slight the displacement. When Hilly had died, Matt had felt for months the strangeness of each room. He wasn't sure that the molecules of their house in Salt Lake had ever satisfactorily redistributed themselves.

When Denise returned, she was holding her flute.

'I'm rusty,' she warned.

Matt looked at her with delight and at the flute as he would an old friend who had moved out of state.

'Why don't we see you more often?' he asked the flute.

Austin watched curiously as Denise organized mouth-pieces. When she began to play he stared at her. Matt climbed on to the sofa and Austin climbed on top of him, without taking his eyes off his mother, as if he wasn't sure the flute player really was Denise.

As the music flowed over him, Matt remembered something Elmer had said about elk. He had said that bull elk like to wallow in spring seeps, plastering themselves in mud. Matt felt like a bull elk right now, lying on the sofa with Austin lying on top of him, the music soaking into every pore of his body. When he got up he would be covered in the new, soft skin which the music had woven him and he would carry it around as long as he could.

He turned to watch Denise's face as intently as Austin did. She was concentrating. Her eyes were closed and a range of expressions he hardly recognized crossed her face. He remembered Hilly at the piano, how the music had also pulled her face into new shapes and how that had scared him: there were already too many Hillys. Maybe that was why Austin was staring at his mother now. But Denise, he thought contentedly as the music rose and fell, as it occupied his mind with its sudden intensity and then released him again, Denise was always reliably the same Denise. He closed his eyes again and allowed the intricacies of the music to engage his mind. Only when the notes had delivered him back to his own thoughts did he remember that he had promised to visit Clem.

'Do I have to go tonight?' he asked Denise as she put her

flute back into its case. He felt too tired and relaxed to get into a car and drive across town.

'I think Daddy would appreciate it.'

'What's worrying him?'

'I don't know. Really. I haven't asked. But I imagine he wants to discuss his medical notes with you.'

Matt sighed. He put Austin to bed and then took the car key off the hook.

'Promise me you won't be asleep when I get back,' he said to Denise and she laughed at him. When she laughed her cheekbones moved higher up her face. He kissed her.

The night receptionist at Mason House beamed at him and buzzed him in.

'Well, how nice of you to call in and see Clem this evening,' she exclaimed. Nice was an important word here. Most of the residents and all the staff were nice. When he had worked as locum right after Africa, where a fair proportion of his patients had been keen to murder one another, Matt had found the glowing white smiles and limitless good nature of the Mormon rest home unsettling, even unbelievable.

As he made his way to the second storey, Matt listened for the sounds of human life. People talking while they played cards, a loud TV, even water running through pipes because someone had just turned on a faucet. But Mason House was eerily silent.

He knocked, and a buzzer revealed that Clem had seen him on the monitor and was opening the door. Matt knew better than to hurry it. The buzzer sounded and then you had to wait for the door to swing open, slowly and mysteriously, of its own accord. When you were inside, it shut soundlessly behind you.

He walked into the apartment. It was, like many in Mason House, over-furnished. People moved into these two- or

three-bedroom apartments from big houses and they generally brought too much stuff with them. As a locum he had
learned to tread carefully whenever he walked inside the
rooms here, with their footstools and coffee tables scattered
around like landmines.

'Hi there,' called Clem's reedy voice. He was in bed and
Matt walked right into the bedroom just as though he were
a doctor on call.

'Thanks for coming over,' said Clem.

The large room was almost wholly absorbed by Clem's
enormous bed and wardrobe and armchair, all of which
looked immovable. Clem, sitting in the great bed in thick
pyjamas, was the only thing in here light enough for you to
pick up. He was so small he made Matt feel too big and too
strong, as though he might inadvertently hurt the old guy.

Clem said, 'Well, I just had to see you now that you've
read my notes.'

Matt wondered if his father-in-law was about to blame
his repeated sexual infections on public toilet seats.

'Because,' Clem went on, 'I know what you're going to
say, so you might as well say it. You might as well tell me
right now that the whole Liguria trip is off.'

Matt was so astonished that he sat down in the armchair
by the bed. 'I wasn't going to say that at all.'

'You must have come to the conclusion that I'm risking
my life. I mean, the flight, the pressure changes, the new
time zone, the weather?'

Matt was unprepared for this. 'Well, naturally the trip
will create pressures and strains on you which you aren't
used to . . .'

'Pressure enough to kill me?'

'No one can say that, Clem. Some people would be killed
by staying in Mason House all day.' Hirsh for one, Matt for

another. 'The change of air and stimulation are as likely to prolong your life as the strain is to end it.'

'I'm worried that this is all the most enormous risk, a terrible, terrible risk,' said Clem, and Matt wanted to ask if the old guy really thought he was going to live for ever but he said nothing.

'The more I think about it, the more daunting it seems,' Clem went on. 'You must have been amazed, when you read my notes, that I've even been contemplating it.'

Matt spoke slowly and carefully to hide a sudden excitement. The entire cancellation of the Liguria trip had unexpectedly become a possibility.

'It depends how much you want to go. If worrying about it outweighs the benefits then I guess you should stay here.'

'But Denise . . .'

'Denise is organizing this trip for you, Clem. If you feel it's too much, she'll be the first to understand.'

'Of course I want to go . . . but my heart . . . I've had some chest pains today.'

'Just today?'

'This weekend. It came on quite suddenly.'

'You should call Dr van Essen,' said Matt firmly.

'I'm beginning to feel this trip is very unwise and should be cancelled. I thought you were sure to agree with me after reading my recent medical history,' Clem said. He looked angry. He pulled the covers up over himself so that only his head was visible. It was easy, now he was cross, to discern the old man's face the way it used to be, before the angles slackened and the skin folded. You could imagine him delivering instructions, making decisions, bullying. Cleaning up, twenty-six years ago, on the Rosebay deal.

'I can agree with you to a certain point, Clem. Because the patient knows what's best in a case like this and if the strain is causing you concern then we should certainly call the trip off.'

'Because of my heart,' insisted Clem. 'We have to call it off because of my heart.'

'Well . . . because of your concerns about your heart.'

'Same thing,' cried Clem in a triumphant, high-pitched voice.

'Well—'

'Because of my heart problem,' the old man repeated with a smile of satisfaction. 'That's why I can't go. I'm so glad you've been honest, Matt, and didn't avoid breaking the bad news to me. Although it's come as quite a shock.'

Matt stood up. 'It's your heart and your decision,' he said.

'I'm basing my decision on your medical advice,' Clem announced happily. 'Will you tell Denise when you get home tonight? Tell her I put up a struggle but I finally had to accept that doctor knows best.'

Matt studied Clem's face. Clem had no difficulty meeting his eye. The old man had already started to believe his own version of events.

'Clem . . .' he said. 'Didn't you ever want to go to Liguria? Have you felt this way all along?'

Clem's eyes widened in disbelief. 'Of course I wanted to go. I still want to go. More than anything. A family holiday with Denise in the place Dora and I honeymooned all those years ago? A doctor to escort me? What could have been more wonderful? I'm devastated that you think we should cancel it.'

Matt, noting his relegation from son-in-law to family doctor, decided it was useless to challenge Clem's new truth. He said, 'Goodnight, Clem.'

He drove home wondering what the real reason was for Clem's sudden withdrawal from the holiday.

Denise was still awake, as promised. She was sitting at the kitchen table, making lists. Matt wasn't sure how to tell her the bad news. He expected her to ask why Clem had requested the visit tonight and then he planned to explain what had happened, but as usual he had underestimated her discretion, forgotten all the things she didn't talk about.

He opened a beer noisily and sat down beside her. 'Are those holiday lists?' he asked.

'No, that one's a shopping list. And this one's a list of people who said they wanted an extra music therapy session this summer. And this is a list of things I have to tell Rosetta. About Austin's food, that sort of stuff.'

'Oh.'

He took a gulp of beer and there was a silence. Matt coughed. He said, 'I had an interesting talk with Clem tonight.'

Denise looked up and smiled. 'Good,' she said. 'It's nice to know you two are getting along.'

He hoped she might ask what they had talked about, but, of course, she didn't. She returned to her lists.

'We discussed the Liguria trip,' said Matt. 'And he's very worried about it.'

She looked up again, sharply this time. Her hazel eyes darkened, as though she knew what was following.

'He hasn't indicated to me that he's worried about anything,' she said. There was a small note of suspicion in her voice.

'He's had some chest pains and he's very concerned that the trip might be too much for his heart.'

Denise raised her eyebrows. 'He is?'

She was alert now, like a forest animal which senses danger and looks all around for a predator.

Matt took her hand. 'This isn't going to be easy for you,

because you've put so much work in. He indicated that he'd prefer not to go to Liguria.'

Her hand, in his, was motionless. She stared at him. She did not move at all.

'Daddy? Daddy has said he doesn't want to go? Or you've managed to persuade him that he shouldn't?'

'No, no, it wasn't like that. I didn't do any persuading. He told me about his worries and finally I had to agree that if he was going to worry that much about it, then the benefits could be outweighed by the—'

But she was up now, on her feet, looking slimmer and taller than usual, her face thin with anger.

'You read five years' worth of medical notes and he changes his mind!'

'I read more than seventy years' worth of medical notes! But that has nothing to do with—'

'Seventy years!' cried Denise, as though Matt had struck out at her.

'The insurance company told the clinic I had to read them all so—'

'Did you ask Daddy if he minded?'

'No! I assumed the clinic had done that.'

Denise was ashen. Her cheeks were drained of their usual warm colour. She sat down again. Matt began to suspect that she must know what was in the notes but she made no further reference to them. When she spoke it was in a voice of slow, deliberate calm.

'I saw Daddy only a few days ago and he was as enthusiastic as ever about our trip. Lacy and Don Chelwell visited and he was telling them where we're going and what we're doing and . . . suddenly, you've read his medical history and he's decided that he's so worried he can't go! You must have said something to worry him . . .'

'Of course I didn't. Why would I do that?'

She stared at him. Her pupils were large. Her eyes seemed black.

'Because you don't want to go. You've made that clear since the beginning.' Her voice came breathily, its measure missing, drained of its usual tones, its musicality absent. 'You must have misused your knowledge of his history in some way . . .'

'Misused my knowledge!' yelled Matt, jumping to his feet.

As the argument progressed, Matt realized that it was their first. There had of course been differences in the past, but this level of anger and accusation was something new. Only the sense of his own rightness and the other party's unfairness was familiar. When he heard himself telling Denise that she was railroading her father into a trip he didn't really want to take, he decided it was time to stop.

This was his first row with Denise, but there had been other women and other rows in the past, and he had over-heard arguments between his parents or other couples and it seemed to him that they all followed the same ugly format, they all tasted the same, as if there were a table of sour food somewhere, ready and waiting, to which people kept returning when they were hungry enough.

Denise withdrew from the argument too by leaving the room, and the molecule displacement became acute. Matt's body felt numb and cold, as though it had been snowing for a while and he'd only just noticed.

When he had turned out the lights and checked all the doors were locked, he moved cautiously into the bedroom. Denise was lying still and breathing evenly in the dark. He did not know if she was already asleep but, encased in her own silence, she was unapproachable.

He lay between the cold sheets thinking how much she

meant to him, and he realized she was everything. They were that ball of love and complication, a family. Matt, Denise and Austin. Hirsh was family too, but he was old and in a few years' time he would leave for ever. Matt's future was with Denise and Austin and, although he knew this was almost impossible, with any more children they might have.

Denise, of course, had Clem, and she had more family besides. She had her three elder sisters back east. When Clem and her mother had converted and moved to Salt Lake, the sisters' conversion had proved short-lived. As soon as they were old enough they had headed east, where they married out, drank coffee and alcohol and didn't observe Family Home Night on Mondays. They lived many miles apart but if you drew a line between New York and Chicago it would pass right by each of their houses. In the weather satellite pictures the same snow fell on all of them. They were linked and Denise was not. After their mother's death they had urged Denise to join them, but she and Clem had already developed a closeness, perhaps a dependency, which had kept Denise in Salt Lake.

Matt rolled over on his side so his back was turned to Denise. He couldn't hear her breathing now.

The sisters were family, they remembered birthdays and offered childcare advice, but they were different. They harboured an eastern superiority to life out west and on their rare visits they took no trouble to hide their disdain. No, Denise was almost as alone as Matt and yet they had argued and were lying silently, angrily, alongside each other.

He rolled again and was going to reach out for her but by now it was clear that Denise was asleep and dreaming. Matt lay waiting for sleep to come to him, too, but instead he became angry with Clem, who had obviously decided for some reason of his own not to go to Liguria and had thus detonated Matt's argument with Denise. Worse, the old man would almost certainly tell Denise that Matt had advised him not to go, since he seemed unable to take responsibility himself for the cancellation.

Anger is the enemy of sleep and it was many hours before Matt slept. When he did, it seemed to him that the alarm rang almost instantly.

17

On Friday after work, Matt picked up Troy from his office. The city was different when summer was at its height. It had nothing to do with the early-evening sun or the leaves or the tourists strolling around the temple or the light clothes he glimpsed as he drove by the windows of ZCMI. You could see it in the way people walked. Shoulders were rounded, steps lazy.

Matt waited, double-parked, outside Troy's office, which was just two blocks down from the temple. Across the road, he recognized the Rosebay Building. It was tall enough so that Matt, from the driver's seat, could not see the top. It was faced in pink rock and its magisterial, classical style suggested that only serious, honest and important business was conducted inside.

The passenger door opened and Troy folded his body into the car. He was dressed immaculately in a suit and tie.

'Sorry I'm late,' he said. 'Court all day.'

His voice sounded metallic. Troy's voice always sounded that way after a day in court. Jarvis said that's because you could only get through eight hours of Salt Lake City's white-collar crimes by turning yourself into a robot. Troy, who worked out almost daily, did often arrive on Fridays with his body stiff as though it had a shell all around it but Matt had noticed his taut muscles start to soften with the first cigarette. Even the skin on his bald head, usually stretched tightly, seemed to slacken a little with the first inhalation.

'You can smoke in my car if you open the window,' Matt offered.

Troy looked at his watch. 'I don't smoke until after seven p.m,' he said. 'What's this thing Jarvis wants us to see tonight? Not a summer blockbuster, I hope.'

'It might have been a blockbuster in Japan,' said Matt.

Troy groaned. 'He's dragging us off to a Japanese movie? Don't tell me it's in Japanese.'

'It's in Japanese.'

They found Jarvis at an outdoor bar near the movie theatre and when they arrived it was easy to locate him. Cigarette smoke rose only from his table. It formed a white, vertical column like an ethereal flagpole. His hair was sticking out from the back of his baseball cap and his amorphous body was spilling over the edge of the chair.

'Seen what happened to your friend Steve's exhibition?' he asked Matt. 'They've finally closed it. For heaven's sake, don't these newspapers understand that when they holler so much about something they just give it publicity?'

'It got some good reviews,' said Matt.

'Huh!' yelled Jarvis. Troy looked at his watch and then placed a cigarette on the table in front of him.

'It's ten minutes before seven,' he explained to Matt.

Jarvis was yelling, 'I mean, good reviews, I don't believe it, good reviews who from?'

'Sylvester Suzuki,' said Matt.

'Sylvester Suzuki!' roared Jarvis. 'Thinks little, knows nothing.'

'He says that Steve's pictures are a major contribution to the debate between art and taboo.'

Jarvis whooped derisively. Troy made a sound like the crash of metal you hear when you drive past a garage with the window down. Matt recognized this as Troy's guffaw but he could see that it had startled people at neighbouring tables.

The waiter appeared and Matt ordered a glass of wine.

'I'm sorry that state liquor laws prevent me serving wine without food, sir,' said the waiter mechanically. 'This establishment is classed as a restaurant and not a tavern and so you have to order something to eat and I have to give you this.'

He laid a card in front of Matt informing him of the dangers to himself and others of liquor consumption.

'I forgot that law,' admitted Matt. 'I don't usually order wine. You can bring me some pretzels.'

'That's not enough to satisfy the state liquor laws, sir. Can I suggest the bruschetta?'

Matt nodded but Jarvis thundered, 'When are we non-Mormons going to rise up as a body and object to the insane restrictions imposed upon us by the Latter Day Scourge?'

The waiter looked nervous and scampered inside the bar. Matt wondered if it was a coincidence that neighbouring tables were emptying now.

'We aren't,' said Troy. 'We're just going to order bruschettes because it's easier.'

Matt knew Jarvis would eat all the bruschette he objected to so strongly and indeed, as soon as they arrived, he grabbed one and began to chew on it savagely.

'Denise didn't want to come tonight, huh?' he asked Matt. He had broken with protocol to suggest that Matt invite Denise to join them for the movie, guessing that she might enjoy it more than either Matt or Troy.

'I didn't ask her,' admitted Matt. 'It wasn't that kind of week. The temperature in our house is down by about fifty degrees.'

'Should save on the air conditioning,' said Troy, placing the cigarette between his fingers but not lighting it.

'Are you telling me,' said Jarvis, 'that you two lovebirds have had A Fight?'

Matt nodded miserably. Since the argument, whenever he spoke to Denise, her replies had been civil but icy. When he had reached out for her in bed she had not responded. He thought she was being unfair. He hated this cold anger. He felt isolated by it.

Jarvis snatched at another mouthful of bruschetta while Matt explained.

'So,' asked Troy. 'Is the old guy really too ill to travel?'

'Well, I wouldn't recommend it. On the other hand, I wouldn't try to stop him,' said Matt. 'But he's already assured Denise that the trip was cancelled on my advice. And I can't argue with that unless I call her father a liar.'

'Which he is,' said Troy.

'He believes his own lies,' said Matt. This seemed to him a more than generous assessment.

Jarvis looked thoughtful. He chewed noisily. 'Hmm. So what's going on here? Why did he really want the trip cancelled?'

'I think I know,' said Troy unexpectedly.

They looked at him but it was seven o'clock and he made them wait while he slowly lit his cigarette and inhaled deeply. Matt watched satisfaction spread over Troy's features. Jarvis watched too. 'You should try it some time,' he told Matt.

But Matt was impatient: 'Well?' he demanded. 'Why's Clem cancelling the trip?'

Troy exhaled slowly. 'He can't afford it any more.'

Matt snorted with laughter. Everyone knew that Clem was more than comfortably off. You only had to look at the Rosebay Building to see that.

'Has the stock market taken a humungous dive?' asked Jarvis.

'No. But Dr Smith's Slimtime has gone belly-up. Finally and officially it breathed its last a week ago.'

Matt stared at Troy. 'So?'

'Clem might have had a lot of money tied up in Slimtime,' said Troy.

'Yeah,' said Jarvis, who had long ago detected Matt's dislike for Weslake. 'Someone had to pay for all those hideous blue and white cans, someone had to pay for lantern-jawed Weslake to smile greasily across our TV screens.'

It was just like Jarvis to relieve you of the burden of disliking someone. Jarvis would do your disliking for you and even, out of sheer loyalty, give you an upgrade to hatred.

'When did Clem change his mind?'

'Sunday. But he wanted to speak to me last Friday.'

Troy gave a smile of satisfaction. 'There you are. It happened last Friday. That's the day he became a poorer man.'

Matt gave a low whistle. 'You think Clem was backing Weslake?'

'Didn't Denise invest in the company?' demanded Troy.

Matt reddened a little. He admitted that he didn't know.

Troy said, 'Let me tell you what people are saying downtown. The FDA decided that Weslake's claims for the product were unsubstantiated and based on spurious medical evidence. Slimtime closed this week and a number of small investors have lost out and one large-scale private investor in particular. Rumour has it that this investor was family.'

'The Smith family, probably,' said Jarvis. 'They're Mormons, they must average at least six to a family and they go back generations. That's about two hundred handsome, smiling lantern-jawed Smiths every fifty years or so . . . that's a lot of lantern-jawed investors.'

Troy inhaled once more. 'Maybe it's a Smith,' he said. 'But I think it's Clem.'

'If you're right that Clem's lost a fortune, why doesn't he just tell us?' said Matt.

Nobody could answer that. Matt remembered the psychiatrist's report on the young Clem again. The document had talked about Clem trying to exercise control over the world. Maybe Clem, using his money, had tried to exercise control over Weslake.

Jarvis and Troy started to talk about an exhibition in Baltimore. Jarvis had wanted to go but Baltimore was unable to provide parking for Arnie within walking distance of the gallery.

'It's discriminatory!' yelled Jarvis. 'It discriminates against truck drivers who want to look at pictures!'

Maybe Clem had held a controlling interest in the company and had used this as a means of controlling Weslake, and maybe Denise had known nothing about it. In this case, Clem would certainly hide the reason for the trip's cancellation. Matt tried, with difficulty, to imagine the successful Weslake Smith as Clem's puppet.

Troy was saying, 'So you had to miss the exhibition?'

'Are you kidding me? I don't miss exhibitions. I parked right outside the gallery and since it was all glass there were reflections of Arnie on some of the pictures!'

'I'm sure that added a whole new dimension to the show.'

'See, wherever you park, you can bet that some bozo in a uniform's going to try to ticket you. So know what I do when this bozo starts walking round and round Arnie? I come running out of the gallery and I'm looking miserable. I say there's some idiot installation art going in there which involves the use of chemicals and I have a truckload of the antidote and the fire department's asked me to stand by for thirty minutes until the installation's complete. God, I am so goddam smart.'

Jarvis congratulated himself with another cigarette.

Troy looked impressed. 'Law enforcement agencies can thank their lucky stars that you never decided to become a master criminal.'

Matt remembered how Stewart, when he talked about the human heart, had said that love has no secrets. Clem loved Denise yet Matt had discovered he kept many secrets from her. Denise loved Matt but she guarded her secrets too.

'And,' said Jarvis, 'the uniform gets real sympathetic. He says, poor you, you got to look at that crap art stuff for half an hour!'

Stewart thought taking on the ownership of someone's heart licensed him to intrude into her life, as though her heart entitled him to her secrets. Once Matt might have been sympathetic but now he was learning that Stewart was wrong. Love has many secrets.

On the way to the movie theatre the others asked Matt about his preparations for Hirsh's hunting trip. He was disappointed that they had been as enthusiastic about it as everyone else. Jarvis, who would never dream of hunting anything larger than a Big Mac, was always saying it was a wonderful idea and that Hirsh was a great old guy.

'I have to train,' Matt told them gloomily. 'I've been running every morning this week.'

He had hoped that Denise might voice objections to this regime since a similar one had led to Weslake's demise but the new, icy Denise had registered nothing more than indifference.

'Training! Great! Training's good for you,' enthused Jarvis, who had never trained for anything ever.

At this hypocrisy, Troy gave a mechanical groan, like a car starting. He told Matt, 'You should run up the hill behind the temple to the State Capitol Building.'

'I already have,' said Matt proudly. 'I'm doing it a couple of times a week.'

'I used to do that every morning,' Troy said, 'but . . . well, something's not right with me at the moment. Next time we meet, I'll have to ask you to check my heart rate and palpate my liver.'

It was Jarvis's turn to groan. Matt, who had investigated numerous phantom illnesses for Troy over the years, said, 'What makes you think there's something wrong with your liver?'

'It sort of hurts when I lie in bed at night.'

'Sort of. I see. Uh huh. Where exactly is your liver, Troy?'

Troy put a hand high on his belly, wincing slightly as though this were painful. The hand was certainly on his liver. Matt hadn't been able to catch him out since Troy had insisted his appendix was bursting while pointing to his left side.

They had reached the movie theatre. It was a small art-house theatre and its doors had only just been opened for the movie. A line of people was shuffling inside. In the line, Matt saw Steve. He detected in himself an instant and reprehensible urge to avoid his old friend but before he even had time to stifle it, Steve had seen him.

'Hey, guys, hey, Matt,' he said.

Jarvis greeted him solemnly. 'Congratulations on your closure.'

'Thanks,' said Steve. 'I'm reopening in two weeks in New Mexico.'

'That's great, Steve,' said Matt. He moved away with Troy and Jarvis to join the end of the line but Steve put a hand on his arm to arrest him. He said in a low voice, 'Did you find out anything yet?'

'Well . . .' said Matt. 'Only a few details. Nothing helpful.'

'Facts are just what I want! Are you free for a sandwich on Monday?'

Matt paused as though thinking. Then he said, 'Go to the cafeteria at twelve-thirty and I'll try to get down there.' He joined the others at the end of the line.

'I can't believe all these people want to spend a hot summer's night watching a movie in Japanese,' Troy was saying miserably.

'They know it's going to be a night to remember,' Jarvis was assuring him.

Matt thought that he could probably expect to see Steve at a lot of the art-house events which Jarvis always dragged them along to. He felt unenthusiastic about seeing Steve on Fridays when he was with his friends. He felt unenthusiastic about seeing Steve at all. Searching for the truth about the Minelli death was one thing when he had believed himself culpable. It was another if Hirsh had been involved.

When they got inside the dark theatre, Matt did not look around for Steve but he nevertheless caught sight of him, a few rows back from the seats Jarvis chose for them. Matt felt Steve smiling at him in the dark.

'How was the movie?' asked Denise when he got home. It was the first interest she had shown in him all week.

'Very good, Jarvis was right to insist that we went. Even Troy had to admit that Jarvis was right.'

Denise said, 'I want to be friends again, Matt.' And she walked right over to him and put her arms around him and pushed herself up against him. She was no longer a stalactite. Her body was soft and yielding.

He enveloped her in his arms and it felt good, this physical contact, this warmth, this wife.

'I don't understand why you were so mad at me,' he said.

'I thought you'd read Daddy's notes and . . . misused them in some way.'

He drew back from her, offended. She reached out to him once more.

'Now don't start again . . .'

But his sense of injustice, suppressed all week, was reasserting itself.

'Why would I do something so mean and unprofessional? Listen, Denise, it was Clem who wanted the trip cancelled, not me. He was the guy who called to ask me over while I was reading his notes, he was the guy who insisted I went over on Sunday. I didn't have anything urgent to say to him.'

'Okay,' she said soothingly, stroking his shoulders. 'Okay, Matt, I believe you. My father doesn't have a halo, I'm well aware of that, I've been aware of it for a long time.'

He looked at her closely. Did she know something of the drink and whores in Clem's past?

'It's just that one day Daddy was wildly enthusiastic about Liguria and the next he wasn't going and it seemed to me that you must have changed his mind. I thought you'd used his medical notes to . . . Anyway, I understand everything now. It was obvious. I should have worked it out before.'

She pushed her head into his chest and he stroked her fine hair and wondered what was obvious that she should have worked out before. If the demise of Dr Smith's Slim-time had changed Clem's mind, had Denise known about Clem's involvement in the company all along? This was the time to ask her, when she was being open and loving, but now they were moving towards the bedroom and the moment to talk about Weslake had, as usual, been lost.

Later, they lay in bed talking softly. Matt felt as though the last few days had been missing from his life, although it was only Denise's affection which had been missing. She told him what Austin had said and done and Matt talked about work. But as he talked he became aware that something was wrong. The house felt wrong. He paused and listened and realized that the background hum was too loud for the fridge and its register too low for the air conditioning. In an instant he realized that there was a car right outside, its engine running softly and evenly, and in the same instant he was out of bed and tearing back the drapes.

'Honey, what's going on?' asked Denise, clearly alarmed by his speed and urgency. 'Are you expecting someone?'

It was Belinda Lampeter next door, manoeuvring inexpertly into her garage. He smiled at himself and got back into bed and closed his arms around Denise. He wanted to ask her if she had seen a red car around. But he knew that if it wasn't already there, just talking about it could introduce it to her life.

'No,' he said. Denise was not satisfied.

'I can feel your heart beating. It's beating in Morse code. Dot dot dot dash dash dot . . . it's saying . . . yes, I do believe it's telling me that you thought you heard someone because you were expecting to hear someone.'

He tried to sound soothing. 'Denise, who on earth would I be expecting late on a Friday night?'

She sighed. There was silence. Then she said, 'When you're working late, when you're out with the guys, especially when you're running, I stay busy. I mean, I get on with things. I don't actively worry about you. But all the time some part of me is anticipating a ring at the doorbell.'

He waited without moving, almost without breathing. When she did not speak, he prompted her: 'Because that's what happened when Weslake died?'

'You only have to experience it once. After that, for the rest of your life, anyone you love just has to walk out of the house and you're ready for that doorbell again. You're ready to answer it and find the police officers. They're standing there with this look on their faces. Sympathy, all mixed up with misery because they're about to give you bad news.'

Matt said softly, 'What were you doing? When they rang?'

Denise shook her head into the darkness. He couldn't see her now but he could feel her shaking her head to free herself from pain, like a dog shaking off water.

'Oh, I was already worried, he was so late. I mean, not at first. I came home from work and everything seemed normal. Weslake . . .' She spoke his name clearly but strangely, with the unfamiliarity of a word often thought but rarely uttered.

'Weslake wasn't there but I assumed he was at a Church meeting. He had some onerous new post in the stake and he was always at meetings. I thought he'd been running as usual and then gone right out again to a meeting and that he'd soon be back. I fixed the meal and he didn't come. I started to get mad at him for not leaving a note or phoning or switching on his cellphone. Finally I ate alone. He still didn't come. I was really mad now, but mixed with anxiety. I called the office. Of course no one was there. I didn't want to phone people to ask if they knew where he was. It looks sort of . . . well, you know. So I didn't call anyone. I just cleaned up a bit, did some laundry, the usual kind of things, but all the time I was waiting. I was getting madder and madder. Then I realized that if he'd been running and come home and showered and gone out, well, his running gear would be in the laundry. It wasn't. That was the point where anxiety overtook anger. I went out to look for him. I drove around the streets where he usually ran but it was dark and I didn't see anyone. I didn't think of going to Yellow Creek. I don't know why he went to run at Yellow Creek that night.

When I got back I was sure he'd be home. But he wasn't. I decided I'd have to call his family, call around no matter what people thought. But by now I had this pit in my stomach and I knew something was wrong. A lot of crazy things went through my head. I went to pick up the phone. But the doorbell rang when I was standing right there in the hallway.'

Her voice was tight now, tight like some stringed instrument. She was speaking in a monotone. She fought for breath. He could see her eyes in the dark. The pupils did not move. Her body did not move.

'I went to the door and there were two police officers standing there and then I knew. I put my hand over my eyes so I couldn't see the expressions on their faces and I said, "Oh God, no." And one of them said, "Are you the wife of Dr Weslake Smith?" And then they came into the house. They said they had some news and asked me if I wanted to sit down. I said, "Just tell me, just tell me what's happened." And they asked me to sit down again but I was sort of frozen. I couldn't even close the door, they had to do it. I said, "He's dead, right? Weslake's dead." And one of them nodded and I felt the breath go out of me. So finally, standing right there in the hallway, they told me. They said, "Ma'am, your husband was running in Yellow Creek Forest when it appears he was hit by a car. The driver of the car did not stop. Your husband was found on the blacktop. He was already dead." And I said, "No, no, he's not dead, he's just hurt, he can't be dead, I'll go pick him up now." But the other one said, "Ma'am, I have to tell you that your husband's body has already been moved to the police morgue."'

Denise stopped talking. She was crying now. Sobs were shaking her whole body, her face was wet, her body was wet, the pillow was wet. Matt fetched a towel from the bathroom. Tissues were not enough for this pool of tears.

When she had stopped crying and his arms were wrapped tenderly around her, she said, 'They asked a lot of questions. They took a look at my car. I showed them where Weslake had hit a deer and I showed them the deer meat. They were checking up on me, they had to. They checked up on everyone who knew him. But they were sure it was just a stranger who knocked into him, panicked, and drove right away. The report said he'd been hit from the front. He would have died almost immediately.'

'From the front? So he must have seen . . .'

'He must have seen the driver. They must have looked right at each other,' Denise said. She began to sob again and this time it seemed to Matt that nothing would arrest her tears until she finally fell asleep.

18

On Monday, Jon Espersen stepped into Matt's office. 'Coming down for a sandwich?' he asked.

Matt declined but felt miserable. In the cafeteria his head of department would shortly see that Matt had turned down his invitation in order to eat lunch with Steve.

'I can get you something downstairs,' offered his secretary five minutes later. 'I'm going right now.'

'I'm going too,' said Matt, looking at his watch. It was twelve-thirty. 'I'm meeting someone.'

'I'm not eating down there because if I do I'll give way to a double chocolate brownie with vanilla cream topping. I'm just going to pick up some apple and low-fat cottage cheese and get right out of there,' she said happily. 'I hate to boast but I've already lost five pounds.'

Matt was pretty sure her diet had something to do with the bald moron in Buildings Admin, who seemed to drop by the office at least twice a day carrying out spurious checks on the partition walling or searching for faults in the air filters.

'You looked nice the way you were before,' he said but she shook her head.

'I have at least another eight pounds to go,' she said firmly.

The busy, noisy cafeteria was a vast underground space but the moment he arrived Matt sighted Steve as though there was no one else in the room. Steve saw him too and waved. Matt stood in line with his secretary to buy his sandwich and coffee and his secretary said in an undertone, 'Is that the guy you're meeting?'

'Yes,' said Matt.

'He's a cleaner.'

'I know.'

'He's the cleaner they want to sack. He took these photos—'

'I know, I saw them.'

'The hospital got his exhibition closed down and now he's going to reopen in Hawaii or somewhere—'

'New Mexico.'

'Anyway, the hospital's trying to get that stopped too. And, they've given him notice for breaking the terms of his contract and invading patient privacy. He's contesting it and they're having arbitration. How come you're meeting him?'

'I knew him when we were kids.'

His secretary was amazed. 'Are you serious?'

'My whole family knew his whole family.'

His secretary looked thoughtful and Matt knew that she was remembering Hirsh, who had actually, on one of his rare trips down to the city, made a brief visit to the department. Matt's colleagues had been friendly, a few had even recalled encountering Hirsh as a doctor. Hirsh, for some reason, had been a big success with all the secretaries. Matt could tell from the surprise on his secretary's face that she didn't think Steve Minelli came from the kind of family which would be friends with Hirsh's family.

'They moved and I didn't see him for years. Now he's just sort of appeared in my life again,' said Matt.

'A lot of people think he's really weird,' the secretary said in an undertone. 'I mean, spooky weird. Keri in Hygiene Resources Admin says that he doesn't blink. So after about two and a half minutes she starts blinking for him. She can't stop herself. She has to keep pretending she has something in her eye.'

'I never noticed that he doesn't blink. And he's not especially weird,' said Matt. But when his secretary had gone back upstairs and he had joined Steve at the table, he wondered if she might be right. Steve was sitting stiff and white-faced. He greeted Matt, then right away demanded, 'So, what happened when you went up to your pa's?'

Matt unwrapped his sandwich. He condensed Elmer's, Stewart's and his father's versions of Mr Minelli's death into one narrative. The shot, the phone call, his father's arrival at the scene. He described Hirsh's attempts to save Mr Minelli in some detail, explaining what tamponade was and how brave and clever Hirsh had been to try pericardial relief. He made the knife wound it required sound like a surgical incision rather than the stabbing force which he knew to have been necessary.

Steve listened intently throughout. Then he started to ask the same questions Matt had asked, about the position and angle of the gun in the car.

'No one seems to remember that exactly,' said Matt. He didn't want to tell Steve how he had parked where Arthur Minelli had parked and how he had mimed the whole event. 'But personally I suspect that the gun was on the dashboard. Your father might have put it there if he'd thought that he needed to grab it suddenly. Then it fell to the floor and that's maybe when it fired.'

'Was a car window open?' Steve demanded. 'Someone could have shot him through the window.'

Matt munched on his sandwich. It didn't taste of anything.

'With his own gun?' he asked. 'I don't think your dad would have handed his gun to someone so they could shoot him.'

'If it was someone he knew well, he might have had some other reason to hand them the gun,' said Steve. 'And how much did they know about ballistics twenty-six years ago? I mean, did they know enough to check that the bullet came from Dad's Remington Mountain and not some other gun?'

Matt shrugged. His knowledge of forensics had at that time been limited to information gleaned from the Hardy Boys.

'I didn't ask if there was a window open,' he admitted. 'But Steve . . . did anyone have a good reason to shoot your father?'

Steve nodded enthusiastically. 'Maybe plenty,' he said. 'He was a very successful businessman. I mean, have you ever looked at the Rosebay Building downtown? It's huge and the design is beautiful. It's a classic, it looks like some of the great buildings from antiquity. Some folk say it's among the finest twentieth-century architecture in the whole state. Now, a lot of people were interested in that building and if my dad had lived to sign on the deal he would have been a rich man. When he died, some other people probably got rich. Plus there were things going on in his personal life . . .'

He looked significantly at Matt and Matt looked away at once because it was clear from the look that Steve knew about his mother's affair with Mr Minelli. Matt felt the same annoyance he had felt watching Hilly in the home movies. She was an exhibitionist who demanded constant attention. She should never have given up her career onstage as a musician. Instead, she had come to Salt Lake where she was always looking for something, and her search had brought her to the unsuitable Arthur Minelli and, inevitably, grief, grief which was resurfacing twenty-six years later as though she had handed them all a time-bomb.

'I don't know what else I can do,' Matt said. 'I asked everybody who was involved for information . . .'

'Your dad sure did try hard to save Pa's life,' said Steve. Matt looked at him again and realized that his secretary and Keri in Hygiene Resources Admin were right, Steve rarely blinked.

'I mean,' added Steve, 'he used desperate measures.'

'It was very courageous,' agreed Matt. 'Probably I wouldn't personally dare to try relieving tamponade with a kitchen knife.'

'Maybe he guessed that someone had tried to kill Pa. And it was very important to him that Pa didn't die. Because your dad didn't want that person accused of murder.'

Matt stared at Steve. 'What do you mean?' he asked. He was tired of veiled references. He wanted Steve to say outright what his suspicions were.

'Like I told you. Your dad guessed who had tried to kill Pa. And for that person's sake he was doing his best.'

Matt shook his head. 'Dad was a terrific doctor. If someone was sick or needed help, he did everything he could to save them. He didn't look for reasons.' He heard his own voice, brittle, perhaps fainter than usual.

'Maybe you can talk to him about it . . .' suggested Steve. His body didn't move, nor did his face, but his eyes had widened.

'It's hard to talk to my dad about that kind of stuff.'

'It won't be hard when you're hunting together. Around the campfire, it won't be hard.'

Denise had said it was easier to talk around the campfire. Was that why the men of Utah set off on these hunting pilgrimages every fall? To exchange confidences around the campfire?

'Where are you going to hunt?' asked Steve. He was

adopting that enthusiastic tone with which practically everyone talked about Matt's trip, except for Matt. Now, though, Matt felt relieved to talk about hunting instead of the Minelli death. Steve's words had left him feeling hot and uncomfortable. He didn't want to examine them too closely. He didn't want to think about what Steve was implying.

'Has the old guy decided just where you're going yet?' Steve was asking now.

'Someplace in the middle of nowhere,' Matt said. 'I'm not sure where it is but it's very topographical.'

'Are you hoping for a three-hundred-point trophy muley?'

'I'm just hoping to get out alive. Dad's hoping to bag an elk.'

'Elk!' cried Steve. 'Elk! Wow! Elk!'

'Why does everyone react that way when I tell them we're hunting elk?' asked Matt drearily.

'An elk's like a prize: you have to win it. First, you need rain. You need rain to green everything up. That brings the big old bull elk out of the forest to loiter around women. And it makes his trail a whole lot easier to follow. And then, remember, he can hear. He can hear you better than you can hear yourself, so don't even breathe. And we've already talked about how well they can smell.'

'Pine sap,' said Matt promptly. 'I have to go scrape pine sap off the trees and use it for deodorant.'

Steve told a few hunting stories. He talked about tracking elk and wounding elk but mostly his stories were about killing elk.

'But you and your old pa won't catch a running elk. I mean, the elk won't stop all day if you scare him. So what you have to do is, you have to scout him and then ambush him. I mean, kill him as soon as you get a clean shot. Connect. Don't stand there staring at him. That's what some guys do. They stare at the elk for fifteen seconds and that's about fourteen seconds too long. Have that gun ready and connect. Have it on your mind all the time: I'm here to kill the elk.'

'Right,' said Matt.

Steve once again offered equipment but Matt assured him he already had more than enough. He told Steve about his fitness training and the Hunter Education course he was doing soon at a local high school. Steve greeted each piece of news with delight.

'How about target practice?' he asked as they got up to go.

'Well,' admitted Matt, 'I don't actually have a gun yet. Dad's sorting that one out.'

When they parted in the hallway near the General Surgical offices, Steve turned to him.

'Thanks for all those questions you asked for me, Matt, I appreciate it. Everything that helps me sweep up the past and tidy it away means a lot to me. Would you try to find out more? I'd like to know more. I'd like to know what your father knows.'

It seemed to Matt that Steve was still a child, eleven years old, trapped in the past, battling to understand an adult would which he could not control.

'I'll do my best,' he promised.

When he got home, Denise suggested that he take a few days off work.

'Now we're not going to Liguria we can take a vacation this summer. And I think you need one. I think this tribunal thing is worrying you more than you're saying.'

'No, oh no,' lied Matt. 'I'm not worried at all.'

But Denise carried right on. 'We could stay here but we could go out every day, hiking in the Wasatch if we felt like it. And we could go visit Hirsh. I'd like to swim in Arrow

Lake and I'll bet Austin would too, and I could see those home movies at last. Oh, and we could take picnics and things.'

Matt hesitated. 'I'm not sure when I could take time off . . .'

'You must be able to find a few days. It's glorious weather, the wild flowers are amazing right now and you need a break.'

'We can't hike with Austin.'

'We get a backpack for him and he falls asleep in it.'

'He's not such a baby any more. He's always running around now.'

'We'll let him run around a little in the mountains and then we hike through the fresh air and he falls asleep right away and it will be like hiking alone together.'

Matt remembered again the summer of Denise's pregnancy, how hiking in the mountains had been such a lyrical, joyful experience. Denise had been almost transcendentally calm and happy and gradually Matt, who was still settling back into America and St Claudia's, had begun to feel the same way for the first time in years. He remembered how they spoke little and walked far, how there had been a sort of perfection in the rotundity of Denise's belly. When they stopped to make love in some green expanse of valley, the mountains seemed to cradle them like a secret. Afterwards they looked up at the white, jagged peaks and the blue, blue sky and these colours had a new intensity as if the rest of Matt's life was in monochrome.

The following day he arranged to take some time off work.

'Good,' said Jon Espersen approvingly. 'You need a break. Aren't you seeing the lawyer about the Zoy case this week? Want me to join you?'

309

'No,' said Matt. 'I'm sure it's just a formality.'

The lawyer's office turned out to be in the Rosebay Building. Matt stood outside on the street admiring the Rosebay's pale pink face, the classical columns at its entrance with their capitals of flowers, leaves and fruit, and the elaborate architraves over each window.

'The front elevation is supposed to be based on the Treasure House at Petra in Jordan,' the lawyer told him. 'Unfortunately it was just like the Treasure House on the inside too: bare to the point of dereliction. I should know, I've been to Petra. So we had to do a total refit when we moved in here a couple of years ago.'

She gestured for Matt to sit down. On her desk was a file with his name on. He didn't know how the file could already be so thick.

'Okay, I've read the report and things aren't looking too bad for us, Matt. What we need are testimonials, lots of them, from colleagues, bosses, professors, students, patients – anyone with whom you've had professional contact. I've already done some checking up on you and everyone says what a terrific doctor you are, so testimonials shouldn't be a problem.'

'Who requests these testimonials?' asked Matt.

'Me. Or, if you prefer, Jon Espersen can organize that.'

'What's the worst thing that can happen at a tribunal?'

'They can issue an official reprimand. That's what we're trying to avoid. Within twenty-four hours of the reprimand the hospital board decides what action to take – varies from case to case. The worst thing is that you could be withdrawn from the hospital's medical staff. Occasionally they suspend for six months, more often they keep you employed but with a warning. If you have an official reprimand, the hospital may have to pay compensation to the patient or his relatives.

And if the patient's really mean, he won't let the case drop there. He'll go on to the civil courts with it.'

Matt groaned.

'I don't think you'll get a reprimand,' said the lawyer, but it seemed to Matt that her tone was less certain than her words.

They discussed the events surrounding Mr Zoy's death in detail. Matt gave her his sanitized version and that seemed to satisfy her.

'We'll probably win this one,' she said. 'But let's not be complacent. I gather that the decedent's son was very angry immediately following his father's death, and if that anger hasn't abated by October then the onus will be on us to present a good case.'

'I think he's still angry,' said Matt. 'In fact, I think he's trying to intimidate me.'

The lawyer had grey hair which was arranged around her head in a gravity-defying style. She looked hard at Matt now and one hand slowly rose to her earlobe. She put her head to one side and stroked her earring between her thumb and forefinger.

'Intimidate you?' she echoed.

Matt told her about the red car. She watched him closely without moving except for her fingers which continued to stroke the earring as though it were a small dog curled up against her cheek. She narrowed her eyes a little as he spoke. Matt knew she was assessing his sanity.

'Has anyone else seen this red car?' she asked.

'My neighbour. But mostly I see it when I'm driving alone,' said Matt. He opened his briefcase. 'Jon Espersen said I should note the times and dates and places . . .' He withdrew a sheet of paper which he had typed and printed. 'Some of the dates are approximate,' he admitted.

The lawyer examined the document and Matt saw her taking pleasure in its detail and clarity. He watched her doubts about his sanity evaporate.

As she read it, he sat in silence. Through the window you could see other downtown office buildings and, further off, you could glimpse the gothic roof of the temple. Below, the traffic hummed continuously. From inside the Rosebay Building you could believe you were in almost any office anywhere. It was true that the developers had not troubled to extend any of the classical details to the interior.

'Hmm. Well, I'd say this amounts to a pretty comprehensive invasion of privacy,' she said, still studying it. 'How sure are you that the car driver is Mr Zoy?'

'Not positive,' admitted Matt. 'I barely glimpse him because his windows are darkened. But I can't think of anyone else who might want to try to intimidate me.'

'Do you generally see the car number?'

'Rarely. I have the make, model and number of a car which I think is the one he uses.'

The lawyer looked thoughtful. Her face was intelligent, her eyes hawkish. She put the pages down and leaned forward, placing her chin on her fist.

'Matt, I'm going to tell you something. It's sort of a secret but I'll tell you anyway. The reason it's a secret is that, if everyone knew it, I wouldn't have any clients left and I'd have to pull my kids out of their schools back east. Almost all the cases I deal with – medical negligence or compensation – are nothing to do with what the doctor did or did not do. They're about how the patient feels about the doctor. How the patient – or in this case, his family – feels the doctor has dealt with them. The reason we've never met before is that you're a genial kind of a guy and you show genuine respect for your patients and their problems, I know you do. But Mr Zoy here, for some reason, feels ill-treated by you . . .'

'I never even met him before his father died!' protested Matt.

'I didn't say you've ill-treated him. I said he feels you have. Dr Seleckis, in my experience, it's the doctors who don't communicate at all or don't communicate enough who wind up in my office.'

'He burst into my consulting room the morning after his father died and I didn't throw him out although there was a line of patients waiting. I spent a long time talking with him and I believe I was sympath—'

'Look, we're dealing with his perceptions here, not the facts. Now, forgive me, I'm no psychiatrist, but try this for size. What he's doing is continually placing himself in your way without actually allowing any contact between you. I think he's showing that he really wants you to communicate and if you can manage to do that, the whole case will change. He may even drop it completely.'

Matt said, 'He never gives me a chance to confront him.'

'Then see if you can move in on him without it feeling like a confrontation,' she advised.

'If he really wants me to communicate, can't he pick up the phone like anyone else?'

'Well, things have gone too far for that, you can't call each other for a man-to-man talk in the run-up to a tribunal. However, if he places himself in your way and you can find a method to communicate directly with him, then it will be hard for him to keep playing this stupid game.'

Matt sighed. 'I thought you might tell me to call the police,' he said. 'I thought you might check out the car number.'

She shook her head. 'You're not sure it's always the same

car. You're not sure about the dates. You haven't seen his face . . . how about this neighbour, what did she see?'

Matt said miserably, 'Not much. The car had been following me on a zigzag route across town for miles, but she didn't see it until it arrived home, so I guess that doesn't amount to much either.'

'He's never gotten out of his car and tried to intimidate you physically, verbally . . . ?'

Matt thought of mentioning the falling rocks. But there were signs up all along the pass warning of rock slides. If he suggested out loud that the bulky Zoy son had scrambled up the mountainside and around it a little way to kick a boulder, the lawyer would probably start to look askance at Matt again.

'No,' he said. 'He's never gotten out of the car.'

'Just keep noting every encounter and get the car number even if it's not always the same one. And try to find a witness. At the moment there isn't enough evidence for anyone to do anything.'

Matt felt disappointed. Noticing this, the lawyer asked, 'Do you feel you're in any real danger from this man?'

'Well, no,' he admitted.

'Then contacting the police could just inflame a situation which is already sore,' she warned. 'So, we'll do nothing about it for now.' Her mouth suddenly widened into a dazzling smile which redistributed the proportions and shape of her face. Her earrings giggled metallically. 'Unless,' she grinned, 'you happen to notice a gun in the car with him.'

About a week later, Matt and Denise and Austin headed off towards one of the National Parks for their first hike. At the first BEWARE FALLING ROCKS sign Matt, who was anyway keeping vigil for the red car, began checking his mirror more frequently. He was looking forward to their hike and did not want the car to glide out of nowhere and ruin their day. He had accommodated a new anxiety into his life the way the family had accommodated Hilly's cancer, like an extra member of the family. But, today, when there was no sign of any other traffic on the road, he began to feel that anxiety lift.

The mountains here in the National Park were different from Hirsh's mountains, barer and completely uninhabited. There were rocky outcrops, hidden lakes and sudden moonscapes. As they neared the park's perimeter, they saw the first slopes filled with fire-coloured wild flowers.

'This is wonderful,' said Denise happily. Matt agreed with her but silently he admitted to himself that it just wouldn't be the same this time as it had been before. How could it be with Austin there?

They parked near a disused piece of blacktop and let Austin scoot around in the sun on his tiny tricycle for a while. Then Denise ran a few races with him to tire him still further. Matt watched them lovingly. Austin thrust his small body forward and ran by rocking from foot to foot so that, although he expended a lot of energy, little of it was channelled into forward motion. Denise pretended to run so Austin could win and Matt saw that, even in play, her movements had their usual fluidity and grace. He decided she was more than musical, she *was* music. And of course today's hike with Austin would be different from the hikes he and Denise had taken alone: it would be better because their son was with them.

In this mood they set off, Austin in the backpack rearranging Matt's hair as though his father's head was an animal in the petting zoo.

'You wait, this mountain air will knock him out,' said Denise.

'It might knock me out first,' puffed Matt, because the trail started steeply.

'Look on this as further training for your hunting trip.'

'I guess I do need some more gradients,' Matt admitted. 'Capitol Hill a couple of times a week probably isn't enough.'

They paused in the steep ascent, turning to look down. The parking lot, their car, looked pleasingly small already. They went over the first ridge and around a valley and after a while the special silence of the mountains fell and they knew they were completely alone. The second ridge took them towards a small lake, ringed by boulders and wild flowers.

'He's asleep,' said Denise, starting to unstrap the backpack.

'What are you doing?' asked Matt.

'I'm going to lift off the backpack and lay it down very gently so Austin doesn't wake.'

'Are we going to eat lunch already?'

'No, we're going to make love.'

Matt turned around and stared at her. She smiled back at him.

'We are?' he said. He was already feeling excited.

They succeeded in setting down the backpack without waking Austin. When they placed him on the grass the child curled his body with the small, instinctive movement of a sea anemone closing.

'I want another one,' said Denise. She was taking off her clothes. 'Don't you too?'

'Another what?' asked Matt, watching her. He thought how perfect her breasts were, full but firm.

'Baby. Let's make one right here.'

Matt sighed. He had regarded Denise's first pregnancy

as a piece of freakish good luck and, although he was always hopeful, he knew that her miserly ovaries were unlikely to yield a second egg at the right time and in the right place.

'Does altitude improve the chances?' he asked now. Probably Denise had read somewhere that conception was more likely where air pressure was lower.

'High altitude and great scenery,' said Denise as if she expected to conceive after an interaction with a poppy or a mountain peak.

Matt glimpsed briefly what it might have been like for Weslake. Always trying to make a baby instead of making love. Anxious husbands attending the fertility clinic where he had spent some time during training spoke of the terrible burden that sex could become when it became a clinical act. Then he looked at Denise and smiled at the idea of sex with Denise ever, ever becoming a burden.

'You're the best scenery,' said Matt, and she did look spectacular now, completely naked, her breasts inviting him, her waist tapering, her hips wide. She held her arms out to him as though embracing the lake and the boulders and the vast blue sky beyond the peaks. Matt descended on her. First with just his mouth and hands and then he wanted, needed, his whole body to engulf her. He wasn't wearing many clothes and afterwards he couldn't remember taking them off, couldn't imagine how his shirt and underpants had ended up so widely scattered across grass and boulders. Denise laughed with pleasure at his hunger.

When they were lying still and entwined, unaccustomed parts of their bodies assimilating the mountain sun, they looked at each other for a long time and Matt thought he was the luckiest man alive. Why did he waste energy feeling jealous of Weslake and angry with Clem and nervous of a red car and agitated by the affair his long-dead mother had with a long-dead man a long time ago? Here, in the mountains, calm and satisfied, he could even understand that one day Hirsh would die and Austin would grow up and he, Matt would grow old and eventually die too. It was just life's natural cycle, you couldn't halt it, you had to acquiesce to it gracefully.

'Well,' said Denise, smiling and stroking his hair. 'That should do it.'

Matt knew what she was talking about.

'It doesn't matter if you're not pregnant,' he told her. 'We've enjoyed it, we love each other, we have Austin, life is sweet.'

She smiled some more at him.

'Oh, but I am pregnant,' she said, laughing a little at herself. 'I can feel it already.'

They lay still, letting the sun and the sky encompass them. Even the mountain peaks looked benign today, towering on all sides like proud parents around a cradle. Death, of Mr Zoy, of Arthur Minelli, of Hilly, of Weslake, lost its tragic edge out here in the mountains. Their passing felt like part of something more immense than humankind. A doctor should understand his limitations. He might be able to massage the lines between life and death but he was ultimately powerless.

'Wasn't your daddy a great doctor?' Sheriff Turner had said. 'Wasn't he just the best?' Everyone always said it but Matt knew Hirsh didn't feel that way. Not so long after Hilly's death, rattled by medicine's failure and his own to save her, Hirsh had retired. Matt closed his eyes feeling, briefly, wiser than his father. Hirsh should have accepted his limitations and life's losses more gracefully.

Eventually, without speaking but both knowing it was

time, they sat up. Matt watched as Denise put her clothes on.

'Sometimes,' Denise told him, 'I've worried that you might not really want another child. When I leave you with Austin for the weekend I know you get frustrated.'

'I'm a much better parent when you're around,' admitted Matt. Denise was gathering garments from distant boulders. She climbed back to him and dropped the clothes at his side and he began to dress.

'But I'd love to have another kid,' he added. 'I've never wanted Austin to be an only child the way I was.'

'Were you lonely?' asked Denise.

'I guess so, sometimes,' admitted Matt. 'That's why it was good to have Steve Minelli to mess about with up at Arrow Lake.'

It seemed to him at this moment that his friendship with Steve had been important to him, and that he owed it to Steve to find out all he could about his father's death, however unpalatable the truth.

They hoisted Austin back up on to Matt's shoulders and he still did not wake. They walked around the lake and through some pine woods. The pines released their sticky, sappy scent into the air. The strong aroma and the warmth and the rhythm of his walk and the presence of Denise right there at his side made Matt relaxed. He remembered that Steve had told him to scrape pine sap off the trees with a knife and put it in a ziplock bag for their hunting trip, and he had even brought the necessary equipment but he did not want to break his stride.

The following day they took a different hike and on the third day they set off early to visit Hirsh. It was a successful visit. Denise and Hirsh were pleased to see each other and Hirsh was delighted with his grandson. For the first time, Austin seemed to recognize his grandfather and treat him like an old friend. They walked into the woods on a fruitless quest for animals, hand in hand.

'Let's leave them to bond and go swimming,' Matt suggested. He and Denise walked down to the lake and made love there.

'Just in case you haven't already got pregnant this week,' said Matt.

'Oh, I have,' Denise assured him. Matt felt sad that she was almost certainly wrong. Having another child would be like winning the lottery twice. Denise's ovaries, for reasons no one could explain, released eggs only grudgingly and occasionally. Her poor ovulation record had not been improved by artificial stimulants and, at the time of Weslake's death, the couple had been considering IVF treatment.

They went swimming. The lake's waters were warmer now. Matt left Denise dozing at the lakeside and went back up the hill to fetch Hirsh and Austin for a swim. He did not take the route which led past the trail where Mr Minelli had parked his car and died. He took the trail which skirted the Minelli lot.

Matt had thought that Steve might suggest Hirsh had killed Mr Minelli. He might suggest Hirsh hadn't tried hard enough to save his father or that he had used a risky procedure. Hirsh had every reason not to try too hard to resuscitate Mr Minelli. But Steve had made a different and quite startling accusation. He had said Hirsh tried desperately to save the patient because he didn't want whoever had shot him to be convicted of first-degree murder.

Of course, there was only one person on whose crimes Hirsh would observe a twenty-six-year silence.

Matt paused on the blacktop between the Minellis' land and Hirsh's. He looked down the road. A few hundred yards away was the trail where Mr Minelli had parked his car. Past that was Stewart's house. He remembered his surprise, on finding Hirsh in the yard with his mother that day. She had been away somewhere and now it was evening. Where had she been all day? Why had she come home moments before the emergency? Why hadn't she looked inside the house to say she was home?

If she had been with Arthur Minelli by the lake and there had been an argument and finally a gunshot, she would have had time to drive back up to the house, park the car and go down through the yard to find Hirsh. When Matt had discovered them with the news and the medical bag, she had already told Hirsh. She had been shocked and tearful at what she had done. Neither had been surprised by Matt's arrival or the news he carried. She had sat on the bench while Hirsh and Matt had hurried down the hill.

Matt tried to remember returning back up the hill to her when Hirsh had sent him away from the accident. What had she said? But all he could recall after that was her silences.

It was much more possible that the quixotic, excitable, passionate Hilly had shot Arthur Minelli than that Hirsh could have done such a thing. Maybe Mr Minelli had ended their affair or started another with the woman in town someone had mentioned. Whatever the reason for her action, it was Hilly's role to blunder and Hirsh's role to save her.

Matt climbed the hill and stopped on the log seat and looked around at the sad remains of his mother's sculptures. He heard voices behind him and he turned, just the way Hilly and Hirsh had turned to find him that day.

'Daddy, daddy, daddy!' cried Austin, throwing himself whole-heartedly into their reunion as usual, although they had only been separated for forty minutes.

'Come on down to the lake,' said Matt and the three of them picked their way through the trees. Austin held Matt's hand and the little boy kicked as he walked at the thick carpet of leaves beneath his feet, just as Matt used to all those years ago.

That afternoon, Elmer and Lonnie came over with some toys for Austin.

'I knew they wouldn't be able to keep away,' said Hirsh gruffly.

'And this,' said Lonnie to Matt, 'is for you.' She held out a ziplock bag which was full of grey fluff.

'Um, thanks, Lonnie. Looks like some kind of detritus. What do I do with it?'

'It's lint from my clothes dryer. I've been saving it for you ever since Hirsh told me about your hunting trip. Doesn't matter how hard it's raining, put a match to some of this and you're sure of a fire.'

'What a good idea,' said Denise. 'I've never heard of that trick before.'

'Never fails,' Lonnie assured her. 'My husband always keeps a ziplock bag full of lint for camping trips.'

'Won't take up much space and weighs nothing,' added Elmer.

'A few drops of pine sap on a ball of lint and you'll soon have a good fire,' said Lonnie.

'That's if you can find dry firewood,' Matt added gloomily.

Denise laughed at him. She said she was going to make coffee and Lonnie went with her. Matt could hear their voices through the kitchen window. He wondered what Lonnie, who so rarely spoke to anyone, was finding to say to Denise.

Stewart appeared, holding a gun. Matt looked at his watch

and gave Stewart five minutes before he started to tell Denise about his heart transplant.

'This is no toy,' Stewart informed Austin, who, as though instinctively, held out his hand for the gun. Hirsh laughed at the boy.

'I brought this for you, Matt,' said Stewart. 'Take it on your trip. Use it. Enjoy it. The Winchester 30–06 is one of the most effective big-game calibres ever developed.'

Hirsh said, 'That's a great offer! A Winchester 30–06 is the best weapon for elk-shooting in my opinion.'

'But,' warned Elmer, 'it's not for the inexperienced.'

The gun felt cool as a surgical knife in Matt's hands. Knives, guns, they were just tools, he told himself, designed to do their sometimes hideous jobs effectively. They only became warm with use, as the hands which held them became warm.

'Well, I am inexperienced,' he protested. He wanted to pass the gun right back to Stewart but Stewart's hands were in his pockets. He was looking pleased, grinning shyly.

'Practise some and you won't be,' boomed Elmer 'Hell, Matt, we were all inexperienced till we practised.'

'That's right. Now you've got a gun we have to start practising,' agreed Hirsh. 'You want to eat out there in the wilderness, we have to know that one of us can hit something.'

Hirsh took the gun and held it up to his shoulder, pointing it away out of the window. Austin, to Matt's disgust, watched with fascination.

'Feels good,' Hirsh reported. 'As light a gun as you'll get for big game, but of course, it does have quite a kick. You'll need to get used to that.'

'It does have a kick,' agreed Stewart, 'but it has a muzzle brake and good recoil pads. Of course, they say some of these new high-tech pads are more effective, you could replace them if you like.'

'Are you really willing to loan Matt your gun?' asked Hirsh, turning to Stewart.

Stewart nodded firmly but Hirsh persisted: 'Do you really want to do this? You're as fit as any of us, you could use it yourself this year.'

'I might use it for deer,' said Stewart. 'But Matt can practise with her this summer and then take her elk-hunting. I'll clean her up for you and you can pick her up next time you come to Arrow Lake. And then make your father very happy, Matt, and kill an elk with her.'

'That's a tall order,' said Matt.

'He says he doesn't have the killer instinct,' Hirsh said, smiling.

'Wait until he's hunted a bull elk for five hours and got real hungry,' replied Stewart. 'We've all got the killer instinct.'

The old sheriff nodded. 'Probably you think you're a good guy and you don't want to know the violent side of your character, you don't want to think about it or even accept it's there. But it is there, Matt. It's in us all. Hunting's an honest sport, it reminds us of our violent nature and helps us to accept that.'

'Well,' Hirsh said, 'this Winchester is a kind and generous offer, Stewart. Thanks a lot.'

'Someone gave me the greatest of all gifts,' replied Stewart, placing a hand over his heart. 'After that, it's not so hard to loan a man something he needs for just a short time.'

Denise appeared to announce that coffee was ready and Stewart added for her benefit, 'You probably don't know this, Denise, but the heart beating inside me now is not the heart I was born with.'

Four minutes and thirty-eight seconds.

Everyone sat on the terrace drinking the coffee Denise and Lonnie had made. They did not look at the view but at Austin, who had a bowl of water and a small tub of wood-chips and some plastic cups. He poured and scooped and mixed, oblivious to the adults.

Elmer and Hirsh told hunting stories. Lonnie even joined in with a few of Robert's tales. Matt looked at their eager, worn faces. Their years had brought them many losses – wives, a husband who lived but was lifeless, children who went east and never came back, even a heart. They knew about loss and tried to protect themselves against it. They kept their lives contained. They exercised, ate well, developed Internet projects and peopled their small world carefully – with one another, the kids at the café, a heart donor's family, the care home staff where Robert lay comatose. They did everything they could to buttress themselves against further loss. But loss was inevitable and all of them knew it.

He caught Denise's eye. She smiled at him.

When the visitors had left and they had eaten dinner and it was dark outside, Hirsh and Matt set up the projector. Denise said, 'Matt, don't watch these movies if they're going to make you miserable.'

Matt remembered how he and Hirsh had watched the movies together after Hilly's death, hoping to find something of the woman they had lost, but afterwards Matt's grief had only been heightened by disappointment. When the movies were over they had sat in the dark. Matt had felt like some sea creature stranded on a dry beach by a high tide knowing that the water would never touch him again.

Hirsh had got up and begun to rewind the whirring film. Matt's mouth was dry, his body drained of all its fluids, his bones leached and bleached by the sun. Then his father had turned on the light and Matt had seen that Hirsh's face was wet with tears and he had envied his father for producing such liquid.

'They don't upset me like they used to,' he said, 'but I guess I'd rather look at the stars tonight.'

So Denise and Hirsh together watched Mr Minelli being a Roman gladiator and saw Hilly swimming and playing ball with a diamond ring on her finger which Matt thought, but only thought, he remembered her finding in a supermarket freezer. Matt sat outside on the terrace with Austin looking for shooting stars. He felt the small boy's body acquire sleep's weight in his arms. Inside, above the buzz of the projector, there was the murmur of voices as Denise asked questions and Hirsh gave background information. Matt didn't listen. He watched the stars and felt at ease with his son sleeping on his lap. The moon was as thin as a blade. Its light revealed little below. You couldn't see the mountains, but where there were no stars you knew this must be because dark peaks were covering the sky.

'Your mother had quite a presence,' said Denise, coming out on to the terrace. 'All that energy and style, did she know what to do with it when she stopped performing on stage?'

'No,' said Matt. 'She should have stayed a concert pianist.'

He waited to see if Denise would say more but she stood silently behind him, looking up at the gallery of stars.

On the way home, Matt asked, 'What was Lonnie talking about with you in the kitchen?'

'Robert. I asked whether she had ever considered terminating life support.'

This felt so much like an emergency that Matt nearly flattened his foot on the brake. 'You said *that*? No one ever says that to Lonnie!'

'Because,' said Denise in that calm, quiet way of hers which always made you see how simple the truth was, 'they feel more comfortable bolstering Lonnie's illusions than they do talking about her choices.'

'So, what did she say? What did you say?'

'She said it felt wrong to terminate someone else's life. I said that withholding active treatment whenever he gets sick, for example, isn't like pulling a plug out. And anyway, sometimes you have to do the wrong thing so the right thing happens.'

Matt thought about that.

'But what would Lonnie do with herself if she wasn't waiting for Robert to wake up the whole time?'

'Live.'

Matt admired Denise for being so incisive about complex moral issues. It wasn't that she didn't see the complexity: she was actually capable of finding a way through it.

'How well can she live if Robert dies and she feels she's responsible?'

'Right now, two of them are living but they're living in a coma. If she terminates, Robert dies, which isn't so different from being comatose. And Lonnie really lives, which is very different from being comatose. There's a net gain. It's hard to take the wrong road to the right place but, well, sometimes it's the only way.'

Matt thought about that for a long time. Finally he asked, 'Did you ever do that? Take the wrong route to the right place?'

She gave no answer and Matt, glancing at her, was unable to see if she was asleep or awake. So they drove silently on into the night, weaving their way between the dark mountains which they could not see but whose presence they could sense. Finally they rounded a corner and the city was laid out before them as though on an immense plate, its straight lines of lights stretching as far as they could see.

19

Matt left Salt Lake to start target practice one Friday a few weeks later. It was high summer and the weather was sweltering. A cloud of yellow pollutants had settled over the city like a tight-fitting lid. Matt had grown so accustomed to this that he only noticed it as the car climbed the mountain and he left the pollution behind. The air cleared, the temperature dropped. As he rounded a ridge, he saw the resort chairlift high on a slope, trapped on its never-ending journey up and down the mountain. The wheels of bicycles hung from its cabins.

He passed Lonnie's house and then the lake. There were swimmers and a rowboat and a couple of inflatable rafts which scarcely seemed to break its still surface.

He stopped at Stewart's house to pick up the rifle.

'I've tightened the screws, cleaned her and oiled her and generally prepared her for you,' reported Stewart, leading Matt through to his office, 'and she's looking good.'

Matt noticed a computer blinking in the corner and remembered Stewart's interest in his heart donor's family.

'I'm entering the surveillance stage,' said Stewart.

'Surveillance?' asked Matt. 'Is this legal?'

'Well, I don't just want to knock on the door and introduce myself as the recipient of their mother's heart. I want to check them out first. I may enter their lives in some other way. They may never know what I'm carrying around inside me, they may just accept that there's someone new in their lives who's kind to them.'

'So, who was your donor?'

'She lived in Salt Lake, in a poor but respectable area on the south side. Her name was Rosalie Jandak and she died at work in a laundry. Her cousin was a chef and she was doing his whites one day with those dangerous chemicals laundries use. She put in a little extra for family, too much extra because the fumes killed her. That's the kind of woman she was. Extra for family. I like to think of her as good-hearted, since I have her heart.'

'Did she have children?'

'Three, all more or less grown now, and at least one leading a rootless, drifting sort of existence. I intend to visit them and make what contribution I can to their lives.'

'I hope you don't get arrested,' said Matt.

'I have Rosalie's good heart and I'm doing what I think she would have wanted.'

'You didn't know her,' Matt reminded him. He wanted to tell Stewart that he was wrong about love having no secrets but Stewart wouldn't have listened.

'I understand you feel, Matt, as a doctor, that we give too much emotional significance to the heart. But I believe that my first heart broke. I kept throwing it at Mara like a big rubber ball until finally it just broke. Now I have Mona and I'm not breaking this heart too. Mona's taking care of it for me and I'm using it the way Rosalie Jandak would have wanted, to do good to those she loved.'

Stewart handed him the gun and encouraged Matt to hold it to his shoulder and point it as though shooting. He corrected Matt's fingers, lifting them and setting them down in new places which felt even stranger than the first places they had landed. He adjusted the rifle's butt against Matt's shoulder.

'Good,' he said. 'You're looking good, Matt. Remember to hold her firm to control that kick.'

Matt didn't feel good. He felt as though he had just been shown some particularly odd yoga position.

'Elbows close to the body. Legs shoulder width,' instructed Stewart.

Matt shuffled his feet around and moved his elbows but nothing he did made his body feel right. It had been the same when he was eleven. The gun, which had been nothing larger than an air rifle, had felt like an unwanted extra limb.

'Now remember. Keep the safety on at all times and never get your finger near the trigger unless you're planning to shoot. That's the first rule of gun safety. If you trip or stumble or if you're just changing position think: muzzle control. That way, it never points accidentally at you or at someone else. Never, ever lean her against a tree or a car or a fence or anywhere else she could fall over and discharge. And, most important of all, treat her as if she's always loaded. She's not now, of course. Hirsh has ammo for you up at his place. Or I could just be saying that. I could be dumb enough to have left something inside her, you don't know, you never know for sure. So treat every gun, Matt, like a loaded gun.'

'Right,' said Matt faintly, thinking of Arthur Minelli.

Stewart smiled at him. 'Didn't your father send you on a Hunter Education course?'

'It starts next week.'

'To be honest, there are a lot of deaths, I mean, human deaths, during the hunting season but it's incredible that there aren't more. Some of these guys waving semi-automatics around . . . well, they just go crazy when they feel a weapon in their hands.'

He took the rifle, opened the action and then gave it back to Matt. Carrying it gingerly, Matt followed him out of the study.

'Once the hunting season starts, you can walk out in your yard around here and just about smell testosterone,' said Stewart, opening his front door. 'There are perfectly normal guys who change personality completely when they're let loose outside with a gun.'

Stewart walked Matt to the car and Matt paused.

'Would you do me a favour and double-check that this gun isn't loaded?' he asked. Stewart looked hard at him through his thick, wire-rimmed eyeglasses. Matt explained: 'I mean, when I think of Arthur Minelli . . .'

Stewart nodded and showed Matt how to check that the rifle wasn't loaded. It wasn't.

'Always good to make sure,' he said. 'Arthur Minelli's death wasn't that unusual. Guys often drive around with their rifles loaded in case they see something they might want to shoot without even getting out of their SUVs.'

Matt got into the car, laying the gun carefully on the back seat.

'Why all the interest in Arthur Minelli?' asked Stewart. 'Is it true you've met up with one of the sons again?'

'Steve. He works at the hospital.'

'Has he been talking to you about his father's death?'

Matt wound down the window. 'I guess so,' he admitted.

'He should try to put the past behind him and get on with his life,' said Stewart. 'He's been up here asking questions. He's a sad sort of a fellow, probably a little unstable.'

'He's been up here?' asked Matt. 'Steve Minelli? Dad didn't tell me that.'

'I guess your father has his reasons but I don't see why I shouldn't tell you. It was last summer. Then he stayed on through the fall and even into the winter. I'm sure he visited his mom in town sometimes but folks said he was basically camping somewhere out near John-Jack's place. The weather really wasn't suitable and they complained about him because he was always wandering around here with a rifle. He kept asking for details about his father's death, as though asking could change things.'

So Steve had already investigated Mr Minelli's death. He had asked Matt questions about Arrow Lake and Hirsh and Hirsh's friends and all the time he had given no indication that he already knew the answers. Matt felt confused and even betrayed. His secretary was right, Steve was weird.

When Matt finally drove up to Hirsh's house, his father was waiting impatiently at the door for him. He held his gun. This was another small indication of Hirsh's age, decided Matt. He couldn't remember Hirsh ever showing such impatience when he was younger.

'Did Stewart keep you talking?' Hirsh asked irritably before Matt could get out of his car.

'Sort of,' said Matt.

'That guy gets worse as he gets older. Are you ready to go right on up to John-Jack Perry's range before we lose any more light?'

Matt agreed and Hirsh climbed into the passenger seat. They headed towards the small range which John-Jack had made when he dynamited his outbuildings for love of Anita. They passed Stewart's place and then there was a break in the trees. The trail, barely wide enough for a car and currently unmarked by tyres, led off the road and then disappeared into the darkness. Matt could not resist staring down it as they drove by. Hirsh must have noticed this but he was talking about ammunition and wind speed and he made no comment.

The range proved to be nothing more than a clearing marked at intervals by piles of sandbags. You could see where once people had used the trees for target practice but someone had more recently erected makeshift targets in front of the trees.

Hirsh went through the same safety routine that Stewart had earlier and then he handed Matt ear protectors.

'We're going to check the sights on your rifle first.'

He showed Matt how to load the gun.

'Okay, forearm and butt stock on the sandbags, keep it firm, see the target, get the target right in the middle of the crosshairs. Breathe out. Relax. At the bottom of your breath, feel that trigger.'

Through the scope the target looked massive. It bulged at Matt. Hirsh had placed a square of thick duck tape across the centre and at this magnification Matt could see its weave. He breathed out and squeezed his fingers and the gun seemed to explode in his hands, a mass of noise and light and shoulder pain. For a minute he was too shocked to move. It felt as though he had some animal locked against his body, wild, vicious, uncontrollable.

'Okay, that's good,' said Hirsh, who was standing by with his screwdriver. 'I won't be needing this. I guess the sights are pretty well adjusted, Stewart must have already done it. I might adjust them up before we get out there for real because realistically you're not going to get much closer to an elk than a hundred and fifty yards. But I don't see you firing successfully from further away than two hundred. Okay, let's get practising. Good shots are made, not born.'

Anything he had learned about shooting as a boy with the Minellis, Matt thought he had forgotten, but there was a certain familiarity about what now followed: the hunting aphorisms which Hirsh and Mr Minelli had seemed able to produce from some bottomless supply, the sharp com-

334

mands, the rebukes, the burst of surprised praise, and the endless coincidence of loud noise with intense shoulder pain.

Hirsh made Matt shoot standing with his gun resting on sandbags, then told him to lie prone, his gun over a log. Next he kneeled and finally he stood in the position Stewart had shown him earlier, offhand, with nothing to support the gun. He missed the target every time this way.

'Well, offhand's the hardest and least efficient way to shoot,' said Hirsh. 'If you can avoid it, you should, by looking for a rest. Now your gun's hot and I think that's moving your shots up the target, so you can just watch me playing until the light goes completely.'

Matt stood back as Hirsh aimed at the target from 300 yards. His shots were mostly accurate (Matt noticed Hirsh was wearing new eyeglasses) but when he changed position he did so with painful slowness and his movements were sometimes stiff.

When they had finished and were driving back around the mountain to Hirsh's house, Hirsh said, 'Target practice is good but it doesn't have anything much to do with hunting.'

'C'mon, I have to learn to shoot straight,' Matt protested.

'You'll almost never get a clear view of an elk from three hundred yards and kill it. Remember, if you can't fire at least twice, don't shoot. Better to leave it than wound it. You'll see what I mean tomorrow when we'll be simulating more natural conditions in our target practice.'

Matt spent the rest of the weekend shooting, running, swimming and studying the various texts on elk habits which Hirsh shoved across the table at him after each meal.

'It was like boot camp,' he told Denise on Sunday afternoon. He was lying on his belly on the living-room floor and Denise was massaging him gently and Austin was massaging him vigorously. There was a children's programme on the TV which occasionally distracted Austin and his small hands went still.

'Are your shoulders still sore?' asked Denise, pressing on the muscles beneath them.

'My shoulders, my legs, my lower back, my arms, my neck, my . . . is there some part of my body I forgot to mention?'

'What did Hirsh do to you this weekend?'

'Scared me. The topo maps are beginning to mean something now and I've realized how arduous this elk-hunting's going to be. I don't just have to walk miles up snowy mountains carrying a heavy pack and a gun, I have to get Dad up there too. He's decided he doesn't even want to take a tent, just a tarpaulin, so we're going to be cold and wet for four whole days. We go to this derelict mining camp he visited about twenty years ago and then we have to find an elk trail and follow it anywhere, even over mountaintops. Then somehow one of us is supposed to shoot the darn thing. Then we cut it up and put it on the tarpaulin and I have to haul it back through the mountains to civilization. And if I fail at any of this, I'll be the world's worst son and only half a man.'

Denise said nothing but he could feel from her fingers that she was smiling.

'And, get this. When I said I was taking my cellphone in case of emergency, Dad told me that it was strictly, absolutely forbidden. He didn't have a cellphone when he was a hunter-gatherer with his dad and I'm not allowed one either.'

'You could take it without telling him,' Denise suggested.

'I will. And I'm taking three times as much food as he

336

wants me to and a full twenty-first-century emergency kit, including some very strong pain relief.'

'Sounds like you could do with that now,' said Denise.

'It's my own fault I ache all over. When I began to understand what he's expecting of me I panicked and got up early and started running up and down mountainsides. I'm not fit enough for that yet. Then I swam in the lake until I turned into a block of ice.'

'What did Hirsh have you do?'

'More shooting. He fixed a target in an old tyre and started rolling it down the hill through the woods and I was supposed to hit it from about a mile and a half away.'

'Did you?'

'Well, there were all these trees in the way and mostly I hit them instead.'

He rolled over to look at Denise. Austin sat on top of him but Matt could see around him to Denise. She looked pale under her summer tan, and tired.

'How are things here? I should have asked. That's the first thing I should have asked.'

She said, 'I have some news.'

The way she said this made Matt sit up. He tried to hold Austin close to him but the child struggled to get away so that he could see the TV screen.

'I'm pregnant,' said Denise.

Matt stared at her with delight and disbelief. 'You . . . are you sure?'

'Well, there's another tester in the kit so we can check. But the first one was positive.'

'You're pregnant!' he cried. 'You're pregnant!'

She laughed. 'I told you those high altitudes would do it.'

Matt threw his arms around her. So she had been right, as usual. She had conceived for an incredible second time

337

because of a change of air pressure. Just wait until news of this got out. The mountains would be full of copulating couples, or even more full than they already were.

'Are you pleased?' she asked.

'I'm so pleased I'm scared to believe it. Let's do the second test in the kit. Right now.'

Austin followed them upstairs curiously. Denise went into the bathroom and closed the door behind her. Austin and Matt sat on the floor together outside. She emerged with a small, plastic stick.

'You can look at it but you mustn't touch,' she said to Austin, holding it up like Show and Tell. Austin and Matt stared at the stick.

'See this little window? If it turns blue then we're all very happy.'

Matt and Austin watched a blue line materialize in the window.

'See!' said Denise. 'It's blue! We're happy!'

Austin smiled. Matt smiled.

'We sure are,' said Matt, hugging them both. 'Can we buy a frame for the tester and hang it on the wall?'

'There's no point telling anyone for a few weeks in case something goes wrong,' said Denise. 'I won't even see Dan Murvitz just yet. I'll go to the clinic when I start feeling sick to my stomach in a few weeks.'

'Can I get you anything?' asked Matt. 'I mean, something to drink or some toast or something?'

She laughed at him.

The baby was due next April. Matt thought that he should cancel October's hunting trip. Not only would he be leaving Denise for five whole days, but he was already away for longer each day, training in the mornings and after work, plus Hirsh had more shooting weekends planned. For the first time, the trip began to seem dangerous. If something terrible happened when he was out there tussling with the merciless mountain elements, Denise would be left pregnant and alone with Austin. But when he voiced these fears, Denise just smiled at him.

'Oh, you'll be all right hunting with Hirsh,' she said. 'He'll take care of you.'

'I thought I was going so I could take care of him!' Matt objected.

'Don't cancel the training, don't cancel the hunting trip,' she instructed him. 'You're looking so fit and well, the exercise is doing you good.'

'Maybe it's given me an astonishing fecundity,' said Matt proudly.

'Maybe,' agreed Denise.

'I could go hunting next year instead,' he suggested.

But Denise was adamant. 'There may not be a next year for Hirsh. You have to go, Matt.'

20

It was the end of summer. The sun was a weakening September sun, arriving later in the mornings, lying lower, creating long, amorphous shadows in the evening.

People had returned from their vacations. They had driven down from the mountains or flown into the airport and begun the resumption of their lives. Lines of traffic throbbed at the lights again. Outside schools, flashing signs reminded drivers to slow down. The schools reopened their gates, cars drew up outside them and children scrambled out with bright new backpacks. Busy, distracted mothers dashed around supermarkets after work.

Maybe it was because the Zoy tribunal was approaching but Matt felt, somewhere in his intestines, an echo of the end-of-summer angst which he used to feel as a boy. He looked with sympathy at the children he passed each morning, draining from yellow buses in the school yard. They looked the same each year, the first graders, the second graders, but each year they were different – a year older, taller, wiser – and the kids who looked like last year's first graders were different kids who had it all to learn.

Interest among Matt's friends and colleagues in his hunting trip grew. He tried to avoid Steve Minelli now and was mostly successful. However, if he did pass him in a hallway, Steve always made some reference to the trip, offering a good compass, for instance, or a hunting knife, which Matt refused. Matt endlessly received hunting tips from everyone, even people who he had no idea ever hunted. Even Jon

Espersen, who had hunted with Weslake but not since his death, had a tip. He recommended taking some of the coffee, milk and sugar sachets from the cafeteria.

Denise insisted that Matt come with her to tell Clem that she was pregnant and so one Sunday they drove over to Mason House. Clem was delighted and amazed by the news. Matt thought the old guy looked at him with a new respect. Matt had achieved the unachievable. Twice.

Clem wanted to talk to Matt about his medication. He gestured to a line of pill bottles which stood on the window sill. There were at least fifteen of them.

'Doctor van Essen has changed one of my heart medications to Chasacon, Matt, and I'm not sure it's a good idea . . .'

'Chasacon's fine, Clem. I'm sure Barbara van Essen knows what she's doing.'

'Well, I tried Chasacon about ten years ago and it upset my stomach. Now she's put me on it again and I'm already feeling a little queasy.'

Matt remembered Clem's notes. 'Your doctor wrote ten years ago that the upset stomach was almost certainly caused by a different medication but at your request he took you off the Chasacon. Now you should give it another chance because it's very good.'

There was a silence.

'How do you know?' Clem demanded coldly.

Matt, who was sitting with Austin on his lap, rearranged Austin's weight.

'Because he's a doctor, Daddy,' said Denise quickly.

'Although,' added Matt, 'I'm not a heart doctor.'

'What I meant was, how do you know I tried it ten years ago?' Clem was alert, his eyes bright now.

Matt and Denise exchanged glances. Denise bit her lip.

Matt said, 'I had to go to the clinic to read your notes, Clem. Remember? For the insurance company?'

Clem seemed to shake a little and his voice, when he spoke, was high-pitched. 'I did not give my permission for you to read all my notes. Certainly not back ten years. I did not give permission for that. I clearly remember that the insurance company requested you read the last five years' notes and that's what I granted permission for, five years, only five.'

Now that he was angry, his face took on its fox-like angles. Once he had been lean and angular and strong. Clem had been a clever, forceful fox who had perhaps controlled even Weslake and his company.

'I'm sorry, Clem,' said Matt. 'When I got to the clinic they said that the insurance company had requested me to read everything, so I did.'

'And why didn't anyone check with me?' demanded the old man.

'Daddy, calm down,' said Denise, but her voice was not soothing.

'So,' Clem demanded, 'you've read all my notes? Right back to . . . the beginning.'

'Well, I guess I moved pretty quickly through the earlier years but since the insurance company requested it and I had to sign to say I'd read them all, then I did.'

Clem looked at him and Matt looked right back.

'Many busy people would have read the last five years and just signed anyway,' snapped Clem.

Matt thought that if he hadn't bumped into Dan Murvitz from his old ethics group when he was reading the notes, he might well have done the same. But he said nothing.

Denise was anxious. 'I'm sorry, Daddy, I don't know how that happened. I gave them the form you signed . . .'

Clem was saccharine again. 'Don't worry, darling, I'm sure it's not your fault,' he said. But he looked meaningfully at Matt as though he was probably culpable.

Then, when they got home, the telephone was ringing. Clem was calling for Matt, asking him to come back over.

'I'll go after work this week,' Matt said wearily.

But it was difficult to find the time, between work and training and his Hunter Education course. On Friday, he had promised Hirsh he would go up the mountain for more target practice and so finally he drove over to Mason House in his lunch-hour. A staff member in an unflattering maroon uniform was just taking away Clem's dirty dishes.

'He likes a sleep after lunch,' she warned Matt.

'This is the only time I have,' Matt told her.

Clem was sitting on the sofa looking, indeed, like a man who had just been dozing. Some religious pamphlets had fallen on to the floor, as though Clem had dropped them when he fell asleep.

The old man greeted him warmly enough. 'I had to talk to you. About my medical notes. Did you really read them all?'

'Yes,' said Matt.

'And have you discussed their content in any way with Denise?'

'Of course not.'

Clem hadn't invited him to sit down but he did anyway. Clem was watching him.

'So,' said the old man. 'What do you intend to do with this information? It seems to me I've unwittingly handed you a stick of dynamite. You could blow me up with it.'

Matt shook his head in confusion. 'There's no way I intend to do anything with the information.'

But Clem disregarded this reassurance. 'You see, it would be a terrible thing for Denise if she learned about some aspects of my past. It would upset her. Cause her so much distress. I couldn't allow that to happen. I would have to do everything in my power to prevent it.'

Matt remembered something Denise had said during their argument. About misusing his knowledge of her father. Without thinking about it first, he heard himself say, 'Has someone tried to blackmail you, Clem?' and he knew, from the way the old man's body straightened, that he was right.

'I wouldn't do that,' Matt said kindly. 'I wouldn't threaten to tell anyone your secrets, least of all Denise. First because it would be wrong, second because I love her.'

Clem stared at him and then his eyes wandered thoughtfully around the room. 'Because you love her,' he echoed slowly. 'Maybe Weslake didn't love Denise at all. I mean, I thought he did and I know that she loved him . . .'

'Weslake?' said Matt. 'Did you say Weslake?'

'He was in possession of the same knowledge about me that you now are. I don't know who told him about certain things in my past which I'm ashamed of . . . although I did enjoy them and even the memories are enough to make an old man happy occasionally . . .' Clem smiled his foxy smile. Matt remembered how his doctor of the time had written: 'I wish he would stay out of whorehouses or at least pay for a cleaner whore'.

'But,' continued Clem smoothly, 'what I did was wrong and certainly not in line with the teachings of the Church. Somehow, Weslake found out about my past. He threatened to tell my friends, the Church, the community. I could have stood all that. But then he threatened to tell Denise. Denise loves me and looks up to me and she's not so strong as she'd like to think. She would have been devastated to know about her father's fallibilities. I couldn't have her hurt, Matt.'

Matt, recalling Denise's shock when she found out he

knew Clem's history and, remembering some reference she had made to those very fallibilities, thought that probably she knew already. Indeed, maybe in a foolish and adoring moment, she had actually told Weslake. Was Weslake really so unscrupulous that he would then threaten to divulge to Denise the very information she had given him?

'Did Weslake ask you for money?' he said.

Clem nodded. And then Matt understood.

'For Slimtime.' he said. 'You're the principal investor in Slimtime, right?'

'I was,' said Clem mournfully.

'That's why you changed your mind about Liguria,' said Matt, 'when Slimtime went under.'

'It wasn't my mind which changed, it was my bank balance.'

Matt revised his idea of a helpless Weslake who, by accepting Clem's offer of money, had relinquished control of his company to his father-in-law.

'I did have chest pains,' Clem was adding defensively. 'What I told you about the chest pains was true. Who wouldn't, when they'd lost that much money?'

'Weslake blackmailed you into investing in his company,' said Matt slowly, incredulously.

'He was starting Slimtime and he needed an investor. You could argue, indeed, Weslake would argue, that he wasn't wholly a crook because he intended to give the money back one day with interest. Except he didn't.'

'But you couldn't tell Denise. Because she had no idea that you'd been propping up Slimtime all along.'

'I couldn't tell Denise anything. I didn't want her to know about my past but I didn't want her to know about Weslake, either. She was married to him and she adored him. It was better that she didn't know the truth.'

Denise had been double-deceived by both the men in her life. She deserved better, thought Matt.

'That suitor, the man who wanted to marry her when she was already engaged to Weslake,' said Clem. 'Am I right in believing that it was you?'

Matt swallowed. Then he said, 'Yes. I went to Africa when she wouldn't change her mind. She didn't want to hurt you, Clem, because she thought Weslake was the one you wanted for her.'

'He was! He seemed a good Saint, he came from the right kind of Salt Lake family, and you have to remember that we're converts from Chicago and so that mattered. Weslake seemed so right for her. I couldn't encourage her affections for you, Matt. You not only were outside the Church but came from a family with a history of opposition to our faith. Denise did love him very much, the way a wife should love a husband, and she suffered when he died, but I now believe I made a mistake all those years ago. And I'm sorry.'

Matt stood up. He knew that he should accept the old man's apology graciously but he remained silent.

'I have to get back to the hospital,' he said at last. 'If you asked me here to reassure you that I'm not going to misuse the information I read in your notes, then be reassured. I won't tell anyone.'

That night he held Denise especially close, cradling her in his arms and kissing her gently. He cupped his hand over her belly as though he could already feel the baby. He spoke as lovingly to her as he knew how. He wanted to make up for the foolishness of Clem, the greed of Weslake. In their own ways they had both betrayed her.

Matt had one last weekend with Hirsh before the hunting season was due to open and their trip begin.

'How was the Hunter Education course?' his father asked as they went up to John-Jack's for target practice.

'They told us about these amazing things called MREs. Meals Ready to Eat. They were developed for astronauts but now they're available to anyone. They're cooked and then packed right away by some amazing process which means they keep for years. You can get fantastic meals like beef teriyaki and all sorts of desserts and you just heat them in their packets or—'

'Stop right there,' ordered Hirsh. 'We're not taking any beef teriyaki into the wilderness, for heaven's sake.'

'Just in case we don't manage to find food out there.'

'No,' said Hirsh. 'It's completely contrary to the spirit of hunting. I mean, hunting the way I've always done it. Is that what they teach you in Hunter Education these days?'

'It was part of the survival lesson.'

'They should have been teaching you about snaring small game in the survival lesson,' snarled Hirsh.

Later they studied maps some more and, in Hirsh's yard, shot at moving targets from every position including standing offhand.

'Relax!' yelled Hirsh in a way which Matt did not find induced relaxation. 'When you're shooting offhand, get into a position where the gun's supported by your bone structure, not muscular tension! It's about that left hand, Matt, the left hand's the thing. Just relax it!'

'If I relax it then I'll drop the gun,' Matt protested.

'Controlled relaxation!' roared Hirsh.

His father made him load and reload his gun over and over, as well as rehearse picking it up and going straight into a shooting position rapidly and silently. They did some scouting through the forest, too.

'Too noisy,' Hirsh would say whenever Matt trod on a twig. The deer rut had started and, stopping to point out rubs and scrapes and footprints, Hirsh led the way, moving between the trees with what seemed to Matt to be uncanny noiselessness. Except for his breathing. As soon as they found themselves on even a slight incline, Hirsh's breathing became alarmingly heavy. Matt thought his father was as fit as a man of seventy-six could be and noticed how much more wiry Hirsh's body seemed after his summer's training, but the old guy was frequently short of breath and by the end of the day it was usually evident that his right side had stiffened.

'Does that stiffness really disappear overnight?' asked Matt anxiously.

'Always,' replied Hirsh.

'Even if you spend the night in a sleeping bag with only a tarpaulin between you and the stars?'

'If I rest overnight I'm fine in the morning,' Hirsh repeated firmly.

In Hirsh's study they laid out most of their equipment and tried stowing it inside the large backpack Matt had brought. It didn't fit. The backpack was overfull and that was without any of the food or medical supplies Matt intended to take.

'We have a choice,' said Hirsh. 'Either we cut down on equipment or I carry a pack too.'

'We cut down,' said Matt quickly, but Hirsh produced a small pack which was sufficient for light supplies and a sleeping bag.

'We should be okay,' said Hirsh, 'if we don't bring too much food. I mean it, Matt. No mountains of peanut butter sandwiches or beer or M&Ms or Orios and strictly none of that food you were talking about which was developed for guys to guzzle in space stations. Just a few sandwiches for the first day, lots of granola bars and hi-carb packs of oatmeal and rice and powdered potato. Maybe a few, a very few, emergency rations. But if we want protein we should snare it or shoot it ourselves.'

'How about a book?' asked Matt hopefully.

Hirsh stared at him. 'A book! What kind of a book?'

'I usually take a good book on vacation with me.'

'You're not going on vacation. You're going into the wilderness to shoot a bull elk.'

'So,' said Denise when Matt got back down to the city. 'Are you guys all ready for the trip?'

'I won't ever be ready for it,' said Matt. But he felt strong and fit and had found this weekend, although demanding, a lot less tiring than the last.

It seemed to Matt in those last few weeks before the hunting season opened that the whole of the city had gone crazy. He had never before noticed how many men hunted. Now everywhere he went people were discussing calibres or arguing round noses versus spitzers or worrying about weather conditions or snowlines or the threat of white-tail invasion, or they were debating mule deer psychology. He went one lunchtime to a hunting store to pick up some Meals Ready to Eat which he would hide from Hirsh and only produce when they were hungry but the staff were so busy and the lines so long that he had to get back to the hospital before he had been served. He returned to the store early the following morning.

And then September was ending and October began, and it was Monday and the tribunal was scheduled for Tuesday. Matt's lawyer called and invited him to her office to rehearse his answers. She examined him closely on what happened the night of Mr Zoy's death, on his final conversation and his exact actions in the dispensary. Matt tried to adhere to his original story but it lacked the sticky surface of the truth and sometimes he felt it slipping away from him.

'Did the patient tell you that he wanted to die?' asked the lawyer in a deep, serious voice.

'Yes,' said Matt.

'No, no, no,' she cried. Matt stared at her in confusion. Was she being his lawyer or was the deep voice a pretence at being the tribunal?

'Matt, this is a minefield and you just exploded. Remember the words in your submission, use only those. Say: the patient indicated that he was ready for death whenever it might come.'

'Oh yes,' said Matt. 'I forgot.'

When they had completed their rehearsal, the lawyer said, 'The tribunal's at twelve. What are you doing before that?'

'Operating.'

'Good, good,' she said happily. 'Will you be wearing those baggy loose things?'

'Scrubs? Well, to operate I will but of course I'll—'

'Don't change. Come directly from theatre looking like you've been saving lives all morning.'

'Come to the tribunal in my scrubs?'

'In scrubs but, please, strictly no bloodstains.'

'Do I get to keep my mask on?'

Her face underwent its dramatic reorganization into a smile. 'I think that's going a bit too far,' she said.

He was getting up to go now. The lawyer asked, 'Is Mr Zoy still bothering you?'

Matt nodded. 'I think I've seen him a few times.'

'Have you managed to communicate with him?'

'It's impossible. He's intent on avoiding me.'

'No witnesses?'

'None.'

She looked thoughtful. She tugged at her earring. 'One sighting after the tribunal, just one, and we'll take action,' she said decisively.

As he was leaving, she added, 'Don't worry about any of this. Don't look worried at the tribunal. Look like the wronged doctor but don't look worried. Because we're going to win tomorrow, okay? You'll come away with your reputation intact and no reprimand.'

Matt nodded, but by the time he was back in his office her confidence had ebbed out of him. He slept badly that night and Denise looked at him with concern in the morning.

'Thank heavens this thing is all going to be over today,' she said. In reply Matt glanced routinely out of the window. No car.

'I wish I could come to the tribunal to support you.' Denise wrapped her arms around him. She had asked to attend several times but Matt had told her that regulations prevented it. He had also refused to let her read his written submission. With her amazing perception, Denise would guess his guilt right away.

He was glad to be operating all morning. That meant he would be concentrating too hard to think about the tribunal for at least three hours. But when he came out of the sterile theatre the sense of dread alighted on him like an infection.

He made his way back to his office where Jon Espersen was waiting.

Jon looked grey. He said, too loudly and too jovially, 'I'm sure everything's going to be just fine.'

'Good luck,' Matt's secretary called. Her voice sounded depleted. It barely reached them as they walked down the hallway, and when Matt opened his mouth to thank her he found his tongue and lips were too dry for words, so he just turned and waved at her and saw then that her hand was resting on her cheek in an unconscious gesture of despair.

'I can't believe the lawyer told you not to change out of your scrubs,' muttered Jon as they neared the boardroom. 'I mean, I'm wearing a new tie and you're making me feel overdressed.'

'I hope there are no bloodstains on that tie,' said Matt. 'The lawyer told me strictly no blood.' They went to the vestibule by the boardroom where they had been told to wait and Jon scanned Matt all over for bloodstains.

Matt kept yawning, the way he sometimes did when he was nervous. Jon kept checking his watch.

'What's going on in there? Where is everyone?' Jon asked irritably. 'Has it started without us? Why's the door shut?'

'It's probably some committee meeting overrunning,' said Matt. He picked up a magazine. It was a car magazine and he put it down again. He had been anticipating the tribunal for months and months and now it was finally happening he felt a sense of numb unreality, as though he wasn't here at all.

'Then why isn't everyone else waiting?' demanded Jon. 'They must be inside. I'm going to find out what's going on.'

He gave the door a brisk double knock and then opened it. Matt heard voices inside.

'Dr Seleckis is right here,' Jon said into the boardroom. 'He's just arrived straight from theatre . . .'

Then a voice must have invited Jon into the room because he disappeared and closed the door and Matt was left alone outside. He looked through the other magazines in the vestibule but his eyes were unfocused. He looked out of the window at the people who were crossing the parking lot, visiting relatives, carrying flowers, hurrying to hear bad news or good. He tried to empathize with the humanity down there but right now the people in the parking lot looked like little wind-up toys and it was hard to feel anything for them. It was hard to feel anything at all, except annoyed with his lawyer who was supposed to be here by his side.

Then he heard voices getting louder and the boardroom door was flung open and his lawyer appeared, flanked by Jon Espersen. The lawyer was smiling. There was a bounce in her walk which made her earrings jingle.

'Sit down, Matt,' she commanded, and Matt sank into one of the low chairs by the window.

'Good news. Very good news. Mrs Zoy has been per-suaded not to take this case any further.'

Matt stared at her. 'But the son?'

'Mrs Zoy has persuaded her son to back down,' said the lawyer. 'She asked for a pre-tribunal meeting this morning and now she's agreed to abandon the whole thing.'

Matt felt relief swamp him as though he had just been through a car wash. 'Abandon . . . ?'

'The tribunal's cancelled,' Jon repeated, grinning broadly. 'You just have to agree to a private meeting with the mother,' the lawyer added, 'and you'll be out of this without a stain on your character or your professional reputation.'

Matt felt his face pulled into unaccustomed shapes by underused muscles. He realized he was smiling. He reached up and touched his mouth. Yes, it was turning up at the edges. An ear-to-ear smile.

'Are you sure?' he kept asking.

'We're sure,' they said.

He stood up and his lawyer immediately hauled him towards the door.

'Let's get down to your office for your private meeting with Mrs Zoy,' she said. 'I estimate that it will take them about twenty minutes to clear up the formalities and then they'll bring her.'

'We'd have won it anyway,' said Jon, suddenly and surprisingly shaking Matt's hand, 'but this is nicer.'

Through the half-open door of the boardroom, Matt glimpsed Mrs Zoy deep in conversation with the medical ethics officer. She looked smaller and older than he remembered.

Downstairs he just had time to phone Denise with the good news and eat a slice of celebratory cake with his lawyer and Jon and his secretary.

'I made it last night,' said his secretary shyly, 'because I knew you'd win.'

'What did Mrs Zoy say about her son?' asked Matt twice before anyone answered him.

'He's always been a difficult character. Tends to go off the deep end. But she's going to try to keep the situation under control,' said Jon at last. It seemed to Matt that Jon and the lawyer exchanged glances over their forkfuls of cake.

'We did agree to be understanding about his problems . . .' said the lawyer carefully.

Matt watched her. 'What sort of understanding?' he asked. 'About what sort of problems?'

'He does have,' said Jon, 'a psychiatric history.'

'What sort of history?'

'Oh, slight,' Jon assured him. 'Very slight.'

'Mrs Zoy would sure like for the police not to hear about how he's been bothering you,' said the lawyer, finishing her cake and brushing crumbs off her hands.

Matt's skin began to itch. He'd forgotten how you could feel insects were crawling all over you even in an air-conditioned office.

'So, he's going to keep driving around behind me?'

'We hope not,' the lawyer said. 'His mother will try to stop him. If you see him, you need to tell us about it. But only call the police if you feel your safety or your family's safety is threatened.'

Matt reddened. He had hoped that today's tribunal would end all his problems with the Zoy family but it seemed that the lawyer had traded one problem off against another.

The lawyer was watching him. 'He's certainly been no threat to your family so far and, since he hasn't even gotten out of his car, his behaviour towards you has been annoying rather than threatening.'

Jon added hastily, 'We're not asking you to ignore it. But the guy's clearly got difficulties and we've promised that we'll be as understanding as possible about them.'

The phone rang and the secretary picked it up.

'Mrs Zoy's on her way down with the medical ethics officer,' she hissed, hurrying to clear away the remains of the cake and all evidence of crumbs.

The secretary showed Mrs Zoy in. She looked so small that next to her Matt's secretary, in her bright clothes and bright makeup, seemed to bloom like a huge, exotic plant.

Everyone shook hands and spoke warmly and then they were gone, leaving Matt and Mrs Zoy alone in his office.

'Well, thank heavens that's over,' she began, and they smiled at each other. Matt had noted that her handshake was firm and now he was glad to hear that her voice was strong and clear.

'Dr Seleckis, I'd like to apologize for everything,' she said. 'The furore over Anthony's death, the accusations, the anger, the difficulties we've caused you . . . I'm not sure any of us is really ourselves at such a time. Now that my son has gone away for a while, I'm embarking on that long journey of grief alone —' Her voice broke and for a moment she was unable to continue.

'I think of grief as a tunnel,' said Matt gently. 'Sooner or later you have to go through it, there's no other way.'

Mrs Zoy nodded.

'But grief,' added Matt, 'is the price we pay for love.'

Mrs Zoy's eyes began to dampen and Matt passed her a tissue.

'Your son's gone away?' he prompted.

'Only for a while. He'll be moving back here from San Diego but he has to go sort things out first.'

'When did he leave Salt Lake?' asked Matt, trying to calculate when he had last seen the red car.

'Yesterday,' said Mrs Zoy.

Matt felt suddenly, ludicrously happy and, to disguise this, he busied himself passing Mrs Zoy another tissue. Mrs Zoy's son was away for a while and, despite what Jon described as a slight psychiatric history, when he came back he might forget all about his campaign against Matt.

She said, 'It would help my journey through the grief tunnel to know what happened. I mean, what really happened the night my husband died.'

Matt drew back a little.

'But I know you won't want to tell me. You've been placed on the defensive. Letters, lawyers, this terrible tribunal. I wish I could have stopped it before, Doctor Seleckis. But my son was so adamant that he wanted you reprimanded, he was like a tidal wave, impossible to halt or dissuade. I'm aware that he's made life very difficult for you . . .' She looked at him with a shrewdness through wet eyes. 'It's been a hard time for him. A time when perhaps he lost his balance. Is your father still alive, Doctor Seleckis?'

'Yes,' said Matt.

'When he dies there will be a lot of unsaid words. That's how it always is, and it's the silences, the unsaid, which can be most upsetting.'

Matt felt the bitterness of Mr Zoy's son keenly in his mouth, around his tongue and his gums. He remembered how the son had stood in his office with his face inflated by anger and grief and how the same anger had been fuelling the man's silent vigil of Matt's world. He thought of Mr Minelli's unsaid words and how that silence had permeated Steve's whole life.

'I think I understand,' said Matt. 'My father's alive but my mother's dead.'

'Ah,' said Mrs Zoy wisely.

Matt recalled how his own parents had hiked to the Mouth of Nowhere shortly before his mother's death. 'We talked and talked and talked. All those words we had to say.' But there had been no special words for Matt. He and Hilly hadn't talked and talked and talked. As she had faded he had watched in a miserable and helpless silence which she had done nothing to relieve. His tongue and his gums swelled and smarted a little at the memory. He thought again that, when he and Hirsh reached the Mouth of Nowhere looking for elk, maybe they would find Hilly and all the unsaid words waiting for them.

'I'm glad you understand how hard it's all been for my son. And I hope that he hasn't been too intrusive.'

'I may have caught sight of him out of the corner of my eye once or twice,' said Matt carefully.

'He never would pose any real, physical threat,' continued Mrs Zoy. 'I just hope he hasn't succeeded in intimidating you. If there are any cracks in your own life, intimidation of any sort can prise them open.'

Matt looked away from her. He had peered down into plenty of cracks thanks to the silent presence of the red car.

'So please, forgive him. I'll try to make sure that he doesn't bother you again but, if he does, I know your response will be typically generous. And now I'm going to ask you to trust me. Nothing you say will be passed on to my son or to anyone, I promise. Not a word will go any further than this room. But please tell me about Anthony's death. I think I'll be able to rest better when I know the truth.'

Matt decided to trust her. He related, in as much detail as he could remember, his last conversation with Mr Zoy. At the end, Mrs Zoy did not move. There was a moment's silence before she began to protest.

'But we had agreed I should be there! We agreed that he wouldn't die alone.'

'Finally, he made a different choice.'

'We didn't say goodbye.'

'Perhaps he couldn't. It so often happens that patients die when a devoted carer leaves the room for a few minutes, I've come to the conclusion that it's a step people want to take peacefully and quietly, by themselves.'

'I guess I'll have to accept his choice,' she said reluctantly.

Mrs Zoy left, thanking him for his courage and humanity. Matt wanted to describe the anxiety which Mr Zoy's death had generated, he wanted to explain that, because he had killed a man, he had suffered all the misery of guilt and in addition had awakened an acute sense of old guilt. He wanted to say that her son's presence in his life had turned some cracks to gaping chasms. But, since he could now hope never to encounter the man or his red car again, he said nothing.

22

Jon sent Matt home for the afternoon and as Matt drove towards the house, he felt his spirits lifting. There was no red car in his mirror. Next week he would go hunting with Hirsh and then it would be all over. And Denise was having a baby in April.

He wound down his window. The fall air felt benevolent, cool but not cruel. The October afternoon sun shone on the distant mountains illuminating the great faces which were flattened by time and shaped by glaciers. Life was sweet.

He spent the afternoon at home. After playing with Austin for a while, a deep tiredness swept over him and Denise told him to sleep.

'It's relief,' she said. 'You've been so tense for so long about this thing and now it's over.'

Matt wished that he could be completely sure his contact with the Zoy son was over but, anyway, it was over for now. He lay down in the bedroom and sleep enveloped him immediately as though it had been waiting for him. When he woke up he knew he should go running.

'Go,' Denise urged him. 'You always come back so relaxed.'

'Jarvis is in town and I'm supposed to meet him and Troy tonight so they can say a fond farewell before my trip. That should relax me,' he said, but he knew he should run daily now that the hunting trip was almost due to begin. Denise found his running gear and threw it at him, smiling.

'You'll feel better once you start,' she said. He knew that was true but today his legs didn't want to climb inside his running pants and his feet didn't want to fit inside his trainers. Somehow they had expanded so that the trainers had to be pulled and shoved. It was already getting dark when he drove through the downtown area to City Creek Canyon.

When he got out of the car and stretched he felt as though something enormous, larger than a locomotive, would have to shunt him along the park trail. Other runners, returning to their cars as the evening thickened, left the faint scent of sweat in the air. A woman greeted Matt as she passed and Matt recognized her as a doctor from some other hospital he had known at some other time. He couldn't remember the woman's name but he admired the easy fluency of her pace. A man ran by at a speed barely faster than a walk. His arms and legs were held tightly against his torso as though running was something which had to be extracted from him like teeth. Matt watched him. He hoped he didn't look like that man when he ran but the man illustrated the way Matt felt right now. He recognized that his exhaustion stemmed from the weakness that relief brings, but it was exhaustion all the same.

He walked past the Liberty Bell. After another full minute he persuaded himself to break into a slow run. First he made a circuit of the park, watching a dog bound into the lake while its owner sat motionless on the grass. Then he started up the hill, waiting for the effort and rhythm of his run to release him from the tyranny of the usual thoughts, the habitual worries. Gradually, as he picked up speed, he felt that the lawyer and Mrs Zoy and her son were all citizens of some other country, far away.

He ran still faster, so that, by the time he was high up the canyon's side, the laden trees of summer's end were a passing blur. When his mind and stride were experiencing a friendly harmony, he climbed up to the traffic at the top of the canyon and there, across a wide expanse of turf, the State Capitol loomed ahead of him, its great dome lit against the darkening sky.

He crossed the street and ran on the grass alongside. Traffic flashed by him. The fat, well-watered blades felt like tiny springs beneath his feet. This was a rolling public space but it was not quite a park, being without amenities and, since a hurricane, almost without shade. The noise and light of the evening traffic dimmed behind him as he turned into the Marmalade District, the area where the streets were named after the fruit that the early settlers had grown here. Denise knew a lot about Salt Lake history and they had walked all around the district, up State Street and down Plum and Quince and Apricot together, looking at the mansions of nineteenth-century moguls and the small homes of the earliest pioneers.

The streets now were silent and deserted. Some of the houses were lit, their drapes closed. The regular rhythm of his pace, the depth of his breathing, the sound of his feet slapping against the sidewalk and the sensation that his leg muscles lengthened with each stride, all gave him a pleasant feeling of well-being. He had no idea how long he had been running.

A car came along. He took no notice of it. His mind was happily blank. He did not know when instinct broke in, like a newsflash, with the information that the car had not passed him but was following him slowly up the street.

He did not slow his stride or turn back but he was alert now. Sure enough, his path was steadily illuminated by headlights. Close behind him, close enough to push him up the hill, was the growl of an engine in low gear. He reached the last house and did not look back. He ran right across the street and back on to the grassland around Capitol Hill. The traffic had thinned now. Apart from the slow grinding of the car behind him, which might have turned left but had followed him to the right, there was nothing.

In this public place, the important dome of the Capitol Building looming above him, Matt believed he must be safe. He relaxed his pace a little. To escape the car, which seemed to be gaining on him, he just had to swerve away from the street. He turned sharply into the heart of the black prairie. For a moment, just one joyful heartbeat, he was in the safety of darkness. Then the car's lights found him. The sound of its tyres indicated that it was mounting the kerb.

Matt's pace slowed. Alarm was robbing him of breath. The car was driving right across the wide, juicy grass. Cars weren't supposed to do that, not at the Capitol Building. There should be police, security guards, sirens, guys yelling into loudspeakers. Instead there was nothing here but Matt and the car. There was no nearby cover to the right or to the left and it was impossible that he could safely reach the state buildings, hundreds of yards ahead. He cursed himself. As soon as he had heard the car behind him he should have turned back into the comforting muddle of trees and houses which was the Marmalade District. Instead he was a lone, vulnerable figure running across an expanse of darkness, helpless to evade the lights of his pursuer.

He continued to expend as much energy as before but his pace was faltering and as he slowed it seemed to him that the car's engine grew louder. With a supreme effort, his legs and arms working like pistons to carry him, he circled to the left, so widely that the driver of the car might not perceive his plan and intercept him. He could see the intersection on

North Main, see the Pioneer Memorial Museum, the glow of streetlamps, the scattered trees. If he could get to the trees, they might delay the driver long enough for Matt to plunge down the hill amidst the houses again.

He felt the car closing on him, slowly but inexorably. Although the gradient was now slightly, very slightly in his favour, his lungs were deflating balloons and it was impossible, despite his gasps, to fill them with air. His feet pounded against the grass with a new painfulness. His legs were numb like detached and uncaring machines. Without looking back, without any visible evidence, Matt knew that the car would not stop when it touched him but continue on its steady path with his body beneath its wheels.

Eyes bulging, body burning, heart bursting, he put on a spurt of speed to near the trees. The car moved to block his exit but he dodged it, without thinking and so without warning. As the car steered between the tree trunks, Matt darted across the blacktop, over the opposite sidewalk and down, down the steep slope towards Center and Apricot and Almond, then into the darkness of a private garden.

The car tried to follow him, swerving into the road as Matt crossed it, but the driver was too late. Matt reached safety and the car continued past him down the hill. At the next intersection it turned right and Matt waited in the dark silence of the garden to see if it would drive around the block. As it had pulled up the hill, he had glimpsed briefly its colour and number plate. Red, MMV.

He lingered in the yard for a while, fighting to breathe normally again. No cars passed. He was at the side of the house where drapes had been left open. He allowed himself to glance into the lit windows of the property owner. A slim woman was cooking while one child watched TV and another, older, sat at a table, perhaps doing homework. A baby lay on a mat on the floor, kicking its legs joyfully in the air.

The domesticity of the scene helped to still Matt's booming heart. He waited, crouched in the dark, for another ten minutes. Once a pedestrian passed. His little dog sniffed out Matt but the owner didn't notice and the dog, after staring at him, walked on. When Matt was sure that the red car was not lurking somewhere nearby he ran as rapidly as he could back to City Creek Canyon.

He drove home to wash and change before meeting Jarvis and Troy. Driving earlier, he had searched his rear-view mirror for the red car out of habit. Now, once again, his search was fuelled by anxiety.

'Didn't running feel good?' asked Denise when he walked in.

He told her that he felt terrific but he shouted this answer from the stairs as he went up to shower. To him his voice, shocked, depleted, undermined his words but Denise did not seem to notice. He showered for a long time, as though the warm water could wash away his fear and confusion. Mrs Zoy's son should have gone to San Diego. And, even if he were still hanging around town, Mrs Zoy had said that he wouldn't actually try to hurt Matt. He experienced a desperation and disappointment so acute that it seemed to date from childhood days when adults were incomprehensible.

When he reached the bar where the others were waiting for him, Troy and Jarvis looked at him eagerly. They thought he had been at the tribunal all afternoon. He had not even reached their table before they had detected his mood.

'Oh boy, oh boy, it didn't go well,' said Jarvis. 'Waiter, bring this man beer.'

'Shit,' said Troy. 'They've reprimanded you.'

'No, they withdrew the case,' Matt said and watched his friends' jubilation as though they were someone else's friends and it was someone else's good fortune they were celebrating.

'So . . . what's the problem, buddy?' asked Jarvis, staring at him closely.

Matt took a deep breath and, for the first time, told them about the car.

'And before you ask me, the answer's yes, I might have been imagining the whole thing. I might be paranoid.'

'We weren't going to ask you that,' said Jarvis.

'How long did you say this has been going for?' asked Troy.

'Since the spring. And he may possibly, but only possibly, have tried to kill me once before.' Matt told them about the falling rocks at the mountain pull-in.

Jarvis breathed out noisily.

'Shit. Holy shit,' he said. 'Maybe the mother thinks he's gone to San Diego and he's just stayed around a few days to kill you.'

'Jarvis, that is not a helpful observation,' Troy told him tartly. 'Why didn't you tell us about this before, Matt?'

Matt sighed. 'I nearly did a lot of times. I nearly told Denise a lot of times. In her case, I thought that telling her would introduce the car into her life as well: even if she didn't see it, she'd be looking for it all the time. And I couldn't tell you guys in case you thought I was paranoid.'

'We never would have thought that,' Jarvis assured him. But Matt remembered the way Jon had looked at him, the way the lawyer had studied him.

He said, 'I suspected paranoia myself. That's been the worst part of it. Then, this summer my neighbour saw the car so I knew it existed. But, of course, I could have been imagining that it was following me.'

'You didn't imagine tonight,' stated Troy.

'No,' said Matt. 'I didn't imagine tonight.'

'And your lawyer's done this trade-off, right? Mrs Zoy drops the tribunal if you don't make noisy complaints about her life-threatening son to the police.'

Matt nodded miserably. He sipped his beer. It tasted sour.

'The police may not listen anyway,' he said. 'All my evidence is pretty weak.'

'Do you have the car number?' demanded Troy.

'I have a number for a car which is red. I almost never catch sight of the car's plate, not all of it . . .'

'Give me the number and I'll check whose car it is,' said Troy. 'Then we should find a way to nail this man, Zoy.'

Matt looked at him incredulously.

'You can do that? I thought only the police could do that.'

Troy looked mysterious. 'There are a few police officers who owe me a few favours,' he said.

'Maybe the guy in the red car isn't anyone you know,' suggested Jarvis. 'Maybe it's just some crazy who chooses people at random to follow.'

'In that case, we'll identify him,' said Troy simply. 'Don't worry, Matt. Your old pals will sort this one out for you. When we know for sure it's Zoy then we'll decide what to do.'

'This guy's vendetta is based on the crazy idea that you killed his father?'

'I gave his father a large painkiller because he was dying and he was in pain. I think Zoy's behaviour has more to do with his relationship with his father, the unsaid words, the unfinished business, the things which might have been.

That's where all this anger comes from. He doesn't know what to do with it so he's directing it at me.'

'Well, maybe if he sees Arnie real close in his rear-view mirror a few times he'll decide to direct his goddam anger somewhere else,' said Jarvis.

Troy and Jarvis started to argue about the wisdom of retaliating in this way. Matt found himself smiling as he listened to them. He began to relax. He should have told them long ago about the red car, he could always be sure of their support. He looked around at the other tables and realized they were surrounded by guys telling hunting stories. Across the room a small group were poring over topographical maps.

Jarvis and Troy began talking about his hunting trip. Worryingly, they were especially nice to him, as though it were either his birthday or he were undertaking some dangerous mission and they feared they wouldn't see him again. Since it wasn't his birthday he supposed he must be going on a dangerous mission. Troy started telling cautionary stories about people dying of hypothermia on rocky mountain ledges because they were too proud to go home without a carcase. Jarvis suggested Matt took two emergency medical kits, one for himself and one for Hirsh. They both repeated, at least twice, that Matt must take his cellphone, despite Hirsh's opposition. Jarvis urged him to take emergency flares as well.

'Anyway, we're not going to starve,' said Matt. 'I've discovered these things called MREs and I'm sneaking a week's supply of beef teriyaki into my pack.'

When they parted for the evening, Jarvis hugged him, wrapping his wide body around Matt's. Troy shook hands stiffly.

'I'm still worried about my liver,' he said. 'Can you arrange for an ultrasound when you get back?'

'You gotta confirm that this crazy Zoy guy's stalking him,' said Jarvis. 'No information, no ultrasound, right, Matt?'

The following day was Matt's last at work before the trip. He saw Steve Minelli in the cafeteria, sitting by himself at a table. He waved for Matt to join him.

'I wanted to say goodbye,' said Steve. 'When are you leaving?'

'I'm driving up to Dad's tonight.'

'I sure hope you have a great trip, Matt.'

'Thanks.'

Steve was finishing up a large plate of food. He saw Matt looking at it. 'I'm refuelling,' he explained. 'I'm just going on duty and I have a double shift right through to four a.m. You're not supposed to do it but they're short-staffed so they let you if you want to.'

He opened a plastic pot of something sloppy and began to fish in it with a plastic spoon.

'How's the target practice going?' he asked.

'Okay, I guess. We've been using the small range up at John-Jack Perry's.' After his conversation with Stewart, Matt did not intend to play along with Steve's fiction that he no longer knew the area.

'That's cool. How's your dad doing?'

'He's fit and he's shooting okay.'

'Are you taking medical supplies?'

'You bet.'

'Taking your cellphone?'

'Against Dad's wishes, but I'm taking it.'

'So, are you going out there on the first day of the bull elk season?'

'Setting off on Saturday.'

'Where are you starting from?'

'A place on the way to Goat Bend. Called Wounded Knee or something.'

'Knee Heights?'

'Maybe that's it,' agreed Matt vaguely.

'I know it. Been there. Very steep for the old guy but steep the way elk like it, plus the cover's thick when you get higher and away from civilization. Where you heading for?'

Matt felt a new, curious hesitation about supplying Steve with information.

'North initially, that's the only way to go. Then we cross a ridge and move west to some forest.'

He knew this to be untrue. Hirsh had shown him on the map that the Mouth of Nowhere was a long journey east. He did not know what instinct had prevented him from telling the truth or describing the Mouth of Nowhere.

'Hmm. North then west. Sort of towards Cold Kitchen?'

Matt made a show of considering this. 'That rings a bell,' he said at last.

'There's a good lodge there,' said Steve. 'The Cold Kitchen Lodge. What kind of a gun do you have?'

'A Winchester 30–06.'

'Hey, that's featherweight. You'll need to pack some 180s inside her if you're going to make a good kill.'

'Dad has the ammo sorted out.'

'Need anything else? Camouflage cover for your gun, space blanket, electrical tape to put across the muzzle and stop the snow getting in . . . ?'

'Thanks, Steve, but Dad's friends have loaned us everything. Probably we're already carrying too much.'

'You got a good coat?'

Matt nodded. 'I'm borrowing the sheriff's old coat.' He decided not to mention the woollen underwear.

'How long you out there for?'

'Probably four days.'

'Matt, don't forget what we talked about. You're going to ask the old guy some leading questions on this trip, remember?'

Matt nodded wearily.

'I wish you luck. May you take home a one thousand-pounder and may his rack make B&C. But just remember, it's not a game. It's life and death when you're out on the mountainside, especially with the old guy. So be careful. I mean it. Be ready to kill at any time. Connect. But most of all, be careful.'

Steve was looking at Matt as he spoke to him. Matt unwrapped his sandwich.

'Thanks, Steve.'

Steve leaned forward suddenly. 'I wanted to tell you something, Matt. It's something I remembered. Something . . .' He looked down shyly. 'Something I sort of want to confess.'

Matt studied Steve's face. He looked too thin. He looked as though he didn't refuel often enough.

'Confess?' he repeated. This conversation was beginning to feel hazardous.

'An old crime, such an old crime that I guess you won't mind any more. You mentioned it the first time we met, well, remet, back in the spring. And I've been thinking about it ever since and I believe I've remembered the truth.'

'Is this anything to do with your father's death?' asked Matt unwillingly.

'Oh no, no, nothing at all. It's about that big glass window, right by your pa's porch door. The one birds were always flying right into.'

'The one we broke?'

'Matt, you didn't break it. I did. I broke it one morning

when I was hanging around outside your house waiting for you to get back from somewhere. I can remember the sound it made now. Sort of scraping and cracking like an earthquake noise. I stood there and stared at it. Maybe I thought it'd paste itself right back together. Anyway, it didn't. So I took my baseball and, man, and I ran real fast down the hill to our place so no one would ever know. Later, our dads blamed us both and they managed to convince you that you must have done it. But you didn't. I did.'

'Come on, kids,' Mr Minelli had said. He had stood right over them and he had looked mean and Matt had been scared. 'I don't like yellerchickens. I don't like kids who don't own up.' And Mr Minelli had shifted his weight around dangerously until Steve, already small at Matt's side, had shrunk back.

'I'm gonna get mean. I'm gonna get real mean if you guys don't tell me you broke that glass.'

By now Steve had been so scared that he had moved right behind Matt. He had hidden from that big, mean bully who was his father.

And Matt, trying to stand tall between Steve and Mr Minelli had said, 'I did it. With the baseball. I broke it.' And the big bully had smiled.

Now, twenty-six years later, Matt felt his face redden with anger.

'You're mad at me,' said Steve sadly. 'You're mad at me for not telling you back then.'

'I'm not mad at you, Steve.'

'I think I told Jo-Jo the truth,' said Steve. 'But I just couldn't tell you.'

As usual, blood had been thicker than water. Matt was silent.

'You're angry with me, I can tell,' said Steve miserably.

'No. I'm angry when I remember the way your father accused us and started shouting at us.'

Steve looked up from his plastic pot.

'Pa didn't shout,' he said very quietly.

'He was furious. He yelled at us. He called us yellerchickens and he said that if we didn't confess he'd get real mean. And we were very, very scared.'

Steve stared. 'I was not scared of Pa,' he said. His voice sounded hot, white-hot. Matt knew he should stop but he did not.

'I confessed because I was scared. And because you were so terrified that you'd hidden behind me and I couldn't stand it. I just wanted it to stop. So I said that I'd broken the glass. I can't remember what the punishment was but it couldn't have been worse than getting yelled at that way.'

Steve's face had narrowed now so it looked like a long, thin, white line of anger. 'I was never scared of Pa. He was a great guy. He shouted sometimes but he was firm and fair and that's how you have to be with boys.'

Steve stood up now. He leaned right over Matt so Matt felt small. He wasn't shouting but his face had rearranged itself into a high-cheeked, jutting-jawed Steve. His brown eyes had a new light in them. For the first time, it occurred to Matt that Steve looked a little like his father.

'He was a great guy and his death was the worst thing that ever happened. You have this fucking fantastic life and you go hunting with your dad and you think you can sit there criticizing my pa. But he was ten times the man you are, ten times the man your dad is.'

Steve turned and threaded his way through the people who were standing in line for food and the old folk who were manoeuvring themselves out from behind tables and the strollers that weren't standing in the stroller park and the small groups of gossiping doctors in blue scrubs. Matt watched him go and eventually he was no longer distinguishable from anyone else in green.

At feeding time, thought Matt, the human descends from the highest altitudes to interact socially with other members of his herd and graze principally on carbohydrates. When angered or replete, he ascends rapidly again, through often hostile terrain.

He put his head in his hands. He felt bad. He never should have ventured near the truth. He had no right to strip away the delusions about his father on which Steve's life was built. Steve's anger, though shocking, had been justified.

His secretary surprised him by sliding down into the seat next to him. 'Mind if I join you?'

'Only if you have a double chocolate brownie with vanilla cream topping,' he said.

'Don't mind if I do.'

'What happened to the diet?'

'I got bored with it.' She opened a bulging cream cheese bagel.

'Bored with the diet, or with Buildings Admin?' he asked, and she laughed.

'I think I prefer Human Resources these days,' she said. 'Apart from anything else, they have lots of fascinating information on people. To be precise, they have some information you might be interested to know. About that guy who was just here, the cleaner you were friends with when you were a boy.'

Matt stopped eating. 'Steve? What about him?'

'Know why you didn't see him for years and years?' she asked.

Matt shrugged. 'Our lives took different routes.'

'His route went to the State Penitentiary.'

'Oh no,' said Matt. 'He was in Seattle and that's not quite the same thing.'

'He was in jail right here in Salt Lake, Matt. Long-term. He only got out last summer.'

Matt swallowed. Stewart said that Steve had appeared at Arrow Lake last summer and had stayed there, apparently camping, into the winter.

'I know it's true, Matt,' said his secretary, watching his face.

Matt sighed. Maybe it was true. It was possible that a single gunshot at Arrow Lake twenty-six years ago had blown Steve all the way to the State Penitentiary.

'Want to know what he was in jail for?' she asked happily. She liked possessing information.

'Don't tell me,' said Matt. 'I'll go ask him myself.'

23

Matt finished work early. Then, instead of going home to pick up his bag for the mountains, he went looking for Steve.

'How do I find out which ward Steve Minelli's working on?' he asked another green-clad orderly. She pulled down her mask and smiled at him, reaching for a clipboard on the side of her trolley.

'You find out by looking at my rota.' Her accent was Spanish. She surveyed the clipboard. 'Oh, lucky Steve, he got Maternity tonight. That's my favourite,' she said. 'Only place in the hospital where the patients are happy.'

Matt thanked her and set off towards Maternity. In April, he and Denise would be walking right in through these doors again, Denise's belly enormous. She would be counting her yoga breaths in time with the contractions. Involuntarily, he smiled. Then he remembered why he was here tonight.

A couple of the nurses recognized Matt and nodded at him. He kept walking until he saw a cleaner's cart outside one of the bedrooms. Inside was Steve.

'Hey,' he said from the doorway. Even before Steve looked up his face was angry. He looked as though he hated people who stood in doorways saying hey. Then he saw it was Matt and he looked as though he hated him anyway. He did not greet Matt but resumed his work.

'Can I speak to you for a couple of minutes?'
'Why?'

'Because there are some things I need to say to you. Like, sorry.'

Steve continued working, his back to Matt.

'C'mon, Steve. Let's talk. Just for a few minutes.'

Steve spoke at last. 'I'm not supposed to talk on the wards.'

'Isn't it time for your break?' Matt persisted.

Steve was silent.

'There must be somewhere you can go for a coffee.'

After a moment, Steve said quietly, 'There's the Operatives' Recreational Point.'

He still did not look at Matt but brushed past him into the hallway. Matt noticed that his face had that same look he'd seen in the cafeteria, thin and mean as a whip. He followed Steve along the hallway and then down some back stairs into the bowels of the building where the corridors were lined with pipes and ducts which perhaps carried cool air to other parts of the hospital but did not release it here. Steve swung through an unmarked door into a room Matt had never seen before. It had wooden seats and a frayed floor rug and no window. It looked like the kind of room where people wait to visit their relatives in jail.

There was a drinks machine in one corner. A misspelt sign on it warned that it was out of everything but coffee or iced tea. The room appeared to have heating instead of air conditioning. It was too hot to drink coffee here. Matt bought them both iced teas and there was a moment when he thought Steve was going to refuse his but the new, angry, hating Steve finally held out a small hand for the cup.

Matt said, 'Steve, I'm sorry I criticized your father. It was unforgivable but I hope you'll try to forgive me. My family had many happy times up on Arrow Lake with your family, you and I had great summers together. Of course there were good times and bad times but mostly it was good, and nothing which happened subsequently can take that away.'

Steve looked into the icy depths of his plastic cup.

Matt continued, 'I just wish that, when we met up again, you'd been more honest with me. About your past.'

Steve looked at him for the first time. His eyes were still lit by anger. 'What about my past?' he said.

'It is true you've been in the State Penitentiary?'

'Who told you that?'

'Not you. I wish you'd trusted me enough to tell me, Steve. But now I know, I just want to say . . . I'm sorry. I'm sorry that everything's been so god-awful for you since your dad died. I understand how important he was in your life and how things have been tough for you ever since you lost him.'

Steve sighed. The sharp angles of his face softened fractionally. 'I didn't do it,' he said. He spoke rapidly now, his voice an undertone. 'I went to jail for someone else.'

'Do what?' Matt asked. 'What did they accuse you of doing, Steve?'

'I had a habit, you know that. I agreed to take part in an armed robbery. I was using, I needed money, a lot of money. I was meant to be just on lookout but this security guard got shot. It wasn't me. But I got convicted. That's all, Matt. I've spent half my goddam life in jail and I didn't even do it.'

'I'm sorry . . .' said Matt again. Steve's face was reshaping itself once more. It was crumpling. Matt saw that he was going to cry.

'Would you tell an old friend where you'd been all those years?' demanded Steve angrily. Tears were starting to flow down his cheeks now but he carried right on as though he

378

couldn't see them or feel them. 'Would you tell people if you were trying to start again?'

Matt passed him a tissue and then realized that was not enough. He got up to put an arm around his friend's shoulders. For a second he felt Steve's body, surprisingly wiry, inside his arm and then Steve, with considerable strength, pushed him away.

'I don't want your fucking sympathy,' he said angrily. 'It's easy for you to hand me sympathy when you've got everything you want. A dad who goes hunting with you, a nice family, a big house, a medical career, everyone looking up to you.'

There was more than anger in his voice now, there was hatred.

'Just remember why you have all that,' he said. 'Because your family destroyed mine.'

Matt started to protest, until he saw there was no point. Steve's face had frozen. He did not look at Matt. His eyes did not move. It seemed his mouth didn't move when he spoke.

'Do you know how hard it is for me to watch you go off on a hunting trip with your dad?'

Matt sat down on one of the wooden chairs. 'I can guess,' he said.

'Huh!' roared Steve. He had stopped crying now but his face was still wet. 'You don't know anything! It all would have been different if my dad had lived. He was the best, the brightest and the best. He had ideas, he had energy, he always came out on top. If he'd lived then we would have had a big house in a good area and gone to the best schools, just like you did, Matt. I would have probably gone into business with Pa and he'd have taught me all he knew, which was a lot. He was a great guy, a big guy.'

Suddenly, unexpectedly, Steve smiled. Matt knew that smile. It was his blood-is-thicker-than-water smile.

'Your father's nothing compared with Pa,' he said, still smiling without humour. 'He couldn't even hit that muley buck from close range. Pa used to laugh at him for that and for everything else. Your father should have died, Matt, not mine. It should have been your dad in that car that day.'

The two of them stared at each other in silence, Steve projecting hatred, Matt receiving it. When he had come to look for Steve in the happiest ward of the hospital, Matt hadn't come looking for this. Although now it seemed inevitable.

The door was flung open and a small group of orderlies walked in. One of them was the woman who had shown Matt her rota.

'Hey, that's great, you found him,' she said warmly to Matt. The women went over to the drinks machine. They ignored Matt and Steve. They were chatting in Spanish and Matt understood them to complain about the machine, about its limited choice, and to discuss the merits of iced tea against hot coffee. Matt watched them with a numb detachment and when he turned back to Steve he saw that he was gone. The door to the room was closing and before it swung shut there was a suggestion of green clothing.

Matt got up slowly and found his way down the hot, pipelined hallway. He went up the first staircase he passed and found himself in Radiology. From here he knew his way to the parking lot. As he drove home through the evening traffic, he thought that he should never have attempted to revive the old friendship. Too many years had passed and now he and Steve had nothing in common but those distant summers. His foolish attempt to resurrect the past had probably damaged both of them.

He was disappointed to find that Denise and Austin were out. He had hoped to spend some time with them before leaving. His bag was ready but now he threw a few more things in. His mood was darkening. Tomorrow he and Hirsh would be checking and packing and probably repacking their equipment. Then, very, very early the following day, Stewart would arrive and transport them to a point higher up the mountain. They would get out of Stewart's car and simply walk off the road into the cold, dark morning forest and, when they could no longer hear Stewart's car engine, they would know they were completely alone in the wilderness.

When Matt thought of all this, his heart beat faster and he wished it was an ordinary evening and he was going to the hospital tomorrow.

The phone rang. It was Dan Murvitz from the Medical Centre and they exchanged warm greetings.

'How was the Italian trip?' Dan asked, and Matt had to explain that it was cancelled.

'A good thing, too,' said Dan. 'It never works, doctoring your own family, in my experience.'

'Want me to give Denise a message, Dan?'

'Well, I just called to remind her to pick up her Subgynon. She hasn't been in for a while and my computer says she's getting dangerously short. Unless, that is, she's made a deliberate decision to stop with the birth control? Maybe you guys are trying for another baby.'

Matt's silence was so long that it alarmed Dan.

'Matt?'

'Sorry,' said Matt. He was trying to think quickly, to respond quickly, but was unable to.

'Are you okay, Matt?'

'Oh, sure, sure. It's just I thought she'd been to the clinic and told you. And I guess she hasn't.'

'Told me what?'

'She's pregnant.'

'That's great! So she already decided to leave off the birth control. Well, congratulations. Send her in to me for the usual checks.'

'I will.'

'As for the Subgynon, she's been on it for years, except when she had Austin of course. I think it would have been time for a change anyway: there are newer, better pills now. We can talk about all that when she's had the baby.'

'I'll send her in, Dan. Thanks very much for taking the trouble to call.'

When Denise arrived with armloads of supermarket shopping, Matt was sitting at the kitchen table.

'We're late. Lines at the supermarkets. Lines at the traffic lights. We were sitting in lines when we wanted to be home here with you.'

She looked at him especially closely and kissed him softly. He saw that all her movements were informed by her knowledge of his imminent absence.

'You haven't even turned the light on,' she scolded. 'Austin's fallen asleep in the car as usual, want to carry him in?'

She looked tired. He said, 'You sit down. I'll carry Austin and the shopping inside.'

She said, smiling widely, 'I've been vomiting all day. Isn't that a good sign?'

'Fantastic,' agreed Matt. He took off her jacket and held her close to him. He realized there was a lot he didn't know or understand about Denise but it made no difference to the way he loved her. Whatever lies she had told Weslake, for whatever reason, if there was a time to question her that time wasn't now.

'Dan Murvitz called,' he said. 'He wanted to remind you about some kind of check-up or something and I told him you were pregnant and would be coming in anyway.'

'I'll go this week,' she promised.

Matt held her tightly. He wanted to kiss her again and again. This would be their first separation for longer than a weekend. He fetched Austin in from the car and held him close too. Leaving was almost unbearable. Then, when he had checked his bag, he threw it into the car. He hugged and kissed them both one more time before he drove away. When he looked back they were standing at the lit window, staring out into the street, waving at his car lights. He felt as though his body was driving up the street but he had left some vital part of it, his heart maybe, lying on the kitchen table.

As he moved slowly through the suburbs towards the mountains, he noticed that garages were lit up and there were big SUVs lined in driveways. Boys were carrying equipment out to vehicles. Men were loading up. He passed at least two people carrying rifles. The whole city seemed to be preparing to move out to the wilderness. The hunting season was beginning.

The Hunt

24

The night was still fuzzy like a blanket when Hirsh woke Matt on the morning of their trip. Dawn, with its light and movement, had not yet begun and the dark felt stagnant. Matt showered, bowing his head and weaving his body from side to side so the hot water covered him all over. The last hot water for days. Even after this, it didn't feel like morning.

His cellphone had been charging secretly under the bed. He stuffed it into his pocket.

There was a light on in the kitchen. Hirsh pushed a coffee towards him in silence and Matt took it, ringing his hands around the mug, feeling its warmth.

'Eat,' Hirsh commanded, producing hot oatmeal and fruit.

'Not sure I can,' admitted Matt but he knew this was foolish.

He forced a spoonful into his mouth. Dried fruit and spice flavours sprang from the unpromising cereal like a secret which just couldn't be kept. In the back of his mouth, around his tongue, raspberries beckoned from the summer, figs spoke of some other country far away, cinnamon told him it was Christmas.

'Good, isn't it?' said Hirsh, watching him. 'This is the super deluxe. I just keep it for special breakfasts.'

Matt wondered what made some breakfasts special for Hirsh. Maybe Sheriff Turner came over at Christmastime or maybe in summer the old guys had coffee and oatmeal out on the terrace.

Stewart arrived looking pale in the porch light. They put on all their outer clothing and their boots. Matt checked in the secret back pocket of the coat Sheriff Turner had loaned him for his illicitly large supply of peanut butter sandwiches. He couldn't see why Hirsh saw peanut butter sandwiches as such a threat to their wilderness experience.

Hirsh fetched the guns. Their backpacks were waiting by the door. Matt braced himself to pick up his, which was stuffed with his secret beef teriyaki-flavoured MREs. He was surprised at how easily he could lift it.

'All locked up, Hirsh? Sure you've got everything?' asked Stewart unnecessarily.

Hirsh volunteered to sit in the back where he wouldn't be such a bad passenger, or at least the driver wouldn't notice so much.

'Could we go over the pick-up routine one more time?' asked Stewart. 'You'll be out there for three nights. Tuesday, depending if your camp's where you think it is, you'll head back towards Rockroll and call someone from the gas station late afternoon. Me or Lonnie or Elmer'll get right over there to find you.'

'It's okay, Stewart,' Hirsh assured him. 'We won't call you on a Tuesday, we'll call one of the others.'

Matt remembered that on Mondays and Tuesdays Stewart devoted himself entirely and unflinchingly to Mona, who closed her restaurant and came up the mountains on those days.

'Oh, that's okay,' Stewart said. 'Mona can come with me to pick you guys up. Now, our safety procedure . . .'

'What safety procedure?' demanded Hirsh.

'If we don't hear by Tuesday night we start to worry but take no action. If we don't hear by Wednesday morning I pick up the phone and call Emergencies.'

If Hirsh hadn't been in the car, Matt would have reassured Stewart that he had a cellphone in his pocket.

'You won't be calling Emergencies,' said Hirsh gruffly. 'You'll hear on Tuesday.'

'Sure we will,' said Stewart. Matt thought his cheerfulness sounded forced 'I mean, you guys are going to have a great time. Weather forecast is for light rain and that's perfect, although I guess it'll get to snowing when you climb a bit higher. And when I pick you up you'll be carrying one big load of elk meat.'

Hirsh and Matt were both silent. Matt was thinking that the chances of them finding, tracking and shooting an elk and then dragging it all the way to Rockroll were virtually zero, unless the animal ran to Rockroll and then obligingly allowed itself to be shot near the road. He wondered what Hirsh was thinking.

It seemed they were at Knee Heights almost right away. It consisted of one small, dark, closed-up restaurant with a closed-up house next door. They passed the house and drove on for another mile. Then, too soon, Hirsh said, 'Around two bends, along some. Now over to that clearing.'

He must have scouted in advance. Matt could barely make out the clearing. Stewart also had trouble finding the small crack in the forest's edge.

'You sure you know where you're going?' asked Stewart anxiously.

Hirsh did not reply to this. He said, 'You'll find the road's wide enough so you can turn around right here, Stewart. Many thanks for getting up early. And for loaning the rifle. We'll make sure we have some good stories to tell you on Tuesday.'

'Take care out there,' said Stewart. When Matt opened

his door the car lit up Stewart's face, paler and thinner than usual, his expression worried.

'We'll be fine,' Matt said unconvincingly.

'Shhhhhh,' hissed Hirsh.

Matt could feel the change in altitude the moment he got out of the car. The air was colder and thinner and, like a cold, thin dog, it could bite. He pulled his hat down over his ears and immediately rolled it back up again. Here in the dark he was almost sightless. He didn't want his hearing muffled too.

In silence they took their backpacks and guns. Matt closed the car door as quietly as he could. They did not wait for Stewart to turn around but plunged right into the dark forest. Matt wondered how Hirsh could see anything. He followed, waiting for his eyes to anchor on familiar shapes, but he could barely make out Hirsh's figure just in front of him.

The route was rocky. It seemed to be either a trail or a dried-up creek bed. It rose steeply from the road. To move silently here, you had to watch your feet or use some sixth sense to detect the boulders in the dark.

Matt heard Stewart's car turning. It already sounded far away. He paused and turned back. Through the trees below him he could see the car headlights shining white. The lights moved down the hill. The tail lights became pinpoints of red. Then there was nothing to see any more. He listened to the sound of the engine disappearing. When there was absolute silence, broken only by Hirsh's occasional footfall up ahead, Matt turned and proceeded up the hill.

There was still no sign of dawn but the darkness disintegrated as Matt grew accustomed to it. He saw the hillside stretching up ahead of him. Around him were the endless verticals of the tree trunks. He easily caught up with Hirsh. His father was moving slowly, probably pacing himself. The small backpack made his figure look squarer. A square of humanity in this vertical world.

It seemed to Matt that they were walking for ever. He knew that Hirsh believed serious hunting was more possible when they were free of their backpacks and that he was anxious to reach their camp. When, eventually, the hill levelled out, the forest thickened. Without warning, Hirsh left the creek bed and turned to the right. Matt stumbled after him. It was a relief not to ascend any more. He had heard himself puffing up the last part of the hill and, probably, so could any animal for miles. The shoulder straps of the backpack had begun to remind him of their presence. His skin felt sweaty. His body felt buried alive in layers of wool and cotton and Gore-tex.

They found themselves in a small clearing. Hirsh stopped right on the edge of it.

'Dawn,' said Hirsh in a low voice. 'It's coming. We'll rest awhile.'

Hirsh sat down on his pack, his back against a tree. Matt was glad to ease the big burden off. Its absence felt so good it made him want to celebrate his release, like Austin running off whenever you lifted him out of his highchair. Matt circled his arms violently, first one way and then the other. He circled his head. He circled his shoulders.

'The sooner we get to our camp the better,' Hirsh said. He still spoke in an undertone and his voice seemed to settle on the air and lie there like smoke on a windless day. 'All this stuff is an encumbrance.'

He reached into his pocket and disencumbered himself of two granola bars. Matt took his and sat down. When he ripped the wrapper the sound seemed to rip the thin air.

His jaws munching on the granola must have been audible from a hundred yards away.

As soon as he had finished the bar he wanted a cup of coffee. Then he realized that the world around him was changing. Somehow, subtly, it was re-forming itself. Dawn was nothing more than the hint of a smile over to the east and its light had not even reached them yet but the forest seemed to know it was coming. It was moving, changing, resettling its limbs. Stealthily at first, then with abandon, noise arrived. Rustling, chirping, scraping, banging. Matt felt stiller than the trees as he watched the light come. He knew it must arrive from the east but it seemed to radiate evenly from inside the earth. Gradually a view formed beneath them, of steep, wooded valley sides. Among the dark pine trees, the broadleaves were a distant block of colour, no longer green but not yet gold. In the distance were high rocks, their peaks muffled by clouds.

They sat in silence. The heavy sky seemed to sink a little closer.

'Rain coming,' murmured Hirsh, getting up.

Far below them, they heard shots.

'Aaah. There they go. The opening shots on opening day,' said Hirsh.

'Do we get to make a wish?' asked Matt.

Hirsh did not reply. He looked out over the expanse of dark trees. 'Those guys are miles away. They're way too low for elk.'

'How long will it take to get to the Mouth of Nowhere?' Matt asked, although he had previously decided not to use his mother's name for their camp, which he thought extravagant in that typically Hilly sort of way.

Hirsh considered. 'Well, we'll be there before dark,' he said at last.

Matt hoisted the pack back up on to his shoulders. He staggered a little as his left arm looked for the strap.

'Want me to take any of that? I've got some space,' said Hirsh.

Matt shook his head, although the pack felt heavier this time. He tried to shift the position of the shoulder straps a little.

'No need to get out the compass, we know which way's east,' said Hirsh. Matt looked over to the place in the grey sky where dawn's glimmer had begun. The steep mountainside fell away beneath them to the south.

'I assume,' said Hirsh, looking over his shoulder, 'that you've noticed some of the rubs we passed.'

Matt did not reply. Although Hirsh had described the way both deer and elk rub scent from the glands on top of their heads to attract females, and although he had pointed out old deer rubs near the house, Matt had failed to notice any on the trees.

Hirsh pointed to a sapling where the bark had been rubbed bare, about four feet from the ground.

'Way too low and way too short for elk,' he said. 'That's a muley. Stay alert and you'll see some scrapes too.'

They were climbing again and Matt did not want to admit it was difficult to stay alert and ascend with the heavy pack. He kept thinking about coffee. Sometimes he even imagined he could smell it.

'Rubs are one of the biggest clues the elk's likely to give us,' whispered Hirsh. 'You have to get in the habit of looking for them all the time.'

Matt noticed that his father was breathing heavily now. They paused on the hill.

'Dawn is peak grazing time for elk,' Hirsh said. 'If I thought there were any elk around here, we wouldn't be travelling like this. General rule is: when your target's on the move, you stay still. When your target's taking a nap, you move.'

They continued. Once they startled a small group of mule deer. The animals disappeared into the forest, bouncing on all fours. Twice Hirsh stopped and got out the map and the compass. He showed Matt where they were and where they were going. It seemed to Matt there was a vast expanse of paper between their present location and their destination. He said nothing but Hirsh, guessing his thoughts, told him kindly, 'These are very large-scale maps.'

They had to plunge down an exceptionally long, steep hill so they could climb the next one. Matt could feel the muscles on the back of his legs objecting. He wished he had done more mountain training. Capitol Hill hadn't prepared him for this.

But gradually the silence of the wilderness seemed to penetrate Matt's heart. The rhythm of his walk began to feel comfortable. Shafts of sunlight penetrated the clouds, he sniffed the unique smells of the forest, sometimes clean, sometimes sappy, sometimes pungent. He watched the changing view and inhaled the clean air. Hunting wasn't so bad. It was like hiking only you had to look for rubs. Down in the city Denise and Austin might be thinking of him, talking about elk as they ate their morning snack. Suddenly he felt happy. He was suffused with love for the family who awaited his return.

They stopped for sandwiches. Matt's watch told him it was almost midday. He tried not to think about coffee while they looked at the maps, which seemed to have shrunk a little.

Soon after they set off again, Hirsh noticed a fresh elk rub. It was much higher than anything they had already seen, as high as Matt, and it stretched above his head. The bark was stripped clean off the tree for at least a foot. There was a little sap weeping from the damaged area.

'A good rack's been around here recently!' whispered Hirsh. 'I never thought to find a bull so soon. Let's see if he's left us a trail.'

The elk had left a trail. Matt was amazed at the way his father followed it. He stooped over hoof prints, at one point measuring both the prints and the distance between them.

'He wasn't ambling,' said Hirsh. 'He wasn't running but he wasn't ambling.'

Sometimes he stopped and sniffed the air. 'I think I even smell him,' he breathed.

From time to time there were more rubs and more footprints. You could see where the undergrowth was trampled in places.

'Do elk always move in straight lines?' whispered Matt. It seemed to him that the elk must soon turn to one side but Hirsh moved straight ahead and always picked up the trail again.

'Unless they have some reason to change course, I guess they do,' muttered Hirsh.

Matt saw that his father was excited. Although his movements were as deliberate as always, Matt could sense the old man's adrenalin. Before they had seen the elk rub, Hirsh's square body had become a parallelogram, listing a little to one side as he walked. Now it was square again. The elk trail was like an anaesthetic and Hirsh had ceased to feel pain in his right hip. He would feel it later, Matt thought, when the long, silent chase was over.

They walked on and on through the forest. They stopped frequently but when they moved they moved fast, faster than they had moved all day, with a new, quiet fluency. Matt lost any sense of how long they had been stalking the bull elk. Matt remembered that Elmer Turner had said the elk could move at more than twenty miles per hour for most of a day.

'Do you know where we are?' Matt whispered once but Hirsh, moving forward soundlessly, examining tree bark, sniffing the air, seemed not to hear him and Matt did not dare raise his voice.

There was an abrupt clearing where the landscape tumbled down to a grassy meadow. Hirsh did not leave the shelter of the trees but stopped so suddenly that Matt almost walked right into him.

'Let's glass it,' Hirsh breathed. 'I don't know where we are but there could be elk around here. It feels right.'

Hirsh held up his binoculars. He focused on one place and then silently passed them to Matt. They filled with bright, blurry fall colours, then the distant swooping peaks. Nearer, where the forest started again, tucked into its edge just the way Hirsh and Matt were, he discerned horizontals. Horizontal lines amid the verticals of trunks and peaks.

'Are they deer or elk?' Matt barely breathed his question although the animals were hundreds of yards away and he was sure could not hear him unless they had the place bugged.

Hirsh pulled him back into the cover of the trees before he answered.

'Too big for deer. We have to get close enough to be sure, and closer still to shoot,' whispered Hirsh. His voice shook a little. 'I didn't expect to find them yet, the country back there didn't feel wild enough.'

'Maybe they don't know it's the first day of the season,' suggested Matt.

'They soon will,' Hirsh said, grinning a little. 'And I think there's another bull elk with his eye on the herd which led us right to them.'

'Where's the other bull?' asked Matt, looking around.

'Hiding in the woods somewhere. Surprised we haven't heard him calling.'

'How do we get closer without them seeing us?'

'Same way as the bull who's planning to mount a challenge. Through the forest. See how the edge of it curves into the meadow a little? That's less than a hundred and fifty yards from the elk. If we go through the forest, move quietly and come back out just on that curve we might, might get one good clear shot at them if we're ready and quick.'

Matt looked around.

'We'll have to swing round and climb up so we're approaching them from above,' added Hirsh. 'That's an elk's weak spot. He looks below, not above, for danger.'

They turned and went in the opposite direction from their quarry. When the trees were thick enough, they swung towards the elk. The forest was densely covered here and there was little undergrowth but a lot of dead branches to snap underfoot. At one point, Hirsh stopped.

'We have to be quieter,' he said.

'It's hard with a backpack,' said Matt. 'Want to leave me here with the equipment while you go ahead alone and shoot?'

Maybe Hirsh would bag a trophy elk right now and their trip would end abruptly here. They could somehow get the carcase to Knee Heights and Stewart would pick them up and they would be back in their beds tonight.

'No,' said Hirsh. 'I want you to take a shot at a bull elk. You might not get another chance like this.'

'I thought *you* wanted to take a shot at a bull elk. *You* might not get another chance,' insisted Matt.

'Are we going to stand here arguing?' asked Hirsh, his whisper turning hissy.

They continued through the forest, more slowly this time. There were a few more rubs but Hirsh didn't stop to examine them. Then he paused. He looked uncertain.

'I'm not sure how far we've come and I don't want to go too close or they'll smell us if they don't hear us.' His voice was less than a whisper. 'If we head down the hill now, think we'll be where we wanted to?'

Matt considered.

'A bit further,' he said finally. They moved ahead for a couple more minutes and then turned down the hill. Hirsh stopped and took off his backpack. Matt did the same, stowing it behind a thick tree. They moved ahead with their guns, slowly, stealthily. Without the weight everything was easier. Movements could be controlled, sound could be controlled, your breath could be controlled. The undergrowth was bushier here. Matt checked for twigs as he walked. He lowered his body and weaved it from side to side to avoid branches, the way he had weaved in the shower that morning.

And then he felt it, for the first time, the thrill of the hunt. The elk was a great wild beast who lived in the wild, understood the wild, lived by its rules. And now he was doing the same. He was moving through the trees like an animal. He was a lion, creeping up on its prey.

His heart beat faster. He felt his hands grow clammy. They were approaching the end of the trees and found themselves in precisely the place they had chosen. They went into slow motion, stopping frequently. Standing only about 100 yards away, while the cows of his herd bedded around him at the forest's edge, was a big, antlered elk. He was sideways on and his eyes were half-closed.

Hirsh gestured for Matt to take the shot. But Matt realized he didn't know how to. If he looked around for a rest, if he crouched into the undergrowth, if he did almost anything but stand right where he was and shoot offhand, the elk would detect him. But he always missed when he shot offhand.

Hirsh touched his arm gently. He pointed to a low tree branch which offered a good rest for the rifle. It was just a few yards away. Matt moved towards it more slowly than slow motion. He didn't look at the elk but turned his face sideways, the way Elmer had shown him. Elmer had said that, just as if you stare at someone in a crowd they're sure to know it, so do animals.

Matt reached the branch. He wedged his rifle across it and clicked off the safety. Through the scope the beast looked enormous, its hide impenetrable. But the animal had detected something now. His eyes were open. He was alert.

'Go,' breathed Hirsh.

Matt positioned the crosshairs so they met over the elk's heart–lung area. He stopped breathing. His body was immobile except for his hand: gently, so gently he thought it rather than did it, he began to squeeze his finger. As he did so, he felt a vibration in the pocket of his jeans.

Then there was music. Computerized, jaunty.

'Waltzing Matilda, waltzing Matilda, you'll come a-waltzing, Matilda with me!'

The elk turned and ran. There was an enormous crash like lightning, a flash, the gun kicked back into Matt's shoulder. But the elk was already gone.

'And he sang as he sat and waited while his billy boiled . . .'

The cows of the herd were on their feet, and within a second, maybe a fraction of a second, they had all melted into the forest. It was like watching evaporation.

'*You'll come a-waltzing, Matilda with me!*'

'Shit, shit, shit!' said Matt.

He fumbled in his pocket to find his cellphone.

'Safety ON,' shouted Hirsh. Matt guessed his father needed to shout about something. He put on the safety and then held the phone to his ear.

'Yes?' he demanded and the tinny music stopped. He could still feel his heart thumping and the adrenalin washing around in his body. His hand was shaking.

'Okay, okay, no need to yell,' came Jarvis's voice. In the background was the roar of Arnie's engine. 'Don't try telling me you were just about to shoot a trophy bull.'

'I was just about to shoot a trophy bull,' said Matt, his voice sounding dead, anyway a lot more dead than any elk around here.

'And my name's Andy Warhol. Listen, I'm just checking you took the cellphone like you promised and just checking that everything's okay with you guys.'

'For Chrissake, Jarvis, we've only just started.'

'I was thinking about you because I'm driving over the Mandlemass Pass right now and guess what I saw? Only a big, mean-looking elk! He was pretty impressed by Arnie. Practically held up his hoof and thumbed a ride. So the moral of the story is, you don't have to suffer in the back country looking for elk. Just drive down the Interstate and you should be able to shoot yourself some delicious McElkburger.'

Matt sighed. 'Thanks, Jarvis.'

'Old guy holding up okay?'

'He's doing just fine.'

'Great. Listen, I have some news for you. You're not going to like it.'

'Is Denise okay?' demanded Matt instantly.

'It's not about Denise. It's about that red car. Troy found out who owns it.'

'Who?'

'You're not going to like it,' repeated Jarvis.

'Who?'

'Guy named Steve Minelli.'

There was a silence broken only by crackles.

'You still there?' yelled Jarvis.

'Yes.'

'Told you he was weird. Told you way back at the exhibition.'

'Yeah,' said Matt flatly. 'Those pictures.'

'It wasn't the pictures. It was the punch. Remember the punch? I knew that guy was trouble from the punch.'

'You were right.'

'I know I'm right, buddy,' roared Jarvis, 'because Troy found out something else about Steve Minelli. He hasn't spent his life in Seattle, he's been down at Draper, Utah. You know what's there, don't you?'

'The State Penitentiary,' said Matt flatly. 'I already knew he'd spent some time there.'

'For first-degree murder. Shot a guy dead. A cynical, cold-blooded and calculated act.'

'It's already dramatic enough, Jarvis, you don't have to dress it up with clichés.'

'Not my clichés. The judge's. Troy got a hold of the trial report and that's what the judge said.'

'Oh.'

'Just trying to be helpful. I mean, I thought you should know. You can spend those long, cold sleepless nights under

401

the stars thinking how you're going to deal with the problem that you're being stalked by a cynical and cold-blooded first-degree murderer.'

Matt sighed.

'At least you don't have to worry right now, anyway,' said Jarvis. 'He can't drive his car up the mountains to bother you.'

'Even if he could, he wouldn't find us. I told him we're going west and we're actually heading east. I don't know what made me do that.'

'Instinct,' said Jarvis. 'We'll sort this one out as soon as you get back, Matt. Troy wants to go to the police precinct with you the second you get down the mountain. In the meantime, stay cool. Stay safe.'

There was a click as Jarvis hung up and then the silence of the forest descended. It was a moment before Matt could turn around to meet Hirsh's eye and then he found that his father was already halfway up the hillside. He stumbled after him and had nearly caught up when his cellphone sang again. Hirsh did not stop but Matt thought he could discern disgust in the hunch of his shoulders.

He opened the phone and greeted the caller curtly. Probably it was Jarvis ringing to say he'd seen another elk.

The line crackled and hissed. There was no background noise of Arnie's engine but the call felt live. Someone was there.

'Hello?' said Matt again. He heard an intake of breath but the caller still did not speak. Standing alone now in the forest, his cellphone pressed to his ear, he felt a tickling sensation in his neck and he slapped at it in case a spider had crawled down inside Elmer's coat. Except he knew it wasn't a spider. It was the small hairs there standing on end because there was a person calling him and something in the volume, the crispness of the phone's silence, indicated that person was nearby.

He looked wildly around but could see no one, not even Hirsh now. The call ended abruptly and his phone made an irritated buzzing noise. He tried to retrieve the caller's number but it was withheld.

By the time he had caught up with Hirsh he had convinced himself that the call had come from some idiot colleague at the hospital who had forgotten that he wasn't supposed to phone this week.

'Okay, I'm sorry. I brought my cellphone in case there was an emergency,' Matt said breathlessly. 'Only I forgot to switch it off.'

Hirsh didn't say anything, a sure sign he was angry. He reached his backpack, sat down on a log and pulled out the map. He began to engross himself in it.

'Dad?' said Matt plaintively. 'I said I was sorry.'

Hirsh looked up at him. 'You wouldn't have shot it anyway,' he said.

'I wouldn't?'

'Nope. You didn't want to enough.'

'I did!' protested Matt, remembering the feel of his sweaty finger on the trigger. He didn't want to admit, even to himself, that Hirsh might be right. He had enjoyed scouting the animal and it had been a challenge to get into position without being detected but, once that was achieved, had he really wanted to take the hunt to its natural conclusion so soon? When 'Waltzing Matilda' had driven the elk off into the forest before he could even fire, he had felt the smallest measure of relief.

'You don't have the killer instinct in you right now because there's nothing driving you,' continued Hirsh, looking at the map. 'I mean, there's no passion like anger or jealousy or the need to show a trophy. And we ate enough sandwiches so that you're not even hungry enough to want the meat.'

Matt said nothing.

'But,' said Hirsh, 'you will be.'

Matt thought of all the MREs stowed secretly in his backpack. He didn't anticipate that he would get so hungry on this trip.

'I know you'll be hungry,' Hirsh went on serenely, 'because I've taken nearly all of those vacuum-packed meals right out of your pack.'

'What?'

'I told you not to bring them.' Hirsh put his finger on the map to mark something, their location Matt hoped, and looked up again. 'That's not the way real hunters go about their work, with a pack stuffed full of food for a week. That's not what the wilderness is about.'

'You took my MREs out? When?'

'Last night when you were asleep. They're in my study drawers for when you want to take them back down to the city with you.'

Matt felt his blood start thumping around his body as though he had seen another elk.

'What else did you take out?' he asked angrily.

'Nothing. I left the medical supplies where they were. I guess they're a wise precaution, although probably a little excessive. I've always carried my own kit but it's a fraction of the size.'

Matt was silent.

'I didn't take *all* your food sachets out,' said Hirsh softly. 'I left a couple for emergencies.'

'So what do we have to eat?'

'Powdered potato, oatmeal, granola bars, rice, and

whatever we catch ourselves. That's what real hunting's all about.'

'They're developed by NASA, they're a mainstay of the US Army, they have interesting flavours like beef teriyaki, but MREs aren't good enough for you,' said Matt bitterly.

'If we were astronauts I'd eat them,' said Hirsh.

Matt sighed. He remembered how his backpack had felt lighter this morning than last night.

He glanced out across the empty meadow. No sun fell on it. The sky was darkened by rain. They could hear the water pattering against the conifers but as yet they couldn't feel it.

'No point following those elk?' he asked.

'No point,' agreed Hirsh.

Matt, who hadn't thought about coffee all the time they were scouting the elk, now felt his need to be acute. He considered suggesting they light a fire then realized that by the time they had found the wood and started the fire and heated the water, the coffee would probably take a whole hour. He never would have become addicted if he'd had to light a fire every time he wanted a cup instead of just heading for the nearest machine.

'So, where are we?' he asked.

Hirsh had his compass out. 'I think we've moved a ways west,' he said. 'I think we're far from where we want to be.'

Matt sat down on the log next to Hirsh and picked up the map where he knew the Mouth of Nowhere was located.

'We're not on that map,' said Hirsh. 'I think we could be here. Look, that peak's marked. It's due west of us . . .'

They spent the next five minutes comparing landmarks and maps.

'I didn't know we'd walked so far,' said Matt.

'That elk took us back towards the edge of the wilderness,' said Hirsh. 'Look, there are houses marked right over there.'

It was true. After walking away from civilization all day the elk had swung them west towards human habitation. As if to confirm this, a distant shot rang out. And then another. There was a burst of fire.

'Someone else will soon be field-dressing our bull elk,' said Hirsh gloomily. 'We're so close to a bunch of other guys now that we should be wearing fluorescents. And I didn't even bring any.'

'Cold Kitchen,' read Matt. 'That's where we're near.' The name sounded familiar. He remembered that Steve Minelli had mentioned it in the cafeteria. Matt had deliberately tried to mislead him by saying they were heading north-west and Steve had understood that as Cold Kitchen. And now, here they were, not so far from the place.

'Isn't there a Cold Kitchen Lodge?' he said suddenly.

Hirsh did not reply.

Matt looked out across the meadow. It was darker now, and raining harder. He looked at his watch, barely visible in the dim forest light. He remembered the silent call he had just received on his cellphone.

'Dad. It's past three o'clock. We can't walk to the Mouth of Nowhere now. It's too late. It's wet. It's going to be completely dark soon. Plus we started at God knows what time this morning and we need a rest.'

'So?' snarled Hirsh. 'What are you suggesting?'

'I'm suggesting we check into the lodge tonight, since it's probably only a few hours' walk away at most. We leave early tomorrow and we don't follow any rubs or smells or footprints, we head straight for our camp. Then we look for elk.'

Hirsh continued to study the map as if sheer willpower would make the Mouth of Nowhere get closer.

'The only alternative,' said Matt, adopting a reasonable tone, 'is to set up camp here. But it's a waste of time camping so close to civilization and a bunch of other hunters. Even I know that. We should go to the lodge.'

Hirsh breathed deeply. 'No,' he said. But he looked tired and Matt knew his resistance was weakening.

'Dad, I think it's the right thing to do.'

'Anyway,' said Hirsh, 'they won't have a room at the Cold Kitchen Lodge. We'll walk all the way there and see a No Vacancies sign.'

'Dad, I really am sorry I left my cellphone on, and I'm sorry that Jarvis called but since I have this thing, let me make use of it.'

He got out the phone again. Its artificial light shone incongrously into the forest.

'I don't believe this,' said Hirsh miserably, but Matt was already dialling inquiries. Then he was calling the lodge. Hirsh shook his head as Matt asked for a room.

'Oh, that's okay,' Matt was saying. 'A trundle's fine. And do I need to book a table in your restaurant?' Behind him, he heard Hirsh groan. 'Okay, that sounds good.'

He gave his name and then snapped the cellphone shut. Hirsh sat on his log without moving.

'Dad?'

'I should have known better,' said Hirsh, 'than to attempt to have a wilderness experience with a city boy like you.'

Matt didn't think this was fair but he said nothing. He was folding up the maps now, confident that he could find the way to Cold Kitchen. He felt the place pulling him as though it had him tied on the end of a long rope.

'C'mon, Dad, let's get going. They had just one room

with one twin bed and one trundle bed and we don't want them to give it to anyone else. Do we?'

'Yes,' said Hirsh, but he hauled himself stiffly to his feet. He didn't look like the same man who had melted through trees in pursuit of an elk just an hour ago. He looked a lot older. Matt suddenly had a cheering conviction that he was doing the right thing.

'Dad, listen,' he said, helping Hirsh with his small pack, 'one of the hunting books you gave me said the most important thing is to recognize your limitations. I know that when we've walked for a couple more hours we'll need a good bed and a good meal and a good sleep. Then we should set off early tomorrow and we'll be at our camp by afternoon. It'll still be light and we can begin scouting for elk immediately.'

He started up the hill. He looked back frequently and saw that, very slowly, Hirsh was following. At the top of the hill he paused. Probably Hirsh should set the pace. He waited and then fell in quietly behind his father.

Hirsh stopped frequently now. The first time was without warning. He suddenly swung around and said, 'Why does it play "Waltzing Matilda", for heaven's sake?'

'I have a colleague from Australia. Big joke, he's pro-grammed everyone's cellphones to play "Waltzing Matilda".'

'Ha,' said Hirsh mirthlessly. 'Who was it the second time?'

'Probably Jarvis again but he's driving in and out of mountain ranges and we lost the signal.'

They stopped soon afterwards because they heard more shooting close by. A third time, Hirsh paused and sat down. He said, 'So what did Jarvis want?'

'To tell me he'd seen a big bull elk from the Interstate at Mandlemass Pass.'

Hirsh guffawed. 'We'd better get right over there.'

It was dark when they arrived at the lodge. Hirsh surveyed the room rates with raised eyebrows while Matt signed them in.

'Have you seen what it costs?' Hirsh muttered.

'I'm paying, Dad,' said Matt firmly.

'Your table in the restaurant will be ready for you in a few minutes,' said the receptionist. 'What time would you like to leave in the morning? How about taking one of our Hunters' Special packed lunches with you tomorrow? They're light, filling and nutritious.'

Hirsh groaned quietly as Matt ordered two lunches.

'We also sell good-quality and tasty top-of-the-range MREs,' she said. Matt stole a glance at Hirsh. His face was stony.

'No thanks,' said Matt. 'But I'd sure like a coffee.'

'All facilities are in your room, sir,' she said, handing him their key. It had a deer horn attached with the room number written on it. They loped off down the carpeted hallways with their backpacks, trying not to bump them as they rounded the corners.

'I feel an idiot walking in here with all our back country gear,' Hirsh said.

'It's okay, no one saw us. And it'll be dark in the morning. All the other guys will be driving off in their SUVs and we'll just slip across the road and into the trees. Like elk,' Matt assured him.

'If elk's on the menu I'm not ordering it,' declared Hirsh. He was walking lopsidedly now. When he sat down on the edge of his bed he looked as though he didn't want to get up again.

'Let's eat now and have an early night,' said Matt when they had made some bad coffee. Hirsh's stiffness was more than evident. It was acute. He moved towards the restaurant as though someone had glued his joints together.

All around them were hunters, their faces reddened by the outdoors. Most looked clean and showered, damp hair combed tidily, clothes dry and mud-free. The noise level was high and while they ate it seemed to rise. Men told one another stories. Groups burst out laughing. A couple of people argued.

There were a number of other father and son teams. Some of the sons looked broad-jawed and handsome like Weslake, who Matt knew had frequently hunted with his father and his brothers.

To keep them both awake while they waited for their meals, Matt told Hirsh how Weslake had been blackmailing Clem. He was aware that he was being indiscreet, even though he took care not to reveal the secrets of Clem's past.

'Well, it's not exactly blackmail if he was using the money for investment purposes and intending to pay it back with interest . . .' said Hirsh.

'Dad! It was extortion! And Clem's just lost it all!'

Hirsh yawned widely and apologized. Then he said, as though the words had slipped out with the yawn, 'Why did you come back to Salt Lake, Matt?'

Matt was so surprised by this question that for a moment he did not understand it.

'After Africa. You had some great job offers in endocrine surgery, why did you hang around in Salt Lake waiting for Jon Espersen to take pity on you?'

Matt reddenened and floundered a little. It wasn't just hard to ask Hirsh personal questions, it was hard to answer them. When he had floundered long enough, Hirsh answered for him: 'Were you here because Denise was here? I mean, you came back to Salt Lake and Weslake died. Were you staying here waiting for Denise to be ready to marry you this time?'

Matt felt his face heating. It was probably pink. It probably looked like the Rosebay Building right now but without the classical features.

'No,' he said quietly. 'That wasn't the reason I stayed in Utah.'

'Did you know Weslake was dead?' Hirsh's face sagged but his eyes were still alert.

'No!' Matt could feel his face was burning now. 'I've already told you. Not until I met Denise again at Mason House, and that was months later. She'd been a widow for a long time, more than six months, by then.'

'Didn't you even try to get in touch with her?'

It seemed strange to Matt that Hirsh, who asked so few questions about his life, had such a curiosity about that bleak post-Africa period, the very period Matt would have been happy to forget. He sighed.

'I've already explained this, Dad. I'd failed to persuade her to marry me. I didn't think she really loved Weslake, I thought she was doing what Clem wanted to compensate for the way her sisters had all gone back east and married out. But I couldn't persuade her to stop the wagon and so we agreed not to contact each other again. Ever. And, that was right because, without me around, the marriage appeared to work. Over four years it had seeded, grown and blossomed pretty spectacularly, at least, that's how it seemed.'

Hirsh propped his head in his hands as though he was so tired it would otherwise fall right down on to the table. 'Seemed?' he yawned. 'Only seemed? What makes you think there could have been anything wrong with that marriage?'

Matt hesitated.

'Well, I guess it was fine,' he said. Except that Weslake had been betraying Denise by blackmailing her father, and Denise had been betraying Weslake by taking the contraceptive pill while apparently desperately wanting a baby. Matt shook his head with confusion.

Their food arrived and they ate rapidly and in silence. Matt had come on the hunting trip because there were a lot of things he intended to talk to Hirsh about but Denise hadn't been one of them.

Back in the room, Matt offered to draw Hirsh a bath.

'Might help take some aches off,' he suggested.

'Matt, it sounds like a great idea but if I got into a tub I probably couldn't get out until morning,' said Hirsh.

When they were in bed and the lights were out, Hirsh added, 'The discomforts of hunting camp really don't matter because when you're this tired you don't notice them.'

'Are you going to be okay in the morning?' asked Matt. He was beginning to worry about Hirsh. He wished they hadn't stalked the elk so far but had stayed with their original plan to get to their camp. Now Hirsh had another whole day of walking before he could rest again.

'I'm just old, that's all,' said Hirsh. 'But not so old a good night's sleep won't make me good as . . .'

He slurred his words and fell asleep before he reached the end of his sentence.

'New?' Matt finished for him.

But in the dark no sound came back except breathing. Matt reached for his cellphone and immediately dialled Denise. She answered sleepily. In an undertone, he told her all about the events of the day, how he had missed the elk and how Jarvis had called, although he didn't mention the news about Steve Minelli. He told her how much he loved and missed her. Before he rang off, he asked, 'You didn't happen to call this afternoon? Sort of mid-afternoon, just before dark?'

'No.'

He shrugged into the night. 'Someone tried to get through. Probably it wasn't important.'

As he hung up it occurred to him that he should switch the phone off now to preserve the charge. But he fell asleep before he could do so.

25

The hunters who had been at dinner came down to an early breakfast in the dark the following morning. Today they looked sunken-eyed. The night had stolen the outdoor ruddiness from their cheeks and the words from their lips. The restaurant was mostly quiet except for the scrape of silverware on china.

'These guys aren't going further than their jeeps can take them,' muttered Hirsh as a particularly rotund hunter attempted to squeeze himself in at the next table. Matt looked around and saw that the men were predominatnly overweight. It was unlikely that any of them was heading as far into the wilderness as the Mouth of Nowhere.

Hirsh finished breakfast first and returned to the room. Matt took advantage of his absence to ask the receptionist for four MREs. There was no beef teriyaki so he took spaghetti with meat sauce and salmon with lemon instead. Hirsh was in the bathroom when he reached their room and Matt had time to stuff the MREs into the pocket of his pack.

They set off into the dark forest with their Hunters' Special packed lunches nestled in their coat pockets. All around them were the slamming doors of jeeps and the sound of cold engines starting.

The air felt cooler this morning than yesterday and the ground beneath them was frozen and unyielding but it seemed to Matt that his night vision had improved. He could see, up ahead, that although Hirsh was stiff he was walking steadily and standing straight.

Their boots skated a little on hard mud. Small branches snapped noisily. The two of them sounded to Matt like a whole army marching through the woods.

Dawn came and from the first hint of light they could hear distant shots. Sometimes just one, sometimes a burst. They did not stop to watch the world light up today. Although they were in untamed terrain, with every shot it seemed the forest was more crowded and they quickened their pace a little. We're elk, thought Matt, escaping to the wilder, higher, most inaccessible places. Probably, though, elk didn't get coffee cravings.

Then they stumbled right across a small group of hunters. The figures were crouched around a miserable camp fire, still in their sleeping bags. Others, supine, were strewn about like giant caterpillars which had just fallen from the trees. There was no sign of tents or any other shelter. Rifles lay haphazardly on the ground or leaned against trees.

'Morning,' said Hirsh, making to walk around them.

'Hey, wait,' one called. 'You guys, wait.'

He sounded young and, when Hirsh and Matt had halted, Matt knew at once that these were a different kind of hunter from the middle-aged men at the lodge and their clean-cut sons. He looked from face to face and saw written there the bleakness which follows recent consumption, maybe of drinks, probably of drugs. One of them got up now and strolled over to a tree behind Matt and Hirsh. Matt wondered what he was going to do. He feared the youth was planning to block their path.

The boy urinated against the tree. Another, by the fire, laughed. Matt saw a third was shivering violently. The supine figures in the sleeping bags had not moved at all. He was sure now: these guys were hungry and cold and possibly feeling mean enough to be dangerous.

The youth who had called after them picked up his rifle.

'Yes, what do you want?' demanded Hirsh and Matt knew from his impatience of tone that his father, so quick to follow trails and to scent animals, had failed to sniff danger here.

'Where you guys going?' asked the kid insolently. Beneath the thick hat, his face retained youth's curves. He was half-smiling in a way which Matt found far from friendly. Matt could imagine him a few years ago, a fat little rich kid playing with his toy guns.

'East,' growled Hirsh, turning to go. But the kid who had peed against the tree was, as Matt had feared, blocking their exit.

Matt tried to adopt a relaxed and friendly tone. He had done so often enough in the emergency room with potentially violent patients. 'If you guys want to shoot animals you might have to move. All the noise is frightening them further into the forest.'

'Is that right?' asked the kid with the gun. He didn't seem grateful for the advice.

Since it was hard to advance with one kid barring their way (a kid, Matt noticed, who now held a gun), Matt knew he had to keep trying.

He said, 'Are you guys okay? Did you sleep out under the stars last night?'

'Yeah, and it was fucking cold,' said one.

'I'm still fucking cold,' said the boy, who was shaking.

'We wanna shoot animals, but you the first motherfuckers we seen around here.'

This wasn't the kind of language Hirsh used or liked to hear and Matt, who guarded his own language when Hirsh was around, though not always successfully, felt ludicrously offended on Hirsh's behalf.

'You'll have to move if you want to shoot,' he repeated firmly.

Hirsh, of a generation to find this behaviour intolerable, said, 'But you won't shoot anything if you leave your guns lying around on the frozen ground. That's no way to treat your firearms.'

The kid with the gun responded by putting it into position. He held it offhand. He didn't aim at them but just past them, into the forest.

'Well, let's see if this baby still works,' said the kid, his words distorted by the stock of the gun.

'What kind of a dumb fool thing to do is that?' demanded Hirsh, but before he had finished speaking there had been an explosion of such magnitude that Matt was amazed to find himself still standing. So that's what the bull elk had seen yesterday when he had missed the shot. All the violence of a mountain storm terrifyingly packed into one tiny place for one fraction of a second.

Matt looked at Hirsh and saw from his face that the old man was badly shaken. And then he felt angry. How dare these spoilt kids scare his father?

He walked firmly towards the boy with the gun. He bent down and, seeing how tightly the kid was grasping the rifle, and how he was shaking a little, Matt did not attempt to remove it. He just slipped on the safety.

'That's dangerous,' Matt said. His voice was soft and without aggression. 'People do that kind of thing when they need help. I think you need help. What can I do for you? Are you short of food?'

The kid stared at him, wide-eyed, but did not move. This close, Matt could see in his pupils evidence of last night's consumption.

Matt reached into his pocket. He pulled at the mighty

417

bulge that was the Hunters' Special. He threw it down at the kid's feet. There was a thud nearby and he realized that Hirsh had thrown over his Special, too. Before the kid could say anything, Matt had pulled off his pack and had fished in the pockets for the four hidden MREs he had bought from the lodge that morning. He dropped them in the kid's lap. Far away, he could hear a volley of gunfire, and then another.

'Eat all this, every bit of it,' he instructed, as though he were prescribing some particularly foul-tasting medication. 'Build your fire. Get warm. If your friend here hasn't stopped shaking within thirty minutes, you wrap him up some more and go that way –' he pointed in the direction he and Hirsh had come from '– and you'll hit a road. On it is the Cold Kitchen Lodge. You go into the lodge and you eat some more and you get warm. This is the wilderness and it's fall and these are serious firearms and hunting isn't a game you play at.'

He swung on his backpack and turned and led Hirsh away past the standing kid, who now made no attempt to impede their exit. They walked quickly and without speaking for about thirty minutes, Matt frequently turning back to glance at Hirsh. His father's face was down as though he was concentrating very hard on his feet. Finally he heard a small voice saying, 'Matt, I need a rest.'

Hirsh was already seated on a large, rotting log. He watched Matt turn back to join him. Matt positioned himself next to his father on the log so he didn't have to take off his pack.

'What you did back there was good,' said Hirsh. His voice was weak and gruff. 'You dealt with it real well. I was old and stuffy and just inflamed the situation. Thank God you were with me or I don't know what would have happened.'

Matt accepted this rare compliment in silence. Then he

said, 'Good thing they were too dumb to guess what I'm carrying in my medical kit.'

'I mean,' continued Hirsh, 'what are their parents doing letting them loose in the wilderness?'

'Their parents probably don't know, maybe don't care.'

'And another thing. What did you give them to eat apart from our lunch?' asked Hirsh.

Matt grinned. 'I bought some MREs at the lodge this morning to replace a few of the meals you threw out.'

Hirsh grinned too. 'Good thing you did that,' he said. 'We really needed them.'

'What is it about MREs that they can't stay in my backpack?' asked Matt as they got up.

This time Hirsh took the lead. He set a noticeably slower pace. Matt felt a sharp, surface pain in one heel with each step he took. A blister. It was annoying, but small enough to ignore.

Suddenly Hirsh stopped. Somewhere nearby there was the crash of undergrowth and the snapping of small trees. Instinctively Matt turned back in case there was a fully armed kid close behind but the noise was coming from one side. Elk, a whole herd of them, on the run from someone else's gun. Hirsh and Matt froze. Hirsh reached for his rifle but the elk saw them and veered simultaneously to their right. Somewhere in the retreating mass of horizontal lines, Matt saw the vertical of a fine pair of antlers. Hirsh's gun was ready now, the bull elk was almost sideways on, but there were too many trees, too many cow elk, and the animals were too rapidly doing their amazing evaporation act, though not silently, into the darkness of the forest.

Hirsh lowered his gun and clicked the safety back on.

'If I'd been a bit quicker . . .' he said.

'You never would have singled out the bull in all that

419

movement,' said Matt. 'You'd have wounded a cow and we'd have spent all day tracking her and we never would have reached the Mouth of Nowhere.'

Hirsh sighed. 'I guess you're right. You're getting good at the theory, anyway.'

'I wish the theory included a cup of coffee,' said Matt.

'When we reach camp,' promised Hirsh.

They were just starting off again when Matt's cellphone started to sing.

'I thought you turned that thing off,' growled Hirsh to the metallic strains of 'Waltzing Matilda'.

'So did I,' said Matt, flipping open the phone.

'So, so, so!' boomed a voice. It was loud and close. 'So the elk came galloping right by and you weren't quick enough to get a shot in! You guys aren't doing too well.'

Matt began to look all around. He peered through the trees but he could see no one.

'Yesterday you missed. And today you didn't even try. Got to improve your performance if you want to eat elk,' said the voice.

'Who is this?' asked Matt, still looking around.

'Can't you guess? You really can't?' Okay, I'll give you a clue. I'll tell you a story. Stories are always nice when you're hunting. This one's about a woman I used to know. Actually, she was a whore. Looked respectable but really she was a whore. Threw herself at men. One day, a man she wanted found a diamond. He found it in the freezer at the super-market. And she wanted that diamond too. She wanted to make it into a ring. But how could she explain it to her family? I mean, a diamond wouldn't just appear from nowhere. So, know what she did? She pretended that *she* found the diamond in the supermarket freezer. God, you should have heard the way she told the story. Everyone

420

believed her. But it wasn't true. It was a lie. This man found the diamond and it was really his! Would you believe it? Well, I hope you enjoyed the story, Matt. See if you and the old man can guess who the woman in the story is! You've had a lot of clues there, see if you can guess the answer. I'll be calling you soon to know if you've guessed it. Oh, and a piece of advice. Be careful! Tell the old guy to be real, real careful! Bye, Matt.'

Matt had stopped looking among the trees for evidence of the caller and was staring at the phone now. Not only had their hunting trip been invaded, his memories had been ransacked as if his very thoughts were being stalked.

Hirsh was watching him.

'Who was that?'

It was a moment before Matt replied.

'I don't know,' he lied.

'Well, what did they want?'

'Nothing.'

Matt took a last look around. 'We should get moving, Dad.'

Hirsh seemed disinclined to go until he had received an explanation but Matt started off decisively. Then it occurred to him that Hirsh would be safer at the front and he waited for his father to pass him. The old man did so wordlessly. He seemed to Matt to be moving with an agonizing slowness.

'Can you go any faster, Dad?' he called eventually, taking care to keep his voice soft. For some reason, the more slowly they moved the more his blister hurt. It was getting larger now.

'No,' said Hirsh.

Before the phone call Matt had begun to enjoy the hike. He liked the way your mind sank down inside itself until you weren't thinking of anything in particular, even blisters.

Probably that was how it was to be an elk. You thought about food or shelter or reproducing when you needed to. The rest of the time you didn't think about anything much, you didn't worry about the weather or question why there was less to eat this year, you just acquiesced in your existence.

But now there was no acquiescence. Matt looked around constantly. Again and again he swung round to watch behind him. He saw no one. Occasionally he stopped and listened. He heard only Hirsh's footsteps. He let his father walk out of earshot and listened again but the sight of Hirsh walking alone through the forest sent worry running down his spine like a current, and he hastened to catch up.

Hirsh looked like stopping a few times. Matt hurried him along, keeping up his vigil. Eventually, when they had puffed their way up steep slopes, they reached the forest's edge. They were looking out over a long expanse of exposed heights.

Hirsh stumbled a little way and then said, 'We haven't even had a granola bar, for heaven's sakes, Matt. Plus I want to check the map.'

They sat down on some cold rocks with their granola bars and some water. Matt, though sweating, was aware that around them the air was cooling. The sky was leaden, hiding all peaks but the closest.

'Is it going to snow?' he asked his father.

'Probably,' said Hirsh, unfolding the map. 'We're high enough.'

These treeless upland heights did not have the jagged edges of the peaks. They were rocky and pitted by great incisions which, except for an enormous crater at the centre, were mostly too small to be canyons, too large to be cracks. Walking across here would take twice as long as you'd expect, thought Matt, because you had to go round the canyon at the centre and around each huge incision. Plus, you were exposed. There were some big boulders but mostly the rocks lay flat in the landscape like sleeping animals. He shivered. He looked back into the forest again but as usual he could see no one.

Then, suddenly, shockingly, there was gunfire. First, Matt thought he actually felt the bullet's proximity. He didn't know it was a bullet, nor did he have time to think about it, but he had the sensation of air displacement, of an immense, unnatural velocity. Almost simultaneously, certainly before you could ask yourself what was happening, he heard the blast of the gun. It echoed across the mountaintops. Maybe it echoed three times, getting a little fainter each time as though it were a mountain train disappearing amid distant peaks.

Hirsh threw himself flat on to the ground. A curved rock afforded a little cover. Matt sat up, staring back into the woods, trying to see the hunter.

'Get down!' hissed Hirsh. 'There's some idiot out there who's shooting at beasts on the other side of the canyon and he hasn't seen that we're right here.'

Matt crawled on to his stomach next to Hirsh.

'How do you know he's not shooting at us?' he asked.

Hirsh said, 'Of course no one's shooting at us! If only I'd brought those fluorescents . . .'

Matt was warmed by his certainty. The phone call from Steve had been crazy, if Steve was the driver of the red car some of his actions had been crazy, their last talk, in the Operatives' Recreational Point, had been a little bit crazy, but surely he couldn't be crazy enough to open fire on them.

He half-expected to hear 'Waltzing Matilda' again but when his phone was silent he concluded that Hirsh had been right. Some lone hunter had set his sights in the distance and failed to notice two small figures making their way across the vast terrain.

After a few minutes, they rose cautiously. Looking all around, they began their journey across the open peak. Tufts of grass peeked from between rocks, otherwise the place had the bleakness of a moonscape. The drama of the higher mountaintops was hidden by a thick curtain of cloud. Snow fell, not large-flaked, gentle Christmas card snow but flakes that were small and hard and serious as though they had been wrung reluctantly from the sky. Matt could feel the mountain wind on his exposed face. He pulled his hat down and his scarf up.

The terrain was deceptive. It was easy enough to round the canyon but the rocky fissures appeared suddenly and you had to be right up against them before you knew they were there. Then they were forced to go back and around. Matt figured that they were making life easy if Steve was following them. A stalker could watch them take the wrong routes, then swiftly select only the right route himself.

He had looked back and around frequently but seen no one. After about an hour, though, he detected in the distance, the far distance, mostly obscured by snow, something which might have been a thin, dark figure. At the sight of it, Matt began to feel angry, far angrier than he had felt this morning with the kids. He and Hirsh were scouting elk and all the time they had themselves, unknowingly, unsuspectingly, been scouted like animals.

Eventually they moved into the shelter of another mountainside. The wind dropped and, although snow still fell, they found themselves in a kinder place. Trees grew in mountain meadows, sparsely at first. Water ran, gushingly, down the hills. Gradually the density of the tree trunks thickened and they were in coniferous forest again. They startled a pair of deer bucks fighting, antlers locked, then a whole herd of mule deer.

'Are those guys lucky we don't have deer tags,' said Hirsh.

A few minutes later, he pointed out a rub. 'Definitely elk!' He was looking at it longingly.

'No! We have to get to our camp,' insisted Matt. All day he had associated camp with safety. He was thinking about safety when his phone rang again.

'Why didn't you turn it off?' demanded Hirsh.

'They said they were calling back.'

He flipped open the phone.

'Oooops!' said a voice. 'Did I give you a scare way back on the rocks? Thought I saw a couple of elk out there eating granola bars!'

'What the hell are you doing?' Matt demanded.

'Hey now, Matt, not so hasty! We're playing a guessing game with clues and everything! Now, did you discuss the last clue with the old man?'

Matt did not reply.

'Did you?' demanded the voice. It was sly, insinuating. Worse, it was close by.

'I have no intention of playing games with my father,' said Matt.

'Oh, but these games are for real. It's Truth or Consequences, only for real. Okay, if the old guy can't guess who took the diamond, let's try another one. Ready now? Who posed nude for my dad, dressed only in a few little itsy-bitsy leaves?'

Steve paused as though waiting for an answer. Matt recalled the envelope he had found in the roof space, and he knew now that it had been addressed and sent by Steve.

'There are some women,' said Steve's voice, 'who'll do anything to attract the attention of a good man. I mean, they meet guys like my dad and they act like cow elks in season. 'Cept cow elks only do it when they're in season and that kind of women, you know the kind I mean, well, they seem to be in season all the time! So who was it? I think you know, Matt. I know you know. But ask the old man. Just to be sure. I'll be calling you soon for the answer.'

'You leave us alone,' Matt shouted but the phone was already dead. He immediately pressed the number recall but the phone yielded nothing. He shook the phone and shook it again. He dialled his home number and it still yielded nothing. A red light appeared by its antenna.

'Oh, shit,' said Matt. 'I've run right out of charge. Or signal. Or both.'

The signal here was either too weak for an undercharged phone to pick up, or they had found somewhere in the world where there was no signal at all. He sighed and put the phone back into his pack.

'What's going on, Matt?' demanded Hirsh.

'Let's get going,' said Matt. 'Let's move into the woods a little further and I'll explain.'

Hirsh saw Matt looking around furtively as he walked, but made no comment.

When they were deep in the forest, Hirsh paused. 'We should eat something. It must be lunchtime.'

Matt was reluctant to stop. He looked at his watch. 'It feels like lunchtime,' he said, 'but it's only eleven o'clock. And we did eat granola bars.'

'We've been on the move for over five hours. So let's eat. And while we eat, you can tell me what's going on.'

Matt looked around. He thought. Finally he said, 'We can eat if we move right off course. I mean, just veer to the left or the right the way the elk did this morning. We have to try not to leave a trail, though.'

'No rubs, scrapes or granola wrappers?' asked Hirsh.

'Not a broken twig.'

Hirsh looked at him searchingly and then turned south for a few minutes.

'I have to stop, Matt,' said Hirsh. But Matt already knew that. The old guy was getting slower and turning into a parallelogram again.

'Just whisper,' Matt cautioned him. 'I sure wish we had our Specials.'

'There's just one sandwich, which we can share. A couple of bruised apples. Some nuts. And more granola bars.'

But at the word sandwich Matt remembered his secret hoard of peanut butter in the back pocket of Elmer Turner's coat.

'Wait till you see this . . .' he whispered.

The sandwiches were mushy. The peanut butter had soaked through the bread. As soon as they were unwrapped they radiated their unmistakable odour.

'That smell must carry for miles,' said Hirsh disapprovingly, but he looked at them hungrily.

'Shhhh,' hissed Matt.

When they had been munching a while, Hirsh said, 'So, who's making these phone calls?'

Matt paused. He had already decided, during their long scramble over the peak, to tell Hirsh the truth, but now it was time to do so he hesitated.

'Steve Minelli.'

Hirsh's face was expressionless. He passed Matt an apple.

'What does he want?' he asked at last.

'He's been sneaking along behind us for a while now. He knew I missed a bull elk yesterday. And he knew we didn't even fire at that herd we saw this morning.'

They ate in silence.

'Gives you a spooky sort of feeling,' said Hirsh. 'You think you're alone in the wilderness. You feel you're alone. And you're not. Some guy's tracking you.'

'Dad . . . Steve Minelli . . . he thinks . . .' It was hard to say this. It was hard to say something that for months you deliberately, painstakingly, had avoided saying. 'He may be following us because he believes that—'

'Oh, he's got problems all right,' said Hirsh. 'He was up the mountain last year, asking questions about his father's death. He came to see me, he came to see Elmer, Stewart, God knows who else. He's a nuisance.'

'Why didn't you tell me before?'

'Because you seemed so pleased to meet him again. You thought he was a regular sort of guy.'

'You could have told me about him,' said Matt bitterly. 'Did he bother you? At home?'

'He bothered everyone. When you said that he'd taken some menial job at St Claudia's, I had to ask myself if it was pure coincidence he'd chosen your hospital. He has an unhealthy interest in his father's death. It's unhealthy because it seems to prevent him from getting on with his life.'

'He was firing at us out there on that rock, Dad. He might have been firing to miss, just to frighten us. I'm not sure. Those kids this morning were dangerous because they were stupid. Steve's dangerous because he's—'

'Crazy?' asked Hirsh. Matt recalled Steve's exhibition, the corpses in the morgue, the operating theatres which looked as though they had been the scene of a bloody battle, the figures in the recovery room, motionless, powerless to protest against Steve's lens. It probably wasn't art. It probably was just crazy.

'He got out of jail last year,' said Matt. 'He was in for a long time for first-degree murder.'

Hirsh nodded but said nothing. There was a long silence. Around them the forest seemed quiet. There were the rustles of small animals and the occasional movements of birds but the place felt motionless. Except they knew it wasn't. There was someone else here too. Another human being who was looking for them, finding their trail, sniffing them out the way Hirsh sniffed out elk.

'Do I understand that now we can't use that phone of yours to call for help?' asked Hirsh. Matt reddened a little and nodded.

'They don't work where there's no signal,' he said. 'Especially if they're running out of charge.' He did not remind Hirsh that he had told Matt not to bring it in the first place.

'What do you propose to do about this guy?' asked Hirsh. 'Will you wait here?'

'Are you going to confront him?'

'Sort of.'

'Leave your rifle!' exclaimed Hirsh, too loudly.

'I can't or he won't take me seriously,' whispered Matt.

His anger had turned icy now. It was frozen and slippery and treacherous. How dare Steve Minelli hound Hirsh, first in his own home and now here, where he was far from any help or protection? He remembered the strange electricity which had passed around the room way back in the spring when he had mentioned to Elmer and Hirsh and Lonnie that he had met Steve Minelli, when he had asked about Arthur Minelli's death. Sheriff Turner had said, when he heard Steve was working at Matt's hospital: Quite a coincidence! But he had meant the words ironically. Steve had come to St Claudia's because Matt was there. He had been the red car in Matt's mirror, he had sent the photos of Hilly, he had awaited Matt in the cafeteria. Steve hadn't been stalking Matt so much as manipulating him.

Matt advanced slowly through the trees. A still-hunter's advance, painstakingly, crawlingly slow, with many stops. He moved soundlessly from tree to tree. He knew that if he retraced his steps he would find his quarry.

He approached the elk rub where he and Hirsh had veered south. He looked to right and left but he could not see Steve. He started to retrace their steps west, back towards the open ridge. The silence of the forest seemed to have the depth of thousands of miles and of many millennia. There was no one else on the mountain or in the whole world.

When he calculated that he had travelled too far from Hirsh, Matt turned and began walking back to the elk rub. Maybe he had missed Steve. While they had been devouring peanut butter sandwiches, Steve must have continued east.

At the elk rub Matt was starting towards Hirsh when he saw a small movement he took to be the sudden flight of a bird. Nevertheless he froze as Hirsh had taught him to do at any unexplained movement. A few moments later Steve's back emerged from behind a tree. He must have somehow managed to pass without Matt detecting a hint of his presence. And he must have discovered that they had swung south at the elk rub because he was now moving silently towards Hirsh and the backpacks. He was an experienced, instinctive hunter who could pick up a quarry's every sound and smell in the forest. Next to him Matt felt large and loud and inept.

Slowly, deliberately, Matt positioned his gun, centring Steve's back in the crosshairs. All he had to do now was flip off the safety and squeeze, very gently, the fingers of his right hand. He could claim it was self-defence. It was an attractive idea but, Matt knew, impossible for him to execute. He lacked the killer instinct.

'Matt, for God's sake!' Hirsh's voice rang out like a shot

in the still forest. Steve, trapped in Matt's sights, swung round. He saw the end of the gun's muzzle and Matt had the satisfaction of watching horror and fear plaster Steve's face. He realized that was all he had wanted.

Hirsh strode right out from the trees, looking taller and stronger.

'I want to talk to you, Steve,' he said. 'I'd be grateful if both of you, Matt and Steve, would put your guns down. I don't know what movie you guys think you're starring in.'

'What do you want to talk about?' asked Steve. His voice was not the sneering, confident voice at the end of the phone. It was stony like mountain soil. His face had been redrawn, its lines thinner, his mouth a slit. Around the eyes the skin was blackened as though Steve never slept.

'There are some things you should know. But this is a private conversation so, Matt, please move away. Please leave us right alone.'

'I can't leave you alone with him,' said Matt.

Steve's lips twisted themselves into something like a smile. How could Matt have forgotten what that smile meant? It had meant the same thing every summer. Not just that blood was thicker than water but that finally Steve cared nothing for Matt, maybe nothing for anyone. It was not a real smile. It was cynical, cold-blooded and calculating.

'Back off, Matt, please,' instructed Hirsh. Matt took a few steps back.

'Further!'

Hirsh waited until Matt was satisfactorily distant, almost out of sight and right out of earshot.

Matt, who had ensured he had a clear if distant sightline and that his gun was ready, could occasionally pick up Steve's raised voice, but it seemed that mostly Hirsh was talking. Nothing in the distant body language of the two

431

men betrayed what they could be saying. The conversation went on a long time. Matt felt his temperature drop and his limbs stiffen. The arm which held his gun was as hard and motionless as the gun itself.

Finally, Hirsh stepped forward towards the smaller form of Steve Minelli. Matt lifted his gun so that the stock pressed against his cheek and then gently lowered it when he saw what Hirsh was doing. Putting his arms around Steve. Matt looked away, trying to remember when Hirsh had last hugged him. The movement had been natural, almost instinctive on Hirsh's part, as though he hugged people every day.

There was more talking and then suddenly Steve turned to go. Hirsh called him back, reached into his pocket, and produced something, almost certainly granola bars. Matt saw Steve take them. Before he went, Steve turned and searched for Matt among the tree trunks. When he had found him he stared right at him and Matt stared back, although he wanted to shrink under Steve's gaze. It was a look of such hatred that it made Matt feel cold and bleak and empty. From now on he had to live with this man's hatred the way you had to live with a scar or a limp, knowing it would never go away.

Then Steve melted into the trees, heading back west. Matt strained his eyes to see where the slim, dark figure had gone, but Steve was a hunter and could make himself disappear instantly in the forest.

Matt found Hirsh putting on his pack.

'What did you do?' he demanded. He helped Hirsh find a shoulder strap.

'I learned a few tricks from you this morning. From the way you dealt with those kids,' said Hirsh.

'But what were you saying to him?'

'The truth. Always the best policy although it can be painful. I sure wish he didn't have a gun with him. Oh well, let's get going. We don't want to get to the Mouth of Nowhere when it's too dark to find firewood.'

'Aren't you going to tell me anything?' demanded Matt.

'Not now.' Hirsh was looking at the map.

'You think he's gone for good?' But even as he asked the question Matt knew that he would never be rid of Steve.

'Anyway, he's gone for now,' said Hirsh. He pointed at the map. 'We are here. The Mouth of Nowhere is right here. See? A couple more ridges should do it.'

'There's an awful lot of contour lines between us and that valley . . .' Matt was saying, but Hirsh had already started walking, folding up the map as he did so. He was heading due east.

26

The snow was still falling although it had barely penetrated the forest yet. Matt was aware that the temperature had dropped and there was an icy breeze to take the temperature down still further. Mostly they were protected from it by the trees but sometimes it found a way to slip between the trunks with the precision of a knife and then the cruelty of its gusts shocked them like bad news.

Matt's blister was starting to bite now. He was aware of it every time he lifted his foot off the ground, as though each step sliced through another layer of thin skin.

A couple of times they thought they saw elk, or signs of elk, but Matt urged them on. He had noticed that Hirsh was getting more lopsided. Once, they stumbled down a steep, grassy bank. Hidden at the bottom was a creek. Hirsh plunged right into it. When he emerged, Matt could see that one leg was soaked.

'Only as far as the knee,' said Hirsh, but he allowed Matt to take his arm and pull him up the bank on the other side.

Matt knew that at these temperatures and when they were this tired, a wet leg could be dangerous. He carefully watched Hirsh's progress through the forest. He could almost see the pain Hirsh was experiencing in his right side and un-fortunately, it was also his right leg which was wet. How-ever, although he leaned, Hirsh retained the rhythm of his walk.

They stopped once to eat. Hirsh spoke very little.

'Dad, are you okay?' asked Matt.

'Fine,' said Hirsh. 'I've got so used to being wet that I don't even feel it any more.'

'I have a blister,' said Matt.

'Want something for it? I brought a mole skin.'

'When we get to our camp.'

They walked on. Matt's blister made his whole foot feel skinless but after a while he found himself numbed by cold against the pain. The forest was darkening now, not because it was so late but because the clouds were low. Matt knew that there were peaks towering close to them on all sides. He knew it from the map but he could see nothing.

Just when he judged that the Mouth of Nowhere had to be quite nearby, he noticed that Hirsh, ahead of him, had ceased to walk in a straight line. He was stumbling a little.

'Dad!' he called. And then, louder, sharper: 'Dad!' But Hirsh didn't seem to hear. Matt ran a few paces and put his arm on Hirsh's shoulder. Hirsh stopped and turned around. He was shivering. Not uncontrollably, but detectably.

'Dad, you're cold,' said Matt. Hirsh shook his head. He smiled, an unusually broad smile for Hirsh.

'Oh no,' he said happily, 'I'm just fine.'

Matt didn't understand how Hirsh could be so cheerful. They were hiking through hostile terrain miles from anyone and anything, except hopefully elk, it had taken two days instead of one to near their destination, and when they arrived there would probably be nothing left of the old ghost town. And it was snowing harder and he wanted a coffee and his blister felt moist now and was probably bleeding.

'Really,' Hirsh assured him, still smiling. 'I feel terrific.'

He walked on and as he seemed to be walking with more stability Matt followed quietly. After a short distance, he saw Hirsh struggling with his pack.

'What are you doing, Dad?' he asked.

'I'm going to have to take this thing off. I'm too hot,' said Hirsh.

'Too *hot?*'

Hirsh dropped his pack and carried on walking. Matt picked it up. It felt light enough to carry on one arm. He realized he should have offered before.

But now Hirsh was taking off his coat.

Matt caught up with him, the small pack swinging clumsily on his arm.

'Dad, don't do that!'

'Stop worrying about me. I feel terrific. Just a little hot and so I'm taking off my coat.' He stumbled drunkenly.

'Dad . . . you aren't hot. You're shivering. Let me feel your hands.'

Matt slipped his fingers inside Hirsh's gloves. The old hands he found there were icy, the skin folded into thick ridges like small, snowy peaks. The shivering had increased.

'I'm going to have to insist, yes, insist, that you put your coat on,' he ordered sternly. He was holding Hirsh up now.

'Now, Matt, don't get sassy with me,' said Hirsh. His tone was mild.

'Coat ON,' roared Matt. 'And then I'm going to put these packs down and I'm going to put my arms around you, real tight, to try to warm you up.'

'I just told you I'm not cold,' insisted Hirsh sulkily but he did as Matt had instructed him.

Matt held his father, slipping his arms inside the open coat and wrapping them around him as though he were a small child, as though Hirsh were his son. They stood in the icy forest near frozen peaks that Matt could not name, feeling winter's blast all around them, Matt clinging tightly to his father, trying to transmit his warmth, as if this could be achieved by willpower alone. He wasn't sure it was achievable at all. Ironically, they were probably both wearing too many clothes for the old trick to work.

After a few minutes, Hirsh pulled back.

'We should get along now,' he said. 'Hilly's going to be real worried.'

Matt felt as though a massive boulder was rolling right over him. He shoved Hirsh back inside the coat but Hirsh resisted.

'Hilly's going to be real worried,' he repeated, 'when she sees it's snowing and we haven't come back.'

'She'll be even more worried if she knows I haven't warmed you up a little,' Matt insisted, and this seemed to settle Hirsh back inside Matt's arms. After a few minutes, he pulled away again.

'I was just falling asleep there,' he announced. 'But I woke up because you're suffocating me.'

Matt touched his father's face. It felt a little warmer.

'Sorry, Dad. But you're too cold . . .'

'You shouldn't go around killing people. Really. No matter how much you love her.'

Hirsh stumbled off muttering and Matt helplessly picked up the packs and followed him. He steadied his father with his free arm. Hirsh immediately leaned on him, so that Matt staggered under the extra weight.

'You wouldn't do it for yourself. Only for love, I know you that well, Matt. But you can't kill and expect to be the same man afterwards. Even if no one knows, you aren't the same. Plus when your car hits a man in that way, well, it's an unforgettable experience . . .' A stream of meaningless words was coming from Hirsh but Matt was barely attending to him. He was wondering what to do. Finally he pulled

437

Hirsh over to the shelter of a big conifer and sat him down underneath it.

'So just why are we here?' asked Hirsh. He sounded querulous and dissatisfied, the way Clem did sometimes if Denise couldn't drop everything and go visit when he wanted her. 'I can't think of any particular reason why we've stopped.'

'Just for a short rest, Dad,' said Matt. He wanted to reach for his cellphone and telephone to the safe world on the other side of the mountain. Except he couldn't.

Hirsh continued to talk, sounding like some other old man but not Hirsh. Matt put his hand to his head.

'Would you stop talking for just a minute? While I think?'

'Sure, sure,' said Hirsh. It seemed to Matt that his father was shivering more violently now. His teeth were chattering. Matt knew that he had perhaps thirty minutes to warm the old man before moderate hypothermia turned acute.

Matt reached for the map. His own hands were shaking. It was hard to hold the map still enough to study it.

'I don't understand,' he said, 'why we haven't arrived.'

'We won't get home yet. We're far from home,' Hirsh informed him helpfully. 'But personally speaking, I feel absolutely fine.'

'Not home. We're going to the Mouth of Nowhere, Dad.'

'Ah. The Mouth of Nowhere. I was hoping your mother might be waiting for us there. She'll be wondering where we've gotten to.'

Matt stood up. He started to take off the lined jeans that Stewart had given him and which, though a little short in the leg, he had accepted because they were baggy and he could pile layers of long underwear beneath them.

'Are you going to bed?' asked Hirsh.

'Take off those wet clothes,' Matt ordered. He pulled a

space blanket out of his own backpack and then Hirsh's and wrapped them around his father.

'Take everything off from the waist downwards,' he said.

'Well, then I might get cold,' said Hirsh lucidly. But, with good humour, he started to fumble with his trousers.

'Not doing too well here,' he said after a moment. He did not sound irritable.

Matt unzipped his father's wet trousers and tugged at the layers of long underwear. Each right leg was soaked all the way up. Then, as Hirsh watched him with detached interest, he pulled his own long pants off (the woollen ones which Elmer had loaned him). He was wearing another pair underneath but it felt as though he was standing naked in the forest. The cold wrapped around him like an icy sheet.

He hastened to get Elmer's long pants on to Hirsh while they still retained his own body warmth. Then he dragged two more dry pairs of underwear from the backpacks and, on top of these, tried to pull Stewart's lined jeans on to Hirsh. It was worse than dressing Austin. At least Austin was occasionally helpful, while Hirsh sat watching him as though it was someone else's body Matt was trying to dress. Matt tugged and swore. Whenever you had to dress another person you discovered that human clothes weren't designed for the human body.

The wet socks clung to Hirsh's feet as though frozen there but Matt eventually managed to pull them free. He took off his gloves and wrapped his hands around the cold, cold skin, trying to transmit his own body warmth to Hirsh's foot. Little swirls of snow which had somehow slipped through the tree's canopy circled them, heat bandits trying to steal whatever warmth was around. Eventually, concluding that he was adding nothing to Hirsh's temperature, Matt pulled two pairs of dry socks on to his father's feet.

439

He took off his coat and the cold pounced as though it had been waiting. He rapidly removed his outer sweater and the cold feasted on him, a ravenous beast, until the coat was back on and closed up. He put the sweater on Hirsh who, uncharacteristically, had made no attempt to protest at all this. Then he bound his father tightly in first one and then the second space blanket. Somehow, with a lot of shoving and very little help from Hirsh, he managed to get his father inside a sleeping bag.

'I can't move!' wailed Hirsh. Matt was anguished to hear him sounding so much like a child.

'Good, you can devote all your energy to keeping warm. Now drink this.'

He tried to heat a bottle of water inside his coat but he wasn't feeling so warm himself any more. He pulled out the stopper, held Hirsh's head back and fed his father the water the way he had fed Austin bottles of warmed milk when he was a baby. When Hirsh began to struggle a little, Matt warned, 'Don't try to use your hands, keep them inside the sleeping bag.'

Hirsh finished drinking. There was still some water left. Matt tucked the bottle into the sleeping bag with his father to warm its contents. Then he fished in the pack for an old pair of sweats which he had thrown in at the last minute because they were light. He gratefully pulled them on and for a moment the cold retreated, snarling. Then it returned again, as fierce as ever. By now it seemed to penetrate Matt's skin, penetrate to his bones and his soft, vulnerable internal organs. Matt knew he had to move to create some more body heat of his own but the cold seemed to be hanging on to him, slowing him down, freezing him to the spot.

'Dad,' he said. His own teeth were chattering and he

could feel his hands shaking. 'Wait here. Don't attempt to go anywhere. I'm leaving the packs with you.'

Hirsh watched him wordlessly.

'I'll be back in a short time. According to the map we should already be at the Mouth of Nowhere. I'm going down that way to check it out and then I'm coming back. Okay?' Matt hoped that the words were coming out in the right order. His mouth had difficulty forming them.

Hirsh did not reply. He closed his eyes. He did not, at any rate, appear to be shivering any more.

Matt looked all around. He should go as quickly as possible to get back as soon as possible but he could not bring himself to leave his father alone in the forest. He made a big circle around Hirsh, staring out into the trees, looking for movement, for a horizontal, for a colour, for a frightened bird, for anything which might indicate the silent presence of Steve Minelli. When he could see nothing he was not comforted. The dark, silent forest stretched behind them for ever, biding secrets, nourishing danger. Matt picked up sticks, brush and fallen branches. He tried to camouflage Hirsh with them, an operation his father ignored. He seemed to be asleep.

Matt took the compass, the map and the binoculars and, after a moment's hesitation, his gun as well. His hand felt frozen to the cold instrument, as though he wore no gloves at all. He did not allow himself to look back at the strange, shapeless bundle which was his father behind a sagging wall of sticks. Hirsh was trussed in so many layers of clothes and blankets, snowflakes gathering on his glasses, that in the face of attack by man or beast he was as powerless as a baby. Matt was able to keep walking away only because he could see a clearing ahead and because he could feel the action of walking heat his bones a little.

441

He knew that the Mouth of Nowhere was an ancient ghost town and that it had been in a state of advanced dilapidation about twenty years ago when Hilly and Hirsh had found it. He understood that the chances of its affording any serious shelter were slim. But if it offered half a roof and a little dry wood that would be an improvement on making camp in the forest.

His watch said it was three o'clock. He gave himself until three-fifteen to find the ghost town. That would mean he would be absent from Hirsh for precisely thirty minutes. Not a second longer.

He glanced behind him. Hirsh was already invisible behind a hundred tree trunks. He halted suddenly, galvanized motionless by another hazard. Then he pulled out one of the old granola bar wrappers from Elmer's pockets and, tucking it into the trunk of a prominent tree, he deliberately littered the wilderness. He paused for a moment, watching, listening, alert. But there was no sign that any other human had walked this way. Ever.

Matt was hoping that, when he reached the clearing, the mountain would start sloping away, just as the map said it should. According to the map, it should slope down to the Mouth of Nowhere. His heart began to thud as he neared it. But when he arrived he found only a large, white meadow, nothing more than an immense break in the trees.

He posted another granola marker and started to cross the clearing but he could soon see that nothing else awaited him on the other side except more trees, an endless, dark, coniferous forest like a great, gaping mouth. Matt wanted to shout or yell or cry with disappointment.

He looked at his watch. Six minutes past three. He had nine more minutes to find the edge of the mountain. He was cold again now. He tried to run. His effort was immense.

His body did not want to run, it wanted to stop and lie down right here in the snow. The cold was freezing his joints. With an act of willpower which felt as though it was sapping his physical strength, he forced his body into a jog. He knew he was running lopsidedly, like a wounded animal. He tried to accelerate and gradually, reluctantly, his body found its pace. He felt once again the slight thawing of his bones, of his heart, his liver, his spleen.

The snow was thicker here without the shelter of the trees. There was a tangled web of shrubs and stalks which reached out to slow him, and there were wet, boggy places which surprised him by giving way beneath their icy surface. He kept running. His rhythm was like a mast to which he had lashed himself. He knew that if he broke his pace the vastness of the wilderness would engulf him.

But as he ran, ugly possibilities took root in his mind. Maybe he had misread the map. Maybe he and Hirsh were nowhere near the place they had believed themselves to be. After all, Hirsh had been leading and he had probably been suffering from hypothermia longer than Matt had realized. Maybe they were on the wrong map. Maybe they weren't anywhere.

Panic seized him and he stopped. He could immediately feel a drop in his body temperature. The silence screamed. He was tired, more than tired, he was burdened by an indescribable weariness. He asked himself if he cared about going on or going back or if he cared about anything. Then he thought of Denise and Austin and the small bundle in the forest which was Hirsh. He reassured himself that he could not be suffering from hypothermia because he was experiencing no sensation of well-being and because he knew he was tired and he knew he was cold. Wasn't the first symptom of hypothermia a complete inability to judge your own body heat? A misleading sense of well-being? Hadn't Hirsh actually started to take off his coat because he really believed he was too warm? Hypothermia was a kind of madness and the very essence of the illness was that you didn't know you had it. Then, gently, you died of cold. Although, really, you were being killed by your inability to know yourself.

Reassured by his own misery, he tried, stumblingly, with slow, imprecise movements, to get out the compass and the map again. Snow fell on the map, making it look far too topographical. Thirteen minutes past three. It was impossible to find the Mouth of Nowhere in the next two minutes. He should retreat, follow his granola wrapper trail through the forest, find Hirsh, make a shelter, light a fire in the snow somehow and dry the wet clothes by it as they now had nothing dry left in the packs. But he knew the effort required to accomplish this was too much. It was all impossible.

He felt hope drain out of him and desperation take its place. He looked up. Small snowflakes hurtled down towards him. They were falling from a great height, they were falling in their hundreds and thousands and millions. You couldn't see the sky they fell from, just the tiny, freezing bombs it dropped on you. Looking up, you became aware of the strange beauty of layer upon layer of white pinheads, pinheads which seemed to blossom into huge white blooms as they neared you. Matt opened his mouth and closed his eyes like a pious communicant. He felt the cold touch of the snowflakes on his tongue.

He admitted to himself, standing in the snow with his eyes closed, that the chances of the pair of them leaving the mountain alive were slim and getting slimmer. Steve Minelli was probably not far away but even without him they had managed to place their lives in danger. Stewart wouldn't be

444

contacting the emergency services until Wednesday, which was too late. And Matt could not trudge back alone because he could not leave Hirsh.

He thought of Denise and Austin, at home together right now in the warm house. They were a million miles away from this bleak mountain. Why had Denise encouraged him to come on this trip when it had plainly been foolhardy? When he didn't come back she would blame herself for ever although, of course, it was all Hirsh's fault, and Matt's. Hirsh was too old for this but he hadn't wanted to admit it. The distance, the energy involved, was too ambitious. The trip had been an old man's folly and Matt's folly had been to go along with it, humouring his father, because up until now Hirsh had always been right about everything and neither of them had wanted to recognize that it was time for Matt to take over Hirsh's role of being strong and right. Now they would pay for this failure, probably with their lives.

Matt sighed his resignation. They had joked about the power of the wilderness to confound them. They had failed to acknowledge its might. Now they knew their own smallness and foolishness. He felt the cold strike at him again like a snake. It was inside him, outside him, all around him. He could not even fold up the map. His fingers were helpless now.

He opened his eyes and saw that a veil of cloud was lifting a mile or two away. He had thought there was just one dense blanket overhead but now he saw that, like the snow-flakes, the clouds were many separate entities. And not so far away, curiously lit by a distant and barely remembered sun, two clouds were parting now to reveal a strange peak, long and pointed. Hirsh had told him the name of that peak. What was it? Matt looked at the damp map again. The Native American name was clearly marked but early white settlers had given it another. Here it was. The Schoolmarm.

Hirsh had said that the Schoolmarm looked down through her long, thin nose at the Mouth of Nowhere.

He knew, then, for sure, that he must be close to the ghost town. He took bearings from the Schoolmarm and saw that he should turn north. That meant swinging sideways across the meadow, where its end was out of sight.

It was three-fifteen. He should return to Hirsh.

His heart beating hard because his decision was a dangerous one, he swung north. He tried to fold up the map, was unsuccessful and so scrunched it up like a piece of litter. He made himself walk and then, stiffly, leaning heavily to one side, he ran. His body felt like a big, slow, metal machine. Once, he fell over and getting up required more fuel and engineering ability than he could muster. Then, after some rolling and struggling, as though some opponent were on top of him, he was vertical again and running on. Just for five more minutes. Five minutes to find the Mouth of Nowhere, then he would certainly go back.

The blister on his foot was shouting at him to stop but he ignored its fury. The intense pain had been incorporated into his worldview now. That and the cold had become a way of life. And he had to reach the far end of the clearing in five minutes.

The horizon, curving acutely as a frown, never seemed to get any closer. He was a ship sailing across a featureless white sea. The faster he travelled, the further the horizon slipped away from him.

Three-eighteen. In two minutes he must turn back to Hirsh.

Three-twenty. Now. He must turn back right now. His wilful pursuit of a nebulous aim was endangering his father's life.

Three-twenty-two. His cheeks bounced as he ran, the

trees which lined the meadow bounced as he ran, the distant, high, white peaks, now revealed, bounced as he ran and, nearer, the Schoolmarm bounced as he ran.

Three-twenty-three. He arrived. The horizon proved to be not the horizon but another edge of another mountain plateau. Their stopping place had been one stratum among many and now, without warning, he was almost plunging over its lip into the valley below.

The drop was steep but slight, perhaps a little more than 100 feet. At its base was the Mouth of Nowhere. Matt recognized it at once from his mother's painting. The valley was shielded from wind and the mountain's wildest elements, watered by a broad, stony creek which, its rocky bed revealed, evidently became still broader in spring. Its path was lined by white-trunked, broad-leaved trees which blazed in red and gold. The ruins of the settlers' houses were evident. There were three visible from here, lying up from the creek at a point where the forest which swept down the hillside met the mountain meadow. Matt didn't need to glass the valley to see that one tiny house was still sufficiently roofed to provide a standard of shelter he could never hope to reproduce in the forest.

Reinvigorated, he turned and started his run back across the white meadow. He did not follow his own footprints but made the perilous decision to cut the corner he had made when he had turned north. He tried to estimate the point at which he had emerged from the forest. Running across the bare, white expanse, he felt as though he was moving on the spot, as though the effort was eating up his energy and getting him nowhere. And then, at last, he saw that he was closer, really closer, and he began to think with increasing anxiety about Hirsh, trussed and helpless on the forest floor, stalked by dangers.

447

He searched the tree trunks for the granola wrapper. When he failed to find it he ran alongside the forest's edge. Had he come too far and missed it completely?

Panic hovered at the periphery of his every thought and decision, he could feel its wings beating now. And then, gleaming at him as though from some urban litter bin, he saw the wrapper. He swung into the forest. He had crossed the meadow in just six minutes: it had taken him almost twenty to venture in, experience despair, change course and discover the ghost town.

It was easy to find his way back. In places where the trees were thin his own footprints were visible in the light snow cover. He left the wrappers to guide their return, jogging past them jubilantly as though they were stewards in a race. But his triumph could not mask his anxiety as he neared the place he had deposited Hirsh. He arrived in less than another six minutes: a glance at his watch told him it was three-forty. He had been gone for forty minutes. In that time, Hirsh could have died. Matt tried to prepare himself for anything but he was still not ready for what he did find.

Hirsh's sleeping bag was still where Matt had left his father and it still bulged in the same places, but something was not right. He surveyed the strange evidence of their stay here. The camouflage branches had collapsed on to the ground. Damp clothes were strewn from branches. His own large pack was on its side, not leaning neatly against the tree the way he had left it. Hirsh's gun was not evident. There were two space blankets in the tree. He went right over to the sleeping bag and found that Hirsh was no longer in it. He grabbed the bag and began to feel it, as though Hirsh could have shrunk in forty minutes. But the bag was empty.

His heart booming, he examined the evidence. Possibly

his pack had just fallen over. Maybe Hirsh had logically hung up the wet clothing. It was harder to explain the space blankets draped over branches, when they could have been placed safely inside the big pack to keep dry. And Hirsh, the Hirsh he had known all his life, that Hirsh would not have left a sleeping bag on the ground, or not unless there had been some hostile intrusion. His father had either been disturbed or he had left the camp in an illogical but not totally crazy state of mind. And if he could walk away, his condition must have improved.

Matt looked all around. He peered through the trees. He listened. He sniffed the air. He looked for footprints. But nothing told him where Hirsh had gone and why.

His blood was throbbing through his body. It made a sound he now recognized too well. Panic's wings, beating hard in his ear. Alone in the mountain forest, suffering from some degree of hypothermia, carrying a lethal weapon but without map or compass, Hirsh didn't stand a chance.

Matt took deep breaths. He tried not to feel the cold but now that he had stopped running he was aware of his own sweat cooling against his skin. His heel, he knew, was raw like meat.

He searched the ground for clues, working in an ever-widening circle from Hirsh's sleeping bag. Not far away he found Hirsh's glasses, bent but not cracked. There were no more clues. He had deliberately chosen to leave Hirsh in a thick part of the forest where the snow barely penetrated but now he regretted this. No snow, no clues. He spotted a thin strip of snow ahead and examined it for footprints. There were none.

He shouted, 'Dad! Dad!'

His voice was hoarse and weak. He coughed and prepared his throat.

'Hiiiiiiirsh Seeeeeleeeeeeckiiiiiiiis! Calling Docccctooooor Hiiiiiiiirsh Seeeeeleeeeeeckiiiiiiiis!'

Then he waited. He listened. And it seemed to him he had never heard such silence.

He tried to reassure himself. Hirsh had dry clothes on, a lot of them, plus an extra sweater plus his big coat, hat and gloves. He couldn't see much without his glasses. He was carrying a rifle, although he was almost certainly unfit to do so.

Matt walked in ever-widening circles until he could barely even see the backpacks any more. Then it occurred to him that maybe Hirsh, for some illogical reason, had decided to start towards home. He returned to the packs, turned west and set off, feeling as though his short run to the Mouth of Nowhere had proved to be nothing more than the sum of a thousand smaller journeys. He walked and jogged but when, after travelling for ten minutes, he had found no evidence of footprints in any snow, he turned back.

The light was fading now. Uncertain what he should do, he returned to their base camp and, just before he reached it, he saw a man's shape, flickering in and out of the trees. Immediately he darted behind a trunk and froze. He peered out cautiously. The shape was invisible now. It must be Steve. Hirsh would not have been capable of evaporating the way Steve could.

Then the figure emerged again. His heart leaping, relief warming him, he saw that it was Hirsh.

'Dad!' he yelled. The figure stopped and he ran towards it. 'Dad, what are you doing?'

Hirsh was carrying a bundle of sticks.

'Collecting firewood,' he said.

'I was looking for you everywhere!'

'We need dry wood.'

'Sure, sure we do,' agreed Matt. 'Didn't you hear me calling you?'

'Yes. But it could have been Steve Minelli, so I didn't reply.'

Matt paused at this but decided to let it go. He handed Hirsh his glasses and Hirsh put them on and then looked around him as though they would offer some kind of explanation.

'Dad, I've found the Mouth of Nowhere. It's about a fifteen-minute walk away. There's an old cabin for shelter. Can you make it?'

''Course I can make it. I'm fine,' said Hirsh, words that Matt did not find reassuring. But he noted that his father's pace, though lopsided, was regular.

'Where's your rifle?' he asked as they neared the camp.

'Steve Minelli came and took it,' said Hirsh. 'I was real mad. Know how many years I've had that rifle? Fifty. Fifty years and then, of all people, Steve Minelli comes and takes it and there's not a darned thing I can do about it because I'm tied into my sleeping bag.'

'Steve Minelli came,' Matt repeated faintly. 'And took your rifle.'

'He just follows wherever you go, asking questions about Arthur, Arthur all the time.'

Was this hypothermia talking? Matt remembered the look of hatred Steve had thrown him that morning. It was not the kind of hatred that walked away. It was not the kind of hatred which, finding its victim helpless in the forest, just confiscated a rifle and wandered off.

'How did you get out of the sleeping bag?' Matt demanded.

'It took a while,' said Hirsh. 'I had to do a lot of wiggling.'

Hirsh waited while Matt put all the wet clothes into a

plastic bag. They fitted easily, with the space blankets, into the backpack. He even found space for the dry wood Hirsh had been collecting. Then he rolled up Hirsh's sleeping bag and tied it to the outside of his pack. He picked up his gun and took one last look around for Steve before leading the way back through the forest.

When they reached the clearing Hirsh was no longer walking so steadily. Matt gave him a drink and then, with his father leaning heavily on him, cut north across the meadow. Once he saw half a footprint which he assumed to be his own but which he now feared might belong to Steve. Otherwise the snowy landscape, except for bushes, was featureless. It had stopped snowing but the wind had smoothed the surface with a near-mechanical accuracy.

The sky was clearer now. Somewhere there was a sunset. It wasn't visible but the whitest peaks were rosy with its light. Others had already disappeared into the night. Darkness was hanging nearby like some guy on a street corner.

The meadow seemed long this time, far longer than when Matt had run across it alone. He noticed, across the other side by the forest, a huge bull elk watching them. He hoped that Hirsh wouldn't see it but mostly Hirsh seemed to be concentrating on walking.

'We're nearly there,' Matt kept telling him, but Hirsh, leaning increasingly on his son, did not reply.

When they reached the edge of the meadow and the hillside plunged away from them it felt as though they were standing on the edge of the world. The Schoolmarm was almost in darkness. He could make out the shapes of the golden trees below. The settlers' cabins were visible if you knew where to look.

'See it, Dad?' he asked. 'Remember?'

Hirsh remained ominously silent.

Matt first got Hirsh down the slope, a stumbling, sliding performance which involved both controlling their speed and avoiding sharp rocks. At the bottom, Hirsh made no attempt to head for the cabins while Matt climbed back up to collect his pack and gun. When he arrived again he found Hirsh sitting on a rock, shivering, patiently waiting.

They followed the dried-up part of the creek bed to the valley's meadow and then they went up to the small, derelict cabin Matt had selected from above to be their shelter.

At the door they paused.

'Hi!' Matt yelled, vestigial manners from that period a few millennia ago when he had lived in civilization reminding him to announce his presence before bursting through a door, even the broken-down door of a broken-down shack.

'Were you thinking your mom might be inside?' asked Hirsh.

'That would be a nice surprise,' said Matt.

He pushed open the door and one of its hinges fell off. He shone his torch around. He saw at once that Kilroy had been here. Hirsh liked to fool himself that no one else knew about the Mouth of Nowhere, but many others had blackened the ancient stone fireplace and slept on these old floors since the settlers had gone. Some had left colourful graffiti on the walls and there were Coke cans and faded pretzel containers. There was no such thing any more, reflected Matt, as a wilderness without a Coke can.

'This is terrific,' he said enthusiastically. His light ran all over the little hut. The roof had caved in at its centre as though there had been a particularly heavy snowfall one day but otherwise it offered the shelter he had longed for. Who had lived out their bleak life here? What had they suffered in this harsh terrain?

'Dad, I think you're still real cold,' he said. 'I'm going to put my sleeping bag in your sleeping bag and then ask you to get inside them both.'

Hirsh did not protest but, as before, he did little to help as Matt manoeuvred him into the bag. Matt used Hirsh's small pack as a pillow and had his father lie down and then he covered him again with the two space blankets. Hirsh lay silently in the dark.

Then Matt lit the fire, using Hirsh's pine sap and the lint Lonnie had saved from her dryer and the smallest twigs that Hirsh had collected earlier. The lint proved spectacular tinder. As soon as he set a match to it the fire flared up and within a few minutes he was adding the largest branches. In the corner of the room some thoughtful visitor had left a small supply of firewood and when this was burning in the big stone fireplace Matt said, 'Dad? Are you awake?'

'Mmm,' said Hirsh sleepily.

'I'm going out to get more firewood. I'll be right back.'

He found some big round creekbed stones outside the cabin, which he carried in and left by the fire to heat, and some larger ones which he put in the fire. He filled the little aluminium saucepan with water and wedged it over the stones. Then he threw the tarpaulin across the place in the middle of the room where the roof had caved in.

Outside it was a clear, cold night. The snow had passed but the temperature had not risen. In the immense silence of the wilderness, a silence as big as the mountains which he knew were all around but could not see, he could hear the occasional trickle of the creek's water.

He used his flashlight to seek out some dead branches from the trees in the forest. There was timber lying around but it looked wet. He took it anyway. Soon he had a small store of wood outside the house which he carried in to dry by the fire.

'Dad?' he said. There was no reply. Panic began to throb noisily in his ears. He went to the supine figure and shook it harshly. 'Dad!'

'What is it?' asked Hirsh.

'I'm going to heat up the emergency meals now,' said Matt quietly. 'They'll be ready in five minutes.'

He felt Hirsh's face and neck. Still cold as the grave. He carried a hot stone from its place next to the fire.

'Pull down those jeans, Dad, put this between your legs.'

'I can't pull down anything,' said Hirsh. 'My fingers don't work properly.'

Matt dragged off the sleeping bag. He put a hot rock between Hirsh's legs and one on his stomach next to the skin and one under each arm and then pulled the clothes back over them and went outside to find some more rocks to warm. They were round and smooth the way rocks were when water had caressed them and worried them over millennia. They felt good in your hand and their smooth edges seemed kind.

He found the two emergency MREs which Hirsh had left in his pack the night before they left.

'Great,' he said. 'Well chosen, Dad. You left a beef teriyaki and a chilli macaroni. Which one do you want?'

Hirsh did not reply so Matt took that to mean chilli macaroni.

He poured some of the hot water into a cup over some pine needles he had collected. Then he dropped the MRE sachets in the pan and waited five minutes. It seemed to him to be the first five minutes of the day in which he had been completely motionless. He watched the fire. Their chances of survival had increased dramatically with their arrival at the cabin. If he managed to get Hirsh through hypothermia unscathed, the next problem would be food. He decided not to think about it.

He opened the sachets and squeezed their contents out on to their plates.

'Mmm, smells good,' he said. 'Time to wake up, Dad. Dad! Wake up!'

When Hirsh did not reply or move or give any indication that he had heard, Matt panicked again, almost upsetting the beef teriyaki in his haste to reach his father. When he had managed to shake the reluctant Hirsh awake he wanted to cry with relief. He sat his father upright in the sleeping bag, took out the cool stones and replaced them with hot ones and then passed Hirsh his meal. Hirsh stared at it uncomprehendingly, so Matt fed it to him, grabbing the occasional mouthful of his beef teryaki while Hirsh munched, as he had seen Denise do when feeding Austin at the table.

'Is it good?' he asked.

'Yes,' said Hirsh.

'Are you feeling warmer now?'

'I never felt cold. But you're not wearing so many clothes, Matt. You should be careful. You get hypothermia and you don't even know about it.'

'Right,' said Matt. 'You'll have to keep an eye on me.'

'Right,' said Hirsh.

He pulled a face at the pine needle tea but drank it.

'Is it like drinking bathroom cleaner?' asked Matt.

Hirsh said, 'People generally drink bathroom cleaner cold.' Matt laughed hard and long at that, not because it was so funny but because it was the first time for many hours that Hirsh had sounded like Hirsh.

He remembered the wet clothes, and laid them out in front of the fire. He wished he had done that before. He finished his beef teriyaki and thought it was the most

456

delicious thing he'd ever eaten in his whole life, better even than Denise's vegetable and chicken soup. Hirsh sat watching him.

'Dad, I'm going to climb into the sleeping bag with you,' said Matt. 'I realize that's going to be a little too intimate for your liking but it's the only way I know to keep you warm enough through the night.'

'The fire's warm,' said Hirsh.

'It isn't going to stay that way and the kind of cold you have works from the inside out.'

'Are you suggesting that I have hypothermia?' asked Hirsh. 'Core cold?' Suddenly all the chill from his body had migrated to his voice.

'You've been giving a few indications,' said Matt carefully, 'and I don't want to take any chances. Remember, the patient never knows he has it.'

Hirsh was silent.

Matt stoked the fire with dry wood and then added the biggest, wettest wood, hoping it would slow-burn through the night. Then he took off all his outer clothing and somehow slid into the sleeping bag with Hirsh.

'You smell of beef teriyaki,' said Hirsh.

'You had chilli but am I complaining? Now go to sleep.'

It was strange, lying here and cuddling his father like a child. It was strange lying here locked so closely to another man. Matt concentrated, as he had that morning, on transferring his heat to Hirsh. He wished he could transfer his energy and his strength and his youth too, and still have enough for himself.

They had made it to Hilly's valley. He listened to Hirsh's breathing as he fell asleep and knew that he had saved his father's life and that his father would probably never be aware of it. Maybe, wherever she was, his mother would

457

know what he had done today. He listened to the sounds of the mountains. The creek outside. An owl. The breeze shaking branches nearby. Maybe this was how the dead spoke to you. Maybe the noises he could hear were Hilly's voice, whispering to him that he'd done well today.

27

They were both very warm when they woke up.

'Will you just explain to me why I have a bag full of rocks?' demanded Hirsh.

Matt scrambled out. The cold in the hut was more than evident, it was palpable.

'Ow, the cold dog bit me,' he said.

He figured Hirsh didn't need two sleeping bags any more. He pulled the outer sleeping bag away from the inner as though peeling off an extra skin and then he crawled right inside it. He hadn't slept well. After a while he had been too hot but he had nevertheless spent most of the night checking Hirsh's breathing and temperature.

'It's already dawn,' said Hirsh. 'We were asleep when the best hunting opportunities were out there. That is not good hunting practice.'

Matt wanted to guffaw. So Hirsh really had no idea that yesterday his very survival had been in doubt.

'What's so funny?' asked Hirsh.

'There are times when it's more important to sleep.'

'What's that supposed to mean?'

'Tell me one thing you remember about yesterday afternoon.'

There was a silence. 'It is sort of hazy,' admitted Hirsh. 'I must have been exhausted.'

'I think so,' agreed Matt.

'Did you give me anything?'

'I thought about painkillers because your hip was probably

hurting. But they weren't the right thing in the circumstances.'

'What were the circumstances?'

Matt was torn between the truth and the need to protect his father's pride.

'Well, you talked a little. And I wasn't sure sometimes whether you were talking about real things or dream things.'

'Like what?'

Matt swallowed. 'For one thing, you said Steve Minelli came and took your gun.'

There was a long silence.

'Was that a real thing or a dream thing?' asked Matt at last.

'Well, I'm not too sure myself,' admitted Hirsh. 'I was so tired . . . I do have memories of Steve Minelli appearing but those memories are sort of dream-like.'

'After you talked with him in the forest when I was there?'

'Yes, long after that. You'd left me somewhere by myself for a while and he showed up. He took my gun and there wasn't a thing I could do about it because I was sort of stuck in a sleeping bag and my glasses were steamed up. Matt, I really don't know if it happened or not.'

'Well your gun's gone, that's for sure.'

'I've had that gun for fifty years,' said Hirsh.

'Yeah,' said Matt, rolling over. 'I know.'

He wriggled to the fire. The clothes there still weren't dry. Another day in his inadequate sweats.

'It sure would be nice to know if Steve Minelli's around,' he said. 'How are you feeling today, Dad?'

'Fine,' said Hirsh.

'That's what you kept saying yesterday when you weren't fine.'

'Well, when you get old you don't enumerate your aches

and pains when someone asks how you are. You assume they don't really want to know.'

'I do. Tell me.'

'I guess I have a slight headache and I feel sort of weaker than usual. Maybe I'm just still tired.'

'How's the hip?'

'I don't generally feel it first thing in the morning but today I would have to admit that I know it's there.'

'You're going to take it easy,' said Matt. 'And I'm going to get some heat going. Just think of that delicious oatmeal we have for breakfast.'

He scrambled into as many clothes as he could as quickly as possible.

'Why aren't you wearing Stewart's lined jeans?' asked Hirsh, watching him from his bag.

'Because you're wearing them.'

'I am? Why?'

'Your jeans got wet. That's another good reason to get the fire going. It's still got a little red glow inside it. I'll revive it with the wood we have here and then I'll go collect some more.'

You had to lift the door right away to get in and out of the cabin. When he did so, the first thing Matt noticed was that the meadow grass was shining. It was reflecting light. He looked up and saw blue sky. Bathed in fall's high-precision sunlight were the meadow, the creek and the mountains around, and he saw them with such an intense clarity that they seemed to jump at him. He was stunned by the crispness of the valley's beauty. And, less than a half mile away at the other end of the valley, was a herd of elk.

'Dad,' he hissed. Hirsh didn't hear him so he had to call louder. It took Hirsh a minute or two to haul himself out of his sleeping bag and find his glasses and the binoculars and get to the door but it didn't matter, the elk were oblivious to their presence. They were grazing the meadow.

They watched the distant animals in silence.

'See any antlers?' asked Hirsh at last.

'Yes. So what do we do?'

'Think,' said Hirsh.

'You can use my gun. I mean, Stewart's gun. Since yours is missing.'

But Hirsh shook his head. 'It's inadvisable to use a gun at all right now. We won't get closer without them seeing us and then we'll have lost them for good. No, we'll have to wait until they come back. Then we'll stand-hunt them.'

'You mean . . . just let them go right now?' asked Matt. He might have confessed to a small feeling of disappointment. Yesterday they had walked past any number of elk signs and on at least one occasion he had sighted a lone bull elk. Now they were at camp and there was a whole herd of elk and they were supposed to ignore it.

'Patience makes a hunter,' said Hirsh. 'They'll be going into the forest to bed down very soon. They'll be back, though, and we should be in position waiting for them.'

'Supposing they don't come back?'

'As long as they think this place is safe, they'll come back. Probably this evening or at dawn tomorrow. Come inside now so they don't scent danger.'

'What about the firewood?'

'It can wait a while.'

They had enough water and probably enough firewood to make oatmeal but no way of cleaning their bowls to put it in, not without disturbing the elk.

'We should have gone over to the creek and cleaned them last night,' said Hirsh, evidently still remembering nothing of last night. 'You should always wash stuff while the dirt's fresh.'

When Matt checked again, the elk were gone. He walked into the silent forest to look for firewood. The bright morning light even penetrated here. Where the trees were sparse, massive shafts of light wedged themselves between trunks, stomping on the thin snow that still lay there.

Matt easily found firewood. He came back to the shack with a great bundle under his arm. Hirsh wasn't there and at first he felt alarmed. Then he looked around and saw a distant figure bent over the edge of the creek. His father was washing the pans. He watched the old man's slow, deliberate movements. He was using a rock, or maybe it was a small stick, for a scraper. He seemed to be talking to someone. Maybe he was talking to Hilly.

Inside, Matt built up the fire some more and then used the nylon line to hang the damp clothes close enough to the fire to dry but not close enough to get burnt. The line sagged. Hirsh's jeans, in particular, were still water-heavy.

'Will you just look at this,' said a voice at the door. 'I caught him without a line, even!'

Hirsh was holding a bowl in each hand and in one of them glistened a small but well-rounded brown trout.

'Did he jump into the bowl and ask you to eat him?' said Matt.

'I tickled him.'

'He's not laughing.'

'Tickling's where you catch them with your hands. My father showed me how but I haven't tried it in years. Couldn't believe it worked first time. Beginner's luck, I guess. I'll show you how, later, and we'll try to catch another one for a fine feast.'

They ate breakfast and when Matt had finished he

produced the tiny sachets of coffee and sugar and milk from the cafeteria which Jon Espersen had suggested he bring.

'It'll take a long time to boil the water for that,' said Hirsh.

Matt fetched the map.

'Wouldn't this be the obvious place for Steve Minelli to head for?'

'Not necessarily. Not unless you knew about it. Remember, these shacks aren't well marked, just the old mineshafts.'

Matt studied the map. It no longer felt like a mass of alien and impenetrable contour lines. It had a familiarity now, like the street outside his house or the parking lot at work. On the map, the wilderness was predictable, decipherable, containable. It was only when you looked outside and saw a distant snowstorm or the threat of some overhanging mountain that you remembered it was nothing like the hospital parking lot.

'He'd need to find somewhere with some protection,' Matt said, tracing his finger over contours. 'I mean, yesterday's weather was harsh and he only had a small pack.'

Hirsh usually ate very slowly and today he was slower than ever. He was only halfway through his oatmeal.

'That boy's used to living rough.'

'How do you know?'

'Because when he was hanging around town we finally worked out that he had some kind of a camp in the woods. And it was last winter, which was a hard one.'

'What did you say to him yesterday?' Matt asked. 'When it seemed he'd turned back?'

Hirsh sighed. 'Well, I'll tell you. But right now I think you should go look for my gun by daylight. Because if it's really not there, then I guess that means that Steve did come and take it.'

'I thought Mom called this place the Mouth of Nowhere because you talked a lot here,' said Matt, getting up.

'She talked, mostly.'

'What did she talk about?'

Hirsh smiled again. 'I'll tell you that, too. We'll talk, Matt, don't worry. There's a lot I have to say. But you should go back up to those woods now because I'm beginning to feel uncomfortable without my old gun.'

'Will you rest?' Matt asked, reaching for his own gun.

'I'll stay around here and try tickling another trout. And I want to set some snares. I have little hope of catching anything before dawn tomorrow but I want to try.'

Matt did not want to leave Hirsh alone. But he didn't want to take the old man back up to the higher plateau and have him hunt around in the forest for the gun when it was clear that what Hirsh needed was rest and access to the fire if he started to feel cold. Tomorrow they would begin their long trek to Rockroll to meet Stewart or Elmer. Hirsh needed to be rested for that.

'Maybe I should leave you with my gun,' Matt said.

'You think Steve Minelli's going around the wilderness collecting unguarded rifles?'

'I think he hates us, Dad.'

Hirsh was silent.

'He thinks we're the way he and his dad would have been if Mr Minelli had lived,' Matt added, and Hirsh sighed.

'He might have tried to kill me in the woods yesterday but he thought you were around and that you were covering me, the way you did while I was talking to him in the morning.'

'He said that?'

'He kept asking where you were and I kept saying, "Matt's right here." He took the gun because he had gotten snow down the muzzle of his own. He slunk off pretty quickly, looking over his shoulder all the time. I think. But I'm not sure. It's like it was all happening in a thick fog. I really don't know if I dreamed it.'

'If I find the gun then I guess you dreamed it.'

The sun was still shining brightly as Matt strode across the meadow. The creek sparkled, the meadow grasses shone, the leaves on the white-trunked trees by the creek shook a little and burned golden. But it was all deceptive. The sun was shedding light but not heat and the breeze which rattled the leaves so gracefully also cooled the skin. Matt asked himself: When was the wilderness ever kind?

He looked back and saw his father standing at the shack door. Hirsh lifted a hand to wave. The gesture, his father's smallness and vulnerability in this great landscape, Matt's fear that Steve Minelli and his hatred were stalking this good man, all of it cut at some tight string inside Matt's body and, unexpectedly, he felt himself to be close to tears.

Hirsh's last words had been, from the shack door, 'Don't spend too long up there. When the mountains are this clear in the morning it generally means the weather turns mean later.'

Matt had no intention of spending a moment longer than he needed to away from Hirsh. He scrambled breathlessly up to the meadow at the top. He remembered that he had forgotten to make the coffee.

As he reached the plateau he saw that there was still a layer of snow here but grasses and bushes showed through so it looked like a threadbare old cloth. He noticed that the wind had once again smoothed out their footprints. He was glad that their trail had been erased. He determined to take a circuitous route which involved a lot more forest floor and a lot less open snow so that, if Steve were around and looking for them, Matt wouldn't lead him right to their valley.

Eventually he arrived back at his own granola wrapper trail. He remembered his cold, his desperation and his fear yesterday. He remembered how panic had stalked him and sometimes seized him. Everything felt different today. Today there was only one threat and it was not posed by the natural world but by a man with a gun who had twenty-six years of anger stored inside him.

With a little difficulty, Matt found the granola wrapper which marked the tree where he had left Hirsh yesterday. There was no other evidence of their stay here. He began to search the way he had searched for Hirsh, in circles that got wider and wider. He was hoping that Hirsh had imagined he saw elk and just stumbled off with his gun and then left it somewhere.

After ninety minutes he still hadn't found the gun. However, he had found a footprint. It wasn't his. It was much smaller than his and, he feared, smaller than Hirsh's. Worse, for the last thirty minutes he had been unable to shake off the unpleasant sensation that someone was watching him. At first he had tried to ignore the feeling and then to suppress it, the way you might actively suppress the anxiety which could surface in a juddery elevator. Then he heard something which could have been a twig snapping and, since he was unarmed, decided to give up the search.

This time he removed all the granola wrappers he could find and then took a route through the forest which involved travelling a long way in the wrong direction, walking right around the clearing and then back through the forest on the other side. It wasn't possible to evade entirely the high, snowy meadow or the evidence of his passage it offered, like an innocent child blurting out a secret. So he made a trail past the valley and, when he hit forest again, doubled back to it. He wished the route he had taken on his way out had been as devious.

He crossed the creek, bouncing from rock to rock. There was a low fire burning behind the shack.

'I've got the fish cooking there,' said Hirsh. He had seen that Matt was empty-handed but had not commented or registered disappointment. 'I don't want the smell in the hut and I don't want the smoke blowing down into the elk feeding ground.'

'Did you tickle any more?'

'Nope, although I tried all morning. But I got the forest snared up and I found us an excellent stand for when the elk come back.'

'When do we get into position?'

'This afternoon. They'll probably come out at dusk.'

Hirsh glanced up. The sky had clouded, just as he had predicted, and the clouds were thickening.

They heated some powdered potato in the pan and ate it with the fish. They sat on rocks by the creek, balancing their plates on their laps. Matt thought it was one of the finest meals he had ever eaten. The beef teriyaki last night had been the food of desperation, of emergency rations. It wasn't real wilderness food. The fish was of the mountains and it was appropriate to eat it with the mountains circling them and the creek which had been home to the fish running right by them.

'This is a fine, well-protected valley,' said Hirsh, looking around with satisfaction after the meal. 'Whoever chose to build their homes in this place chose well.'

'You think they were polygamous Fundamentalists who split from the Church in Salt Lake?'

Hirsh nodded. 'I expect this was a place of prayer and reproduction.'

'In just three cabins?'

'There used to be more. If you go up a bit and into the trees there's a clearing and you can see the remains. That's where the mineshaft is. 'Course, just because it was a good place to live doesn't mean the mine was productive.'

They drank a coffee from Matt's sachets at last. It tasted of mountains instead of hospital cafeteria.

'What size are your boots?' Matt asked suddenly.

'I forget. Why?'

Matt shrugged in reply.

In the early afternoon, Hirsh surprised himself by taking a nap. While he slept, Matt examined his father's boots. The tread was different and they seemed bigger than the footprint he had seen in the forest. To be sure, he should have carried a tape and measured the footprint the way Hirsh had measured elk prints when he was scouting.

He sat on a boulder outside the shack and watched the clouds gathering around the mountains. Maybe he would bring his family here, when Austin and the new baby were older, and try to persuade them that cloud formations were more interesting than TV. He thought how he would describe the place to Denise in a couple of days' time.

He went into the forest. Hirsh's hanging snares, empty, decorated almost every nearby tree. After a few minutes he found a little evidence of the other huts: their crumbling stone fireplaces. Probably visitors had burned the rest of the cabins for firewood. The mineshaft was boarded over, but part of its curious zigzag pulley system still remained. There was a series of mighty timbers to take the weight of the ore which the settlers had extracted. Matt was examining them when, suddenly, the hairs on his neck stood up. He was being watched. He swung around and it seemed to him that there was the distant movement of a distant shadow. He stared after it, but there was no further disturbance and it was possible the movement had been a bird in flight.

Then he made his way back to the hut, closed the door and kept his gun on hand until Hirsh woke up.

He was almost certain someone had been there. He couldn't explain the feeling in words but he knew he shared it with deer and elk and probably other wild animals. That's why you couldn't look at them full-face. They didn't need to understand how or why they knew, they just knew when you were watching them.

The hut was quiet. Hirsh breathed deeply. Matt told himself to stop being so fanciful. Yesterday had been fraught with danger but the danger was mostly over and he should jettison his fears now. Except that Steve Minelli was still out there somewhere.

To stand-hunt, since they had only one gun, Hirsh had chosen one immense tree, its trunk thick and its leaves mostly shed already. It had two significant branches.

'If the guy with the gun doesn't have a clear shot then he might just be able to pass it across,' said Hirsh.

'You can be the guy with the gun,' Matt told him. 'After that fish I'm not hungry enough to find my killer instinct.'

Hirsh had them cover themselves in tree sap outside the cabin. It was starting to rain when they got into position. Matt helped Hirsh up the tree and then climbed up himself. Hirsh took the gun. And then they waited.

At first Matt was alert. He seemed to feel every small sound of the forest on his skin. Like the hunted, he looked everywhere.

Evening gathered around them and no elk appeared. The rain thickened. On the branch above, Hirsh did not move.

Matt did not move. Sitting so still for so long induced a trance-like state. After a while the itch on your nose didn't long to be scratched and you didn't even care to change position. By the time it was dark, Matt had become a part of the tree. He no longer knew where the wilderness ended and he began. When suddenly Hirsh spoke, announcing that they might as well leave because it was getting too dark for elk now, Matt was almost unable to respond. He had long ago ceased to look for elk but he had grown accustomed to his own stillness.

They were walking quietly towards the hut when they heard a strange, deep cry. Hirsh spun around.

'What was that?' whispered Matt.

'An elk bugling. There's an extra male or two hanging around that herd.'

'Where did it come from?'

'Right where we were sitting. We should have stayed there another ten minutes,' sighed Hirsh.

'Should we go back?'

'Nope. We should get up real early tomorrow and get into position before dawn.'

'Hunting sure is frustrating.'

'Only for the impatient. Hunting isn't for the impatient or for the noisy or the violent or for any of those things people seem to have become these days.'

When they were well away from the elk part of the forest, they shone their flashlights. They looked at Hirsh's snares. Hirsh was a lot more surprised than Matt to find a squirrel hanging in one of them.

'Who'd have thought it!' he said. 'Who'd have thought one of my little loops would work so quickly!'

'Are we really going to roast that poor critter?' asked Matt, but he was hungry now and didn't really mind.

'Want to learn how to skin it and bone it?' offered Hirsh.

'No,' said Matt. 'I'll organize the fire and start cooking the rice.'

He went into the hut and took everything out of the big pack and the small one too, but he was unable to find the rice. The fire was ready, the water was hot, but the rice pack was nowhere to be seen. Since he had noticed it only that morning, he searched both packs with his torch again.

Hirsh came in.

'Never, ever, go into the wilderness without aluminium foil,' he instructed, wrapping up the squirrel meat and placing it on the fire to roast.

Matt watched him, his face puckered a little with worry.

'And,' Hirsh was saying, 'we'd better get all the rest of those snares down before we leave in the morning. Otherwise it's going to look like Golgotha out there after a few days.'

Matt said, 'Dad. Did you move the rice? Or use it for anything?'

'No. We had potato for lunch.'

'There's oatmeal and some packs of powdered potato left. And that's all. No rice.'

'Well,' said Hirsh carelessly, turning over the squirrel with a couple of stones. 'I guess we forgot to pack it.'

'But I saw it only this morning.'

'It's potato for dinner then,' said Hirsh.

'Also,' persisted Matt, 'there was a whole box of water purification tablets. And I can't find that either.'

Hirsh smiled.

'Right here,' he said, producing the box from his pocket. 'Why are you so jumpy?'

'Steve Minelli,' said Matt shortly. 'I mean, I never did find your gun.'

472

'You think he could have come in here while we were stand-hunting and stolen our rice?'

'Yes. If he was hungry and planned to make a fire somewhere.'

Hirsh seemed unperturbed. 'If he's hungry he's welcome to a piece of squirrel. A small piece, that is.'

A silence fell. They watched the fire and from time to time Hirsh turned the squirrel. Matt began to feel he should speak. He sensed that Hirsh was waiting for him to say something. He had, after all, promised they would talk here in the Mouth of Nowhere. The silence between them went on and on until it seemed to echo around the hut and echo around the valley.

'Dad,' said Matt, 'I think the problem with Steve Minelli is that he's become obsessed by his father's death.' He spoke so suddenly that Hirsh looked up at him in surprise.

'That's certainly true,' he said.

'I mean,' continued Matt, more slowly, 'what's obsessing him is that he finds the circumstances of that death suspicious. And, maybe . . . maybe they are suspicious.'

When the words were said they felt enormous, as enormous as all the things you couldn't see out there right now, the creek, the valley, the mountains.

Hirsh said nothing but he looked at Matt shrewdly, his dark eyes lit by the fire.

'The killer instinct . . .' Matt began. 'You said that you have to be driven to kill. I mean, maybe by hunger, you said, or a need to show someone your trophy, or by anger or by . . . by jealousy. Jealousy, I know, can be a very strong force. An overwhelming force. That's one thing that could make you kill someone.'

Hirsh was sitting on the stone ledge by the fire, still looking intently at Matt. His face was expressionless. Matt wished his father would say something so that he didn't have to go on.

Finally Hirsh spoke. He said, 'Matt. If you're trying to tell me that you've killed a man through jealousy . . . I already know. I've suspected it for a little while now. If you're trying to tell me that my suspicions are correct, well then, we should discuss what we're going to do about it.'

Matt gaped. He opened his mouth and no words came out.

Hirsh said, 'It's taken me a long time to accept that Weslake's death was no random accident. I haven't enjoyed my suspicions, Matt, they've caused me some suffering.'

'Suspicions?' echoed Matt.

'I fear,' said Hirsh softly, 'that you were the driver who ran him down. Am I right?'

'No!' said Matt.

'Matt. This is the place and the time for the truth.'

'But it isn't true! I mean, it just isn't!'

Hirsh sighed and studied Matt's reddening face.

'So it's just a coincidence. That Weslake died right after you got back from Africa.'

'I told you, Dad! I didn't know he'd died. I didn't meet Denise again until Weslake was dead, until months after Weslake died!'

Of course he'd thought of it, but only thought of it. He had assumed she'd be the proud mother by that time of at least four little Weslakes.

Hirsh did not take his eyes off Matt.

'I still don't understand why you came back to Salt Lake. After Africa. You had a great job offer in Boston and you came back here and worked as a locum before you could work at St Claudia's. It just doesn't make sense to me. I think it must have been Denise pulling you back.'

474

'She would have done if I'd thought there was a chance,' said Matt 'But I didn't.'

'Matt, maybe Denise knew that Weslake was blackmailing her father. Maybe there were other problems in the marriage, as she had no children.'

Matt did not meet his father's eye.

'Didn't she contact you to tell you how bad things were? Didn't she make you think that maybe you could get Weslake out of the way?'

Matt was quiet now. He said, 'No. None of that's true. I don't know how you could have thought it, Dad. I don't know how you could have thought I killed Weslake.'

Hirsh turned the small packet of foil over again. He said nothing. Matt felt both offended by his father's accusation and anxious to insist once more on his innocence.

'Remember way back when I got my driver's licence and you told me how it was when a car ran down a pedestrian? Well, that story's haunted me. I've dreaded doing such a thing in error. I never could have gone out and run a guy down in cold blood.'

Hirsh sat up straighter. 'I'm relieved to hear that, Matt. But, of course, you've been thinking the same thing about me for a long time. Right?'

Matt looked at him but said nothing. Suddenly he was clean out of words.

'You've suspected that I killed Arthur Minelli,' said Hirsh. 'You've been silently accusing me and maybe even forgiving me, without once actually asking me.'

Matt hung his head. He picked up one of the big, round stones which he had heated and slipped into Hirsh's sleeping bag last night when his father had been old and vulnerable and cold, not the strong eagle of a man who confronted him now. He felt the stone's ancient surface, rubbed smooth by time and water, with the pads of his fingers. He fitted it snugly between his palms. He stroked its hard, unforgiving curves.

'I did think that for a while,' said Matt. 'But now I believe that Mom might have killed him.'

Hirsh stared straight at Matt and then threw back his head and looked all around the room and spoke into the darkness. 'Hear that, Hilly? Did you hear that?'

Matt said, 'She had an affair with Arthur Minelli. Right?'

'Right. It was brief. It lasted one summer. It caused me pain beyond words.' Hirsh's voice broke as he spoke. The change was fractional. A stranger wouldn't notice it but Matt did, and it made continuing still harder. He looked around the room at the darkness that was Hilly. He invited her to witness Hirsh's pain.

'You didn't do anything about it,' said Matt. 'Because you didn't want to lose her.'

'I couldn't do anything. I just had to watch and wait. Believe me, Arthur Minelli was a sensational performer. Capable of charming the birds from the trees. The kind of man who always gets what he wants. He found a diamond in the freezer at the supermarket and he wanted her to have it but, of course, they had to explain it. So she had to go through the ludicrous charade of pretending *she* had found a diamond at the supermarket. He wanted her to play the piano, she demurred, he had a piano delivered on to our terrace and she gave a concert, her only concert. He wanted to play ball, everyone played ball. He wanted to swim, everyone swam. He wanted an affair, they had an affair.'

Hirsh's tone stayed curiously even. He spoke dispassionately as though he were reading words someone else had written.

'She could have said no,' Matt suggested, very quietly.

'I wish she had. But she was a woman who devoured life and who was always looking for new experience. Arthur was her only affair, I believe. She soon tired of the game. His demands, that crazy edge to him, it all got too much even for Hilly. Until then I thought she never could get enough attention. But even she had a limit and by August it was over for her.'

'Mom ended the affair?'

'She ended the affair. She gave him the ring back and it ended up in the possession of his wife, I imagine.'

'She wears it still,' said Matt. 'Steve said it was Mr Minelli's last gift to her.'

'Ha,' said Hirsh. 'She never acknowledged the affair in any way, not even when they were both being blindingly obvious.'

'So she took the ring and wrote the affair right out of history. Did Mr Minelli really love Mom? Or was it just . . .'

'Lust? No, I think for a period he was genuinely, crazily, in love with her. And remember, he always got what he wanted, so he didn't like Hilly ending the affair.'

Matt watched his father take the foil-clad squirrel off the fire and prise the folds open delicately.

'That day he died,' Matt said, 'I took the call, Stewart phoned our house and said Arthur Minelli had been shot in his car and I sent Steve right home and then I got your bag and found you on the hillside. Mom had been out all day so I was surprised when I saw you sitting together on the log seat. And then I saw you'd both been crying. And when I told you about the accident, you said, "I know."'

'And you figured I knew because I'd killed him? Or, correction, because your mother killed him?'

'She could have met him down by the lake and fired the shot and then driven right up to the house . . .'

There was a long, long silence. Hirsh put the squirrel meat on to their plates and spooned some potato.

'That's what Steve Minelli believes happened,' said Matt lamely. 'I mean, he thinks that when you tried to save Mr Minelli, you were doing it because you didn't want your wife facing a murder charge.'

'Oh,' said Hirsh. 'Well, that's an interesting idea.'

Matt threw some more wood on the fire. They began to eat in silence.

'Matt, it wasn't an accident. Steve's right about that,' said Hirsh at last.

'Oh, Dad.' Matt's voice was dulled by sadness. All his suspicions, now he knew they must be right, had turned into a great weight of sadness.

'I didn't kill him,' said Hirsh. The bright brown eyes were staring back into Matt's.

'It really wasn't you?'

'Nor your mother, for heaven's sake. The police report said it was an accident and we made it look like an accident. Steve's right that we did falsify the evidence to some extent, I mean the angle of the gun and that kind of thing. But we were just saving his family from the truth. We made a pact that we never would tell anyone the truth and I've kept that pact all these years.'

'What is the truth?'

'He killed himself. It was obvious the moment I got to the car. Stewart and Elmer saw it too. Arthur's hand was still on the trigger.'

'Because of Mom? He died because Mom ended their affair?'

'I don't think so. By September his life had changed. A property deal in the city had gone seriously wrong for him and he was deeply in debt and may have been facing

478

prosecution. Hilly had made it clear she had no intention of resuming the affair weeks earlier and there were rumours he was involved with someone else. Who knows what was in his mind and in his heart that day he pulled the trigger?'

'Was there a note?'

'No. I wish he'd said something loving and kind to that poor wife of his. But I guess we never could have faked an accident if he'd done that. I've had sleepless nights, wondering if we did the right thing, worrying that she should have been told the truth. But by then we'd rearranged the evidence and we couldn't turn back.'

'Did you tell Steve Minelli in the woods yesterday that his father had killed himself?'

'I didn't see I had any other option. His anger and suspicions are making him very dangerous. But he's wrong. His father killed himself and, if he wants to be mad at someone, I guess he should be mad at Arthur Minelli.'

'Did he believe you?'

'He was so shocked he didn't question it. But when he came back later – if he came back later – I think he'd decided not to believe me. The fact that I had confessed to a cover-up just seemed to confirm his old suspicions. He thought we were covering up a murder, not a suicide.'

Matt ate his meal without even noticing it. Afterwards he wished he could remember how squirrel tasted. He had always hoped squirrel might taste of nuts but he had no memory of the experience.

'I know how you tried to save Mr Minelli,' Matt said. 'Elmer told me. Relief of pericardial tamponade with Stewart's kitchen knife.'

Hirsh nodded.

'Medically speaking,' he said, 'I guess I'm probably more proud of that than almost anything else in my career.' He

479

grinned at Matt a little sheepishly. 'I'm not gifted like you, Matt. I'm not a surgeon.'

Matt said in surprise, 'I've no gift, Dad.'

Hirsh smiled. 'Oh, sure you have. Sure. That was obvious from an early age. You've got a surgeon's hands. I could see it even when you played the piano. You've got talented hands, a very good brain and the right kind of antennae to pick up on what a patient's really telling you. You're a good doctor, Matt, very good, and I'm proud of you.'

At this tribute, Matt felt something buzzing inside his eyes, heating them up, making them water. Hirsh had never, not once, indicated that Matt might be good at his job. He had always been the camp follower, the son dwarfed by his father's stature. He opened his mouth to speak, to thank Hirsh, but no words came out. Hirsh seemed to have detected his difficulty.

'I guess it wouldn't have been so hard for you to deal with tamponade, you've probably done it a lot of times, but, I can tell you, I could hardly bear to attempt to shove that knife into the pericardial cavity. I mean, Stewart's kitchen knife, for heaven's sake. But Arthur was failing fast, so I had nothing to lose.'

'How did it feel, stabbing your rival?' asked Matt.

Hirsh grinned. 'Well, it didn't feel good if that's what you mean.'

'But Mom had an affair with him! You must have hated him! Why did you try so hard to save him?'

'The affair was over by then and I was feeling sorry for him, actually. Although it's true I hadn't been too partial to him all summer. A better reason, in my view, for not saving him was that he had chosen to kill himself. It was his choice to die. After years in medicine, I do believe people have a right to die if they want to. If we passed a man trying to kill himself here in the forest, I'd have a real moral dilemma, whether to interfere or respect his choice. You must have saved suicidal patients only to have them curse you for it.'

Matt nodded.

'But Arthur was dying and in pain,' Hirsh went on, 'and there was always the possibility that he'd meant to pull a stunt and not actually to kill himself. That would have been very Arthur. Plus there was his family to think of, plus people knew about his affair with Hilly and I couldn't have them saying I hadn't tried. So, all things considered, I tried. Hilly always suspected that I might not have done. We didn't talk about it for years. Then we came here shortly before she died. And we said all those things we should have said before. I was able to reassure her that I'd done everything for Arthur and I think that was a relief to her.'

Matt looked around as if he expected to see Hilly sitting by the fire with them. 'Did you come to this very cabin?' he asked.

'No, we camped in the meadow. And we talked. How we talked.'

'Why were you upset the day Mr Minelli died? When I found you on the bench, you looked as though you'd been crying before I even told you the news. And then you said, I know.'

'I knew something had happened from the gunshot. I didn't know it was Arthur. And we were upset because Hilly had just got back from the city. She'd insisted on going to the hospital alone. I stayed with you.'

'The hospital?'

'For the Minellis it was the summer they lost Arthur. For me it was the beginning of losing Hilly.'

'She was diagnosed that summer?'

'I'd been barred from her bed because of Arthur, so I

didn't detect the lump on her breast until the August. By that time you could almost see it with the human eye. It was diagnosed as malignant at the beginning of September.'

Matt was silent as his father banked up the fire and climbed into his sleeping bag. Matt climbed into his. Their bodies were hidden now but their faces were still lit by the firelight.

'Does it make you sad to come back here?' Matt asked.

'No. I had a happy time here with her. Saying all those things at last. And that's one reason I wanted you and me to get here. I knew we had some things to say and I figured that if we said them anywhere it would be here.'

His father lay down and closed his eyes. He was silent for so long that Matt thought he was asleep. Matt lay down too. He didn't sleep. When, much later, he heard Hirsh putting more wood on the fire he opened his eyes again.

'What else did you and Mom talk about when you camped here?' he asked.

'Oh, let's see. Well, we talked about playing the piano.'

'She never should have stopped.'

'All those years she'd stuck to the story of how she gave up studying with Ozolins to marry me and move to Salt Lake. She had sacrificed her career for us. But when we were here in the wilderness she told me the truth. That Ozolins had stopped teaching her because he said she would never make a concert pianist.'

Matt was so shocked at this challenge to long-established mythology that he sat bolt upright.

'She wasn't good enough to be a pianist?'

'She was very, very good. But not exceptional enough to be one of the few soloists. Or maybe he decided she didn't have the application. Anyway, her whole life must have felt as though it was buckling under her when he rejected her.

But she never told a soul the truth. Not until the end of her life when we came here.'

Hirsh lay down again. Soon the hut was quiet and it seemed Hirsh was asleep. Maybe Matt slept a little too. But later, when he opened his eyes to the light of the dying fire, Matt could see that his father's eyes were open too.

'Are you awake?' Matt asked.

'Yes.'

'The reason I came back to Salt Lake and didn't take the job in Boston, since you ask, wasn't Denise. It was you.'

'Me?'

'I like living near you,' said Matt and there was a long silence.

Hirsh said hoarsely, 'Well, thanks. I guess I never thought of that.'

Matt said, 'You believed I killed someone. And I believed you did.'

'I'm very happy we were both wrong.'

They grinned at each other by the firelight.

'There's no way I could have done it,' said Matt. 'I just don't have that killer instinct. I've always been jealous of Weslake but I never thought of killing him.'

'That's what's worrying me,' said Hirsh.

'What?'

'Well, if you didn't kill him then someone else did.'

Matt lay very still. If he rearranged himself at all the sleeping bag would make its soft, padded sounds up around his ears and he might not hear Hirsh's explanation. But no explanation came. He suddenly felt tired. His eyes seemed to be sinking inside his head. He may even have fallen asleep waiting for Hirsh to speak again.

'You see,' said Hirsh softly, and Matt started a little, 'Weslake's death wasn't an unfortunate random killing by a bad driver. He was killed by someone who wanted him dead.'

'Like who?'

Hirsh was silent for a long time while Matt tried to think of someone who might have wanted Weslake dead.

'Weslake would have bled Clem dry if he'd lived. So I guess Clem benefited from his death . . . but, I mean, the old guy can hardly get out of bed. Let alone drive a car.'

'Think harder,' said Hirsh.

Matt rehearsed every name that Denise had ever mentioned in connection with Weslake. He even thought of Jon Espersen and then laughed at himself.

'I can't think of anyone,' he admitted.

'Matt, remember the deer meat that you gave me from Denise's freezer? Weslake's roadkill? The roadkill that had left its mark on Denise's fender for the police to find?'

'Yes.'

'It wasn't hit by a car. That deer had been killed by a bullet. I nearly broke my tooth on the evidence.'

The fire crackled. Matt struggled with this information.

'I remember you hurting your tooth. But you said it was just a piece of metal because someone had taken a shot with the wrong kind of ammo and wounded the deer . . .'

'That's what I thought. Since you said it was roadkill. But when I cooked the next piece, I found the whole bullet. It packed a lot of power and it was lodged in the animal. It was certainly the bullet which killed the deer.'

'So . . .' Matt was groping for the significance of this.

'So the car hadn't hit a deer right before Weslake died.'

'But it was dented.'

'By Weslake's body. I understand Weslake had just come back from hunting. He brought a deer carcase. Denise was able to use it to explain the dent left by Weslake's body. She smeared deer blood on the fender to cover any evidence.'

'No, Dad, no, you've made a mistake!'

'I don't think so.'

'Listen. Denise adored Weslake. She worshipped the guy. She can't even talk about him because she . . .'

'Because she's scared she might reveal how she really felt?' suggested Hirsh.

There was a long silence. The fire wrapped its tongue around some wet wood and the wet wood hissed.

'There were these bruises,' said Matt slowly. 'At least, her doctor told me there were bruises. He looked right at me and told me she used to get bruised doing yoga. So did Jon Espersen. But I'm not sure you can get bruised from the lotus position. I suspect the bruises were caused some other way.'

Hirsh said nothing and Matt heard his own voice, talking on, but slowly, as though somebody was extracting the words from him, pulling them out of him.

'She was on the pill,' he said. 'She pretended to want a baby and that she had fertility problems and all the time she was on the pill. I found out last week.'

'So, she didn't want a baby with that guy. We can't guess why but we can guess she might not have loved him. I think Denise would put up with anything for herself, maybe even bruises. But, if she knew he was blackmailing Clem . . . I don't think she could have stood that.'

Denise had said, after that row: I thought you were misusing information about my father. And Matt had felt surprised and offended. And, on the same occasion, she had said something about knowing for years that her father was no angel.

Nevertheless, Matt found himself shaking his head vigorously now. 'Dad, Denise loved Weslake.'

'What makes you so sure?'

'Well . . . because Clem says so.'

'But she wouldn't have burdened him with the knowledge that her marriage was unhappy or that she already knew his secrets – which I assume involve some kind of behaviour not generally approved by the Mormon Church – or that she knew he was being blackmailed. Now, if they'd just been open with one another, Weslake couldn't have taken Clem's money. But they were both trying too hard to protect each other.'

The fire hissed some more. The silence was long and Hirsh's breathing even.

'Denise couldn't kill a man, Dad. She just couldn't. She always tries to do the right thing . . .'

But before he had finished speaking he had remembered Denise's words to Lonnie. How you sometimes had to take the wrong road to get to the right place. She was the only person who had ever dared to suggest to Lonnie that withdrawing Robert's life support was the right thing to do.

'You think she doesn't have that old killer instinct, eh?' smiled Hirsh. 'You think you don't have it, either. But if the circumstances were right, you'd find it inside yourself. And I believe Denise, reluctantly, found it in herself, too, for her father's sake. It must have been so hard for her. There are natural killers but she's not one of them.'

'Are you basing this whole theory on a bullet you found in some deer meat which got put in the freezer three years ago?'

'Yes,' said Hirsh. 'It was the pain in my tooth that got me thinking.'

Matt did not want to think any more. He wanted to sleep.

'I'm sorry that I've put suspicions about your wife into your head,' said Hirsh. Matt made a low, guttural sound that was part animal and part snore. 'But,' Hirsh's soft voice pattered against Matt's head like light, persistent rainfall, 'if you think she might have killed a man, you have to decide what to do with the suspicion.'

A moral dilemma. Matt needed to discuss it with Denise. She was the person you discussed your dilemmas with. You laid them out before her like a meal you wanted her to digest.

'We suspected each other, Dad, and we were wrong,' he mumbled. At least, he thought he mumbled it. He wasn't sure he'd spoken at all until Hirsh replied, 'I guess being wrong about you is how I know I'm right about Denise.'

Matt must have fallen asleep. He was awoken by a sound like footfall outside the hut. The fire was out and Hirsh was breathing deeply. Matt lay in the dark, alert, straining to listen. He thought he should probably go outside and look around but decided it was too cold to leave his sleeping bag. He reached for the rifle and laid it alongside him. When he heard a second noise, he was sure it was the sound of a foot slipping a little on the rocks outside the hut. He got up at once and squatted by the door, alert, unmoving. After five minutes of silence, he got back into bed but his heart was still thumping. He remained at the ready. Ready for anything.

If the impossible really was true and Denise had killed Weslake, should he do something, say something?

Eventually he fell asleep again and woke with a start to find Hirsh dressing.

'We have to get into position,' said Hirsh. 'We're going to shoot an elk.'

Matt remembered their conversation in the night. He remembered that Denise had killed Weslake. She had been unhappily married to a man who may have been violent and who was ruthlessly blackmailing her father. And she had done the wrong thing to make the right thing happen.

He lay for a few minutes fighting exhaustion, the kind that seems to start inside your bone marrow. He thought he had barely slept at all. His head ached.

'Do we have time to make a coffee?' he asked.

'No,' said Hirsh. 'Just the smell of it would drive an elk up to the top of the Schoolmarm.'

Matt tried to dress inside his sleeping bag but gave up and wriggled out. All the wet clothes were dry now and he could take back Stewart's lined jeans.

'What should I do about Denise?' he asked his father. 'What should I say?'

Hirsh paused. 'In most circumstances, if you believe that a murder has been committed, you tell the police.'

'You thought I'd killed Weslake but you didn't get right on the phone to Sheriff Turner or whoever sits in his chair now.'

'I decided I should talk to you about it first. Maybe you decided the same thing when you suspected that your mother or I had killed Arthur Minelli.'

'I guess I also knew we had to talk about it first,' admitted Matt. 'But it was hard to know how to start.'

'Good thing we came to the Mouth of Nowhere. Is the rifle loaded? Have you got the extra ammo?'

They made their way through the forest towards their stand. It was still very dark but Matt seemed to have developed night vision in the last few days.

'Are you sure this isn't too early?' he asked, yawning.

'I'm sure.'

They took up their positions in the cold tree. The night air was thin and Matt felt his body heat evaporating into it. He was waiting for first light to thicken it up. He sat in his tree, not looking for elk or even thinking about them. He was thinking about Steve Minelli, about the possibility that in the night he had heard Steve outside the shack. Then he thought about Denise. She had driven a car right into Weslake. Had driver and victim experienced a hideous moment of eye contact? And in that moment had Denise suffered too or had she retained her incisive belief that she was doing the wrong thing to make the right thing happen?

'In most circumstances, if you believed that a murder had been committed, you'd tell the police.' Those had been Hirsh's words.

The sky ripped a little and, through the rip, dawn broke. From the very first light the elk came. You could hear them crashing through the undergrowth. You could hear the stamping of their feet. A few cows appeared with their young. Then more cows. Then the bull elk, surrounded by a whole group of cows.

The bull had a magnificent rack of antlers which he carried above him as though the points could touch the sky. His body was immense. His flanks were firm and his coat was sleek. He moved with the ease of the very fit. His great brown eyes were alert. Matt had never expected to see a wild animal so close and so clearly. He had the binoculars but he didn't need them. He glanced up at Hirsh. The gun was poised, waiting for a clear shot.

The herd grazed a while as the sun came up. When the grass of the meadow was sparkling, they moved over towards the creek. They stood under one of the great white-barked trees. Overhead the leaves blazed like golden banners. The brown coats of the elk gleamed in the light. The calves gambled at their mothers' feet. The bull sank down on to his knees as though worshipping the scene. He drank. Then he stepped up on to a boulder in the creek and lifted his great head and surveyed the valley, his mouth dripping with the clear, clean mountain water. Matt thought he had never seen anything so beautiful as those animals in the sun but he knew the bull had now fatally exposed his lungs to Hirsh's rifle.

He looked up again and saw to his amazement that Hirsh had put down the gun. He was watching the elk intently. When the bull had finished drinking, the herd moved back into the meadow and continued to graze and play as they made their gradual return to the forest. When the elk had passed back into the trees, almost beneath the tree where Hirsh and Matt sat hidden, Matt looked up to Hirsh for an explanation. Hirsh avoided his eye until they were both down.

'The killer instinct,' said Matt. 'It deserted you.'

Hirsh nodded.

'I'm glad you didn't shoot,' said Matt. 'Very glad.'

They walked slowly back to the hut.

Hirsh said, 'There are times when you have all the power. And the bravest, biggest decision you can make is not to use that power. To take no action at all.'

Matt wasn't sure if Hirsh was talking about elk. He might have been talking about Denise. She had, after all, done the wrong thing not for herself but for Clem. And now, the bravest, biggest decision he could make was to take no action at all.

As he rekindled the fire to boil water for coffee, he began to feel happy. They were going home today. Tomorrow he would see Denise and Austin and lay a hand gently on Denise's belly where the baby lay in its small sac.

He took the coffee out to Hirsh, who sat meditatively by the creek.

'Are you thinking about Mom?' asked Matt.

'I guess so.'

'Thanks for telling me her secret. About the piano.'

Hirsh smiled at him. He looked tired.

'I didn't tell you mine.'

'Your secret?'

'When she said that Ozolins had rejected her as a concert pianist, I told her my secret.'

Matt waited, his eyes fixed on Hirsh over the rim of his cup.

'What was your secret, Dad?'

'That I knew. I'd known all along.'

'The whole time you were married you knew that—?'

'I wanted to marry her, a lot. I was doing my stint with the very deprived in New York but I had a job waiting for me back home here in Salt Lake. I couldn't believe my luck when she said she was giving up her whole career to come to way-out-west Utah and be my bride. With a trembling hand I called the great Ozolins himself. I said that I would find a way to stay in New York even if I had to take a job in a carwash if he really wanted her to continue studying with him. And he told me the truth.'

They looked at the creek, the relentless progress of its water through the valley. The water you had stared at yesterday was already miles away but the creek looked just the same. It was like the kids you saw when you passed the school. Each year, kids grew and changed, and then there were different kids climbing from the bus, although they always looked the same.

'There sure were a lot of secrets in your marriage,' said Matt at last.

'The best marriages,' said Hirsh, 'have secrets.'

They looked at each other and smiled.

'I'm not going to say anything to Denise. I'm not going

to do anything,' Matt said. 'Just because you have all the power, doesn't mean you have to use it.'

Hirsh smiled, and Matt knew he was agreeing.

'Now,' said Hirsh. 'Once again we have to wash last night's dinner plates in the morning. I'll do that and start making our oatmeal and packing up camp. You go and remove all the snares. If you don't find thirty then you haven't found them all.'

Hirsh picked up the coffee cups and headed for the hut. Matt picked up the rifle. He went into the trees. About ten minutes later, when he had found twenty-four snares, Matt looked out from the edge of the forest and saw Hirsh once again leaning over the side of the creek, scraping the bowls clean with a stone or a stick. Was he talking to someone? It seemed he was saying something or nodding as though listening. Was he conversing with Hilly? He looked small in the great panorama. The mountains seemed to swell above the tiny, industrious figure. The landscape here had a thousand moods, but it never changed, thought Matt. The mountains, the valley, the meadow, they would all be here in the next millennium when he and Hirsh were not.

He wished that in this place which his mother had somehow made her own, he had experienced more of her. He had learned a lot about her but felt not much closer to Hilly than he did to the settlers who had built the shacks. Maybe what he had learned from the trip was that he never could hope to know her better: she was all Hirsh's. Her facial expressions, the sense of her body in motion, occasional phrases, fragments of memories, she would never be more substantial, no matter what facts were revealed about her. He began to look up and down the valley as though, if he were quick, he might glimpse her there.

And in the corner of his eye, he did detect movement.

Holding his breath, his heart beating with excitement, he tried to locate its source. High up where the valley abutted the mountain, almost hidden in the trees, something was moving furtively. He pulled the binoculars from his pocket. An animal. Its movement, its stealth, made him sure it was prey-seeking, perhaps a mountain lion. When he focused on the animal he saw it was a man.

Steve Minelli. So he had been here all along, lurking in the forest, watching them, wandering around their valley at night, stealing out of the trees to take a pack of rice and then evaporating back into the darkness.

Steve carried a gun. He moved with the slow, deliberate, careful pace of a hunter along the forest's edge, his body frequently masked by trees. For a moment Matt thought that he had melted into the woods. Then the shape re-emerged, further around the steep slopes, where the trees funnelled steeply into the valley. Steve took out binoculars. He was sighting his prey down in the meadow. Then he moved among the trees again, Matt sensing his direction only from the occasional intimation of movement.

Matt looked across the meadow. There was no animal here, only Hirsh, scrubbing pans, chatting to the absent Hilly.

Matt was seized by a fear and an anger which he didn't stop to analyse. He didn't think at all. He moved noiselessly through the trees. He controlled his breathing but otherwise his body was loose, relaxed, the body of a man who can bend and roll through rough terrain beneath overhanging branches without stumbling or breaking twigs. He was moving fast, so fast that it must be impossible to maintain this soundless speed, but his body was focused now as it had never been before. He was a hunter in the mountains and he was stalking his quarry, and his blood, his bones, his skin, every cell and corpuscle, were focused on Steve.

493

He paused from back among the trees and saw, where the forest curved ahead of him at the mountain's edge, something which looked from here like an eye blinking rapidly. It was Steve, moving. He was glassing the meadow. When he slid into the trees again, Matt turned to look at the meadow's expanse of water and grass but there was still no animal to shoot here. Only Hirsh.

Steve reappeared again, still further around the base of the mountain. He paused and then slowly, deliberately, he lifted the gun to his shoulder. It was pointing down the creek. He had positioned himself right behind the unsuspecting Hirsh now and it took only a fraction of a second to know that the gun was aiming at Hirsh and another fraction of a second for Matt to lift his own gun to his shoulder.

Through the sights Matt recognized the rifle Steve was aiming as Hirsh's own. He could see Steve's face, too white, too tired, too thin. And Matt knew that this was no joke shot, nor was it intended to frighten or even to intimidate. Steve was going to kill Hirsh. Just as they had scouted and then intended to stand-hunt the elk that morning, Steve had been scouting too. And now he was stand-hunting. So Hilly was here with them at the Mouth of Nowhere. Her affair and whatever its role had been in Arthur Minelli's decision to die had started in motion a chain of events which culminated here, now, with the muzzle of his own rifle pointing right at Hirsh.

Matt was overtaken by a monumental fury, a rage so massive that it rose from inside him like a roar. It came from some immense dark cavity in his body which was buried so deep that not even the most brilliant surgeon could find it. His rage was the rage of grinding teeth, shaking hands and hideous noises, but it was bound by an imperative.

He had to keep perfectly still, aim carefully, slip off the safety, keep the distant figure of Steve trapped in the crosshairs like a butterfly pinned to a card; his left hand had to support the rifle without tension and he had to squeeze the trigger. He must fire the rifle and he must do this in less time than it took Steve to do the same to Hirsh.

The shot echoed through the valley more than once, more than twice, maybe a thousand times. It continued to ring in Matt's head long after the valley was silent.

Matt looked from Hirsh to Steve to Hirsh. He did not breathe. He was waiting for one or, worse, both to fall. And then, so far away that the manoeuvre seemed to be conducted in complete silence, the body of Steve Minelli slid rather than fell to the ground. Hirsh, over by the creek, stood up, looking around him in bewilderment.

Matt knew that Steve was dead. He did not approach the body right away. Instead he walked across the meadow towards his father. Hirsh watched him getting closer. The turf sprang underfoot. The sun sparkled on the grass. The massive, towering mountains leaned right over them but did not block the sun. It was a long time before Matt felt the crunch of dry rocks underfoot as he reached the edge of the creek bed. He heard the water babbling and giggling frivolously on its long journey towards sea level.

Hirsh stood waiting, stooped slightly, elderly, confused, but unharmed. He watched throughout Matt's approach. He waited patiently for an explanation. He watched and waited because Matt was his son and Hirsh trusted him, and he seemed to know that, when Matt arrived, he would place an arm around his father's shoulders.